54 MILES

A Novel

LEONARD PITTS, JR.

A Bolden Book
AGATE
Chicago

This novel is a work of fiction. Names, characters, incidents, and dialogue, except for incidental references to public figures, products, or services, are imaginary and are not intended to refer to any living persons or to disparage any company's products or services.

First printed in July 2024

Printed in the United States of America

10 9 8 7 6 5 4 3 2 1   24 25 26 27 28

Library of Congress Cataloging-in-Publication Data

Names: Pitts, Leonard, Jr., author.
Title: 54 miles / Leonard Pitts, Jr.
Other titles: Fifty-four miles
Description: Chicago : Agate, [2024] | "A Bolden book." |
Identifiers: LCCN 2023058193 (print) | LCCN 2023058194 (ebook) | ISBN
   9781572843370 (trade paperback) | ISBN 9781572848849 (ebook)
Subjects: LCSH: Selma to Montgomery Rights March (1965 : Selma,
   Ala.)--Fiction. | Civil rights movements--Fiction. | African
   Americans--Civil rights--Fiction. | Children of rape victims--Fiction. |
   Alabama--Fiction. | LCGFT: Novels. | Historical fiction.
Classification: LCC PS3616.I92 A615 2024 (print) | LCC PS3616.I92 (ebook)
   | DDC 813/.6--dc23/eng/20240325
LC record available at https://lccn.loc.gov/2023058193
LC ebook record available at https://lccn.loc.gov/2023058194

Bolden Books is an imprint of Agate Publishing. Agate books are available in bulk at discount prices. For more information, visit agatepublishing.com.

For my aunt, Mildred Jenkins, in loving memory.

"You know, my friends, there comes a time when people get tired . . ."
—Martin Luther King, Jr.

prologue

So she walked with him into Bienville Square, a public green from which, as a Negro woman, she was barred by law. On her hip, Thelma Gordy balanced Adam, her toddler son, a plump cherub with skin so light that sometimes, on the rare occasions she ventured downtown, white people mistook her for his governess. They were usually affronted to learn that she was, in fact, his mother. "Oh," they would sniff, and it was as if a sudden veil hooded their gazes, "he must be a mulatto, then." And she would smile—smile, even though it made her feel like dirt—and nod, and leave that department store, that doctor's office, that pharmacy, as fast as she could.

Now, she and her mulatto son entered this park that was for whites only and she tried to ignore the siren voice of conscience—no, of simple self-preservation—that reminded her she had no business here, no business walking alongside this white man into a place where the law said she did not belong.

Girl, she asked herself, *what are you doing?*

The Square, largely empty at this late hour, was festooned with light. It was Christmas Eve, the first yuletide of peace after four terrible years of war. And George Simon, still in his marine dress blues, had just returned home to Mobile after two years in a Jap prison camp. And on his first night back, the first thing he had done was to come find her. It was a frightening thought.

He led her to a bench facing a department store window across the street. The display showed a train endlessly looping a track to the delight of a mannequin white boy in an engineer's hat. Next to him, his

1

mannequin white sister cuddled a doll with pink skin and curly blonde ringlets. Above the window hung a metal sign depicting a rosy-cheeked Santa Claus drinking Coca-Cola.

George and Thelma sat watching, Adam between them like a bridge linking distant shores. There seemed to be no words.

Then a portly white man approached, finger already pointing. "What's she doing here?" he demanded.

George looked up. Thelma looked down.

And George bolted to his feet. He put his nose a half inch from the other man's and yelled in his face. "What's she doing here? What are *you* doing here? She's a human being and she's taking the air in a public park, that's what she's doing! If you don't like it, you can go to hell. You think I fought the Japanese master race so I could come home and have to fight the white cracker master race?"

It was like a storm that blew up out of nowhere. George Simon, whom she had known as a gentle, soft-spoken man of God, was ready to punch this man for insulting her.

She called his name tentatively. "George . . ."

He ignored her, grabbing the stunned man by the collar. "People like you make me sick!" he cried. "There's a whole world out there, full of all different kinds of people, and most of 'em, they just want the same thing anybody else wants. But people like you just can't see it. You're too busy staring down at your own bullshit lives, your bullshit hate! You need to look up sometimes. Goddamn it, just look up for a change!"

She had never known him to curse. Much less to take the Lord's name in vain. Adam watched with huge eyes.

Thelma tried his name again. "George," she said, standing.

When he didn't respond, she took hold of his bicep and pulled at it. Still George ignored her, glaring at the fat man, whose eyes had gone wide in a face that was slack and pale. Finally, George shoved him. The man stumbled. Then he gathered himself and walked away at a quick step, glancing over his shoulder once to make sure George wasn't following. George scowled after him, his chest heaving. Finally, he allowed Thelma to lead him back to the bench and they sat. They didn't speak.

Thelma and Adam stared at him. He wouldn't meet their eyes.

The park had gone silent. The world had gone silent. Would they sit there all night without speaking? Thelma tried to think of what to say. No words presented themselves.

And then there came a sound of childish delight. "Look!"

Adam had just noticed the window display. He was pointing a chubby finger and his whole face was alive with excitement. "That's a choo choo," Thelma told him in a cooing voice, glad for the distraction. "You want to see the choo choo?"

She was speaking to Adam, but she kept her eyes on George. Now he looked at her. He nodded.

And Thelma knew that something had just happened. Something had passed between them like a current. She could not put words to it, but she knew it was there as surely as she knew her own name.

"Let's go see the choo choo," George said. They each took one of Adam's hands and together, crossed the empty street to the department store window. There, they stood for a long time, framed together in the light from the window, the little boy laughing, transfixed.

All around them, the world was still. Nothing moved, except the train continuing its endless loop and the Santa Claus sign creaking gently in the breeze.

And then, George spoke her name. She looked up to find him staring at her. There was weight to his gaze. "Yes?" she said.

He swallowed. He looked terrified. But his voice was firm. "What would you think if I asked you to marry me? Would you think I was crazy?"

Thelma felt something thump hard against her breastbone. Her mouth fell open. "Marry you?" She laughed. "George, I don't even know you."

His gaze was resolute. "Yes, you do," he said. "You know me."

She laughed again, plowing through the frightening truth of it. "Besides," she said, "that's not even legal in Alabama."

He shrugged. "To hell with Alabama," he said. "Alabama isn't the only place in the world."

She stared up at him, this blond marine, two years her junior. She remembered how, when the military declared him KIA—killed in action—somehow, her heart had known that he was not.

George met her gaze. "You didn't answer the question," he said.

"Would you think I was crazy?"

Thelma didn't hesitate. "Yes," she said, "I sure would."

George took this in. Then he gave her a soft smile. "What if I asked anyway? What would you say?"

It was a long moment before Thelma replied.

one

THE CONGREGATION SANG A HYMN, "GOD WILL TAKE CARE of You." To Adam Simon, the words felt hollow and thin, an assertion of confidence he did not feel, but he followed along in the hymnal anyway, joined his voice to all the others, throwing the words against an apprehension, a certainty of doom, that made his stomach ache. *"Be not dismayed, whatever betide,"* he sang, *"God will take care of you."*

But was God here in Selma, Alabama? Could even God keep a rein on that crazy sheriff, Jim Clark? Or were they all just kidding themselves?

He knew the thought was blasphemy. His mother would be disappointed in him, though of course, that was nothing new. He had lived his entire life with a pervasive sense that he had somehow let Thelma Simon down, though he could never say just how. And as to his dad, well . . . if the Reverend George Simon ever caught wind of those sacrilegious thoughts, he'd probably disown him, only child or not.

But Adam couldn't help what he felt—or, more to the point, didn't feel. After a moment, he stopped singing. The other voices crested on without him, a grainy mix—not quite harmony—of men's uneven baritones and women's trembly sopranos. *"Beneath his wings of love abide,"* they sang. *"God will take care of you."*

Above the pulpit, a cross made of light beamed down on the congregation. Several of the bulbs were burned out, leaving splotches of darkness on this symbol of Christ's suffering and victory. It seemed apropos. Adam had never been so scared. And he questioned, not for the first time, exactly what it was he was doing here.

He was supposed to be a senior at the City University of New York.

Instead, he had slipped out of town on a Greyhound bus without tell-ing his mother or father, knowing they would never have approved of him taking the semester off to join SNCC—the Student Nonviolent Coordinating Committee—in trying to register Negroes to vote in some one-horse Alabama town nobody ever heard of. He should have been preparing to accept his diploma this spring as part of the school's first graduating class. Instead, he was here in this chapel with hundreds of other people, singing words he did not quite believe, wondering if he would survive the day.

Jimmie Lee Jackson certainly hadn't survived. It was just over two weeks since Alabama state troopers had chased that unfortunate young man and his mother and grandfather into a Negro diner after they joined a protest march. Jimmie Lee, who was unarmed, had tried to keep the cops from beating the old man and his mother. One of the troopers had shot him twice in the stomach and he had died days later of an infection.

The shock of it was still fresh, especially coming just six months after those three missing voting rights workers were found dead over in Mississippi. The year before that, an NAACP official named Medgar Evers was assassinated in his own driveway.

It seemed like every few months, the news brought another stark, if unnecessary, reminder of how dangerous this work was. These crackers down here would kill you just as soon as look at you if you stood up to them. The realization made you check yourself, made you ask if you really believed what you said you believed. If you believed it enough to put your body on the line for it.

After Jimmie Lee's death, Adam's mother had called long distance and begged him to come home. He had assured her he would be just fine, but in some shameful secret crevice of his mind, the call had pleased him. Adam knew that was wrong and it made him feel guilty. Still, her worry proved that she cared about him, didn't it? There had been many times in his almost twenty-two years when he wasn't quite convinced she did.

Adam was a gangly, round-faced young man, his hair a fine, curly fringe the color of muddy water that he kept cut short; its texture was, he had always thought, nature's compromise between the black in him and the white. As was his skin. He was so light-complexioned—"high yella," was the phrase Negroes used—that kids in school had nicknamed him Whiteboy. He had borne it through middle and high school, smiling and pretending it didn't bother him.

Ultimately, though, it wasn't his skin color that most set Adam apart. Harlem, after all, was home to the whole rainbow of brown that constituted what the world called Negro. To walk its crowded streets was to rub shoulders with high yella, blue black, redbone, chocolate, coffee, almond, cinnamon, and tan. The taunting of his classmates notwithstanding, Adam knew that, in and of himself, he was not so odd.

His parents, however, were another matter. Even in Harlem, one did not often see white men holding hands with black women.

Leaning drunkenly against them, laughing too loudly, a hand resting possessively upon a curvy hip rented at a fair market rate, yes, certainly. It was nothing to see white men who came uptown seeking their jollies by taking black women on what were euphemistically called "dates."

But to see them walking together *holding hands*, walking like any respectable married couple on their way to church, on their way to dinner, on their way anywhere—*that* made people turn their heads. That made people talk. Especially when they were with their half-white son, a boy whose very skin color provided the exclamation point at the end of the sentence:

This Negro woman and this white guy are together!

Not on a "date," but together.

At how many school plays and restaurants had he seen the shock of it in people's eyes? How many times had he stood on the playground at ground zero of a jeering crowd of kids, hands balled into fists as he defended his mother's honor? Too many to count.

His parents made a point of not caring what people thought about them and had always encouraged him to do the same. After all, they were quick to remind him on the rare occasions he said anything about it, they had plenty of friends—at Dad's church, at Mom's job, even at his school—who didn't gawp when they saw them. That should be more than enough, shouldn't it? Why should they care about the opinions of people who did not even know them?

But Adam cared. He knew he shouldn't, but he couldn't help it. And by the time he hit his teens, he had begun to distance himself.

He declined to go to restaurants with them, pleading lack of appetite. He stood apart from them at church, he walked ahead of them on the street. It wasn't that he didn't love his parents. It was that he was tired of standing out, sick of being the exclamation point on a sentence he didn't even write.

Mom didn't seem to care that he didn't want to be seen with them. He wasn't even sure she noticed. But Dad did.

"Are you ashamed of us?" he'd asked once. "Or maybe you're just ashamed of me?"

Adam had shaken his head vigorously. "I just didn't feel like going out to eat, Dad. I'm not ashamed."

Which was a lie. Adam *was* embarrassed by them—not individually, but as a unit, as a pair, as a white man and a black woman walking down Lenox Avenue holding hands like it was nothing, oblivious to the way people stared. He was humiliated by that—and angry with himself for feeling that way.

But how to say that to his father? And saying it to Mom wasn't even a consideration.

They were not close. Away from the prying eyes of the street, he had always enjoyed spending time with his dad, whether listening to a ball game on the radio, playing checkers, or building a volcano for the science fair. He had no such memories with his mother. Her rare embraces were quick and perfunctory, over before they began. Their conversations were brisk; she spent more time instructing him on how to comport himself in the world than asking his favorite color or what he did in school that day. More than once, he had seen a vaguely accusatory expression in her eyes when he looked up and caught her watching him.

Adam didn't understand it, but he tried not to take it personally. He knew, mostly from his father and uncle, that her life had been seared by tragedy from early on, what with having her parents lynched back in 1923 when Uncle Luther was nine and she herself was not yet three years old. She had suffered such devastating loss at such a young age. It was perhaps inevitable that she was a bit . . . scarred.

Still, it was hard not to let it hurt him. She was his mom, after all. And you want your mom to like you.

It was as he was thinking this that Adam abruptly became aware of a loud silence. After a moment, he realized that the song had ended and belatedly replaced his hymnal in the pocket on back of the pew in front of him, glad that the singing was finally over. It occurred to him that maybe he was turning into an atheist. Wouldn't Dad love that? But Adam couldn't help himself. Especially standing here in this church, getting ready to do what they were about to do.

God will take care of you?

He hoped. He even prayed. But he could not quite believe. Adam had an awful premonition that he was going to die today.

The meeting broke up then, and he shuffled out of the sanctuary with the rest of the marchers. It was a cool, sunny day. The breeze was a welcome kiss on his sweaty brow.

A classmate from CUNY came up to him as he stood there on the steps, savoring it. "I hope you brought your swim trunks," said Jackson Motley, a cigarette bobbing between his lips. "You Negroes 'bout to end up in the Alabama River."

"That's not funny, Jack," said Adam.

"Ain't meant to be funny," said Motley. "It's the truth."

Buttoning his coat, Adam stepped down, following the crowd across the unpaved dirt street to the playground of the housing project facing the church. There, they would assemble their march lines. "I'm doing this," he said, trying to perform conviction he did not feel.

"This ain't us," retorted Motley, falling into step beside him. "This some of de Lawd's foolishness."

"Us" meant SNCC. "De Lawd" was Martin Luther King.

It was Motley who had brought Adam to SNCC, though Adam hadn't needed much convincing. Kids in school could call him "Whiteboy" all they wanted; he knew he was a Negro, and he knew what that meant. How could he not, when it seemed like every day, the headlines blared some new atrocity—snarling dogs, high-pressure hoses, burning cigarettes against bare skin, sniper fire in your own damn driveway—against Negroes whose only demand was that America be what America said America was. And how could any self-respecting Negro sit safely on the sidelines while others were putting their lives at risk for the benefit of them all? So Adam, Motley, and other members of SNCC had been down here for months, quietly organizing Negroes to go over to the Dallas County courthouse and register to vote—something white people had made an intentionally arduous and intimidating process.

You want to register?

Explain article 8, paragraph B of the Alabama state constitution.

You want to register?

Name the sixty-seven counties of the state of Alabama.

Tell me how many bubbles are in a bar of soap.

Tell me how high is up.

Small wonder practically no Negro was registered here.

Still, SNCC members resented the way King and his Southern Christian Leadership Conference had swooped down on their campaign, a contrail of reporters and TV cameras following close behind in expectation that the preachers would deliver some dramatic confrontation, some indelible moment of street theater like in Birmingham two years ago. It had led to an intense debate within the student group—Motley said that he, for one, would "not let those damn preachers use me for cannon fodder." In the end, SNCC had decided to have no official role in today's demonstration. Any member, like Adam, who chose to participate did so as a private citizen—not a representative.

"I understand how you feel," he told Motley. "But see, I don't care if we get the credit. I care if these Negroes get the vote."

Motley's face shrank into an expression sour as gone-bad milk and Adam knew he had struck a nerve. "Well, of course, I want 'em to get the vote, too," said Motley. "I just don't see how you all getting dumped in the Alabama River gon' help that cause."

"Stop saying that," said Adam.

Motley gave him a look. He took his time answering. "I guess you done already thought about that," he finally said.

"I guess I have," said Adam. He glanced around the playground at the somber faces and focused gazes of the colored men, women, even children getting ready to march. "We all have," he said.

He might have said more, but a pretty young woman he recognized as one of the march organizers hooked his elbow. "We need you to line up right here," she said, moving him to a position in line next to a girl—Adam thought she was maybe sixteen—in cat-eye glasses, her hair swept back in a ponytail. They were organizing the marchers in pairs.

The organizer looked at Motley. "You're not marching, right?"

He shook his head. "No, ma'am," he said, "I am not."

"Then I need you to stand over there," she said, pointing.

Motley touched two fingers to his brow in a mocking salute, then did as he had been told.

Adam realized with a jolt that he had been placed just three rows behind the leaders of the march. He could see King's lieutenant, Hosea Williams, conferring with John Lewis, the SNCC chairman, who, like Adam, would be marching today without the backing of their organization. Adam couldn't hear what the two men were saying, but he noted John's quiet, bulldog intensity. He was a small man, not physically impressive, but he had a way of making himself felt.

The girl next to him said, "I hear Reverend King isn't here."

Adam had heard the same. "Preaching at his church in Atlanta," he said. "That's what I hear."

She shrugged. "I'd feel better if he was here."

"Me too," said Adam. As a member of SNCC, he hated to admit it, but it was true.

"I'm Emma."

"Adam," he said. They shook hands.

"You from around here?"

He shook his head. "New York City. Well, that's where I grew up. I was actually born in Mobile."

"New York, huh?" She lifted an eyebrow, impressed. "You a long way from home, then."

"What about you? Where you from?"

"Right here in Selma," she said. "Born and raised. Never been too much of nowhere else."

"Aren't you supposed to be in school, then?"

She gave him a direct look. "This more important," she said. "Even the teachers say so."

Adam nodded. "Can't argue with that," he said.

The line began to move. They walked in silence, two blocks down Sylvan to Water Avenue, where they turned right. Adam glanced at Emma. She was staring straight ahead, her gaze resolute.

White people on the sidewalk gaped after them as they passed. Cars slowed. Still, there was quiet, save for the soft scraping of their feet and the low rumble of the support vehicles following their procession.

Two of those vehicles, he knew, were ambulances. Three were hearses.

The hearses were only being used to ferry supplies. Still, they were hearses.

They turned left at Broad Street, and there stood the bridge looming above them, a tower of girders and bolts lifting the empty ribbon of asphalt, which had been closed to vehicle traffic, over the Alabama River. "I wonder who Edmund Pettus was?" Adam asked no one in particular as he read the name emblazoned across the structure.

Emma said, "He was some Confederate general. Grand dragon of the Alabama Klan."

Adam shook his head. "He was in the KKK, so they put his name on a bridge. I guess if he lynched somebody, they'd have elected him governor."

The girl met his eyes and Adam had the impression that on any other morning, she might have laughed. "Like I told you," she said, "you a long way from home."

The line continued forward, climbing the narrow sidewalk on the left side of the bridge. Adam glanced over the railing and saw fractured sunlight rippling on the muddy water below. The Alabama River was a long way down.

And he couldn't swim. He tried not to think about that.

At the crest of the bridge, the line stopped. Adam couldn't quite believe what he saw below him: a phalanx of law enforcement officers stretching across all four lanes of Route 80. He'd have sworn every cop in Alabama was down there waiting for them: state troopers, sheriff's deputies, possemen. Emergency lights flashed on the police cars. About a dozen troopers were mounted on horseback.

And there were spectators—white people—everywhere. Some crowded the parking lot of the Chicken Treat restaurant, others stood out in front of the Pontiac dealership and the mattress store. Some had climbed up on the hoods of their cars. Confederate flags billowed. It was like a football game.

Adam tried to swallow, but his throat was too stiff. "Jesus," said the girl. She spoke it in a whisper. Or maybe, he thought, it was a prayer.

And the line moved forward. Up front, John had his hands in the pockets of his raincoat, a small backpack over his left shoulder. Hosea said something to him then. Adam couldn't make out what it was. John shook his head slightly. His expression radiated a resolute intensity, the focused determination to face whatever needed facing.

The two men led the line of marchers to within fifty feet of the state troopers. There, they stopped again.

Some of the troopers, Adam saw, were busy affixing strange contraptions over their heads. Latches clicked shut. The devices made them look like alien invaders: large insectoid eyes, long elephantine trunks. "Gas masks," he whispered.

The girl said, "Jesus," again.

A trooper stepped forward, speaking into a bullhorn. "It would be detrimental to your safety to continue this march," he said. His amplified voice sounded thin and vaguely unreal. "And I'm saying that this is an unlawful assembly. You are to disperse. You are *ordered* to disperse. Go home or go to your church. Is that clear to you? I've got nothing further to say to you."

Hosea Williams said, "May we have a word with the major?"

The trooper said, "There is no word to be had. You have two minutes to turn around and go back to your church."

And for a moment they stood there facing one another, the white man bristling with all the authority of the sovereign state of Alabama, the Negro men and women facing all that power with only bone and flesh. Finally, John said, "We should kneel and pray."

Hosea nodded and began to pass the word. Which was when the trooper barked an order into the bullhorn. "Troopers, advance!"

They came on at a march, billy clubs held chest-high, parallel to the ground, as if to push the marchers back. But something seemed to come over the state troopers as this hammer of white power met the wall of Negro resistance. The moment teetered as if on a fulcrum. Then police discipline and order broke like something brittle, and the white men began to stampede, a tidal wave of blue uniforms and helmets sweeping over, sweeping *through* the line of Negro protest. From the sidelines, a rebel yell went shrieking up from the spectators in the parking lot like their team had just scored a touchdown.

Adam went down under the wave of uniformed authority. As he scrambled clear, a state trooper lunged for him, truncheon high. Adam threw up his arms to ward off the blow, but the trooper tripped on a scrum of black and white humanity tangled together on the ground and staggered to his left. Adam took the reprieve, clambering to his feet. He heard the clop of horse's hooves. More rebel yells. "Get them goddamn niggers!" someone screamed. It was a girl's voice.

To the left, Adam saw John on his knees, dazed. To the right, he saw Hosea running flat out, some little girl wriggling in his arms as he apparently tried to help her get away. He finally put her down and she sprinted ahead of him. A club thudded into the side of John's head and he dropped. A mounted man with a bat wrapped in barbed wire was chasing after some young Negro man. "Get back here, nigger!" he cried.

Adam stood there stunned as chaos broke wide all around him. It seemed like some terrible waking dream. Then the reality of the thing came home with the crack of a bullwhip and a slashing pain across his back. He wheeled about and saw a man on horseback riding down on him. Adam flinched to the side, avoiding a direct collision, but was staggered by the animal's flank. Somehow, he kept his footing. Somehow, he ran.

Or he tried to. Adam took two steps, then stopped short when he saw the girl, Emma. She was standing there on wobbly legs, shrieking at the madness that swirled around her. No words, just palpable terror and rage. Adam started toward her, but a white man on horseback got there first. A booted kick to the head broke her glasses and dropped the teenager to the pavement, where she did not move.

Adam took another step, trying to reach her. There came a sharp cracking sound and he whipped around in disbelief, his brain screaming. They had opened fire! The white men were shooting at them!

But no. Bullets weren't flying. Instead, clouds of white smoke began to billow over the bridge. Tear gas. Even as he realized this, Adam sucked down a lungful of the noxious cloud. It was like sucking down fire. He couldn't breathe. He couldn't see. His eyes burned so badly he would have gladly ripped them from his head with his own hands. Adam stood there coughing, blind and helpless, his ears reporting carnage all around him.

Horse's hooves.

Screams.

Feet moving in every direction.

Moans.

"Get them niggers!"

Adam Simon was going to die on this bridge. He knew it as surely as he knew his own name.

But he couldn't just stand here and wait for it to happen. Arms outstretched, hoping to touch any landmark, anything that might give him guidance, he staggered about in the mist. Then his foot struck something yielding. Adam strained to get his eyes to focus. Through tears, he realized it was her, the girl, Emma. Her face was a bloody mess.

He wasn't sure she was conscious.

He wasn't sure she was alive.

Adam gave a violent cough. Nausea was a snake burrowing its way up from his gut. Snot and tears dripped down his face. He patted Emma's cheek roughly. "Are you okay?" he cried. Her eyes flickered. "Come on," he said. "We got to get out of here."

On the southbound lane of the bridge, some man was doubled over, retching.

From somewhere far away, white people were laughing and cheering. "They really showed them niggers, huh?"

Adam could not bring Emma to. She was a rag doll.

Horse's hooves made a thunder on the asphalt. The troopers were chasing marchers through the chemical fog—apparently, all the way back to the chapel.

Adam didn't want to carry this girl. He wasn't even sure he could carry himself. But he had no choice. He hooked her armpits and began dragging her body through the white cloud. It was slow going. His eyes were still tearing. His chest was a firepit. He thought of his mother and all the tragedy she had lived. She deserved better than this. He wished he hadn't snuck out of town to come here. He wished he hadn't been embarrassed by her and Dad. He wished a lot of things.

I'm sorry, Mom.

Which is when he heard the horse coming at full gallop. Adam spun just in time to see it emerge from the cloud, like a specter from some nightmare, a trooper in a gas mask sitting astride, his club already on its downward arc. Adam's brain ordered his body to move, but he never had a chance. The truncheon struck his head with a solid crunch. He dropped Emma. The world spun away from him. He saw blood flying up. Then the pavement was coming at him.

And that was the last thing Adam Simon knew.

two

Luther Hayes, carrying his black barber's case, pulled open the door of the West Haven Rest Home at half past three. Some white man in his forties was coming toward him, wheeling a woman whose scalp gleamed beneath shreds of thin, gray fuzz. He was trailed by a stoop-shouldered teenaged girl whose expression broadcast resignation and petulance. Luther stepped back and held the door for them. The white man acknowledged neither Luther nor the courtesy as they passed. The girl's gum cracked like a whip.

Shaking his head, Luther stepped through into the lobby, a room of indirect light with seascapes on the walls. A listless old white man leaning heavily on a cane regarded him without interest. The blonde receptionist looked up from her movie magazine, saw who it was, and looked back down. Luther came here often. That fact notwithstanding, he hated the place. There were few things more depressing than a building full of old people waiting to die.

He supposed part of it was just the fact that he was getting older himself—he would be fifty-one in May; already his joints ached and he found himself standing over the toilet four times a night. Hardly worth it trying to sleep anymore.

But it wasn't just the reminder of his own inevitable decay that made him depressed. It was also the reminder that somehow, he had managed to make it this deep into life only to find himself more or less alone: no child, no wife, few friends. Just his sister and her son. And he barely knew either of them since they lived in New York, a town so far from Mobile and so utterly alien that it might as well be a moon colony. If he ended up in a place like this, who would even come to see about him? What middle-aged man and bored teenager would come to take him for Sunday dinner?

Luther wondered where the years had gone. He marveled that he had managed to do so little with them. The thought made him sigh. He had been coming here for six months and it always had this effect on him.

He passed through the dayroom where half a dozen residents were sitting and an old episode of *I Love Lucy* was playing on the television. Lucy Ricardo had her head stuck in a loving cup and was bumbling about the New York subway system. The studio audience howled with laughter. The West Haven audience was silent and still.

Two corridors branched off either side of the dayroom. Women residents had the hallway to the right, men to the left. Plush carpet swallowed the sound of Luther's steps as he entered the hallway on the men's side. He paused at the first door on the left and knocked, then pushed it open. The old man was in an easy chair watching television. He looked up. The hesitation was minute.

"Luther," he said.

"Hey, Johan," said Luther. He held up his case. "Haircut day."

Johan smiled and waved him forward. "Come on in," he said. "I was just watching the news."

In a place where some people walked around in robes and putting on blue jeans counted as dressing up, Johan wore what he always did, what he always had: a tailored suit, this one navy blue, with a crisply knotted tie. On his lap was the inevitable matching homburg. If you didn't know better, you might think he was going to court to try a case. But his days of going to court were done. In fact, his days of going anywhere were done.

Once, he had been one of the most important men in town. Now this sad place constituted his entire world. It did not seem fair.

For many years, Luther's barbershop had been one of the places Johan had regularly gone. He'd made a habit of coming in every two weeks for his trim, arriving in a chauffeured Packard. He cut an odd figure, sitting there awaiting his turn, an overdressed old white man in a room full of boisterous Negro men who laughed and argued about women, politics, and sports. More than once, some customer had inclined his head toward Johan and whispered to Luther, "What this old honky doing hanging around here?"

Luther would shrug and say, "I guess he like the way I cut his hair."
Because, really, how to explain Johan and how they knew one another
without taking the whole afternoon to do it?

They had met back in '42 when Luther was in jail for refusing
induction into the army and Johan Simek—still calling himself John
Simon back then—was the lawyer Thelma had somehow conned or
arm-twisted into representing him. Luther had distrusted him on sight,
sitting there ramrod straight in that interrogation room with his expensive suit and hat, hands folded on the table, reeking of a white man's
imperiousness, his bred-in-the-bone sense of his own essentialness.

But Johan had impressed him when he did something white men
did not often do: he listened to a colored man. Indeed, his eyes grew
intense with horror as Luther explained why he refused to be inducted
into the U.S. military. Namely, because he could not fight for a country
he loathed, a country where his parents had been lynched at their own
front door and the law refused to do anything about it.

When Luther was done, Johan, who was always more of a deal-
maker than a lawyer, had offered him a surprising bargain: if Luther
would agree to military service, Johan would get the charges against
him dismissed and find a way to make sure his parents' killers were pros-
ecuted. "Why should I trust you, man?" Luther had demanded.

And Johan had shrugged as if the answer was obvious. "Because
I give you my word," he said. He had offered his hand and after a
moment, Luther had reached across the table, his handcuffs rattling,
and taken it.

Each had honored his part of the bargain, with Luther going on
to serve in Europe with the 761st Tank Battalion and Johan somehow
managing to wheedle and bribe the district attorney into prosecuting
the man who had led the murderous mob. Not that it had done any
good in the end. A jury of white men had heard the incontrovertible
evidence—eyewitness testimony and even a photograph of the crime
and the perpetrators—over a three-day trial, then deliberated for less
than an hour and returned a verdict of not guilty.

Something about the experience had changed the imperious white
man, though. Luther never quite understood what it was—Johan
would not talk about it—but he knew it was real. It was after this that
Johan had decided to go back to the birth name he had cast aside after

coming to America as a boy from Central Europe—"I was trying to be a white man," he had explained to Luther once—and had become a vocal and energetic advocate for Negro civil rights, no easy thing to be in Mobile, Alabama. He lost clients, he lost friends. Once, in 1948, he'd even had a cross burned on the front yard of his mansion. Yet whenever it was suggested he should be more circumspect about such dangerous activity, Johan had waved the idea away. "Ach," he would say, "I have spent enough time being afraid."

So he had kept right on doing what was dangerous to do in Mobile. He joined the NAACP, he gave money to support the Negro bus boycott in Montgomery and the desegregation campaign in Birmingham. When the boy Emmett Till was brutally murdered in Mississippi, he wrote a check to the child's mother and had it delivered to her in Chicago by an intermediary from the NAACP. He showed Luther the note he sent with it.

"I was not born in this country but when I came here in 1895 as a boy from Europe, I thought I had arrived in Heaven. I carried with me in my heart the American promise: that this was a land of freedom and opportunity where anyone who was willing to work for it could achieve anything he could dream. Sixty years later as an old man, I have come to understand the hypocrisy and lies embedded within that promise. Please know that a stranger in Mobile grieves with you the murder of your son. I know that no gift and no words from me can soften the ache you must feel at what those monsters in human form did to your beautiful child. But it is my hope that this small token of commiseration will encourage you and fortify you in your quest to make America finally honor its promise. May you someday find peace."

But for all of that, the moment Luther considered Johan's finest had come in response to a crisis of a different sort much closer to home.

On that Christmas Eve after the war, when his son George had impulsively proposed to Luther's sister, Thelma, and she had just as impulsively said yes, it had torn two families apart. Luther had known the boy was sweet on his sister, but still, they hardly knew each other. He and Thelma had argued well into the night, then picked it up again as Adam was opening Christmas presents beneath a meager tree the next morning. It was too soon for something like this, Luther told her. While George was nice and all, he was a white boy. She couldn't marry a white boy—it wasn't even legal. But the more he tried to reason with her, the more stubborn and resolute Thelma became.

As Luther would later learn, it was even worse at George's house. When the young white marine broke the news to his family over breakfast, it shattered Christmas morning like glass. George's mother, Lucille, yelled that she was damned if she'd stand by and allow her son to ruin his life with "some nigra woman." His kid brother, Nick, who had grown up worshipping George, cursed and disowned him. His sister, Cora, fled the room crying.

His father, Johan, had watched all this with grim, quiet dismay. The next day, he went out early and rented a moving truck. He spent the day filling it with furniture from the after-Christmas sales and brought it rumbling to a stop early that evening in front of Luther and Thelma's little shotgun house on Mosby Street. He crossed the plank that served as a bridge over the open sewer, marched up to their front door, and knocked. When Luther answered, he spoke without preamble.

"I assume she has told you?" he said.

Luther nodded. "Yeah, she did. They both crazy if you ask me."

"Perhaps they are," said Johan. "Or maybe it is the world that is crazy and they are the only ones who are sane. It is not for me to say. But the one thing I know is, if they are determined to do this thing, they cannot stay here in Alabama." He nodded toward the truck. "There is furniture in there, enough to set up a household. You and I must drive them someplace north—I think, perhaps, New York City—where they can do as they please. And we must do it as quickly as we can."

Luther had glanced around at the sound of movement behind him. Sure enough, his sister stood there, listening. Her gaze dared him to say no. Luther had sighed, suddenly exhausted. "Yeah," he said, "I think you right."

They started out early on the last day of the year. They drove through the night, taking turns at the wheel, following George and Thelma in George's little sports car, and arrived in New York City on the evening of January 1, 1946. Johan and Luther spent a week in the city. They stood witness to George and Thelma's vows, helped them find a place in Harlem, and moved them in.

It was an act of generosity that drove a wedge between Johan and the rest of his family. Johan didn't like talking about it, but Luther knew the break between him and his wife had never quite healed, even though Lucille Simon lived another seven years before dying of breast cancer in 1953. And though it had all happened almost twenty years ago, Johan's two other children—Cora was a housewife in Huntsville, Nick, a marine serving in Vietnam—barely spoke to their father to this day.

Yet Luther had never once heard the old man complain, much less second-guess what he had done. Whenever Luther brought it up, he invariably gave the same response. "It was the right thing." For him, that had always settled it. Eventually, Luther just stopped raising the subject.

Now, as the old man watched with expectant eyes, he opened his case, unfolded his barber's cape, and draped it with a practiced flourish around Johan's neck. Then with his shears and comb, he began trimming the old man's coarse, graying hair. "What's that you watchin'?" he asked. On the screen, a phalanx of state troopers was rushing, batons swinging, over a group of Negroes.

"Ach," said Johan with a wave of his hand, "terrible news. There was a march for voting rights for Negroes. The state troopers met them on a bridge and beat them like savages. Terrible, terrible thing."

"Where was this?" asked Luther.

Johan pointed to the floor. "It was here. Right here in Alabama. In Selma."

Luther shook his head. "Bad shit always seem to happen in Alabama, don't it?"

"Well, I could do without the coarse language," said Johan, "but yes, of course, you are correct."

Luther smiled at the familiar rebuke. "Well, coarse language fit a coarse situation, don't you think?"

"The situation is more than coarse," said Johan. "It's evil. I don't know why President Kennedy doesn't send in the army. Or federalize the National Guard."

It made Luther wince. "Johnson," he said.

"Eh?"

"It's President Johnson now, remember? Kennedy was assassinated two years ago."

"Ah, yes, just so. Johnson. That's what I meant to say. President Johnson must take action."

Johan was getting senile. It made Luther sad to see—another reason he hated coming here—but he felt that somebody who knew the old man should bear witness, and with his wife gone and his three children scattered elsewhere in the world, Luther was the only one left to do it.

"Johnson," Johan was saying. "Johnson, Johnson, Johnson." Like repetition might make it stick.

He had ended up here in September after a fire at the house where he had lived alone, but for household help, since his wife died. Johan had put the skillet on the stove, intending to fry himself an egg. He had turned on all four burners, then went up to his room, got dressed for bed and fell asleep. The resulting fire had destroyed the kitchen and would have taken the entire house but for the quick action of a passerby who kept a fire extinguisher in his car. The firemen had found Johan sleeping peacefully.

Cora, coming down from Huntsville to investigate, had heard from his neighbors of her father's increasingly erratic behavior—he forgot the names of people he had known for years; he repeated himself; he laughed inappropriately; he got angry for no reason—and had promptly deposited him in this place. The idea of finding a facility for him in Huntsville had apparently not even crossed her mind. Then, she'd put the mansion up for sale and returned home. The whole process had taken her less than a week.

Johan still had good days, but they were becoming fewer and further between. A doctor had warned Luther once, out of Johan's earshot, that Johan would only get worse. "He'll have peaks and valleys," he had said, "but the condition itself is terminal. He won't recover from this." Even worse, the doctor said he would likely linger for years, the fog encasing his thoughts getting thicker by the day until he withdrew from life completely, alive only in the technical sense of drawing air.

Luther could not imagine a more terrifying fate. Johan would slowly be entombed within his own body.

"You know what you are doing with my hair?" asked Johan.

"You know I do," said Luther. He had been the old man's barber for almost twenty years now.

"Don't leave it too long. I don't want to look like one of those rock 'n' roll singers. Have you heard any of them? With all the 'yeah, yeah,

yeah'? I feel sorry for the young people today who will never know what real music sounded like."

"Erskine Hawkins," said Luther, naming the Alabama trumpeter who'd had big hits in the late thirties and all through the war.

The old man cut him a look. "I was speaking of the classics," he said. "Wolfgang Amadeus Mozart, Johannes Brahms, and of course, Ludwig van Beethoven. You get back to me when your Erskine Hawkins composes something as transcendent as 'Ode to Joy.'"

Luther grinned. "I don't know about 'transcendent,'" he said, "but that one song of his, 'Tippin' In,' used to get everybody out on the dance floor."

"Ach. You are a philistine," said Johan.

"And you a snob," said Luther.

"Don't leave it too long in the back. I don't want to look like one of those Beatles. Have you heard them?"

"I heard them," said Luther. "Nothin' but a bunch of 'yeah, yeah, yeah.'"

"Benjamin, are you sure you know what you're doing?"

Luther paused in his clipping. Benjamin Johnston was the Negro man who, with his wife Alice, had been Johan's live-in cook and butler for many years. Benjamin had died in 1958, Alice in 1960. It wasn't the first time Johan had made the mistake—he'd done it twice before. But each of those times, when Luther corrected him, telling him that his longtime butler was dead, Johan—a stoic man whose emotions were ordinarily more impregnable than Scrooge's wallet—had broken down, sobbing and wailing as if it had just happened. And for him, Luther supposed, it had. Now, he considered briefly whether it was worth putting Johan through that ordeal again and decided it was not.

"Yes, sir," he answered, "I know."

"Don't leave it too long in the back," said Johan. "Lucille will think she's married one of those Beatles."

"No, sir," said Luther. "We wouldn't want that." He kept clipping.

After a moment, Johan said, "I saw him, you know."

"Who's that you saw?"

"Bitters. I saw Floyd Bitters here."

Again, the scissors in Luther's hands paused in their cutting. Floyd Bitters was the leader of the mob that killed Luther's parents. He and

Johan had had some sort of confrontation while Luther was away in Europe. Johan would never say exactly what happened between them, but Luther knew it had left him shaken and afraid. Now Luther prayed to a God in whom he did not believe.

Lord, don't ever let me get senile.

And his hands went back to cutting.

Another moment passed. Johan said, "You're not Benjamin." It was almost an accusation.

"No, I'm not."

"Benjamin is dead."

"Yeah, he is."

"My mind," said Johan. "I hate what is happening to my mind."

His voice broke and he wept quietly. Luther pretended not to hear.

After a moment, Johan said, "Don't leave it too long."

"No sir," said Luther. "Don't want you to look like one of them Beatles."

"Ach, have you seen them?"

"Lot of 'yeah, yeah yeah,'" said Luther.

"I pity the children today. They don't know what real music is."

"Beethoven," said Luther. "'Ode to Joy.'"

"You know 'Ode to Joy'?"

"Yeah," said Luther, "sing it all the time at the barbershop."

"You have a barbershop," said Johan. A statement.

"I do," said Luther.

"It's on Davis Avenue."

"Sure is," said Luther. "Right there on the Avenue."

The old man smiled, pleased with himself for remembering. He said, "I saw Bitters."

"Really? How he doing?" Luther was whisking the hair from Johan's neck.

"He's a terrible man. He beat me up, you know."

Luther stopped. This was new. "Really? What happened?"

Sudden tears were leaking down the old man's face. "I went to the town where Luther's parents were killed. This man Bitters, he heard my accent. It comes out sometimes when I get agitated. He called me bohunk. He said, 'You are no white man. You only look like one.' And he slapped me into the dirt and stomped on me. Broke my ribs. I was in so much pain. And I could do nothing. I was too weak. Ever since then, I've been afraid of him."

"You ain't got to be afraid," said Luther, his voice soft. He had been nine years old when his parents were murdered. He knew what it was to fear Floyd Bitters. "That was more than twenty years ago when all of that happened."

Johan's face brightened. "Really? What year is this?"

Luther whipped the cape off him, flakes of hair falling to the linoleum. "It's 1965," he said. "Brand new day." He went to a closet, retrieved a broom and dustpan he kept there, and began sweeping up.

Johan pointed at the television. The news was once again running the video of state troopers charging into a line of Negro protesters, bodies tumbling to the pavement, clubs flashing down, white clouds of gas drifting across the highway like ghosts.

"A terrible thing," he said. "I don't understand how they can treat people like that. People who just want their freedom."

"I don't understand it, neither," said Luther.

"President Kennedy should do something about this."

"You right," said Luther, emptying the dustbin into a trash can. "President Kennedy need to get off his ass."

He replaced the dustbin in the closet, repacked his barber's tools, then took a seat on the bed. As difficult as it was being here, Luther always made himself stay at least an hour. It felt like a duty, some hard but honorable thing he was obligated to do. Especially considering that no one else would be coming to see the old man until Luther returned midway through the week.

George, at least, tried. He had been down to see his father four times since Johan had been placed here, but Luther knew it was difficult on a preacher's salary. Plus, there was the matter of getting the time off. The logical thing, as George had confided wearily on his last trip, would have been to simply return to Mobile; he could tell his sister to take the house off the market and he, Thelma, and Adam could move in.

But of course, the neighbors would complain at having Thelma and Adam there. And the state might intervene since it wouldn't recognize them as married and the law prevented people of different races from spending a night under the same roof.

Even if those problems could have been resolved, though, there was also the fact that Thelma would never agree. She had not stepped foot in Alabama even once in the twenty years since she left it. Thelma hated her home state with an incandescent passion. Saw the whole thing off and set it adrift in the Gulf of Mexico and she wouldn't give a damn.

Still, thought Luther, this was her husband's father and that ought to count for something. He hoped George would get a chance to come down again soon. The old man's memory was going fast. How long before there would be nothing left? How long before his oldest son would walk through that door and his father would look up and not know who he was?

Luther did not envy George that moment.

They sat together for a few minutes. Johan mentioned the Beatles twice more. But what riveted his attention was the footage from the bridge, which kept repeating. Apparently, this carnage had happened today.

"Terrible thing," said Johan, shaking his head. "Terrible."

"You got that right," said Luther. He glanced at his watch. "Well," he said, "time for me to go."

"So soon?" The old man looked crestfallen. He always did.

"I'll be back before you know it," said Luther.

Johan's voice turned sharp. "What is this place? Why am I here?"

"This where you live now."

"I live here? Why?"

Luther was at the door. "Because you need help," said Luther. "And they the ones can give it to you."

"And then I'll go home?"

"This your home now," said Luther.

"This is my home?"

"I'm afraid so," said Luther. He pulled open the door. "But I'll see you soon," he said. He stepped into the hallway without waiting for a reply. He felt almost as if he was making an escape. In a sense, he supposed that he was.

Luther stood in the hallway for a long moment, thinking. The day-room was to his right. From the television, he could faintly hear Ralph Kramden threatening to send his wife to the moon. He rubbed his chin. Then he turned left.

The first door he opened, he found two old men playing checkers.

They looked up in confusion. "Sorry," he said, closing the door. "Wrong room."

In the next room, a man was lying in bed, his hand moving vigorously beneath the covers. At Luther's entry, the hand abruptly stopped what it was doing and the man looked up sheepishly. "Sorry," said Luther, closing the door. "Wrong room."

This was crazy, he knew. He could get in trouble. But something drove him on.

In the third room, a man was sleeping in a chair. The fourth room was empty. In the fifth room, an old man and a woman were watching television. "Sorry," said Luther. "I got the wrong room."

The sixth room was dark. The figure on the bed was only a shape, a mountain range of shoulder and legs. The last of the day's late-winter sunlight filtered in and Luther saw with a start that the man was turned toward the door and that he was looking at Luther, pale eyes alert and curious in the drooping, colorless face of someone who has suffered a stroke. His right hand jittered aimlessly. He made an inarticulate sound that might have been a greeting.

And Luther's heart stumbled.

The man in the bed had been big once, had been powerfully built. But age and infirmity had carved the power out of him, left the skin sagging limply on his bones. Now he was just the leavings of the man he once had been. A thin thread of drool connected his flaccid lips to his bed shirt.

He pulled those lips up into a smile then, eyes still watching Luther, hand still moving without purpose. It was meant, Luther supposed, as some sort of acknowledgment, as a way of saying, "Hello, I see you there." Or maybe, "What a fine mess this is, huh?" Something harmless and friendly like that. But Luther backed up a step. The man didn't recognize him. Luther knew him, though. Indeed, Luther would never forget him.

All at once, he felt hot, he felt dizzy, he couldn't breathe.

Johan's voice: *I saw him, you know.*

At first, Luther had dismissed it as just more evidence of the old man's crumbling memory, his fading hold on reality. But this was no hallucination or fantasy.

Luther was in a room with Floyd Bitters. He was in a room with the man who murdered his parents.

three

From somewhere far away, the telephone rang.

Luther heard it but did not hear it. The sound did not quite reach him in the place where he lay sprawled out on the porch of the old house on that steamy night in August of 1923 when he was nine years old. Torch flame made bizarre, dancing shadows of the mob of white men in the yard and of his shrieking, hysterical parents, held fast. Above him loomed the monster Floyd Bitters.

The telephone rang again, rang into a cacophony of horror that silenced the crickets in the trees, but still Luther did not quite hear it. Luther froze. Luther did not breathe.

And then the white man saw him. Floyd Bitters bent down, way down from the sky, it seemed, and with one hand, lifted Luther by the arm. He held him up, and for a moment, man and boy were eye to eye. The sweat on the white man's face reflected the flickering orange glow of the flames. His breath smelled like whiskey and onions. Blood dripped on his lips, staining his teeth black in the uncertain light.

Yet again, the telephone rang.

Luther peed on himself. The warm trickle slid down his leg to puddle on the porch. He wasn't even aware.

Mama shrieked. "Leave him alone! Leave him alone!"

Bitters regarded him like a prize fish. "Look here," he yelled. "I done caught me a pissy little nigger cub."

"You call that a niglet," yelled some man behind him.

Bitters laughed. And then he flung Luther away. Didn't drop him, but threw him, like something useless and soiled. The boy landed at his grandfather's feet, bawling like a baby. Not-quite-three-year-old

Thelma was crying, too, her eyes glittering with tears, her mouth gaped with wailing.

"Ma-ma," she cried, reaching chubby arms forward.

Again, the telephone rang. Now Luther heard it. He turned this way and that, moaning, wondering what the awful sound might be.

Gramp held both the children back from running to their parents. "Please, sir," he said, "please, sir, please, sir." Like an incantation of some impotent magic. "Please, sir. Please, sir. Please, sir. She got the little ones. He my only son. They ain't meant no harm. Please, sir, don't. Have mercy on them. Please, sir."

Bitters didn't even bother to answer. He had his back to the door, lifting high the hand with the half-full bottle of brown liquid. "Let's get on with it!" he roared.

And again the phone jangled its harsh metallic alarm, like coins falling down a pipe. Luther bolted upright in bed, the sound of his own strangled cry filling his ears. He was immediately sorry. His head felt grotesquely swollen, every contraction of his heart matched by a hard throb of misery in his temples. His mouth tasted like something furry had crawled up from his gut and died on his tongue.

The bottle that was the cause of this extravagant misery lay on its side on the nightstand next to a vase full of pocket change Luther kept there. The neck of the glass bottle was pointing toward him like an accusing finger. Luther saw with a grimace that the bottle was empty. He had sworn off drinking while in basic training—hadn't had a drop in over twenty years, a fact of which he had been distantly proud before last night.

It took him a moment to reconstruct the night. Then he recalled. How he had stepped into that room to find an elderly Floyd Bitters smiling at him—*smiling* at him. How all the old terror and hatred had welled up in him, pushing through his gut like a fist. How he had staggered out of that place needing alcohol with an animal desperation.

Something to fog the clarity of the mirror. Something to make everything stop hurting. Not that it had helped. He had spent the night drinking and collapsed in his bed, but the old monster had followed him down into his dreams, dreams that had returned him to that awful night—August 28, 1923—when white men set his entire world on fire.

And now, the bill for a night of drinking to forget came due. Luther touched his temple and was surprised not to feel it pulsing obscenely beneath his fingers.

The phone made its jangling noise again and he snatched up the receiver. He wasn't sure he would survive another ring.

"Yeah?" he said.

"This is the operator," said a white woman's officious voice on the line. "I have a person-to-person long distance call for a Mr. Luther Hayes from Mrs. Thelma Simon."

Something cold spilled in his chest. It made his head hurt even more. A long-distance person-to-person call, especially during the week, when the rates were highest, could only mean trouble. "This is me," he said. "Put her on."

The operator said, "Go ahead, caller."

Then Luther heard his sister's voice. "Luther? Are you there?"

"I'm here, Thel. What's wrong?"

"It's Adam," she said. "He's missing. I can't find him."

"What are you talkin' about?"

"That march yesterday. He was in it."

"Thelma, you not makin' any sense. He was in what?"

She sounded shocked. "Luther, where have you been? Haven't you seen the news?"

The memory came back only slowly. Before he wandered down the hall. Before he found Floyd Bitters lying in that bed smiling and waving vaguely. Before he sought oblivion at the bottom of a bottle. Before all that, he had been sitting with Johan. And he had seen the footage on television. White troopers beating Negro people. "You mean the march on that bridge?" Luther scowled from the pain of his own voice.

"Yes," she said. "It was one of those civil rights protests they've been having. It was in Selma."

He interrupted her, surprised. "Adam in Selma?"

Thelma didn't bother hiding her impatience. "What do you think I've been trying to tell you."

"How long he been there?"

"Since January. I told him he couldn't go, but he sneaked his ass out and went anyway."

"January? That's . . . two months!" His nephew had been that close for that long and he hadn't even bothered to let Luther know?

"I *know* it's two months, Luther!"

"I'm sorry," he said.

She sighed. "No, I'm the one who should be apologizing," she said. "I shouldn't yell at you. I'm just so worried about him. You know how it is down there. You know how they treat us."

"I know," said Luther.

"But see, he *doesn't* know," said Thelma. "That's the point. Adam has spent his whole life here in New York. I'm not saying it's perfect, but I am saying it's not Alabama. He doesn't know Alabama. He just knows he wants to fight for civil rights."

"A lot of young folks doing that these days," said Luther. "Some of the old ones, too. That Martin Luther King, he's got a lot of people stirred up."

"You saw the news, right? They broke into the TV program last night to show it. Those troopers, they were riding over them with horses. They were beating them with clubs. They shot them with tear gas. You wouldn't treat a dog the way they treated those poor people."

"Was anybody hurt?"

"They say on the news nobody was killed. But you think those Alabama crackers would tell the truth about that?"

The language was not like her. After all, Thelma was married to an Alabama cracker—or at least, to a white man from Alabama. He took it as a measure of how scared she really was.

"You're sure he was in this?"

"I spoke to him Saturday night and he told me they were marching the next day. He was frightened, trying to put on a brave face. He doesn't like me checking on him and he doesn't want me to be afraid. But I tried to explain to him—I've been telling him ever since he first went down there—that he doesn't know those people like I do. He's young."

He heard another sigh blow out of her. "Then I tried to reach him last night, after we saw the news footage. He's staying with some family—someplace called the Carver Projects—and I couldn't get through. I tried again and again and this morning, I finally called the church and they sent someone over to the family's apartment to check. A few minutes later, I get a call that the family doesn't know where Adam is. He didn't sleep there last night and nobody's seen him since the march. That was a whole day ago."

His sister paused then, and Luther knew she was weeping.

"It's okay, sis," he said softly. "It's okay." He was acutely aware of how empty his words were.

"Luther, what if he's hurt? What if he's . . ." She didn't finish.

"He ain't," said Luther firmly. Another emptiness of words.

"How can you be sure?"

"I just know, all right? Your boy is fine."

"Will you go look for him, Luther? That's what I called you for. I know you and Adam aren't close. To tell the truth, you're practically strangers, what with you being there and him growing up here, so I know I don't have the right to ask, but I'm asking anyway. Will you do it for me? Will you find him?"

The quaver in her voice split his heart like an axe through cord-wood. "Of course I will, Thel. You know that. I'm your brother. And we may not be close, but me and your boy, we still family, right?"

"Oh, God. Thank you, Luther."

"You ain't got to thank me."

"You'll call me? Soon as you know anything?"

"Count on it," he said.

"And you'll be careful, right? Those white cops, they're out of their minds."

"Yeah, I'll be careful," he promised.

She paused. Then she said, "Luther, are you all right? You don't sound good."

"Just a headache," he said. "That's all."

"Are you sure? I mean, you really sound awful."

"I'm sure," he said.

There was another moment and he feared that she was going to push him on it. But she didn't. "Well, all right, then," she said, and her dubious voice expressed the skepticism her words withheld. "You take care of yourself. And Luther, thank you for doing this."

"I'll talk to you soon," he said and hung up the phone.

He climbed out of bed, grunting at the pain in his joints. That small bit of exertion made him dizzy and he braced himself against the wall. He would never drink again. He promised himself this, while waiting for the world to stop spinning around him. Never again.

When he thought he could manage it, Luther let go of the wall and walked with careful steps to the bathroom. Back when he was still drinking regularly, he had believed in a little hair of the dog as a remedy for morning-after regrets. But there was nothing else in the house to drink, so he settled for dry swallowing four aspirin from the medicine cabinet. He studied his face in the mirror. His eyes were red-rimmed and sad—probably a fitting match for whatever it was Thelma had heard in his voice.

Floyd Bitters reaching down from the sky . . .

Luther stood over the toilet, suddenly aware of the urgent need to do so. Yet despite the urgency, his bladder made him wait. And wait. Another sign, he thought ruefully, that he was getting old. When he was finally done peeing, Luther took a quick bath, shaving in the tub. He dressed himself—blue jeans, white shirt, jacket—then went into the kitchen where he fixed coffee and scrambled three eggs. Just looking at them made him nauseous, but he forced himself to swallow them down. He hadn't eaten since lunch yesterday and here it was—he checked his watch—a little after ten in the morning.

When he was finished eating and reasonably certain he wasn't going to bring the eggs up again, he went back into the bedroom, picked up the phone, and called Smitty Logan, who often managed the shop in his absence. Luther's shop was closed on Mondays. But he told Smitty he might not be in on Tuesday and appointed him to open up and collect chair rental fees from the other barbers.

"Everything all right there, Lu?" Smitty's voice was wary. Luther wondered just how bad he sounded.

"I'm fine. Just got to do somethin' for my sister, is all. You seen that story on the news yesterday? Them state troopers beatin' up all those people on that bridge?"

"Yeah, I seen it. Everybody seen it."

"Well, my nephew was in that shit. My sister just called and said she hasn't been able to get him on the phone. Want me to go find him."

"Damn," said Smitty. "You be careful up there. Them honkies ain't playin'."

"Yeah," said Luther. "I know."

He hung up the phone, grabbed his keys, and headed toward the door.

There, he stopped. Thelma's and Smitty's words came back to him, telling him to be careful, telling him these damn Alabama crackers had lost their minds. Both of them knew like he knew, and like Adam had just learned, that bad things happened when white people lost their minds.

Luther returned to his bedroom. He opened the top drawer of his nightstand and pulled out the pearl-handled revolver he kept there to greet anybody who might come through his door in the dead of night looking for something to steal. With his thumb, he popped open the cylinder release and spun the wheel once to confirm what he already knew. The weapon was fully loaded.

Then Luther closed the cylinder, engaged the safety, put the weapon into his right jacket pocket. Now he was ready.

A few moments later, Luther settled behind the wheel of his Buick, turned the key, and heard the engine roar to life. He glanced at his watch. It was ten thirty. If he hurried, he could be in Selma before two.

four

SITTING THERE AT THE KITCHEN TABLE IN HER SMALL APART-
ment in Harlem, Thelma lowered the phone to its cradle and wiped at
tears straying down her cheek. God, how she wanted a cigarette. But
a year ago, the surgeon general said the damn things gave you cancer
and she had been trying to quit ever since, something George had been
pestering her to do for years.

She glanced over to her husband, who stood in the hallway across
from their bedroom, watching her. He had a bedroll under his arm, a
suitcase in hand. "He says he'll look for him," she told him.

"You didn't have to ask Luther," said George. "I'll be there myself
by morning. I could have done it."

He spoke in a neutral monotone, something he often did when
they had been arguing and he didn't want her to latch onto something
in his voice and get angrier than she already was. The irony—and he
had never quite grasped this—was that it was his very caution that usually made her angrier. She hated being treated like some ticking bomb
he had to tiptoe around for fear of blowing himself to pieces.

"I know that," Thelma replied, trying to keep the impatience out of
her own voice. "But Luther can be there in three hours. That's a four-
teen-, fifteen-hour difference. A lot can happen in fourteen or fifteen
hours."

It annoyed her that she even had to say this. George was smart and
he had the purest heart of any man she had ever known. But Lord, he
could be obtuse sometimes.

"Thelma," he said, still sounding as if he was addressing a bomb,
"I'm sure he's fine."

"That's easy to say," she told him.

"You saw the news, you read the papers. They all say nobody was killed."

"You really believe that? Just because those people down there claim it's true?"

"You don't trust those Alabama crackers, huh?"

Thelma knew her husband meant it as a joke, an attempt to disarm the bomb. But it felt mocking all the same. Maybe it was just her. Lord, maybe she really was a ticking explosive. She looked at him. "No," she said simply, "I don't."

A pause. She nodded at his suitcase. "You've got everything you're going to need?" A change of subject. Her own way of lowering the temperature between them.

"Yes," he said.

"Toothbrush and toothpaste?"

"Yes."

"Socks?"

"Yes."

"Underwear?"

She looked up in time to see him grimace as she had known he would, then disappear into the bedroom. Thelma almost smiled. He always forgot underwear. The things you learned about a man after nineteen years of marriage.

Thelma stood and went to the doorway of their bedroom. He was rummaging in the dresser. "Top left," she said, as if she didn't put his drawers in the same place every week after washing them.

The things you learned . . .

Thelma Gordy had loved George Simon before she knew she did, before she realized such a thing was even possible between some poor black girl on a dirt road and a white man who came from money. They had met not long after Pearl Harbor. Her first husband, Eric Gordy, had died saving George's life during the Japanese attack. The War Department had thought it would be great for Negro morale to have the white marine visit the colored widow and express his gratitude and condolences. She had refused to play along with their charade, but even so, she and George had somehow become friends. And then, they had become something more.

"What would you think if I asked you to marry me?" he had asked her, sitting on a bench in Bienville Square that Christmas Eve. "Would you think I was crazy?"

And she had said yes, because of course it would be crazy. The idea of them getting married was downright insane. But to her surprise, that had not ended the discussion. Instead, he had smiled. "What if I asked anyway?" he said. "What would you say?"

She had gaped at him. Then she heard herself reply. "I would say yes."

Because apparently, she was crazy, too.

"You'll call me when you get there," she told her husband now. She made it a statement, an instruction.

"First chance I get," he said. He stuffed the underwear into his suitcase, then scanned the room for anything else he might've forgotten.

Thelma heard herself say, "I really wish you weren't going down there."

His gaze came back to her. "Thelma, we've talked about this."

"You've talked," she said. "I've listened."

She hated the soft accusation in her voice—why poke the embers of argument just when the fire had finally died down?—but she couldn't help herself. Thelma felt whiplashed by how fast this trip had come together. The marchers on the bridge had been beaten yesterday afternoon, not even twenty-four hours ago. Last night, they had seen on the news where Martin Luther King was calling for clergy to come to Selma for a defiant second march on Tuesday. An hour later, she and George had been awakened by a call from their pastor. Reverend Columbus Porter had announced excitedly that he was going to rent a car in the morning and drive down to Selma with some men from the church; they would be driving straight through, taking as few breaks as possible, to make sure they arrived on Tuesday. Would assistant pastor Simon like to join them?

George said yes without even consulting Thelma, which made her furious. They had argued about it half the night, woke up arguing about it some more. Bad enough she had not been able to stop her son from going down there. Bad enough she couldn't reach him by telephone. Would she now sacrifice her husband as well? George seemed incapable of understanding the danger.

He answered her now with that same careful voice. God, how she hated that voice. "Thelma," he said, snapping the suitcase shut. "I don't know what else to tell you. This is something I feel called to do."

"Called," said Thelma. Sometimes, she hated being married to a preacher. "Called" was their all-purpose excuse. How could you argue against something a man said he felt called to do? It was like arguing against God.

"Thelma, please don't be that way. I don't want to leave on bad terms."

She gazed at him. She turned away.

George sat down on the edge of the bed, looking exhausted. "Thelma," he said, "I'm sorry I didn't discuss it with you. You're right, I should have. But honey, there are some moments when a man can't just sit on the sidelines and watch. At least, I can't. There are some moments that decide everything that comes afterward. I think this is one of them—not just for me, but for the whole country. You know better than I do what it's like for Negroes trying to vote down there. And if you have no vote, you have no voice. Which means you get ignored by the people making the decisions. That's what's at stake here."

She turned to glare at him. "I know that. You think I don't know that?"

"Then what are you so mad about?"

"Why does it have to be you? Those white people down there, they aren't fooling around. I don't think you understand that. You say you do, but I don't think you really do."

"I'll be careful, Thelma. I already told you I would. But I couldn't live with myself if I didn't respond to Dr. King's call."

"You and your damned conscience," she said.

"I'm sorry," he said, helplessly. He stood, lifting his suitcase and bedroll. "Try to understand."

"What I understand is that nobody knows where my son is. He's lost down there, don't know if he's dead or alive. And now, my husband is going to the same damn place for another damn march."

"You just sent Luther in there to look for Adam. Aren't you worried about him?"

"Of course I am," she said. "But at least he's not going to some damn march. He's not daring those white people to hit him. Luther is going to go in there, get Adam, and get right out. He understands the danger and he knows how to avoid it."

"Whereas I don't? Is that it?"

Thelma didn't back down. "You don't," she said. "You couldn't."

"Because I'm just a dumb white guy."

"You're not dumb," she told him.

He sighed. "You think I'm going to be the only white man who answers Dr. King's call?"

"The only one I'm married to, yes."

"Thelma . . ."

She turned her back on him. He put the suitcase and bedroll down and came up behind her, taking her by the shoulders. Thelma allowed him to bring her gently around. "I know you're worried," he said. "But I promise I'll be careful." With an index finger, he drew an imaginary x across his heart. A child's gesture, she thought. "You'll see," he told her. "It'll be fine."

He was waiting for words, she knew. Words of balm to cool the tension between them. But she had no such words in her.

"Thelma, I've got to go. We're meeting at the church in fifteen minutes, and I don't want to be late."

She recognized it for what it was, a plea for her to say the words he needed. Words they both needed. But she still didn't have them. She would not have given them if she did. Instead, she said, "Then, you'd better go."

"I hate leaving with you angry at me," he said, now making the plea explicit.

She looked up at him. She gave him nothing. A moment passed. He sighed. "I've got to go," he said again. And he kissed her cheek. "I love you."

Even that, Thelma did not answer. George finally gave up with a tired shrug. "Love you," he repeated softly. He lifted the suitcase, tucked the bedroll under his arm, and walked past her, crossed the living room and opened the door. "I'll call from Alabama," he said. The door closed behind him.

Thelma heard him on the stairs, his steps growing fainter. She spoke to the empty room. "I hate Alabama," she said.

Actually, she hated the whole damn South for the petty, creative ways it found to demean you for being black. Can't walk here. Can't sit there. Can't go through that door. Can't even put your dime in this slot of the damn Coke machine, have to put it in that other slot over there.

The whole South could go to hell, as far as she was concerned.

But she hated Alabama the most. Alabama was where her parents had been butchered and burned like meat at their own front door. Leaving that hateful place had felt like rebirth, like rising from some pool of sticky filth into something clean and new.

She still remembered the long drive, New Year's Eve day, 1945, the three of them in George's little sports car, her brother and George's father lumbering behind in a big moving van, dawn breaking over Mobile Bay, taking turns behind the wheel, eating bread and cold chicken from a paper bag, making a toilet of the woods, all so that they could make as few stops as possible, answer as few questions from nosy, dangerous white people as possible. She had felt guilty about it, putting Johan and Luther through so much trouble on their account.

But she had felt giddy, too. Through two long days of driving, she and George had not been able to stop laughing. There had been an unreal quality to the whole enterprise. It was as if they had become fugitives from gravity, from the rules that had defined their entire lives. It felt like a fairy tale.

New York City returned them unceremoniously to earth. Thelma had thought she was ready for it, thought she understood that it was a big, busy place. But she realized as they drove north through Manhattan and went apartment hunting in Harlem that she'd really had no idea. The city was big and grimy and loud and frightening as it rushed by you, pushed past you, nearly walked right over you, in a never-ending, God-almighty hurry. Poor Adam, clinging to her hand as to a lifeboat as they walked down the street, couldn't turn his head fast enough to see all there was to see.

They found a preacher. They filled out some papers. The preacher said some words. George kissed her. And just like that, they were married.

Their first months were difficult. As much as she loathed Alabama, Thelma kept finding herself nostalgic for a life that was not lived to a rhythm of jackhammers and a melody of sirens. She kept wishing New York City would just slow down and let her catch her breath.

After a while, though, she finally got used to it. They found a church, she got a job waitressing in a diner and did temp work in an office. George, who had declined on principle all further offers of assistance from his wealthy father, worked as a security guard and managed a gas station. They alternated taking night school classes, a semester on, a semester off, so that one or the other was always home with Adam. It made getting their degrees take years longer than it otherwise would have, but in the end, he graduated and was ordained, and Thelma passed the state bar exam on her second attempt and went to work for the Legal Aid Society of New York.

And life was life.

She never went back to Alabama. For her, it was never even a consideration.

Even when George's mother died, she made an excuse to avoid accompanying him to the funeral—the woman had hated her anyway. And she never joined him when he went down to visit his father. She felt terrible about sending George down there by himself, but she couldn't help herself. She absolutely hated Alabama.

And it hit her then, as she stood there in her living room wishing her husband would come to his senses, wishing her son had never snuck out to go down there, that that wasn't quite right. It was what she had told herself for years, but there was more to it than that. Oh, she hated Alabama all right, but it wasn't only that.

It was also that she feared Alabama. It was that Alabama scared her to death.

That's why each click of the odometer, each mile that put first Mobile and then the whole damn state further in the rearview mirror, had felt like a vise squeezing her chest was loosening by increments until finally she was able to breathe. And maybe that was why she had been so giddy—she and George both. They were happy, yes. They loved each other, yes. But they were also high on oxygen, on the simple joy of finally breathing.

That had been years ago. And for the first time since then, she was finding it hard to breathe.

It wasn't that New York City was paradise.

They drew stares, even in Harlem, when they walked down the street as a family. It still rankled her to recall the time one of those sidewalk preachers on 125th Street had yelled something about "so-called Negro women who pollute their bodies with the white man's seed" as she and George and Adam walked past. George had flushed a bright crimson. Adam, who was twelve at the time, had also turned colors; he refused to walk with them after that. Thelma hadn't known at the time who that preacher was, but years later when she saw him again on television, she realized it was a man from the Black Muslims who called himself Malcolm X. He had been shot to death just last month and while she was sorry to hear that, while she prayed for his widow and his daughters, she still held those words against him.

So no, this city was not paradise. But it had become home, a place where they could at least *be*, openly and unafraid, a small grace impossible even to dream in the state where she was born. Indeed, she and George were not even considered married down there. Never mind that the full faith and credit clause of the Constitution—Article IV, Section 1, she could recite it by heart—required each state to respect the "public acts, records, and judicial proceedings" of the others. In other words, if you were married in New York, then you were also married in Alabama.

Never mind that, because the South simply ignored any rules it did not feel like obeying. It was like Appomattox had never happened; those states just went on their merry way as if they thought they were still some other country, bound by some other set of rules, as if constitutional commandments did not apply to them and Supreme Court decisions were merely suggestions they were free to accept or reject as they pleased. When challenged on its lawlessness, the South reacted as unthinking animals do—with savagery.

Now the three people most important to her were converging in that awful place. And she had just sent one of them, her husband, down there without so much as a reminder that she loved him, that he meant all the world to her. He had needed the words, had all but pleaded for the words, and she had withheld them.

Thelma felt something curdle in the pit of her stomach. What if that turned out to be the last time they spoke? What if she never saw him again on this side of life?

What might Rita Schwerner, widow of Mickey, give for the precious chance Thelma had just spurned? What might Myrlie Evers give? Or Mamie Till?

Lord, what have I done?

And she was out the door. And she was flying down the stairs. And she was walking at a brisk step down the street, hugging herself against the March chill.

All the while, she was bargaining with God to let her be in time, let her be in time, please let her be in time. Dear Lord, what had she been thinking? They couldn't part like that. She could not send him down there like that.

By the time she reached the church, she was almost running. Temple of Praise AME—situated between a beauty parlor and a record store on a side street four blocks from their apartment—was little more than a glorified storefront. Thelma pushed through the front door and crossed the vestibule into the sanctuary. There, she stopped. It was empty. But maybe they were meeting in Reverend Porter's office?

"You just missed them," said a voice behind her.

Thelma turned. Mary Porter, the pastor's wife, was a thin, nervous-looking woman with big eyes that, just now, regarded Thelma with concern. "They just left," she said. Then she inclined her head. "Sister Thelma, are you all right?"

Thelma tried to lie with a nod but even as she did, she felt her face betray her, felt it tell the truth. Her mouth contorted, her eyes spurted tears. "Oh, dear," said Mary. She wrapped arms around Thelma and held her close. "Thelma, what are you crying for? Shush, now. It'll be all right."

But the assurance just made Thelma bawl all the more. It wasn't all right. It would never be all right again. She sagged against the confused woman, made helpless by the collision of guilt and fear within her. She had bargained with God and God had said no.

And Thelma felt herself crumble in the grip of a sudden crushing certainty that she would never see her husband or son again.

five

THE WORDS CAME TO MIND AS LUTHER guided the BUICK
over the Edmund Pettus Bridge.

"We have come over a way that with tears has been watered."

It was from "Lift Every Voice and Sing," the so-called "Negro
National Anthem," that he had learned in school as a child, a songwriter's figurative description of three centuries of Negro struggle. But it
occurred to Luther as he crested the bridge that after Sunday, the line
was no longer merely figurative. Surely, this otherwise unremarkable
stretch of asphalt now fit the description quite literally.

A shiver climbed through him at that thought, even as the road
brought him down into the town proper, a drab cluster of low buildings huddled on a bluff above the meander of the Alabama River. Every
doorway and street corner seemed to contain white men in uniform—
police, sheriff's deputies, state troopers. Not a Negro in sight.

As he piloted the Buick slowly through town, Luther could not
help remembering the times he and his fellow tankers—Books, Jocko,
Arnie, and Friendly, all of them dead in the war—had rumbled down
the main drag into some European town bristling with menace. The
streets would be empty and artillery blasted, but you could smell the
krauts watching you, knew that at any second, all hell might rain down.
He had never felt so vulnerable or exposed. Until now.

Luther's grip on the wheel tightened. He checked his speed, willed
the car and himself invisible. The pistol made a somber weight in his
pocket.

He drove through the commercial district, such as it was in a
nothing town not half the size of Mobile. The buildings were old and

ramshackle. Other than men in uniform, there were few white people about. Still no Negroes. Luther was filled with the sense of an impending something he could not name. He finished a cigarette and rolled down the window to toss it out, then thought better of it and crushed the butt in the ashtray instead. Best not to give these cops any excuses.

A few blocks from the bridge, Luther finally spotted a Negro man—dark-skinned, with a gleaming scalp and a fuzzy gray mustache and beard—exiting a Rexall drugstore with a small brown paper bag in hand. Luther pulled to the curb next to him, leaned across the seat, and cranked his window down.

"Excuse me," he said.

The old man's step hitched, but he did not stop. His expression was that of some small animal, cornered.

Luther nudged the car forward. He spoke fast. "Look, man, I don't mean no harm. I don't know my way around, is all. Tryin' to get to the Carver Homes."

At that, the old man finally stopped. He gave a furtive glance up and down the street, then leaned into the car. "Carver Homes?" he said. "That's where I'm going."

"I could give you a ride," said Luther. "Solve both our problems at the same time."

The old man needed no further invitation. He pulled open the door and deposited himself on Luther's front seat, already pointing. "Make a right up here," he said.

Luther followed the direction. A clutch of state troopers stood watch at the corner. For an instant they filled the windshield, watching Luther's Buick with baleful eyes. Then they slid from view as the car completed the turn. He glanced into the rearview mirror and when he saw no official cars following them, released a breath.

The old man nodded approvingly. "You right to be nervous," he said. "I wouldn't be out here myself if I didn't have to go to the Rexall for my old lady. She need her heart pills, boycott or no boycott."

Luther nodded. "Same here," he said. "I'd be back down in Mobile, except my sister called from New York and asked me to come find my nephew. She ain't heard from him and she got worried."

The old man's glance hardened. "Your nephew was one of them out there on that bridge yesterday?"

"Yes," said Luther.

"Then your nephew one of the ones caused all this trouble."

Luther pushed down an instinctive flash of anger. What was the point of arguing with this old man? And besides, it wasn't as if he himself believed in all this nonviolence shit. Let some cracker hit you in the head and don't hit back? That wasn't for Luther Hayes. So instead of defending his nephew, he said, "You got no use for the civil rights movement, I take it?"

The other man sucked his teeth. "Bunch of young niggers got these crackers riled up. And you seen the result. Got they asses beat all to hell. Take this right turn up here."

"They say they fightin' for freedom," said Luther, guiding the car around the corner.

"Yeah, that's what they say," the old man said. His voice was sour. "Don't know why they can't just leave well enough alone. Stay in a nigger's place. All they done is make things worse. Got these white mens down here mad as a hive of bees."

"You don't want the right to vote?" asked Luther, who had never sought to register.

The other man lifted an eyebrow. "What I care about votin'? All I care about is to be able to walk to the Rexall without being scared some cracker gon' hit me over the head with a billy." He pointed. "That's it up yonder. Might as well park here, though. You won't be able to get no closer."

As Luther pulled in at the curb, he saw what the old man meant. The street ahead was congested with cars, buses, and bodies. All the Negroes who had not been over on the main drag were here. Many white people, too.

"I thank you kindly for the ride," said the old man, already out of the car.

Luther nodded, preoccupied by the sudden realization of how daunting his task might be. How was he supposed to find Adam in the midst of all this?

He stepped out of the car and stood for a moment surveying the scene. The George Washington Carver Homes was a complex of two-story red brick structures, each surrounded by a lawn and connected by a grid of concrete walkways. There was something regimented about the layout. The place looked less like homes than barracks.

Luther walked toward the commotion. Across the street, several men were nailing plywood over a broken window; apparently, the state troopers' rampage had extended all the way back into the neighborhood. Nearby, an olive-skinned young man in a white kufi was having a spirited debate over some point of religious orthodoxy with an older, heavily bearded white man in a long black coat and hat. A group of white women in nun's habits stood quietly watching.

On one of the Carver lawns, a group of young people, Negro and white, were crouched on their knees, heads down and hands clasped at the nape of their necks. A young Negro man stood over them saying, "Excellent. The idea is to make yourself the smallest target you can. And always remember: you must rise above the urge to strike back. If you don't feel you can accept the blows without returning them, then please do not join this march. There are other ways you can help."

"Sheeiiit," whispered Luther to himself, drawing the word out into two syllables of scorn. He had to find Adam and get the hell out of here. Let one of these crackers hit him and there'd be no "rising above."

"I take it you're no fan of nonviolent protest," said a sudden voice at Luther's elbow.

Startled, he turned to find himself facing a bright-skinned young Negro man with a short Afro and a guarded smile. "Beg pardon?" he said.

"I understand," the other man said. "It's not for everybody. But I would ask you to respect what we're doing here."

"What are you talkin' about?"

The man pointed to the bulge in Luther's jacket pocket. "This is a nonviolent protest. We don't need guns here, brother."

"I ain't here to protest," said Luther. He thought about the guarded smile and added, "Ain't here to cause y'all no trouble, neither. Just here to find my nephew, is all. He was in that march yesterday and ain't nobody heard from him since."

The man's smile relaxed only fractionally. "I can help you with that," he said. "But if you wouldn't mind, I'd still appreciate if you got rid of the gun. You won't need it here and it sends the wrong message."

Luther considered ignoring the man. After all, how could a group of nonviolent protesters stop him from carrying a gun anywhere he damn well pleased? Then he decided that, like arguing with that other fool, this would be a waste of time. It was their show. All he wanted was to find Adam.

"That's not a problem," he told the man. "I can leave it in the car. Like I said, I just come to get my nephew."

"I'll wait for you," the man said.

Luther returned to the car, where he deposited the weapon in the glove compartment. When he returned, the younger man was still there as promised.

"Thank you," he said. "As I'm sure you can imagine, things are very tense right now, people are very much on edge, and we don't want to introduce any element that might make matters worse. Now," he added, clapping Luther on the back, "let's see if we can find your nephew. I'm Andrew, by the way. Andy, they call me."

He extended his hand and Luther took it. "I'm Luther. Pleased to meet you."

Andy led Luther across the street to where a pretty young woman with hazel eyes was standing before a church, fielding questions from some white reporter. After a minute, the reporter nodded, closed his notepad, and wandered away. She turned to the two of them without a pause. "And what can I do for you gentlemen?" she asked. Her smile was disarming.

"Diane," said Andy, "this fellow could use your help."

"Looking for my nephew," explained Luther, as Andy slipped way. "His name is Adam Simon. High yella, curly hair. He from New York City, work with SNCC. Joined in the march yesterday and his mother ain't heard from him since."

"So she got worried and sent you to find him," said the woman, already consulting a clipboard. Apparently, it was a story she had heard before. Luther found that comforting.

He nodded. "I come up from Mobile," he said.

"Well, you can tell his mother we had no one killed yesterday. Mostly broken bones and cuts. That should put her mind at ease."

"I already told her that. She don't trust it. She said these Alabama crackers might be lyin', trying to cover their backsides." Diane's eyebrow arched. "Her words," said Luther.

Diane laughed. "Well, that information came from us, not from our brothers of the pale persuasion, but I understand her caution." As she spoke, she was running her finger down a list. Then she looked up.

"I don't have any information about him being injured. According to this, we housed Adam with a family name of Baker. You might want to check with them, see if they've heard anything." She gave him an apartment number and pointed across the street. "First building over here on the left."

Luther thanked her, but she was already engaged in solving someone else's problem and didn't hear him. It struck Luther as he trotted across the street ahead of three boys on bicycles that he had seen staging areas in Europe that were not this busy—or this mission focused. The movement might be nonviolent, but in every other aspect, these people were fighting a war.

He found the Baker apartment and banged on the front door. After a moment, it was pulled open by a heavyset Negro woman Luther's age, drying her hands on an apron. "Yes?" she said. Luther got the sense he had interrupted something.

"Beg pardon, ma'am," he said. "My name Luther Hayes."

"Yes, Mr. Hayes? What can I do for you?"

"I'm lookin' for my nephew. They told me he was stayin' here?"

"You must be Adam's uncle," she said. "Come on in."

She didn't wait for him to answer, leaving him at the door as she rushed back to attend to something in the apartment. Luther stepped into a heaven of aromas—chicken frying, greens with fatback simmering. "I'm sorry," said the woman from behind the stove in her tiny kitchen as she prodded the chicken with a serving fork. "Don't want my food to burn."

She lifted a plump chicken breast from the skillet and placed it in a pan atop a mound of perfectly browned poultry. "Look like you feedin' an army," Luther said.

The woman smiled, a gold tooth winking. "I near about am," she replied. "We all pitch in to cook for these people done come down here to help us get the right to vote. And after yesterday, they surely deserve a good meal. My name Dora, by the way."

He was standing in a small living room. A portrait of Jesus—long blond hair, soulful, suffering eyes turned toward heaven—watched him from a wall. There was a brown settee that had seen better days and a coffee table strewn with a chaos of overflowing ashtrays, empty glasses, books, newspapers, and magazines. Luther counted four sleeping bags and makeshift pallets of pillows and blankets rolled up against the walls.

Dora saw him looking. "I usually keep a much neater house," she said.

Luther said, "All these people to take care of, it's got to be runnin' you ragged."

She smiled. "It's not so bad. Besides, it's gon' be worth it."

"You talkin' about voting?"

"I'm talking about being a full citizen, yes. Done lived in this country forty-eight years and ain't never been a full citizen. I think it's about time, don't you?"

"Yeah," said Luther, "I guess you right."

"You're the uncle was in the war?" she asked. She went on before he could respond. "How you must feel, done fought all over Europe, risking your neck to get rights for other people, get back to Alabama and ain't got no rights for yourself."

Luther was surprised. "He told you about that?"

"Your nephew talk about you a lot." A smile. "Apparently, you won the war all by yourself. Well, you and his daddy."

"Well, we had a little help," said Luther.

"He's proud of you," said Dora as she lowered a drumstick into the skillet, the hot oil crackling and sizzling.

And Luther wondered how that could even be. They barely knew each other. Adam had been a toddler, not yet two years old, when Thelma and George moved away. Sure, Luther had seen the boy a few times when George brought him down for visits. Once, Luther had even ventured up to New York and spent a few days. But they had never really talked, didn't really know each other. So, he could see no reason the boy would be bragging on him.

Dora seemed to read this on his face. "You look surprised," she said.

"I guess I am," Luther replied.

"Don't know why you would be. You his uncle, ain't you?"

Luther shrugged. "Yeah," he said, "I'm his uncle."

Again, she read him. "You don't sound sure."

"I am his uncle," said Luther, more firmly. "Just . . . we ain't never been close, is all. New York a long way from here."

Dora smiled. "Ain't that the truth." She speared a fat brown drumstick on a serving fork. "Fix you a plate?"

Luther was tempted, but he would feel guilty eating food bought and prepared for the civil rights marchers. Lord knew he was no nonviolent protestor. "No, thank you," he said. "I'm actually looking for Adam. His mother got worried after all the fighting yesterday. She says she's tried to call, but she ain't been able to get through."

"Yeah, I know." Dora was rolling chicken parts in seasoned flour. "Phone's been out. Been waitin' for the repairman to come, but you know how that is. His mother—I guess that's your sister—had someone come over from the church this morning to ask. Tell her not to worry. She raised a good boy, got a good head on his shoulders. I'm sure Adam's just fine."

"You're 'sure'? You mean, you still ain't seen him?"

Up to this moment, Luther had considered his trip to Selma just a way of placating his worrywart sister. Now, for the first time, he felt a prickle of real anxiety.

Dora saw. "I wouldn't worry," she said. "Things been confused since yesterday."

"But you ain't seen him," pressed Luther.

She shook her head. "Not since he left out of here yesterday morning. He went to the service at the chapel, then I saw him when they all lined up in the yard to walk over the bridge. 'Cept, of course, they didn't quite make it."

Luther said, "Can you think of where he might be?"

Her shoulders lifted in a negative response. "Lot of places he might have gone. Might have sacked out in the church over there. Sometimes they do that. Might have made friends with one of these young women and went to find someplace they could be alone for a while." Her smile was sheepish. "Sometimes they do that, too. But I'm telling you, don't worry; he's fine. If he wasn't, we'd know it. You know how it is with young people; they don't always think about checking in."

He knew she was right. But it was thin solace.

"I still need to find the boy," he said. "His mama kill me if I don't."

She smiled. "I might feel the same way if I was her," she admitted. She thought for a moment as she turned the chicken. Then she said, "I know he has some friends in SNCC that he runs around with. Maybe one of them could tell you where he got to."

She gave him four names and the apartment numbers of the families they were staying with. Luther thanked her and set off across the complex. There was no answer at the first two doors. At the third, he met a young man who introduced himself as Jackson Motley.

"Yeah, I know Adam," he said, as he and Luther stood on the front stoop smoking cigarettes. Out on the street, a bus was disgorging a group of men in clerical collars.

"You saw him yesterday?" asked Luther.

"Before the march," said Motley. "Not after. I gave him some grief. Told him don't let them crackers throw him in the river."

Luther cut him with a glance and Motley stammered. "I ain't sayin' that's what happened," he said. "I'm sure it didn't."

"But you ain't seen him since."

Motley shook his head. "No, sir, I have not."

"You got any idea what could've happened to him?"

"Well, I don't know for certain, but way I hear it, he got knocked in the head on the bridge."

The words drove a spike through Luther's chest. "What?"

Motley shrugged. "That's what I hear," he said. "They say he was trying to drag some girl to safety after she was knocked out. This trooper on horseback caught up to him and gave him a whack with his club."

Luther gaped. This brought another shrug. "I told him not to go out there," Motley said, his tone defensive.

"What happened next?"

"Don't know," said Motley. "Like I say, I wasn't there." Pause. "But if I had to guess?"

"What?"

"He probably ended up in the hospital, right? I mean, they say he took a hell of a shot."

Twenty minutes later, Luther walked into the emergency room of Good Samaritan, the Negro hospital in Selma. The waiting area seemed to have been decorated by a tornado. Chairs were askew, magazines and newspapers littered the tables. The trash cans and ashtrays were full. The bitter scent of tear gas—faint, but unmistakable—filled the room. Half a dozen people sat, either waiting to be seen or waiting for word of loved ones.

It struck him that just a few hours before, this would have looked like a frontline army surgical hospital after some big battle, the bloodied and broken streaming in, carried in, standing and sitting all over the place as they waited for medical care. The room was quiet now, but it was the heavy quiet that comes in the aftermath of chaos.

Luther went to the reception desk. "Lookin' for my nephew," he told the nurse who glanced up expectantly at the sound of him. "I think he was brought in here yesterday. Name is Adam Simon."

"That sounds familiar," she said. "Hold on."

There was a moment while she checked some paperwork on a clipboard. Then she frowned. "Hmm," she said. "No Adam Simon."

"But you said you knew the name."

"I said it sounded familiar," she said. "Wait a minute."

She ran her finger meticulously down a list. After a moment, she stopped. "That's why it sounded familiar. We have a Simon Adams here. No Adam Simon, though."

Luther grunted in frustration. The woman said, "You sure he's here?"

"I don't know where else he could be. They told me he got hurt on the bridge."

Her expression turned thoughtful. Then she said, "Come on back. I've got a hunch."

Mystified, Luther stepped into the exam area and followed her through a maze of hospital beds, each partitioned off from the rest by sliding curtains. She paused in front of one, peeked around to ensure the patient was decent, then swept the curtain open with a metallic rasping of the track in the ceiling above.

And there lay Adam. He was unconscious, mouth gaping, a heavy bandage on his head.

"That's him," said Luther. "That's my nephew. Is he okay?"

She consulted her clipboard. "We have him as Simon Adams," she said. "Things were really crazy yesterday, as I'm sure you can imagine. Apparently, the intake nurse made a mistake when they checked his ID. I'll get it corrected."

"But is he *okay*?" insisted Luther.

She went back to the clipboard. "It says here he had a scalp laceration that required eight stitches. And he has a concussion. Doctor wants to keep him another night for observation. They're going to move him to a room as soon as one's available."

"So I can take him home tomorrow?"

"Well, that's going to be up to the doctor, but I expect they'll probably discharge him in the morning, yes." She shook her head and added, "Pretty sure he's not going to be up to any more marching any time soon, I can tell you that."

"I see," said Luther. He marveled at the gangly length of the young man lying before him. The last time he had seen his nephew, Adam had been a pudgy fifteen-year-old boy with acne. Time was a relentless master. "Is there a pay phone?" he asked. "I need to call his mother."

Minutes later, he found himself standing in a phone booth outside the hospital, shifting his weight as he listened to his sister weep. Her soft gasps made him feel awkward and useless—a broadaxe trying to do brain surgery.

"Come on, Thel," he said. "Ain't got to do all that. I told you, he's okay."

"I know," she said. "It's just . . . I've been so worried about him, so scared. You know, Luther," she added, and her voice had grown small, "I haven't always been the best mother to him. It's hard because, of, you know . . . what happened."

The confession set off an alarm bell inside him. "Come on, Thel," he said, again. "Ain't got to go into all that." A note of pleading had entered his voice.

There was a silence. Finally, she said, "I guess you're right."

"'Course I'm right," he said.

"Thank you, Luther. That's all I really wanted to say. I don't know what I would have done if it hadn't been for you."

"You ain't got to thank me," he said. "That's what family for. Now, I'm gon' say goodbye, because I know this call costin' you an arm and a leg."

She was reluctant to let him go, kept pressing for more details, more assurances, but finally, Luther got her off the phone. He returned to his car but didn't start it immediately. Instead, he lit a cigarette and sat there, smoking and thinking.

As far as he was concerned, this so-called voting rights campaign was leaving nothing but disaster in its wake. First, that boy Jimmie Lee

Jackson had been killed. Then Adam and all those others had been beaten bloody. Now, here was Luther's poor sister, traumatized so badly that she was saying things she knew her brother had no way to hear.

And all of this for what? To appeal to white people's conscience? Luther's laugh came out as a bitter grunt.

He could not deny the guts it had taken those marchers to confront Alabama state authority with nothing but their bones and flesh to protect them. Idealism made them brave, he supposed.

But there were times idealism was indistinguishable from foolishness. Hadn't his own father proven that? Walking among white men in all his starchy dignity, only to die with his wife, sheathed in flame, writhing in the dirt, with that enormous white man towering above, braying laughter into the night. The memory of it took Luther away, as it always did. For the shadow of an instant, the stench of burning flesh painted the back of his throat.

When he came back, he found tears standing in his eyes. He brushed them away and shook his head, chuckling at his own softness. It was just exhaustion, he assured himself as he turned the key and heard the engine crank to life. Seeing Floyd Bitters after all these years, drinking himself into a stupor, driving up here to find Adam . . . the exhaustion had brought his emotions too close to the top, that was all. He needed some rest. In the morning, he'd be fine.

Luther was pretty certain this was a lie, but he decided to believe it, at least for now, at least for tonight. And he wheeled out of the parking lot, hoping Dora Baker's offer of a fried chicken meal might still be good.

six

For the first hour, they hardly spoke.

It wasn't a comfortable silence. Rather, it was the silence of things unsaid, the silence of Lord, where to begin. It was a silence flowing from that brand of kinship shared by strangers with blood ties, but no frame of reference in common. Of "family" with nothing to say to one another.

Yet though it was a bad silence, Adam was grateful for it just the same. His head was throbbing as if a convoy of eighteen-wheelers was driving down the middle of his skull. And simple sunlight felt like someone dumping hot coals on his eyes. Even in the balm of shadow—the hospital had given him a pair of disposable sunglasses—he had to squint to see.

He had a bad concussion, the doctor had said. He was over the worst of it, but he would still need a few days to recuperate. And there was no way he would be able to participate in today's march. The doctor had said this as if bracing for resistance. But Adam had only nodded and mumbled, "Okay." Even if he hadn't been in excruciating pain, he had no interest in facing down white men with clubs again any time soon.

So he sat there next to his uncle in the front seat of the careening Buick, peeking through the flimsy plastic shades, giving thanks for the blessing of a silence broken only by the grumbling of rubber against asphalt. Not even the radio played. His uncle lit a cigarette, cranking down the driver's side window to lure the smoke.

Adam had been surprised to find Luther waiting for him when he was discharged from the hospital. He had supposed he'd have to call one of the Negro cab companies or try to reach someone in SNCC to give him a ride. Instead, Luther was there, announcing that he'd been dispatched by Adam's mother to take him back to Mobile and let him rest up for a few days.

It had caught Adam by surprise. He knew that even two months later, Mom was still angry he had slipped out of town a semester short of graduation and come down here to join the voting rights campaign. Whenever he saw her again, he knew he would catch a basket full of hell for that. But your mom is always your mom, he supposed. When you're in trouble, she sends help.

Even when she's angry with you. Even when you've never been close. It was a reassuring thought.

At length, Luther spoke out of the silence.

"Ain't got but the one bedroom," he said.

"I remember," said Adam. "The apartment over the barbershop."

"That's right. But the couch in the living room folds out. You can sleep on that."

"That'll be fine, Uncle. Thank you."

"Your mother was real worried about you."

Adam didn't know what to say to this, so he didn't say anything.

"She said you sneaked out of town without her knowin'."

"I guess I did. Wasn't like it was that hard, though."

Adam felt, rather than saw, Luther's gaze tighten. "Mmm," he said.

There was another silence. Then Luther said in a mild tone, "I was surprised to find out you were here. Been here a couple months, Thelma said. Why didn't you call?"

"I was going to wait till we were done with our work up here. Come down and surprise you."

He was relieved when his uncle simply nodded, accepting the explanation without pushing for more. Because what Adam had said was truthful without being honest. The fact was, he had not reached out because he was intimidated by his mother's brother—almost as much as by his mother herself. For some reason he could never quite explain, he always felt like he was on trial when he was with them. Luther had never mistreated him, never even raised a voice toward him, but Adam was pretty sure all the same that his uncle did not like him. In fact, if his mother's brother had ever so much as smiled at him, Adam couldn't recall.

Luther was getting older. He was thick around the middle, flecks of white colonizing the hair he kept cut short enough to make an army drill sergeant smile. But his face was still all hard angles and eyes that seemed to see everything but give away nothing. He still made you want to take a step back and not give him any grief.

Now Luther said, "You may see George while you're down here. Your mother say he and your pastor and some others comin' down to join this next march."

Adam brightened. "Dad's coming?"

Something unreadable crimped Luther's lips. "Yeah," he said. "But don't ask me about driving you back to Selma to meet him. He can come down to pick you up in Mobile if he want, but I'm for getting out of here fast as I can—and staying out."

"Me too," said Adam.

This seemed to catch his uncle by surprise. "Really?"

Adam nodded, wincing from the pain. "I've seen enough of Selma to last awhile," he said. He tried to smile, wasn't sure if he made it.

Luther regarded him for a moment. "I guess that make two of us," he said. "And I ain't even been hit upside the head with no billy club."

"It's not something I recommend," said Adam.

This brought a snort that might have been laughter, then his uncle turned his attention back to the road. He finished one cigarette, lit another from the lighter on the dashboard. A moment later, Adam lowered his window. He had always hated the smell of cigarette smoke, but this morning, it made him downright nauseous. Another effect of the concussion, he supposed.

They drove. Ramshackle homes alternated with farm fields. Luther seemed in no hurry to speak again, but the silence suited Adam just fine. After a moment, he closed his eyes. The motion of the car, the hiss of the tires on asphalt, were therapeutic, hypnotic. Time passed. Safe in the darkness, Adam was lulled, pulled into tranquility's embrace. He almost slept.

Then the gunshot brought him wide awake.

He bolted upright, looked over at Luther. His uncle was grimacing, hands curled hard upon a steering wheel that was trying to wrench itself from his grip. There was the ugly *flap flap flap* of deflated rubber on asphalt as the vehicle slowed. And Adam realized he had not heard a gunshot after all. Just a tire blowing out. He dry swallowed. Tried to get his breathing under control.

The Buick rolled to a stop on the side of the road next to a winter-dead field where stray puffs of white fiber still clung to brown stalks. "Shit," said Luther. "Shit, shit, shit, shit, shit."

"You got a spare?" asked Adam.

A deep sigh. "Yeah, I got a spare."

He turned the ignition off, pulled his keys. Adam said, "You need help?"

"Best help you can give me in your condition is to stay right where you are." Luther was already out of the car.

"You don't have to tell me twice." Adam sat back and closed his eyes.

The world became sounds. The creak of the trunk popping open. The clanking of the jack as it was pulled out. A grunt of effort from his uncle. The whisper of the spare on asphalt as Luther rolled it along.

The flat was on the driver's side in the front. Adam heard the metallic groan of each lug nut as it came loose. The jack scraped as it was put in place. After a moment, Adam felt the car rising beneath him. The ruined tire came off and the spare went on. Then Luther said, "Oh, shit."

"Don't tell me," said Adam, his eyes still closed. "Your spare is flat."

Luther's vice was rigid. "Open the glove box. There's a gun in there. Give it to me."

Adam's eyes opened. "What?"

"Do what I tell you. Do it now." Uncle Luther was standing straight as a plumb line next to the driver's door, his right palm splayed wide behind him, reaching into the open window, waiting for the gun. Adam followed his uncle's gaze to where a pickup truck was slowing to a stop behind them. A dirty Confederate battle flag was draped across the grill.

Adam said, "Shit." He fumbled the glove compartment open and was just sliding the pistol into Luther's hand when the doors of the truck opened on both sides and three white men came out. Using his body to shield his actions from their view, Uncle Luther tucked the weapon in at the small of his back, covering it with his shirttail. The three men moved with the unhurried authority of police making a traffic stop. But these men, in their overalls and jeans and rough work shirts, were not law enforcement. Their authority stemmed from the fact that they were white—and Adam and his uncle were not.

Two of them confronted Uncle Luther. The third came up by Adam's door.

One of them, a bear of a man with a reddish-brown shrub of beard hanging to his sternum, addressed Luther. "Havin' car trouble there, boy?" There was a smile down in the tangle of his facial hair, but it was as false as the friendliness of his voice.

"Flat tire," said Uncle Luther. He returned the false smile with one of his own. "Nothin' I can't handle. Got to tighten this spare here and we'll be on our way."

"You from here?"

"Mobile," said Uncle Luther.

"That's where you headed back to?"

"Yeah."

"Y'all had some business up here?"

Uncle Luther was still smiling and it was still as false as a car dealer's promises. He wanted to tell the man it was none of his damn business what business he had here or anywhere else. Any fool could see this and there was a crazy moment when Adam thought his uncle would give in to that temptation. Instead, he said, "Yeah, you might say that."

The bearded man cocked an eyebrow like a gun. "I might?"

The man behind him piped up now. "Danny, this one's plumb got a attitude. Can't you see it? I don't think he like you much."

Another fake grin. "Really? You got to be mistaken there, Buddy. Everybody like me. Hell, I'm the easiest guy in the world to get along with."

"Ain't got no attitude toward you," said Luther. And then he added, as an afterthought, "Sir." He had held the false smile so long that it was just a grimace with teeth showing.

Any second now, the man would see that. Any second, he would call Uncle Luther on it. Then, the one next to Adam spoke. "Hey, what's with Ray Charles here?" He reached in and snatched the flimsy sunglasses from Adam's eyes. Adam recoiled from the sudden explosion of light, brought his hands up to cover his face. He heard the one next to him say, "Hey, y'all, look at me," and supposed he must have put the sunglasses on. The supposition was confirmed when he heard the moron start singing in a toneless approximation of Ray Charles.

"*Georgia . . . Georgia . . .*"

"What's wrong with your friend?" asked Danny with what sounded like genuine curiosity.

"Eyes are messed up," said Uncle Luther. "The light hurts them."

"That ain't all." This was the one called Buddy. "His head's all bandaged up."

Adam heard the big man give a low whistle. "I do declare, you're right. How'd you get all banged up, boy? You ain't one of them protesters was makin' all that racket, are you?"

Adam forced his eyes open in narrow slits. He was about to reply, though he had no idea what he would say. Then Uncle Luther beat him to it. "Yeah," he said in a hard voice, "he one of 'em, all right. My sister's boy from New York. When I heard he was here, stirrin' up trouble, I was plenty pissed off, I tell you. Drove up here ready to kick his ass all over lower Alabama, then I found out one of them state troopers done saved me the trouble." Uncle Luther's hand rested casually on the door frame, just inches from the gun in the middle of his back.

"Is that a fact?" The man called Danny was scratching at his beard reflectively.

"It is a fact, sir," said Uncle Luther. "Takin' him home with me so he can rest a few days, then I'm puttin' his ass on a bus back to New York City where he belong. I done already told him, don't come back down here till he know how to stay in his place."

The one named Buddy said, "That's a right smart idea." He yelled to Adam. "You hear that, boy? Pay attention to your uncle here. He's smart. He'll keep you out of trouble."

The moron said, "We should beat him up anyway. Make sure he done learned his lesson."

Danny regarded Luther for a long moment without speaking. Adam saw his uncle's hand move fractionally closer to the center of his back. Then Danny smiled, and for the first time, there was genuine humor in it. "Nah," he said. "We can mosey along. His uncle got things in hand."

And then, to Luther: "You can carry on. We just wanted to stop and make sure you wasn't one of them so-called 'nonviolent protestors.'"

Uncle Luther gave another lying smile. "No, sir," he said earnestly, "I don't believe in that nonviolence." And as the white man had not seen the falseness of the smile, neither did he hear the duality of the words, the threat sleeping quietly within them like a viper in a woodpile.

Danny waved at the other two. "Come on, fellas, let's let these boys be on their way."

They made their way back to the truck, the moron still wearing Adam's hospital glasses, walking with his hands out before him like a blind man, as the other two guffawed. "Willard, you're such a fool," one of them said.

The truck came to life with a roar. Moments later, it swept past the Buick in a great gust of road debris. Uncle Luther stood there until they were gone. Then he went back to changing the tire, his movements as brisk as if he were on a pit crew.

When he was done, Luther cranked the jack down. He returned it to the trunk, which he slammed. Then he slammed the car door as he took his seat behind the wheel. For a moment, Luther just sat there. Adam feared to speak. Abruptly, Luther turned, spearing him with his index finger. "When I tell you give me my fuckin' gun, boy, you give it to me, you hear? Don't be hesitatin'. Don't make me ask you twice."

Adam nodded. He could manage nothing more. For a moment they sat facing one another, still as stone. Then, whatever he saw in his nephew's face slowly gentled Uncle Luther's gaze. He reached up to his sun visor, produced a pair of sunglasses and handed them across. "Here," he said, "put these on."

Adam did as he was told. The shade was like a kiss of grace. His head was throbbing. He hadn't realized it until just this moment. "I'm s-sorry," he stammered.

Uncle Luther sighed as he started the car and wheeled it onto the road. "No," he said, "I'm the one sorry. Ain't had no call to yell at you. It's just . . . I hate dealin' with these country-ass crackers. Think they can talk to you any kind of way, treat you any kind of way, like you ain't just as much a man as they is."

"That was slick the way you handled them," said Adam.

"Done had lots of practice," said Uncle Luther. "Too much practice. If you a Negro in Alabama, you learn." He was lighting a cigarette. "Don't make it easy," he said, blowing out smoke. "Ain't easy by a long shot."

"Mama hates it down here," said Adam.

"Yeah, I know."

"Says she got out once and 'ain't never goin' back again.' Dad used to try to get her to come with him just for a visit and she wouldn't even do that."

"Can't say I blame her."

"How come you stay? How come you never left like she did?"

The tip of the cigarette glowed fiercely orange as Uncle Luther took a long drag. His eyes were distant as he blew out smoke that was instantly shredded by the breeze. He said, "We look at it different, your mother and me. She don't want nothin' else to do with Alabama and I understand that. But me? These motherfuckers drove us off our land when I wasn't but a boy. I'll be goddamned if I'll let 'em drive me out the whole state. I got as much right to be here as they do."

Adam was silent for a moment. Then he said, "You know, Mama won't talk about that. What happened, I mean."

Luther said, "She was only a baby. Not even three yet. She don't remember it."

"No," said Adam, "I mean, she won't *talk* about it. None of it. Not at all. When I ask her, she changes the subject. If I ask her again, she gets mad."

"Well, you can't blame her," said Luther. "That ain't easy to talk about. Even for me, it ain't."

"I know," said Adam. "But they were my grandparents. And I don't know a damn thing about them."

"No way for you to know," said Luther, nodding.

Adam hesitated. Then he said, "Would you tell me about them?"

Luther glanced over. Then he returned his eyes to the road. "You don't know what you askin'," he said.

Adam felt like a trespasser. "I'm sorry," he said, softly. "I guess I don't."

His uncle did not respond. After a moment, he pulled over. They sat by the side of the road. A hawk drifted lazily overhead. The trees were filled with the sawing of insects. Uncle Luther gazed inward. Adam feared to speak. Finally, his uncle's mouth twisted, a decision made. He wheeled the car around in a great wide arc and turned it back north.

"Where are we going?" asked Adam.

"You want to know about your grandparents," said Luther. "Fine.

You got a right. I'm takin' you to their farm." He turned so that their eyes met. "I'm takin' you to where they died," he said.

seven

THERE WAS NOTHING TO DO NOW BUT WAIT.

The three Harlem preachers—George, Reverend Porter, and Reverend Lester Williams, another member of the ministerial staff— had already checked in and been assigned housing. George had borrowed the phone in the pastor's office at Brown Chapel and called Thelma collect, learning to his relief that Adam had been found and was safe with his uncle—beaten and bruised but, thank God, whole. The three men had even walked to a nearby café for a late breakfast, careful to stick to the route that had been sketched out for them by SNCC staffers to avoid straying into the white part of town.

Now, as they joined a crowd milling about on the lawns of the Carver Homes, they waited. There was, they had learned, some question whether the march would even take place. Two white men in dark suits and armbands had shown up, climbing out of a black sedan with a government decal on the door. They were federal marshals, bearing an injunction barring Martin Luther King from leading a march to Montgomery. "What do you think?" George had asked his colleagues. "This won't stop them; King will march anyway, right?"

Lester had agreed with him. But their boss had not.

"I know the man." Reverend Porter, standing just above them on the first step of the church, watching the marshals weave through the crowd, had spoken mildly. "Well," he appended, smiling as they turned to him in surprise, "that is to say I knew him in passing. As you're aware, I got the calling relatively late in life. I'm a bit older than he is so we certainly didn't socialize in the same circles, but we were, in fact, students together at Crozer Theological Seminary up in Pennsylvania back in

'48. He and I were two of a very small number of Negro students in the school, so naturally we were aware of one another. We had a couple of classes together. Systematic theology and advanced pneumatology, as I recall."

"You know King." Lester's voice was flat.

"Yes, as I said. Not well, but certainly in passing."

"Why didn't you ever tell us that before?" A million questions surged within George, but that one found its way to the top.

The older man smiled, his eyes large and owlish behind the thick lenses of his bifocals. "Well, I never wanted to seem as if I was bragging or claiming fame by association. In fact, I would not have spoken of it even now, but I wanted to make the point that the Martin King I knew was a careful and meticulous young man, very orderly in his thinking. He was the opposite of impulsive. Now, this injunction has apparently been handed down by a federal court, correct?"

The other two men nodded. "Well," said Porter, "the federal courts have been King's ally throughout this entire movement, ever since Montgomery. He has disobeyed injunctions before, yes, but they came from state courts. Even worse, they came from state courts here in the South. He loses nothing by alienating them because they will never be on his side to begin with. But will he really risk angering a federal judge? With Johnson talking about putting forth a voting rights bill? If I had to wager, I'd say no."

"You don't think he's going to march," said George.

Porter shook his head. "No, I don't."

Lester waved his hand to encompass the crowded street. "But he got all these people to come down here. What's he going to tell them?"

"Yes," Porter had said, "that is the million-dollar question."

Two hours later, they still had no answer. Two hours later, nothing to do but wait. George glanced at his watch and gave a sigh. Lester chuckled. "All these years you've been at a Negro church, and you still don't understand CP time?"

George's smile was more of a grimace. "It will happen when it happens," Reverend Porter assured him. "Or not."

"Or not," agreed Lester.

And they waited.

At one point, George's attention was snagged by two Negro men who went sauntering by wearing hard hats. He was wondering what construction crew they might be part of, when one knocked a fist against his helmet and said, "Them trooper boys hit me in the head again, I'm ready for they asses this time!" And both men laughed.

"I'm going to take a walk," George told his colleagues.

"Good idea," said Porter.

And he drifted across the lawn, thinking of Thelma, wondering if the news of Adam's safety would free him from her doghouse. Certainly, her voice had sounded loose and friendly over the phone. That, he figured, was a start.

He was allowing himself to feel hopeful when a white man approached and identified himself as a reporter from the *New York Times*. They had a brief interview and George spoke of why it was important for white people to bear witness for Negro freedom. A few minutes later, he fell into conversation with a soft-faced white minister from Boston and found that they had a shared interest in housing programs for the poor; they agreed to compare notes if they got a chance. After the two of them parted, George spent a few minutes watching a group of Negro boys playing a lively game of basketball, focused on their hook shots and rebounds, oblivious to the commotion around them.

The boys were arguing a call when George heard a man's voice, both thinned and magnified by an electronic bullhorn, roaring at a crowd that had massed itself against Brown Chapel. The speaker exhorted the people to action.

"That is *your* bridge," he cried. "Your taxes built it, your taxes maintain it. And you are free to march across *your* bridge any time you get good and ready. If Sheriff Clark tries to stop you from marching across *your* bridge, what are you going to do?"

"March on!" the people cried.

"If these Uncle Tom Negroes around here try to stop you, what are you going to do?"

"March on!"

"If yo' mama tries to stop you, what you going to do?"

"March on!"

George wandered closer. He saw fists churning the air, heard mouths filled with righteous thunder.

"March on!"

"March on!"

"March on!"

Then the speaker on the steps brought them to an unthinkable peak of defiance. "If Martin Luther King says don't march, what are you going to do?"

"March on!"

"March on!"

"March on!"

"He's certainly got them worked up."

It was a young rabbi standing next to George in the back of the raucous crowd. "He does at that," said George.

"I take it you've heard about this federal injunction?"

George nodded. "Yes."

"What do you think? Will King violate it?"

"Well," said George, "my boss knew him when they were both in seminary. He seems to think he'll obey it."

"Of course, that isn't the real question," said the rabbi, sucking thoughtfully on his pipe. "The real question is, what will we as clergy do? Where does our duty lie?"

He gave George a searching look. George had no answer. Somehow, he hadn't even given that aspect of the problem a thought. "I don't know," he said with a shrug. "I suppose we'll find out."

"Yes," the rabbi said, smoke leaking from the side of his mouth, "I suppose we will."

More time passed. George's stomach began making noises and he found himself wondering if he had time to find a sandwich somewhere. He was looking at his watch when a loud cry went up from the crowd massed at the door to Brown Chapel.

"Almighty God," came the sudden, amplified voice of Martin Luther King, "thou hast called us to walk for freedom even as thou did the children of Israel."

George craned his neck, searching the crowd. And there King was, standing in a crush of people in front of the church, speaking into a handheld microphone. "We pray, dear God, as we go through a wilderness of state troopers, that thou wilt hold our hand."

By the time he said "Amen," the people were revved up like a race car engine, erupting in a chaos of freedom chants and songs. They were ready to march across their bridge. George thought they were ready to march across the water beneath the bridge if need be.

Organizers lined the marchers up two abreast in the playground of the housing project. George looked around for Lester and Reverend Porter, but he didn't see them. He found himself standing instead next to a young blonde woman with fidgety eyes.

George smiled a greeting. She said, "I guess this is it, huh?"

"You're nervous?" he said.

"Actually, I'm scared shitless," she admitted with a laugh. Then her eyes widened as she took in his clerical collar. She covered her mouth. "Oop. Sorry."

"Don't worry about it," said George. "Would you like to pray?"

"Thank you, Father, but I'm not a believer."

"That's okay," said George. "I'm not a Father."

King was moving by them, still addressing the people through the bullhorn. "I say to you this afternoon that I would rather die on the highways of Alabama than make a butchery of my conscience!" he cried. So apparently, thought George as the line began to move forward, Reverend Porter was wrong. Apparently, they were marching after all, going all the way to Montgomery, fifty-four miles away.

All at once, George felt a butterfly air dancing in his chest. For years, he had idolized Martin Luther King the way his sister did Frank Sinatra back during the war. He had read his books, pored over his speeches. Now, finally, he would have the chance—the honor—of marching with him.

George could hardly believe his good fortune to be there, on this dusty street, in this little town. He felt as if he had stepped off the edge of the Earth, untethered by previous anxieties and fears. He felt strong and unafraid.

The marchers sang freedom songs as they walked. An older white woman ahead of him introduced herself to the Negro teenager next to her. She said she was the widow of a United States senator. The teenager introduced himself as Cedric, a custodian at a local five-and-dime. George thought it fitting, somehow, that two people at such opposite ends of the social spectrum should find themselves walking shoulder to shoulder in Selma.

"Hey, King!" some white man jeered from the sidewalk. "Hey, you nigger son of a bitch! If you want to vote, why don't you act like a human being?"

The young woman next to George looked up at him. "What does that even mean?" she asked.

George shrugged. "None of this is about logic," he said. "If logic had anything to do with anything, you and I wouldn't even need to be here."

"I suppose you're right," she said.

From the sidewalk came still more jeering.

"Go home, nigger lovers!"

"Get out of here, you black bastard!"

A group of adolescent white boys followed along, scratching at their armpits and making monkey sounds.

"God, I absolutely loathe white people sometimes," the white woman said.

"They do make it hard to love thy neighbor," conceded George.

Then the parade stopped. And there, looming above them on the left, was the Pettus Bridge.

"What's going on?" asked the young woman.

Craning his neck, George could see that King had been confronted by one of the U.S. marshals. The white man was talking, reading to King from a piece of paper. King listened impassively.

"I'm not sure," said George.

"That's the government man," said the young janitor, Cedric. "They're reading the injunction. They're telling King not to march."

"Do you think he'll march anyway?" the young woman asked.

"I don't think he has any choice," said George. "Look at all these people."

After a moment, the marshal finished reading. There was a brief exchange with King, and then the white man stood aside and King led the marchers forward again. The line of people, of pastors, priests, nuns, rabbis, bookkeepers, beatniks, students, bus drivers, mechanics, housewives, janitors, and George turned left and began to climb the Pettus Bridge. When he reached the crest, George saw, far below, a sight that made his heart stammer painfully.

A group of Alabama state troopers in their powder blue helmets had lined themselves across Route 80. King led his marchers right up to the major in charge. George was too far away to hear the exchange between them. He saw reporters scribbling furiously in their notepads. Shoulder-mounted cameras with film magazines on top recorded every move.

He steeled himself. This was it.

This was it.

After a moment, King and the other ministers with him went down on their knees and one of them—George recognized him as King's aide, Ralph Abernathy—began speaking in words that didn't reach this far back in the line. "What are they doing?" asked the woman next to George. She was standing on tiptoes, trying to see.

"They're praying," said George.

The silence of the moment felt unearthly. He didn't know what to do with himself. This far back in the line, none of them did. They waited. They watched.

The ministers rose from their kneel. They faced the state police, the armed and arrayed authority of the state of Alabama. The major barked an order to those men.

And then, the unbelievable. The troopers stepped aside.

George felt his heart surge within him. It was as if the very hand of the divine had reached down to take hold of human events. The troopers were standing down. They were the Red Sea and Martin Luther King had become Moses, personified.

A moment.

A moment.

And then, hard upon that miracle, the unbelievable happened again. Instead of leading the marchers triumphantly through their adversaries, King spun around and began to make his way back through the crowd, trailed by his aides.

They were turning around.

"What are they doing?" asked the senator's widow.

"What's happening?" asked the teenage janitor.

"They're turning around," said George, not believing what he was seeing.

"We're not going all the way?" The teenager's voice brimmed with disappointment and hurt.

"Doesn't look that way," said George. He struggled to keep the emotion of out of his voice.

"But the road was open! They were letting them pass!"

George shrugged. "I don't know," he said.

He saw King draw closer, his face grim. George wanted to stop him, wanted to ask him a million questions. Instead, he just watched as King passed him by, leading the ministers back the way they had come.

People looked at one another. No one had any answers.

The young woman next to him glared at George as if this were somehow his fault. "I didn't come all this way to turn around," she said. "What a waste of time."

She held his eyes for a beat, then walked off with a disgusted shake of her head.

George stood there a full minute, struggling for mastery of his own feelings. He knew he should have been prepared for this. After all, Reverend Porter had predicted it. But he had allowed himself to believe, and now, disappointment cut him like a razor. Down at the foot of the bridge, the troopers milled about and photographers ran after the retreating marchers, snapping photos. No one seemed to know what to do.

George had never felt so . . .

He struggled for the word.

. . . *betrayed*.

Disgust escaped him in a soft exhalation. Finally, he turned, head bowed, and began walking back the way he had come.

eight

LUTHER BROUGHT THE OLD BUICK TO A STOP ON THE SHOUL-
der of an empty country road a few miles southwest of the tiny town
of Kendrick, Alabama. This was his second pass down the same weath-
ered stretch of blacktop, having made a U-turn and circled back because
nothing in the landscape seemed to match his memories. Now he
pointed uncertainly to an overgrown field on the other side of the road.
"I think that's it," he said.

"You're not sure?" Adam sounded surprised.

"It's changed," said Luther. He reached over, popped open the glove
compartment and retrieved his pistol.

"Why do we need the gun?" asked Adam.

"Ain't no tellin' what's livin' over in that grass. Now, come on."

Luther pushed open the car door and stepped into the lonely road.
He tucked the gun in the pocket of his jacket and for a moment, just
stood facing the field. Steeling himself. Adam came up beside him.

"Ain't been here since 1945," said Luther. "Johan brought us and
we stopped on the way to the trial. You was with us, in fact."

"Dad wasn't with you?"

Luther shook his head. "George was still in a hospital in San
Francisco."

Now Adam paused and Luther could tell he was working up the
nerve for something. After a moment he said, "Uncle Luther, you mind
if I ask you something?"

"Go ahead."

"Do you not like my dad? Do you have a problem with him or
something?"

Luther stared at his nephew, surprised. "George? No. I ain't got no problem with him. He a good guy, he take care of my sister; that's all I can ask. What make you think I don't like him?"

Adam's shoulders went up. "I don't know," he said. "Just a feeling. Just something in your face when you talk about him."

Luther tried not to grimace. He promised himself he would be more careful from now on. He'd never spent much time with his nephew, but he could see the boy was smart. He paid attention. And he knew there was something there, something he had not been told, even if he couldn't quite figure out what it was.

"I like George just fine," said Luther, striving to sound definitive.

"Okay," said Adam. "I didn't mean to make you mad."

"I ain't mad," said Luther. "Now, do you want to hear about your grandparents or not?"

"I want to hear," said Adam.

"Then come on." Without waiting for a response, Luther crossed the road and plunged into the field, Adam trotting to keep up. Grass scraped at their knees. Beer cans crunched under their shoes. "Used to be a driveway right about here," said Luther. He pointed off to his left. "It's hard to tell because everything is growing wild, but if this the right place, then the house be somewhere right over—"

And then he saw it. Or rather, what was left of it.

The structure maintained its nominal shape, but it would never be a house again. Now it was just a ruin, the blackened skeleton of his father's dreams. Fire had torn holes in the roof, left jagged beams of wood jutting to the sky. Two walls sagged against one another like drunks staggering home from a bender. Grass was growing through the empty sockets where the windows had been. Incongruously enough, the front steps and most of the porch were intact.

"What happened?" asked Adam. "It caught fire?"

Luther shook his head. "Somebody burned it," he said. He didn't know how he knew this, but he did. "I guess they just couldn't stand looking at it anymore. Maybe reminded them of what they did."

He had no way to prove this was true, but it felt true and he decided to believe it. Doing so gave him a distant, bitter pleasure.

He moved closer then, stepped cautiously up on the porch and peered through the black rectangle where the front door had been. The floor inside was a carpet of grass and weeds. The sun probed through two jagged tears in the roof.

"This place," he said.

And then he stopped, the memory too powerful to speak. Adam had the good sense not to prod him. After a moment, he tried again. "This place was your grandfather's pride. They owned this land—in fact, they was some of the only Negroes to own property back then, and that's only because my daddy worked like a demon to buy it. Always said a man got to own somethin' in this world if he want to get ahead. He *always* preached that."

Luther turned from the door and looked across toward a gnarled oak tree looming above the grass. "That's where they killed him," he said, with a nod of his head. "Killed them both, I should say."

He crossed what had been the yard, paused before the tree as a penitent before an altar and touched a hand to the rough bark of the trunk. Just over his head, a heavy bough jutted off at an angle. "This branch," said Luther, pointing. "That's where they did it. Me and your mama watching from the door yonder. And Floyd Bitters . . ."

He stopped. About a hundred miles south, at West Haven Rest Home down in Mobile, they would be serving lunch to the old people right about now, he figured. And in a room a few doors down from where Johan Simek sat quietly losing his mind, some nurse or orderly would be spooning porridge into the mouth of a wasted old man who, before he was rendered feeble and mute by cerebral hemorrhage or some similar misfortune, had come into this yard and destroyed nearly everything Luther loved. The world, he told himself bitterly, made no sense.

"Who is that?" asked Adam.

Luther started. He had forgotten his nephew was there. He said, "Floyd Bitters was a county commissioner. He the man who led the mob that night. Came here into the yard and killed your grandparents."

"Why did he do it?" asked Adam. "I've never understood that."

"He did it 'cause he could," said Luther. "He did it 'cause he a evil motherfucker."

Luther turned and saw Adam's uncomprehending stare. "A hog," he said. "He did it over a hog."

"I still don't understand."

Luther gave him a bitter smile. "That just mean you ain't crazy," he said.

He went back across the yard and sat on the steps. He grunted, they creaked. Everything getting old.

After a moment, Adam sat beside him. There was a silence. Then Luther said, "They didn't want you to be no man. Not if you's a Negro. If you's a Negro, they expect you to be a boy, to be a nigger. They expect you to do all that duckin' your head and yassuh bossin', all that smilin' when ain't nothin' funny and scratchin' when don't nothin' itch. Some colored men, I guess, were so beaten down they could do that with no problem. Some of 'em, they plain forgot they was just supposed to be pretendin'. After a while, it come natural to 'em. That might not be a fair thing to say, but that's the way it always seemed to me.

"But your grandfather . . . ain't none of it come natural to him. Man had a natural dignity, a natural stick up his ass, if you want to know the truth. And when I seen him smilin' and duckin' his head, I could always tell how hard it was for him to do. I could always tell he really cussin' they asses out in his mind. He'd give me this look and it be like this secret between me and him. Always surprised me white folks couldn't tell he was puttin' 'em on."

Luther regarded his nephew. "If my father had any real sense," he said, "he would have taken us out of here. He would have gone to New York, Chicago, Detroit. But he decide he gon' make his stand here in Alabama. He not gon' let these crackers run Mason Lincoln Hayes out of town."

The thought of it made Luther smile a sad smile. "Guess that's where I get it from," he said.

Luther lit a cigarette, fanned at a fly that was buzzing around his head. "So while he yassuh bossin' and smilin', he also workin'—and I mean, workin' *hard*. Seem like I hardly ever saw him as a child, 'cause he was always gone to one job or another: porter, barber, farmer, janitor, mechanic, you name it. The first war come and he volunteered for that and went to Europe for a year. Say he an American, good as any other American, so he got a duty to fight in America's wars."

Luther shook his head at his father's foolishness. "Your grandmother, her name was Annie Chisholm before it was Annie Hayes, she had me to take care of—Thelma didn't come along till a few years after

Papa got back from the fighting. But Mama also taught at this school-house they had for colored, kept house, tended the crops. So they was both busy—industrious, you might say."

Luther sucked hard on the cigarette. Exhaled a blue cloud, fanned again at the fly. "All that workin', they did well. They prospered. Some of my clothes was even store-bought, right out the Sears catalog. That was a big deal back in them days. In fact, we all was dressed right nice when-ever we went to town, though that wasn't very often, since Papa didn't like bein' around white folks all that much. Still, whenever we did, you could tell it pissed them off. They hated to see us like that: lookin' good, doin' good. Then Papa, he bought his self this old Tin Lizzie, and that only made it worse."

He stopped when he saw the confusion on Adam's face. "Tin Lizzie," he repeated. "That what they called the old Model T Fords. He bouncin' up and down these roads in that thing while most of them walkin' or ridin' mules. Something else they didn't like him for. See, wasn't no colored man s'posed to be doin' well enough to have a car. They s'posed to been sharecroppin' and scufflin' and lettin' white men cheat 'em out what they done earned. Papa, he didn't have to 'crop or scuffle, nor be cheated. He did well—did better than most of them, to tell the truth—by keepin' to his self and workin' hard. So they already thought he was forgettin' his place. Already said he was gettin' uppity. Then come that business I told you about."

"You mean the hog?"

Luther nodded. He blew out a last stream of smoke, crushed the cigarette butt beneath the toe of his work shoes.

"The hog," he said. "Where Papa got it, I couldn't tell you. I don't remember the thing myself, but Gramp used to say it was black as a crow at midnight. Weighed seven hundred pounds if it weighed one. He said, half the time, he wasn't sure if we was gon' be eatin' it or it was gon' be eatin' us. Turned out to be neither. That man I told you about, that Floyd Bitters, he got it in his head he had to have that hog. But Papa wouldn't sell it to him, see? Said he was gon' butcher it to feed his family. And the more he say no, the more that man push. 'Mason, I got to have me that there hog,' he say. 'You name your price.' It's like he can't accept that he ain't gon' get what he want—especially if the one tellin' him no is some Negro."

Luther didn't speak for a long moment. He pulled in a breath. Lord, this was hard. Harder, even, than he'd thought it would be. And he'd thought it would be hell.

Was Floyd Bitters done with lunch by now? Had someone fluffed his pillows or led him to the bathroom? Was he lying there watching television? Was he taking a nap?

"So what happened?" asked Adam.

Luther sighed. "What happened is that one day, your grandfather forgot to bow and scrape. You know that poem, 'We wear the mask that grins and lies'? Well, he let the mask slip, let them white men see that he thought he was a man, too. He in town this one day with Gramp and ol' Floyd Bitters ask him one time too many to sell him that damn hog. And he says, with just a little edge in his voice, 'I done already told you, Mr. Bitters, he ain't for sale. I'm gon' hold on to him. Butcher him for my family.'"

"That's all he said?"

"Yeah. 'Cordin' to Gramp, at least. That's what he told me, years later, when I start askin' questions like you doin' now. And he say Papa knew right off he done made a mistake, talkin' to this white man like that. And he start tryin' to put the mask back in place. Duckin' his head and sayin', 'Oh, suh, I'se sorry. Ain't meant to be so peckish. Got this corn on my foot and it done put me in a right frightful mood. You know how it is, suh. Nigger can't take no pain.'

"But Bitters and them other white men, they ain't buyin' it. It's like they seein' for the first time who he really is, and they ain't liked it one little bit. This was August of 1923. I was nine years old. Your mother, she turned three that October. But see, even though we ain't nothin' but children, we could tell somethin' was wrong when he got home. The next few days, there was all this tension in the air, all this worry and fear. Mama and Papa and Gramp huddlin' together all the time, talkin' in these low, scared voices. Even Thelma could feel it. Them few days, seem like she just cried all the time, wanted to be picked up, wanted to be held. But Mama was snappish and short-tempered, even with her. When I asked Papa what was goin' on, he told me mind my own business, stay in a child's place.

"Whatever he was mad about, I could tell it wasn't me. I could tell he was scared. And that scared *me*. When you a boy, ain't nobody in the world bigger than your daddy. So when you see somethin' big enough to scare him?"

Luther didn't finish the thought. He couldn't. He fished another cigarette out of the pack in his breast pocket and lit it. His hands shook. He glanced over and saw Adam seeing this.

"Uncle Luther . . ."

Luther ignored it. "They come for 'em three days later," he said, blowing out smoke. "August 28. It was a Tuesday night. Been hot and sticky all day. Now it's dark and it's still hot and sticky. Me and your mama, we shared a bed. I'm wide awake. She kickin' me in the ribs like she always do. Gramp snorin' on the other side of the room like he always do. It's a peaceful night. And then: bam! bam! bam! He come bangin' on that door."

"This Floyd Bitters."

Luther nodded. "Floyd Bitters," he said. He made his voice rough, puffed it up with peckerwood authority to approximate what he'd heard that long ago night. "Mason! Come on out here, boy! We know you in there, boy!"

"And then again, bam! bam! bam! I thought his fist was gon' come through the door. Woke Thelma up. Woke Gramp up. He fumblin' for his glasses, askin' what's goin' on. Then Papa and Mama come down the hallway tellin' us it ain't nothin'. Tellin' us go back to sleep. But I know he lyin' 'cause I can hear in his voice how scared he is."

Luther looked at Adam. "Like I say: you don't never forget it when you see your father scared."

A pause. A long drag on the cigarette.

Then Luther said, "Mama beggin' him not to go out there. And he tellin' her he ain't got no choice. He don't go out there, they gon' come in here. And sure 'nough, you hear the voice from out on the porch. "Mason, get your black ass out here!"

"Floyd Bitters," said Adam.

"Yeah," said Luther. "Floyd Bitters."

Probably lying in a soft bed at the rest home this very minute, drooling on himself while *I Love Lucy* reruns played on TV.

"So what did your father do?"

"What else could he do? He went out there. Mama told him to take his gun, but he said that would just make things worse." Luther sucked his teeth. "Don't know how they could have got any worse, though. He open the door and there he is—Big Floyd, they called him, 'cause he stood a good six foot five with a big ol' belly sloppin' over his belt. I wasn't nothin' but a boy, but I swear, lookin' up at him was like lookin' up at a mountain. He standin' there, staggerin' from a half-drunk bottle of whiskey in his fist. And behind him in the yard, where you see all this grass growin' now, it was nothin' but white people with torches and guns, howlin' and laughin.'"

"White men," said Adam in a disgusted voice, as if he wasn't half a white man himself.

Luther smirked. "Wasn't just men," he said. "Women and children, too. I had a white boy I used to pal around with, Jeff Orange. Me and him used to hunt mudbugs down to the swamp. He was out there with his mother and his sister and his father."

Adam gave him another stare of utter incomprehension. Something about it made Luther angry. "This was *entertainment* to them," he said. "Fun for the whole family."

Luther held Adam's eyes till he felt heat on his fingers and saw that his cigarette had become a teetering tower of ash. He tossed it down, stomped it out, pulled out another and lit it.

"My Papa," he said, behind a fresh exhalation of smoke, "he out there pleadin' with them white men, grinnin' at 'em, tellin' him he ain't meant no harm. He wasn't tryin' to disrespect them. Yassuh boss, nossuh boss, and all that shit."

Luther studied the smoke curling off the cigarette burning between his fingers. "But it was too late for that," he said. "Floyd, he wasn't havin' it."

Luther transformed his voice again, filled it now with a peckerwood's wounded propriety. "Offered this nigger good money for that there hog. But he too good to accept a fair offer. Come talkin' to me like he was the white man and *I* was the nigger. He as much as said to me, 'You gettin' on my nerves, Big Floyd. Shut up and leave me alone, Big Floyd.' This *nigger* as much as said that to me. Are we suppose to stand still for that? Is that what we're lettin' this country come to? Are we gon' be the niggers now and let the niggers act like they're white?"

Luther fell silent for a moment. He sat there smoking, remembering, gathering himself to give this boy what he had asked for, what he deserved to have, and yet, what hurt so much to give. Finally, he said, "Big Floyd, he grabbed Papa then. Papa pulled back from him, and that only made him madder. He grabbed him again with one of them big hands of his and yanked him out of the house. And them white men came up, right here on this porch where we sittin', and they all took hold of him. Grabbed his arms, grabbed his legs. One of 'em had a fistful of his hair. And they took him off. His feet didn't touch the ground. I always remembered that."

He glanced over at Adam. His nephew's eyes were nearly invisible behind the sunglasses, but his mouth gaped and his chest was still as a stone. Luther gave a rueful chuckle. "Breathe, boy," he said. "Story gets a whole lot worse."

As Adam obeyed, Luther took another long drag from his cigarette. "So anyway," he said, "they got your grandfather out in the yard and your grandmother, she start screamin' at this big monster who done come to her front door and took her husband. 'You doin all this over a hog, Floyd Bitters? You're doing this over a goddamn hog?'

"Mama didn't cuss, but she sure cussed that white man that night. And something about it almost seemed to reach that mob. I remember the yard went still, like maybe they was really thinkin' about it, like they was wakin' up from a bad dream. You could see on they faces, they almost askin' themselves, 'What the fuck we doin' out here in the middle of the night, about to kill a man over his own goddamn hog?'

"Mama, she kept at 'em. Papa yellin' for her to get back inside, obey what he tellin' her. But she kept right on. 'You want the hog that bad? Then you take it! You can have it! It's all yours. Just leave my husband alone, you hear me? You give him back to my children and me.'

"She almost had that mob convinced," Luther said. "You could tell. Floyd Bitters could tell, too. He said, 'You better go back inside. I don't want your damn hog no more. I just want him.'

"But Mama, she wouldn't back down. Papa yellin' at her to go back in. Gramp prayin' to Jesus, me pullin' at her nightdress. She ignored it all. Stood there in front of that giant man and told him he was nothin' but a coward. You could tell she was gettin' to him, gettin' to all of 'em. Floyd, he speaks to her in a low voice, like it's just him and her. 'Last time I'm gon' tell you, bitch. Listen to your old man. Go on, get back inside, 'fore you get yourself hurt.'

"I think he thought that was gon' be the end of it," said Luther. "I think he thought she would back down. But Mama whispered right back at him, 'I will haunt you the rest of your life for this. Do you hear me? *The rest of your miserable damn life*. I don't care what I have to do or how far I have to go. I swear before God, you will never know a second of peace.'"

"That's why he took her?" asked Adam.

Luther shook his head. He dropped his cigarette, crushed it out, and blew out a last stream of smoke. "No," he said. "He took her because she spat in his face."

"What?"

Luther nodded. "Uh huh." He touched an index finger to Adam's left cheekbone. "Right there," he said. "And then she punched him in the nose."

"What?"

Another nod. "Your grandmother was a little woman, stood about five foot two. She had to get on tiptoe to do it. But she clocked his big ass, landed a punch that would have made that Cassius Clay fella proud. Blood gushin' everywhere. First he looked shocked, like he couldn't believe it had happened. Then he looked crazy. I mean, *crazy*. He reached out and grabbed her by her head, palmed it like a basket-ball and pulled her. Mama went flying out into the yard. And that's when . . ."

Abruptly, Luther stopped. To his horror, he found himself blink-ing back tears. *Tears*. He turned away so that Adam couldn't see and cleared his throat. "I was holding on to her, you see. Had hold of her nightdress. And when she went flying off the porch, I went flying, too. Landed right at the feet of that monster. I'm nine, remember. Small for my age. And he's this big giant of a white man. He reaches down, all the way down and . . ."

Luther stopped. He shook his head. "I pissed myself. You believe that?"

He tried to read Adam's face. Couldn't. He shook his head again, laughed to cover his shame. "I don't know why I'm tellin' you this. Ain't never told nobody none of this. Well, except for Johan. I did tell him, the day we met in that drunk tank when he agreed to be my lawyer."

"Uncle . . ."

Luther waved him off. "Let me finish," he said. He inhaled a lung-ful of air to steady himself, blew it out. Then he pulled out a cigarette and held it in his hands, turning it over and over without lighting it. Another glance at Adam, which was a mistake. He couldn't say this part while facing the boy's honest horror. So Luther looked away.

"He pulled me up till we was facin' each other. Mama and Papa both goin' crazy. 'Get your hands off him! Leave him alone!' And Floyd Bitters grins and he says, 'Look like I done caught me a pissy little nig-ger cub.' He laughs and they all laugh and then he flings me away like a piece of trash."

Adam said, "Jesus."

Luther finally lit the cigarette. He gazed at his nephew through the haze of smoke and shook his head. "Still ain't the worst part of the story," he said.

He let a silence intervene, sat smoking quietly for a while, his hands still shaking. Birdsong drifted down from the old oak tree. Insects in the high grass made a rhythmic, rasping noise.

Lord, this was hard.

Adam said, "Uncle, you ain't got to talk about it if you don't want."

Luther glanced at him, then away.

"They took their time killin' 'em," he said, finally. He crushed out the cigarette. "Must have took two hours, at least. And they had fun doin' it. All of 'em. All them good white people, right here in our yard. First they beat them. The whole mob of them, stompin' and kickin' at two people, lying there on the ground. Children leaning through to make sure they got their licks in. Mama and Papa covered with blood. Then somebody pulls out a machete—"

At this point, Luther saw his nephew cringe, but he continued right on.

"—and he says, 'Who wants some souvenirs?'"

Luther shook his head. "People laughin', children raisin' their hands, we standin' in the doorway, watchin'. I hear Mama and Papa start screamin' in pain just as Gramp close the door. He say, 'Y'all don't need to be seein' this.' And he probably right. Hell, I know he was right. He took us back to our room. He holdin' hisself like if he don't, his body gon' fly apart. And he rockin' back and forth and cryin' out to Jesus. But Jesus ain't there. Even I can see that.

"And after a moment, I tell Thelma come on, and we go down the hallway to our parents' room and we get up there on their bed and look out the window. By this time, Papa lyin' on his back, holdin' up his right hand." Luther held up his own hand as illustration, fingers splayed wide. "And he ain't got nothin' but bloody stumps where his fingers and his thumb used to be. Jeff Orange, the little white boy I told you about, one who used to hunt mudbugs with me, he's got Papa's pinky finger and he's laughin' this demented laugh."

Luther stopped. He blew out another lungful of air.

"And Mama . . ." He paused, had to clear his throat. "Mama, she's on all fours, they done stripped her almost naked. And these men done gathered around her. 'Where you goin' honey? Ain't so feisty no more, is you? Wow, get a load'a them tits.' That's what these motherfuckers doin' while she crawlin' in the dirt"—he pointed to a spot in the yard—"right there."

"Some white bitch got jealous then and kicked her in the face. Kicked her so hard, she flopped over on her back. She lyin' on her back in the dirt. And that's when she see me and Thelma, watchin' all this from inside. And my mother"—he felt his voice growing raspy; he coughed it clear and pushed through—"my mother, she smiled at me then. My beautiful mother, she all busted up, all bloody, teeth broken, one eye swole shut, nightdress ripped to rags, she smiled at me, like to say, 'It's okay, baby. Mama be all right.' You hear what I'm sayin'? She been tore all to hell, she near 'bout dead, and she worryin' about *me*."

Again, Luther paused. He thought about lighting another cigarette, but didn't. Smoke couldn't take this away. Nothing could. His head came around and he glared at his nephew. "I hope you gettin' all this," he said. "I hope this answer your questions, 'cause I ain't never tellin' this story again, you hear me? Ain't *never* tellin' it again."

Adam nodded. His eyes, still barely visible through the green tint of the plastic shades, were wide. Luther clamped a hand on the boy's forearm by way of a silent apology. "Almost done," he said. "Almost done."

"They went then and got the rope. Made hangman's nooses and put 'em around Mama and Papa's necks. Tied their hands behind them. Some bitch start whinin' then that she never got no souvenir, so somebody cut off Papa's right ear—just like snippin' a rose from a rosebush—and handed it to her. She holdin' it up, grinnin' like Christmas morning."

Luther pointed to the old oak. "They hauled the rope up over that there branch, then. They lift 'em up off the ground, Mama and Papa strugglin' in the air. They let 'em hang like that for a few seconds, let 'em almost die, then they bring 'em down, let 'em lie there and get some strength back. Me, I'm watchin' this and I'm thinkin'—really, I'm *hopin'*—this is the end. They done had their fun and now they'll leave 'em alone. But like I told you, they just wanted to take their time with it. So they let 'em lie there a minute, then they haul 'em back up over the branch again, let 'em dangle there a few seconds. Then they let 'em down again. Up and back down, up and back down. I don't know how many times they repeated this. I'm just sittin' there in the window trying to figure it out: Why don't they get it over with? Why they keep doin' this? Why is this fun to them?"

"Sick bastards," muttered Adam.

Luther nodded. "Sick bastards," he said.

Again, he allowed silence to intervene. Then he said, "Finally, they got tired of that. That's when they set 'em on fire. I think Mama was already dead by then. But I know Papa was still alive, 'cause I seen him throw back his head and scream."

Luther faced Adam. "Pretty sure you ain't never smelled human flesh cookin' and you should be thankful for that. Wish I could explain to you what it smelled like. Best I can tell you is, it smell like evil. Like pure evil.

"Fire burned through the ropes and they fell. Sparks flyin'. White folks stayed in the yard, drinkin' and laughin' till the fire went down. Before they left, they got their guns and they shot what was left of Mama and Papa. They shot up the old Tin Lizzie, too, and turned it on its side. Someone took a picture of them all, posed around the bodies, grinning like fishermen do when they got a prize catch. Then, last thing they did, they shot the hog."

There was a moment. The two of them sat there, just breathing. "Never tellin' this story again," muttered Luther. "Never again." He stood and walked to the middle of the yard.

"None of them were ever punished?"

Luther shook his head. He didn't feel like speaking.

"And the jury let this Floyd Bitters go free."

Luther nodded.

"It's been forty-two years," said Adam. "At least they're probably all dead by now."

Luther whirled on the boy. Something angry sprang to his lips. But before the words could come out, he suddenly found himself on his knees in the high grass. To his horror, some wrenching, anguished sound was ripping out of him, some roar that fused rage and sorrow into some undefinable third thing. His face was awash with tears and he was pounding the ground with his fist. And he couldn't make himself stop.

Adam was off the porch. He was frozen in surprise, and then he was stepping tentatively forward.

Luther managed to raise his hand. "No," he rasped through his cries. "*No!*" Bad enough to be seen like this, *humiliating* enough to be seen like this. But it was unthinkable to also be touched, to be comforted.

Adam stopped, uncertain. Luther struggled to master himself. It was Adam saying that surely they were all dead by now, that was what had done it. Luther had been okay—or at least, had managed to make it safely—through the beating, the cutting, the rope, and the fire. But he could not make it through this boy saying with airy certainty that the murderers were probably all dead, when Luther had seen Floyd Bitters just Sunday afternoon, Floyd Bitters, who had escaped judgment all these years, Floyd Bitters, who was lying in a comfortable bed, probably sleeping at this very moment. Floyd Bitters, who was certainly alive, even if not quite well.

And wasn't that always the way? White people never paid, did they? It was the great unspoken truth of American life. Beat a nigger, kick a nigger, burn a nigger, kill a nigger. Didn't matter. They never paid for the shit they did. They never had to. Hell, that was the whole point of America.

Luther knelt there in the grass until the tears passed. He knelt there a long moment more. Finally, when he couldn't avoid it any longer, he climbed to his feet, chest heaving and ashamed. "I'm sorry," he whispered. He kept his head down. Couldn't look at Adam, couldn't bear seeing the compassion on his nephew's face. He said it again: "I'm sorry."

"No need," said Adam.

"It ain't easy," said Luther. "Bein' here, talkin' about it. Ain't easy at all."

"I understand," said Adam.

And even that was more solicitude than he could bear. "Come on," said Luther. "Let's go. It's two hours down to Mobile."

He spun around decisively without waiting for an answer and plunged back through the grass the way they had come, leaving the blackened ruin and the old tree behind. He didn't look back.

nine

FROM THE JUKEBOX, DAVID RUFFIN'S VOICE, ALL YEARNING and sweetness, faded out over a cascade of harmony and a swirl of violins. *"Talkin' 'bout my girl,"* he sang. There was a pregnant silence. And then, sure enough, there came the now familiar wash of strings and horns rising to meet the soft, solemn rumble of a bass drum, and Sam Cooke—shockingly murdered in some seedy Los Angeles motel just three months ago—filled the café with keening lament, singing of a change long forestalled.

"But I know, a change gon' come," he prophesied.

Lester, who had predicted this, grinned and spread his hands in a gesture that said *I told you so*. Reverend Porter nodded and smiled, and George chuckled dutifully as "A Change Is Gonna Come" played for the fourth time in the half an hour they had been sitting there. Not that any of the New York ministers minded. Not that any of the other diners, packed elbow to elbow in the little Negro café, seemed to mind, either. A song of resilience and the promise of ultimate victory felt appropriate to the moment—indeed, *necessary* to the moment—a soundtrack well suited to disappointed people at the end of a disappointing day some had already taken to calling "turnaround Tuesday."

"So," said George, "now what?"

The three Bethel ministers were gathered around a table containing the remains of their feast: bones from pig's feet, fried chicken and oxtails, a smattering of hog maws, hoppin' John, and collard greens. Lester, who was born in Harlem and had never ventured further south than Philadelphia, had contented himself with a cheeseburger and French fries.

Porter's smile was rueful. "I suppose that's what we'll find out at the meeting," he replied, prompting George to glance at his watch. King had asked participants in that day's march to gather at Brown Chapel at seven thirty. It was six fifty-four.

"Well, I hear they're going to court to get the injunction lifted," said Lester. "I hope they're able to. And I hope we're able to stay and see it through. We came all the way down here to accomplish something. I don't like the idea of leaving with the job half done."

"I quite agree," said Porter. "Let's just play it by ear for now. See how the Lord leads us."

Lester's nod was noncommittal. He made a show of picking disconsolately at his French fries. "Can't say I'm much impressed by the local cuisine," he said. The modest café was, they had been told, the only place nearby that served Negroes.

George was about to defend the honor of Southern cooking when a finger tapped his shoulder. He turned and found himself looking up into the bespectacled face of the white preacher from Boston he had met that afternoon on the housing project lawn. He tried to remember the man's name, then realized he'd never learned it. "Sorry to interrupt you all," the newcomer said with a friendly smile and a nod that took in the whole table. And then, to George: "I was remembering what you said earlier, about housing programs. I don't know why I didn't think of it before, but there's a pilot anti-poverty program being launched by the federal government that you should probably look into. It's a public-private partnership, part of Johnson's Great Society. I've already applied, but I remember the administrator telling me how disappointed they were to get so few applications from the New York and New Jersey area. You said your church is in Harlem, right?"

"Our church," corrected George, gesturing to include Lester and Reverend Porter. "But yes."

"Well, I'm sure they'd welcome your application. Why don't you walk back over with me and my friends? I can give you the details. That is, if you gentlemen don't mind letting me borrow him for a moment."

"By all means," said Porter with an open-handed gesture. "We'll see you at the chapel, Reverend Simon."

"Save me a seat," said George. He stood, dropping three singles on the table, and accompanied the other man. He extended his hand as they moved toward the door.

"By the way," he said, "I'm George."

"Jim," the other man said, and they shook. Sam Cooke was reaching the end of his song as they passed through the door—"*Oh yes, it will*," he sang of the coming change he would not live to see—and sure enough, the record began all over again.

"Somebody in there really likes that song," said Jim with a smile.

"Well," said George, "it catches the mood. You've got to give it that."

Two more men—Jim's friends, George realized—joined them on the sidewalk. "Give me just a second, fellows," said Jim, pointing to a nearby phone booth. "I should call my wife and let her know I've decided to stay on an extra day."

George waited with the other two men—Clark and Orloff, they said their names were—while Jim made his call. Seeing him standing there in the lighted booth with the receiver to his ear reminded George that he should probably call his own wife. He checked his watch and decided he would do so after the meeting.

After a moment, Jim finished his call and rejoined them. The men walked north, which put the river at their backs. This raised a faint alarm in George. "Are you sure this is the right way?" he asked. "My friends and I, we came from the other direction."

Clark tapped his watch. "The meeting begins at seven thirty," he said. "Want to make sure we get good seats, and this is a little shorter."

George shrugged. "Long as you know what you're doing," he said.

Darkness was just beginning to pull itself across the sky. The streetlamps were flickering to life, bathing the world in a mellow glow. The night was so still that George could hear the faint tick of insects hurling themselves against the phosphorescent bulbs. Jim was explaining the application process for the federal program, which, like all federal programs in George's experience, seemed needlessly complicated.

They crossed an alley, passed a building marked Barnes Music Company, and came abreast of a corner restaurant. A big sign over the swinging, western-style saloon doors announced that this was the Silver Moon Café. The same sign promised "Steaks Chops Chicken Seafood." George was thinking that this might be a good place to get lunch tomorrow when a glance through the window made the flesh jitter on his arm. Hard white faces glared back at him. It was a jarring sight. These people, he realized with a start, hated him deeply and personally without even knowing him. It was, he supposed, something of what it meant to be a Negro.

In the same instant that realization hit, the stillness was broken by the scuffle of feet. A group of white men was crossing the street, coming up from behind. Out of the corner of his eye, George saw that one of them was brandishing some sort of club. And there came a braying cry, "Hey, you niggers!" A fist of ice punched through George Simon's gut.

"Just keep walking," hissed Orloff.

"Don't look at them," said Jim. "Don't run." It reminded George of advice his father had given him once for handling a bad dog.

But these particular beasts would not be so easily dissuaded. The scuffling of feet drew closer. "Hey, you niggers!" the voice cried again. "You white niggers! We're talkin' to you!"

George was just turning when he saw the man swing the club, like a home-run hitter laying into a fat, slow pitch. Jim never saw it coming. It smashed into his left temple with an audible crunch and he went down, so stunned that he wasn't even able to brace his fall. George reached out for him, but in that same instant, something hard and heavy slammed into his right side, driving the air from his body with explosive force. His knees unlocked and he went down.

Above him, around him, he heard voices crying out, heard the heavy thudding of men landing blows against the bodies of other men, elongated shadows moving under the lights. Someone ran. Someone else chased. "Here's how it feels to be a nigger down here," one of the white men growled, and there came another heavy blow.

Then, as suddenly as it had begun, like a sudden squall on a spring day, it was over. George heard footsteps receding at a run, the white men returning to the shadows that had spawned them, chased by their own giddy laughter.

He staggered to his feet, disoriented, holding his side. "Is-is-is everyone okay?" he cried. In times of stress, George sometimes stammered.

There was no immediate answer to his cry. Then he heard someone yell, "Jim!"

George spun, his eyes finding the Boston minister, who was leaning against a building, one hand to his temple. There was a small cut above his left ear, but it was his eyes that frightened George. They were unfocused, fixed on nothing, as if there was no animating intelligence behind them. Jim was making sounds that he seemed to believe were words, but it was as if his mouth and his mind were disengaged from one another; the sounds had no meaning.

"Jim," one of the other men said sharply, as if the sound of his name might re-tether him to a reality he seemed to have lost. "Come on, Jim, snap out of it."

After a moment, Jim seemed to do just that. "My head," he said. "Oh."

The words, spoken in recognizable English, made George weak with relief. "We've got to get him to a doctor," he said.

Orloff said, "The SCLC office is not far. They'll know what to do."

He and Clark hoisted Jim between them. They braced him as they staggered together down the darkened street. George, his right arm pinned against the pain in his ribs, followed them. He glanced back at the Silver Moon Café as they passed. The hard faces still stared after them. He'd have sworn he felt the darkness itself closing in.

When they lurched into the SCLC office, the same young Negro woman he'd met that morning at the church—Diane was her name— looked up from a typewriter. "What happened?" she asked.

"Gang of thugs attacked us," said Clark. "We had just come out of that black diner."

Her eyes narrowed. "Were you on the route I told you to take?"

"No," admitted Clark. "We were hurrying to get back to the church."

George braced himself for her to say how foolish they had been— strangers in an unknown and hostile town, veering from the directions they had been told would ensure their safety—but Diane simply nodded and picked up the phone. "He doesn't look good," she said with a nod toward Jim, who was once again muttering in a language that did not exist. "I'm calling an ambulance. He needs a doctor."

Anxious minutes later, a long, black station wagon pulled to a stop in front of the building. The ambulance, George saw, was a hearse pulling double duty. Clark and Orloff got Jim into the back seat, where they sat flanking him. George sat up front next to the driver.

"My head," Jim said again as the vehicle took off with a lurch. It was the first time he had spoken for long minutes. "My head is killing me."

The car raced through the night-darkened streets of Selma. George thought it would be just their luck to get pulled over for speeding by some local cop. "Maybe we should go back to the chapel," mused Orloff.

Clark nodded. "Maybe we can find some help there."

The driver shook his head. "Even if you could get some help there, you couldn't get close to the place. Dr. King is holding his meeting. Police have the street blocked off."

George looked back at Jim. His skin was gray, his eyes were closed. He seemed unconscious. George closed his eyes and began a silent prayer. A tense voice interrupted him.

"We've got company," said Clark.

As the driver checked his mirror, George looked out through the back of the station wagon. Oval-shaped headlights hovered in the darkness, about half a block back, keeping pace. "They've been with us the last mile," said Clark. "Turn for turn."

"Police, you think?" asked George.

Clark hunched his shoulders. "I have no idea. I suppose, under the circumstances, that would be the best-case scenario."

"Maybe," said Orloff, "but not by much."

Minutes later, they braked to a stop before an old frame house in a Negro neighborhood. George questioned the driver with a look.

"This is it," he said. "It's called Burwell's Infirmary."

"What happened to our friends?" asked Clark, nodding toward the street behind them. The oval lights were gone.

"Don't go asking the gift horse any questions," said George.

"Amen," said the driver.

Inside, a doctor examined Jim, shined a light into his eyes, checked his vital signs. "He needs X-rays," he said, and a nurse wheeled him away on a stretcher, leaving George, Orloff, and Clark to pace nervously in the hallway. "You think he's going to be okay?" asked Clark, speaking to no one in particular.

Orloff, holding against his head an ice pack he had been handed by a nurse, shrugged helplessly. "I don't know," he said. "He looked pretty bad."

"I think he's going to be okay," said Clark. "I think he's going to be fine." George recognized the note of forced hope in his voice. A glance at Orloff showed that he did, too.

George tried again to pray. But just then a young intern approached, indicating with a nod the arm George still held wedged against the ache in his side.

"Doctor says I should look at that," she said.

"Don't worry about me," said George. "Just take care of him."

"How about if we do both?" she said.

She had phrased it as a question, but she took hold of George's arm in a way that left him little room to refuse and led him into an exam room. "Take off your shirt," she said.

George did as he was told. An angry purple bruise had bloomed on his torso. With brisk efficiency, the young woman prodded him for pain. When her fingers found the spot, he winced and grunted. "Ow," he said.

She nodded. "I think it's broken," she said. "Broken ribs usually heal up on their own, but this will help." George glanced up and saw that she was holding up a roll of elastic bandages.

Moments later, his ribs wrapped tightly and having swallowed a couple of aspirin for the pain, George was finally allowed to put his shirt back on and rejoin Clark and Orloff. Two police detectives were standing with them in the hallway, notepads open. One of them cocked his head in George's direction. "This here is the third guy?"

Told that George was, in fact, the third victim, the detective introduced himself, flipped his notepad to a fresh page and said, "Okay, Reverend, why don't you tell me what you saw?"

It soon became apparent to both of them that George had seen very little of use. "They came up from behind," he said. "And I didn't get a good look. It happened too fast." He shook his head ruefully, feeling useless. Then, with a snap of his fingers, he remembered. "Wait a minute, there were witnesses, though. They were watching us from the window of some café . . ." He snapped his fingers again, trying to recall the name of the place.

"The Silver Moon?" one of the detectives asked.

"Yes," said George pointing at him, "that's the one."

The detectives looked at each other, then the first one shook his head at George. "That's a Klan hangout," he said. "We'll talk to them, but I can pretty much guarantee ain't nobody in there seen a thing. Not that they'll admit, at least."

George was absorbing this when Clark and Orloff approached him. "I don't suppose you have an extra $150 tucked in your shoe, do you?" asked Clark.

"What are you talking about?" asked George.

"Doctor says Jim needs a neurosurgeon," Orloff explained. "But the nearest one is in Birmingham and the hospital there needs $150 before he can be admitted."

"You've got to be kidding me," said George.

"I wish I was," said Orloff with an exasperated shake of his head.

"Maybe SCLC can help," said Clark. "Let's go back over there."

George looked from one to the other, disbelieving.

"Have you got a better idea?" asked Clark.

George did not.

The ministers and the doctor helped load Jim's stretcher into the capacious rear of the black station wagon. The doctor drove the three ministers back to the SCLC office in his personal car as the ambulance followed.

As he watched the dark streets of Selma blur past his window, George found it hard to believe what was happening was actually happening—that instead of taking a stricken man for help, they were driving around this hateful little town trying to raise money. It felt surreal. Granted, $150 was no small amount, but wasn't a man's life worth more? And this was taking so long.

He thought of Jim lying on that stretcher in the car behind them and the thought repeated itself. It was taking far too long.

When they reached the SCLC office, Diane listened to their explanation, then wrote out a check to the hospital. The men all piled back into the station wagon—George and the doctor in the front seat next to the driver, Clark and Orloff in back with Jim—and set out for Birmingham, siren screaming. Very quickly, the city fell behind them. The driver silenced the siren and the hearse-turned-ambulance followed a cone of its own headlights down a two-lane Alabama road, the crunching of wheels against asphalt the only sound to be heard.

"How far to Birmingham?" asked George.

"Close to two hours," said the driver. "Maybe less, being it's late."

George glanced at his watch. It was well after eight thirty. Too long. This was taking too long. But at least, he reassured himself, they were finally on their way.

Which is when there came a loud bang and the back of the vehicle jerked. "Look like we lost a tire," said the driver, as he coasted to the shoulder of the road. "And we don't have a spare."

George's eyes went to the ceiling of the car. He felt it again, this sense that he was living some absurdist nightmare, the three of them passing through a gauntlet of trials, each more jarring and bizarre than the one before. It was like something out of Job. Heck, it was like something out of Kafka.

"Uh oh," said Clark.

"What now?" said the doctor.

George looked over his shoulder, his eyes following Clark's gaze. What he saw made his body clench like a fist and flooded his mouth with the taste of metal.

A pair of oval headlights had pulled up behind them.

"Oh, God," said the doctor.

"Oh, shit," said the driver.

And George's mind jeered at him in accusation.

She warned you, didn't she? She tried to tell you.

Was it really just yesterday? It seemed so long ago, him standing there righteous and self-assured in the safety of their apartment in Harlem.

"*You just sent Luther in there to look for Adam. Aren't you worried about him?*"

"*Of course, I am. But at least he's not going to some damn march. He's not daring those white people to hit him. Luther is going to go in there, get Adam, and get right out. He understands the danger and he knows how to avoid it.*"

"*Whereas I don't? Is that it?*"

"*You don't. You couldn't.*"

"*Because I'm just a dumb white guy.*"

"*You're not dumb.*"

But maybe he was. Maybe as a functional matter, "dumb" and "white" were pretty much the same thing in matters like this and nobody had ever bothered to tell him. Or maybe Thelma had tried to tell him, and he'd been too dumb and white to listen.

George stared at the white men in the car behind him. They sat there, just watching.

Thelma, he thought, would be home from the Legal Aid office by now. Maybe she was having the leftover spaghetti for dinner. Maybe watching Joey Bishop on television while she proofed some legal brief during commercials. Or maybe right now she was just sitting there watching the telephone, waiting for it to ring, waiting for her dumb, white husband to call and assure her that he had somehow managed to not get killed on his first day in the war zone into which he had come skipping with such blithe self-confidence.

Who would deliver the news to her if he died here? How would she take it? Would she mourn his memory or would some part of her be furious with him for the rest of her life?

Ah, honey, I'm sorry. I am so sorry.

Still, they waited. And still, the doors of the car behind them did not open. The white men did not move. They simply sat there, watching.

"What do you think they want?" asked Clark.

"What are they going to do?" asked Orloff.

Sitting next to George, the doctor lifted the transmitter for the vehicle's radio telephone off the dashboard and punched a button on the device. "Hello," he said. "Hello? Is anybody there? Is anybody receiving? Hello? Hello?"

"It's busted," said the driver. "They were going to get it fixed."

"Lot of good that does us now," said Orloff, as the doctor replaced the transmitter.

"Maybe we can run for it?" said Clark.

George shook his head, still looking back at the unmoving men in the mystery vehicle. "We run, we die," he said.

"Yeah," conceded Clark.

A moment.

"Hell with this," said the driver. He put the car in gear, checked his side-view mirror, and gave it some gas. The vehicle limped back onto the road, wobbling unsteadily.

"What are you doing?" asked Clark.

The driver pointed. "Used to work at a radio station a mile or two up the road," he said. "We get there, we can call for help. Have 'em send out another car."

George looked behind them and saw the mystery car pull out and follow them. "We've still got company," he said.

The driver glanced at his rear view. "I see," he said.

Long, tedious minutes passed, filled only with the scrape of metal on metal mixed with the disconsolate flopping of ruined rubber. The car rocked gently with the motion of it. Jim's head wobbled loosely. This was not good. George prayed another silent prayer. This was not good at all.

Finally, the driver said, "There it is," and pulled into the parking lot surrounding a small red brick building bearing a radio station call sign. The unknown vehicle parked nearby.

The ambulance driver popped open his door. "Here goes nothin'," he said.

Leaving the vehicle running, he stepped out of the car and walked at a measured pace—he didn't run, but he didn't linger—to the door of the radio station and rang the night bell. George kept an eye on the mystery car. Still no movement. After a long moment, the door to the building opened, and someone let the driver in. George released a breath. He looked into the back of the car.

"How's Jim?" he asked.

"Same," said Orloff.

"Alive," said Clark. "About the best we can hope for."

A moment passed. A moment sitting in a crippled vehicle with a stricken man in the rural darkness north of a country town filled with people who hated them without even knowing them, people who would be just as happy to see them all dead. George had not been this scared since the war. It was a sobering realization.

"Uh oh," said Clark.

"What now?" said George, exasperated by the thought of yet another misfortune. He looked back and what he saw answered the question. The doors of the unknown vehicle had opened. The ragtag band of white men climbed out. One by one, the doors slammed.

George scanned their hands for weapons. Saw none. Thanked heaven for a small favor.

"M-m-make s-s-sure the doors are locked," he said. "W-w-windows up."

The men came on behind stupid grins that contained no humor. "Hey, what y'all doin' in there?" cried one.

"Hey, who's that in there?" cried another. "What y'all boys up to?" Knuckles rapped against George's window. "Y'all boys hear me talkin' to you? I ast you a question."

It was the knuckles on the window that did it.

In the months after he returned from the war, George had often felt like a man walking a tightrope. He spent his days pretending to be normal, pretending to be what everyone else around him was, just another Joe going to work and raising his family. But inside, he had often felt like some brittle thing strung together with high-tension wires, his nerves so taut that on bad days, he'd have sworn he could feel them humming.

Things set him off. On the bad days, it didn't take much. A rude customer, a backfire, or, God help them both, some innocent person with a Japanese face. That was all that was needed and suddenly, George was hurled back to the heat and stench of Guadalcanal, to the brutality and degradation of a prison camp at Nagasaki, to the day the city was blown to pieces by the second atomic bomb.

It took years for him to get past that: lots of prayers, lots of Thelma, lots of time. But finally, there came a day when he realized it had been years since his guts felt like they were strung with wire, years since some innocent happenstance of modern life threw him back into the mud and muck and the constant, omnipresent fear. He had not forgotten the ordeal, not one second of it. But he had learned to control it. Learned to live with it.

Or at least, he thought he had.

With the rapping at his window, George felt his heart start jack-hammering his broken ribs, felt his breathing come shallow and fast, felt his fists clench and unclench, felt the sweat bubbling on his skin, and he was scared, Lord, so scared, and the Japs, the miserable goddamn Japs, swarmed his position and he reached for the old Springfield bolt-action rifle they had been issued, which was better than no weapon at all, but not by much, and his head swiveled this way and that, and his wide eyes scanned the stinking wet jungle and he braced himself to kill or be killed, to shoot some sonofabitch cocksucker in his Jap face and . . .

"George!"

. . . and watch his brains fly out the back of his skull and . . .

"George!" The cry came again. George blinked. He found himself in a disabled ambulance in a radio station parking lot. The doctor was shaking his shoulder roughly.

"Are you all right?" he asked.

George felt his chest heaving. He nodded, dumbly.

"What happened to you?"

"Sorry," said George, feeling humiliated. "Flashback from the war. I used to have 'em all the time. Haven't had one in years."

"Must have been a doozy," said Orloff. "You were muttering about 'Japs this' and 'Japs that.'"

George blinked again. "I'm sorry," he said again.

He looked out through the window to escape their stares. The white men from the mystery car were still circling the station wagon. One of them knocked again on the window, which made George flinch. "Yoo hoo," he cooed in a girlish falsetto, "y'all want to come out an' play?"

Raucous laughter filled the air. And then, so did the screaming of a siren.

A replacement ambulance turned into the parking lot. It was followed closely by a sheriff's patrol car. The ambulance driver stepped out of the radio station then. He had been waiting at the door. Moments later, a sheriff's deputy flashed his light into the ambulance. Another knocked on a rear door and Orloff opened it.

"What happened to this man?" demanded the second deputy.

"He was beaten up back in town," said Orloff. "He has a brain injury. We're trying to get him to Birmingham."

He glanced back at the white men from the mystery vehicle. George followed Orloff's gaze and saw to his horror that where there had been a handful, now there were at least ten. "We sure could use a police escort," said Clark.

The deputy shook his head. "We'll radio ahead. That's all you'll need."

George was not at all sure, but no one had asked them. The back of the vehicle swung open. The two drivers pulled Jim's stretcher out, locking the wheels in place, then rolled it across the lot to the second ambulance. George, Clark, and Orloff piled out and followed.

"Who's that?" demanded one of the white men, pointing to the stretcher.

"Where y'all takin' him?"

"What's happening here?"

Clark faced them. He lifted his palms and spoke a tired plea. "Please don't," he said. "Please, just don't."

His eyes held the flinty eyes of the white men behind them. There was a moment. Finally, George touched his shoulder. "Let's go," he whispered.

The three of them walked toward the new ambulance. Their driver met them there. "We got a problem," he said.

"Of course we do," said George.

"No brackets in back to hold the stretcher in place."

Clark and Orloff shared a look. Then, without a word, they climbed into the rear of the vehicle with Jim's stretcher. They braced themselves on either side of it, each gripping the railings to hold it steady. "Let's go," said Clark. "Let's get a move on."

With a shrug, the new driver slammed the back of the station wagon. George and the doctor climbed in and the vehicle roared off into the darkness of the night.

It was eleven o'clock when George saw the sign for Birmingham University Hospital. He felt no relief. Only numb exhaustion and fear. It had taken so long. There had been so many delays—so many needless, stupid delays. The ambulance pulled up outside the emergency room, but even as the back gate was pulled open, even as Jim's stretcher was being wheeled into the emergency room, he was half convinced something else would happen.

Maybe the stretcher would buckle and Jim would fall on the floor.

Or the doctors would choose this moment to go on strike.

Or the power would go out.

He was braced for this new absurdity, whatever it might be, but it never came. Bare minutes after his arrival, Jim was whisked into surgery.

The three ministers stood there helplessly, looking at one another. Their mission finally accomplished, they had no idea what to do with themselves. George spoke for them all. "What now?" he asked.

"Y'all are the three ministers from Selma?" A short, chunky white woman in a nurse's cap was coming toward them.

"Yes," said Orloff. "I guess that's us."

She waved them to follow her. "There's some people here want to talk to you."

A mystified look passed between the three men. Then they followed her down a hallway, through a set of double doors. They opened it into a lightning storm of flashbulbs. Men started shouting questions at them. "I don't want to do this," said George.

"We have to," said Orloff. "God forbid, if the worst happens to Jim, we owe it to him to let the world know what those people did to him."

There was no arguing with that. George conceded with a nod and the three men spent the better part of the next hour answering reporters' questions. They spent an hour after that being interviewed by agents of the FBI.

It was after one in the morning when, dazed and exhausted, they at last found themselves alone again. No one asking questions for the first time in two hours. No one forcing them to relive and remember. George asked a passing nurse about Jim and was told he was still in surgery. "Y'all are the three from Selma?" she asked.

George nodded. "Yeah," he said, "that's us." He must have looked as exhausted as he felt, because she offered to let them sleep in the room reserved for doctors on call. Clark and Orloff politely declined. They had called a local couple from their denomination, the Unitarian Universalists, who had agreed to put them up for the night. When the couple pulled up outside the emergency room a few minutes later, they offered George a bed as well, but he said he would wait at the hospital.

He shook hands with the other two men as they parted. Orloff said, "George, wish I could say it's been a pleasure."

"Same here," said George.

Clark said, "He'll be all right, don't you think?"

"I hope so," said George, trying to sound hopeful. But he couldn't help himself. "Took such a long time getting him here, though."

"Yeah, it did," said Clark.

George gave a desultory wave as the two men passed through the doors.

When they were gone, he picked up the pay phone in the waiting room, empty at this hour but for a young woman cradling a weepy toddler with a fever. A television mounted on a wall beamed a test pattern into the room. George fished from his pocket a piece of scrap paper where Reverend Porter had scrawled the number of the apartment where he was being housed, then dropped a dime into the slot and dialed it.

"Sorry to call so late," he told the woman who answered.

"Nonsense," she said. "We been waitin' to hear from you. Dr. King announced what happened. Y'all all right?"

"Jim's still in surgery," said George. "My ribs ache something terrible and Orloff got conked in the head."

"Thank God you're all still in the land of the livin'," she said.

"Yes," said George. "Amen."

She put Porter on the line and George had to go through it all again. He tried to be patient. He knew it was only to be expected that people would be concerned, that they would want details. But Lord, he was tired. Finally, when Porter ran out of questions and was certain that George was all right, they agreed that he would drive up first thing in the morning and retrieve him.

Finally, George dropped another dime in the slot. He took a deep breath and dialed 0, ready at last to place the call he had been dreading. Moments later, he heard his wife assuring the operator that she would accept the charges and the operator said, "Go ahead, caller."

"Hi, honey," he said. "I'm sorry to call so late."

"George," she said, and to his dismay, there was no fog of sleep in her voice. "Are you all right? I've been so worried."

"I'm fine," he said. "Well," he amended, "I've got a bruised rib"—he couldn't bring himself to say "probably broken"—"and I'm exhausted. But I'm all right."

"I saw it on the news," she said. "Some white minister from the North, was all they said. George, I was so scared."

He heard the faint accusation in her voice. "I'm sorry," he said.

"What happened?"

"I was with him," said George. And he felt the sudden tears sliding down his cheek. "I was with him," he said again, struggling to keep his voice steady. "There were four of us. And these white guys, they came out of nowhere."

"George, I told you . . ."

"I know."

"George, I tried to warn you . . ."

"Honey, please," he said. And something in his voice caused her to fall silent.

George cleared his throat, mashed at the tears on his cheek. "I know what you told me," he said. "And I promise you, we'll have that conversation. But I can't do it right now. Do you understand? I just can't do it right now."

After a silent moment she said, "I understand." Her voice had softened. She took another moment and then she said, "Are you all right, George? I mean, are you *really* all right?"

He took a moment to think about that, to recall how a night that had begun with a song of reparative hope—"*But I know, a change gon' come*," sang Sam Cooke in the theater of his memory—had spun itself about and become a night of absurdist terror awful enough to catapult him back to the war. Now, here he sat in this room with this young woman and her sick toddler and this TV test pattern and this awful sense of exhaustion and weight. He felt as if he might just sit on this orange plastic chair in this nondescript space for the rest of his life.

"I don't know," he finally admitted.

"George . . ."

He cut her off before she could get started. "I'm tired," he said. "Let's talk about something else. I'll feel better in the morning. I promise."

"All right, George," she said, "if that's what you want." He could tell in her voice that she didn't believe him for a second, but she was willing to let it go for now and he was so thankful for that. They talked another few minutes about nothing, words they forgot even as they spoke them. Finally, George said good night. He hung up the phone and sank into the chair. Then he leaned his head back until it met the wall, closed his eyes, and made ready to wait out the night.

ten

THE SMELL OF BREAKFAST—BACON FRYING WITH EGGS—
lifted Adam's head from the tangle of blankets on the pull-out couch.
He reached to the coffee table for his watch and was not surprised to
find that it was just a little after six. His uncle believed in getting an early
start. Adam believed in sleep, but knew there was no sense resisting. So
he dutifully climbed out of bed. He yawned and stretched, then went
padding into the kitchen, where Luther, in boxer shorts and T-shirt,
stood over the gas stove, stirring the eggs.

"Morning," said Adam. He was careful not to say more. It was two
days now since they had stopped at the remains of the farm in Stubbs
County, two days since his stoic uncle had shocked them both by collapsing in the high grass, bawling like a lost child. Adam knew Luther
was mortified to have been seen that way. As a result, they had coexisted
since then in a cold silence broken only to say what was absolutely necessary to say, and even that in a tone of stiff impatience on Luther's part,
as if he resented whatever question or need required him to expend
some part of his meager store of words.

When they hit Mobile, Luther had stopped at a package store and
picked up a bottle of amber liquid. He had sealed himself in his room
that night and, apparently, proceeded to get epically drunk, because the
following morning, he had emerged dressed for work but walking as
carefully as if walking were new to him, fingers pressing lightly against
his temple, scowling at the kitchen light, scowling at the television,
scowling at the sound of traffic from the street. He had also scowled at
Adam as if the hangover was his fault.

In a way, Adam supposed it was. They would not have gone to the farm if not for him, and if they hadn't, Uncle Luther would not have had to drink away the pain. Adam had spent every moment since then making as little sound as cotton, trying to be invisible as air whenever Luther was in the room, to draw no more attention than a wallpaper design. Now, awakened by the smell of breakfast, he went into the cupboard for plates, opened a drawer to remove a pair of forks, and set two places at the table.

"Don't get too used to this," said Luther as he lifted a spatula full of eggs onto Adam's plate and forked four pieces of bacon on to keep it company.

The unexpected words almost made Adam fumble the bottle of orange juice he had just retrieved from the refrigerator. "Sir?"

"Me givin' you room service. Your arms ain't broke. You can fix your own breakfast tomorrow."

"Yes, sir."

"And you ain't got to 'sir' me. 'Luther' is fine."

"How about 'Uncle Luther'?" asked Adam, who had not been raised to be on a first name basis with an elder.

"'Luther' is fine," Luther repeated, as he fixed his own plate. He gave Adam a look. "Just ain't much for formality is all," he explained.

"Okay," said Adam, who doubted he'd ever be able to be so familiar with his uncle. He poured two glasses of orange juice, took his seat, and started automatically to bless his meal; having grown up with a preacher for a father, it was an ingrained habit. He caught himself when he realized that Luther was already eating.

"What happened at the farm the other day, that ain't your fault," Luther was saying around a mouthful of eggs.

It was, Adam realized with a jolt, an apology of sorts. Or at least an explanation, which was likely as close to an apology as Luther could manage. He saw that his uncle was waiting for a response, but Adam didn't know what to say. Finally, Luther grunted. "Just wanted you to know that," he said. "Ain't your fault."

"Yes, sir. I mean, Luther."

They ate in silence for a moment. Then Luther said, "You're feelin' better?"

Adam nodded. "Yeah. Headache's mostly gone. The light doesn't bother me."

"So, what you plan to do now?" asked Luther. "You going back to Selma?"

"I'm not sure yet," said Adam, pausing a forkful of eggs on the way to his mouth. "King's people are trying to get the injunction lifted. If they're able to do that and they march again, I want to be part of that. Like to see us finish what we started. But if they don't beat the injunction, I'll probably just go back home."

"That'd make your mother happy."

"I know," said Adam. "Right now, all I can do is wait and see."

In response, there came another grunt. Emboldened by the fact that they were apparently on speaking terms again, Adam nodded toward a cheap bookshelf next to the couch; it was so jammed with paperbacks and hardbacks that some were double-shelved and more than a few were piled haphazardly on the floor. The shelf had intrigued him from the moment he arrived, but with his head pounding and his eyes hating light, he hadn't been in much shape for reading. Besides, given Luther's mood, he had been scared to touch any of his property, much less ask about it. Now he said, tentatively, "You got a lot of books."

"Yeah," said Luther, following his gaze. "I read a lot. That stuff on TV'll rot your mind. *Gilligan's Island? My Favorite Martian?* Who thinks up that bullshit? Rather have me a book."

"I like to read, too," said Adam. "I was hoping you wouldn't mind if I look through your books?"

Luther regarded him as if trying to think of a reason not to allow this. Finally, he shrugged. "I don't mind," he said. "Just put 'em back when you finish. But don't think you gon' spend the whole day with your head in no book. I expect you down to the shop every couple hours or so to sweep up, maybe do the lunch run for the barbers. Make yourself useful."

"Okay, Uncle Luther."

"Done told you, 'Luther' is just fine."

He looked as if he might say more, but the telephone rang in the bedroom just then and he got up to answer it. Adam stuffed a last forkful of eggs into his mouth. He drained his glass, then cleared the table and ran dishwater.

"Hello?" he heard his uncle say. "Hey, George. Yeah, he here. He washin' the dishes. Nah, he was shaky the first day or so. He fine now."

Adam tried not to eavesdrop, but in such a small place and with the bedroom door open, it was impossible not to.

"Uh uh," Luther was saying, "I hadn't heard about that. Somebody was hurt? Shit, that's too bad. I'm sorry to hear it. How about you? You okay? Oh, I know how that is. Had my ribs busted one time, too. Took about a month and a half to get right again. You told Thelma?"

Alarmed by this turn in the conversation, Adam turned off the water. He went over and stood by the open door to better hear what was being said, no longer worried about eavesdropping. Luther acknowledged him with a glance.

"Uh huh," said his uncle. "I can imagine. Well, you can't hardly blame her. Uh huh."

Adam made an imploring gesture. Luther raised his index finger. *Wait.*

"Uh huh. So, what you gon' do now?" Pause. Adam heard the indistinct murmur of his father's voice. Luther said, "What time you be here? Uh huh. Okay. Hold on, Adam standin' right here. He fit to bust if he don't talk to you." Luther extended the receiver and Adam took it eagerly.

"Hello? Dad? Hello?"

"Hey, son. How are you?" His father's voice sounded washed out.

"Forget about me," said Adam. "What's happening with you?"

"Just a rough couple of days, is all."

"What do you mean?"

"Have you seen the news?"

"Not really."

"Read the paper. It'll tell you the details. But briefly: I'm here in Selma."

"I heard you were coming down."

"Yeah. I guess we got in about the same time you were leaving with Luther. We did the march—well, sort of—and I was with these three ministers afterward and we got jumped, beat up pretty badly."

Adam's heart jumped. "Dad, are you . . . ?"

"I'm fine. Well, outside of a cracked rib. But one of the other fellows has a brain injury. They had him in surgery, but it's really touch and go at the moment. His wife has flown down from Boston. The poor guy has four kids."

"So, what are you going to . . . ?"

"We're waiting to see if the injunction will be lifted so that we can march again. In light of what's happened, Reverend Porter is determined—we're all determined—to see it through to the end. Meantime, I'm getting a Greyhound down to Mobile. I'll be there this afternoon. While I'm waiting to see what happens, I thought I'd visit my father. Maybe you'd like to join me?"

"Yeah, Dad, sure."

"All right. I'll see you then."

Adam returned the phone to its cradle, looked up to see his uncle watching him intently. "He'll be all right," said Luther, reading his mind. "Busted ribs, that ain't nothin.'"

Adam nodded dumbly. "Yeah, I suppose. But he said the other guy, he was hurt pretty bad."

Luther shrugged. "Just be glad it wasn't George."

"I guess."

"Take a lot of guts to do what he's doin' . . . what you doin', too. I respect Dr. King and all, but if one of them crackers try to hit me, I'm hittin' back. That nonviolence stuff . . ." His voice trailed off. "Ain't everybody can do that," he said finally. "Ain't everybody even want to." A pause. Then Luther said, "You think it'll make a difference?"

"I think we'll get a voting rights bill, yeah."

"But do you think it'll make a *difference*?" pressed Luther.

"I don't follow."

"Read your history. They done passed laws before. Hell, they even had constitutional amendments before. But somehow, don't never seem to make no real difference. Colored people always end up gettin' tricked. Been that way since my grandfather left the plantation at the end of the war. Thought he was free, but them paterollers taught him different. Tol' me once they arrested him for 'vagrancy' *while he was walkin' to his job*."

Luther's laugh was bitter as smoke. He shook his head. "That's the way it always is when we try to get so-called 'freedom.' We *always* get tricked."

"You think that's what will happen this time?"

Again, Luther shrugged. "That's what done happened before. But you think it'll be different now."

It wasn't a question this time, noted Adam. More like a judgment. He considered it for a second. Then said, "Yeah. I do. I have to."

Luther regarded him for a moment, his expression unreadable. Then he said, "I'm goin' to get ready for work."

Minutes later, freshly bathed and shaved, Luther walked out the front door and trotted down the exterior steps. Moments later, Adam heard the radio come on in the empty barbershop downstairs. It was tuned to some station playing swing jazz from twenty-five years ago, but Adam knew from experience that by the time the shop opened at ten, Luther would have turned to a station playing something hip—some Motown or some James Brown—as a reluctant concession to his customers.

With his uncle gone, Adam felt able to breathe for the first time all morning. Somehow, when Luther was in a room he seemed to suck up all the air. Adam flipped on the television. On the *Today* show, anchor Hugh Downs was reporting the arrest of three men in connection with the attack his dad had told him about. Downs then cut to an interview with the wife of the man who'd been most badly hurt. Marie Reeb, they said her name was. She seemed dazed. The reporter questioned her gently.

He asked, "Do you think the cause for which your husband came to Selma was worth it?"

She said, "I don't feel that I can answer that for myself. I can only answer for Jim, that any consequences that might occur did merit this."

Her sad composure moved something inside Adam. And, not for the first time, the terrible portent of what the movement was doing here—of what he, personally, was doing here—struck him like a fist. They were standing against the forces of white people and their white power, and those forces were declaring, clearly and unmistakably, in the words of a Negro freedom song, that they, too, would not be moved.

But the Negroes who sang that song and the bastions of white power they were contending against could not both be right, could not both be immovable. Something had to give.

"You think it'll make a difference?" Uncle Luther had asked him—*challenged* him.

As far as Adam was concerned, it had to. The alternative was unthinkable.

Partly to free his mind from such grim thoughts, Adam lowered the volume on the television and went to explore his uncle's bookcase. The contents surprised him. There was *The Fire Next Time* and *Nobody Knows My Name* by James Baldwin. One shelf contained copies of *The Crisis*, the magazine of the NAACP, going back a good fifteen years, plus a smaller collection of *Muhammad Speaks*, the newspaper of the Nation of Islam. Then there was *Black Reconstruction* and *The Souls of Black Folk* by W. E. B. Du Bois. A collection of poetry by Langston Hughes. Another by Gwendolyn Brooks. *Black Skin, White Masks* by Frantz Fanon, *The Mis-Education of the Negro* by Carter G. Woodson, *A Voice from the South* by Anna Julia Cooper, *Why We Can't Wait* by Martin Luther King, Jr.

Paging through some of the books, Adam was further surprised to find them dog-eared and heavily notated. Scribbling in the margins in his cramped handwriting, Uncle Luther—just "Luther," Adam reminded himself—was given to debating the great thinkers or expanding on their points. His observations were often trenchant and incisive.

"Bullshit!" he wrote, next to a passage in which King claimed that American history taught the Negro "that nonviolence in the form of boycotts and protests had confounded the British monarchy and laid the basis for freeing colonies from unjust domination."

"What really freed those mf's was muskets and sabers," continued Luther's note. "We're nonviolent with people who are nonviolent with us. But we are not nonviolent with anyone who is violent with us."

Adam recognized the last part as something Malcolm X had said. Taciturn to the point of abruptness and with the ungrammatical English so often found in undereducated Negroes from the South, Luther, it turned out, was nevertheless a well-read man with an agile intellect. This was something Adam would never have guessed.

He was replacing the King book on the shelf when he noticed it had been resting, not against the back of the bookcase, but against a small white metal box. Curious, Adam removed another few books and pulled the hidden box out. It was not locked. With faint foreboding, Adam opened the clasp and lifted the lid.

Inside, he saw photographs, military insignia, and paperwork. It took him a moment to realize that he was looking at memorabilia from the war. On top was a shoulder patch. It depicted the profile of a snarling black panther and beneath that, the words "Come Out Fighting." Adam guessed that this had been part of his uncle's uniform during the war.

Beneath were a series of black-and-white photos. Adam recognized his uncle in some of them—younger, thinner, often caught staring down the camera as if it were some kind of enemy. In one photo, his uncle stood with four other men next to a tank. In place of his usual grumpy expression, Luther's face in this picture reflected a grim and even swaggering pride. In fact, he was almost smiling. There was an emblem painted on the tank. Adam had to squint to read it. "Lena Horne," it said. Apparently, this was what they had called their tank.

Adam put the pictures aside. Digging deeper, he found discharge papers and a faded military ID. At the bottom was a bundle of letters bound by a rubber band; it was so brittle and old that it broke when he lifted the envelopes out.

"Shit," hissed Adam. He would have to scrounge a new rubber band if he didn't want his uncle to know he had been snooping.

Adam was vaguely ashamed of what he was doing. Uncle Luther, whatever his faults, had driven across the state to rescue a nephew he barely knew and had given him a safe place to recuperate. He deserved better than to have that same nephew, first chance he got, invade his privacy by rifling through his things.

But Adam couldn't help himself. As Luther barely knew him, he barely knew Luther. This was a chance to shed some light on the mystery of his mother's brother, to learn something about a man who, along with Mom, Dad, and his father's father, was the only family Adam had. That was, if you didn't count Dad's brother and sister, which Adam did not; from family stories, he knew that his aunt and uncle had made it clear the moment his parents got together that they wanted nothing to do with a brother who married a black woman. They had disowned Dad and his wife and kid.

Adam was happy to return the favor.

So yes, he reassured himself, since Luther was part of what little family he had, he had an absolute right to know more about him. Thus justified in his own mind, Adam began examining the envelopes. But it soon became apparent they were all from the same person, all from his mother and written to Luther between 1942 and 1945 while he was serving in Europe. This was what finally made Adam pause.

It was one thing to invade his uncle's privacy, but it was quite another to do the same to his mom. For some reason, that felt like a greater violation. He argued with himself, tried to convince himself otherwise. He told himself maybe it would be all right if he just read the first letter she had written after February of 1944—when he was born—just to see what she said about her new son? Surely reading just that one wouldn't be such a sin, would it?

Adam tried to convince himself, but he couldn't. So in the end, he put the letters down, went into his uncle's bathroom and scrounged up a rubber band, then came back and stacked them and bound them more or less as he had found them. He replaced the other contents of the box and returned it to the shelf. He opened the Frantz Fanon book and began to read, determined to ignore the curiosity that gnawed at him like some burrowing animal.

It was after five when Luther came back up the stairs. Adam had spent the day with his head in Fanon's book, notwithstanding four forays down to the shop to sweep up hair and empty ashtrays. He glanced up at his uncle's entry. "Want me to sweep up again?" he asked.

Luther shook his head. "Nah, they still down there cutting. They'll take care of it when they close up at six. You and me, we need to go pick up your daddy."

They rode together to the Greyhound station where they waited on the platform until the bus from Selma came wheezing into its slot. Dad was the fifth person to climb off. He looked worn and preoccupied, but smiled when he saw Adam and Luther. They shook hands all around—some old white woman pursed her lips in disapproval—Dad picked up his bag but winced and touched a hand to his ribs when he did so. Adam took the bag, waving off his father's objections, and they were off.

West Haven Rest Home was on the west end of town, where the lawns were vaster and the homes they encircled more capacious, where the trees canopied the streets and there was a sense of peace and order one was hard put to find in parts of town where there was less money and more colored people.

"So," said Dad, as they turned into the parking lot. "You've seen my father more recently than I have, Luther. How is he doing? Is it any worse?"

"Depend on the day," said Luther. "Never know what you're going to get. Some days, he clear as a bell and you'd swear he got no business even being in a place like this. Other days . . ." He finished the sentence with an eloquent shake of his head.

"Well," said George, opening the car door, "let's go see what kind of day this one is."

It seemed to be a pretty good one, as near as Adam could tell. When the door opened, Johan Simek, dressed as always as if he might be going to court at any minute, stood up from the chair where he had been watching television, a broad smile of recognition splitting his face as he shook each of their hands in turn.

"George," he said, happily. "And Luther. And my goodness, is this Adam? You're all grown up. I would not have known you if I had seen you on the street."

"Hey, Grandpa," said Adam.

"Sit, sit," said Johan. There were only two visitor chairs, so Adam stood as his father and uncle took their seats. "So, what brings you to town, son?"

"We drove down overnight on Monday," said Dad. "We came down to join Martin Luther King's march."

"His march?" Grandpa looked mystified.

"The march for voting rights," said Dad.

"Is that why Adam is here?"

"Yes," said Adam, nodding.

"And you, Luther?"

Uncle Luther shook his head. "I live here, remember?"

"Ach," said Grandpa. "Of course, you do." He made a vague gesture. "My mind," he said in a low voice, his head bowed. "My mind isn't what it used to be."

"That's okay, Dad." Adam's father laid a hand on his own father's shoulder and repeated himself. "It's okay."

Dad looked as if he might say more, but then there came a knock at the door. Looking up, Grandpa smiled. "So popular I am, today," he said. And then he called out to the unseen newcomers. "Yes, by all means, please come in and join us."

The door opened and a white man and woman stepped through. She had dark hair and was probably in her thirties, dressed in a stylish jacket and skirt the color of cream and a blouse the color of coffee with matching hat and gloves; he was about the same age, with short-cropped blond hair, and was wearing green fatigues. They had been talking animatedly to one another, but pulled up short when they saw Adam, Dad, and Uncle Luther.

For a moment, nobody spoke. Everybody stared. The man and woman looked vaguely familiar to Adam, but he couldn't place them. When he looked to his father for a clue, he was surprised to see that he had risen from his chair, his posture tense, as if to confront a threat, eyes filled with wary recognition.

"Cora," he said. "Nick."

Only then did Adam realize that these two were his aunt and uncle. As far as he knew, his father had hardly seen or even spoken to either of them in years. Uncle Luther came slowly to his feet, standing alongside Dad.

"Well," said the man. "Well, well, well."

"Nick . . ." The woman's voice was a warning.

"What are you doing here?" Dad asked his younger brother. "Last I heard, you were overseas."

"Vietnam," said Nick. "Killing gooks for Uncle Sam. I got leave when I heard about Pop."

His eyes traveled to Luther. "So I suppose, this'd be your brother-in-law, huh?" Something in his tone mocked the words. Then he swung his eyes toward Adam. "And I guess this is him?"

Him?

Somehow, the word made Adam feel as he if wasn't really there. He straightened. "My name is—"

Dad cut him off. "Stop it, Nick."

Dad's brother didn't say anything else. But he stared at Adam like meat. Now Dad turned to Luther. "Would you mind . . . ?" he asked, nodding toward Adam.

Luther spoke without taking his eyes off Nick Simon. "Are you sure?"

Dad nodded. "Yes, I'm sure." Still, Luther hesitated a moment. Then he moved to Adam. "Let's go," he said. "Let's leave them to it."

Adam was surprised. "Uncle Luther? I don't want to."

Luther gripped his bicep in a way that said he had no choice. "Let's go, boy."

"But..."

Before he could get another word out, Luther had opened the door and steered him through it, brushing against Nick, who turned to watch them go. The door closed behind Adam, and immediately he heard his father's voice. The words were indistinct, but the tone was furious. He tried to remember the last time he had heard his gentle father speak with fury. He couldn't.

"It's about me," he pleaded. "I should be in there. Why can't I be in there?"

"This is somethin' they got to do on their own," said Uncle Luther. "Probably somethin' they should have done a long time ago."

"It's about me," repeated Adam.

"No, it ain't," said Uncle Luther. "Not really."

Which was so obviously a lie that Adam could only stare. Luther met his gaze, but something flickered in his eyes, and after a moment Luther turned away. He made a point of reaching for a cigarette and lighting it, but there was no mistaking it. Luther Hayes, who had driven tanks through Nazi shellfire, had turned away rather than face him.

"Come on," muttered Luther, cigarette bobbing in his lips. "Let's wait in the parking lot. They likely gon' be a while."

They retreated through the front door and into the coolness of an early evening in spring. His uncle, never the most voluble of men, seemed to struggle for something to say.

"Look like it might rain," he said, gazing up at a fleet of tattered clouds passing across the moon.

"Yeah," said Adam, uninterested and not bothering to disguise it.

"Done rained a lot lately."

"I guess," said Adam. He looked back at the building. "What do you suppose is going on in there?"

"I don't suppose," said Uncle Luther. "Ain't my business to suppose."

He leaned against the trunk of the Buick, smoking his cigarette. After a moment, Adam joined him.

"What you want for dinner?" asked Uncle Luther.

And since when did his uncle ask a question like that? Adam stared at him. "I don't know," he said. "I've got no idea."

"Catfish might be nice. Got to defrost 'em first, though. That might take too long."

"I don't care." Adam's voice was sharp.

Luther looked at him. "Okay," he said, carefully. "You don't care."

"I should be in there."

"If George wanted you in there, he wouldn't have told me to take you out."

"But they're talking about me."

Luther nodded. "I expect they are," he said, abandoning the lie. "Expect they talkin' 'bout a whole lot of other shit, too."

"Did you hear what he said? 'I suppose this is him.' 'Him.' Like I ain't got a name."

"I heard."

"I'm his damn nephew. And he acts like I don't have a name?"

"That's fucked up," said Luther. "You got a right to be mad."

"I've got a right to be in there."

"Maybe," said Uncle Luther, crushing out his cigarette. "Ain't my call, though. Ain't yours, neither."

They were silent for a moment. Then Adam said, "Why would he treat me like that, Uncle Luther? What did I ever do to him?"

Luther gave him a look. "You askin' me to explain white people? Might as well ask me to explain an atom bomb."

And this was a truth Adam could not deny. He was white himself. Half white, at least. But white people were the Mariana Trench. White people were the far side of the moon.

They waited.

Uncle Luther lit another cigarette. Smoked it down.

They waited.

The door of West Haven flew open. Nick Simon came stalking out, his sister trotting to keep up. He had a cigar clenched so tightly in his jaw that it was a wonder he didn't bite clean through it. The two of them walked toward a shiny black Cadillac parked on the other side of the small lot.

And Adam couldn't help himself. "Hey, man," he yelled, "what did I ever do to you?"

Nick's head came up and he spun toward Adam. Uncle Luther came off the trunk, ready for confrontation, but Cora Simon hooked her brother's arm and steered him back toward the car, whispering something in his ear.

Dad stepped through the door then. He looked drained. And Adam's fury surged all over again. "Hey, man," he cried. "What did you say to my dad?"

Now Nick wrenched his arm loose from his sister's and whirled around. He closed the gap between them with three angry strides. Uncle Luther moved to intercept him, but there was no need. Nick stopped short of Adam and gave him a hard stare. His voice was like concrete slabs.

"Nigger," he said, "I've never even met your 'dad.'"

He waited. And then, apparently satisfied by whatever it was he saw on Adam's face, he turned and allowed his sister to lead him away. She had backed out her Cadillac and was pulling into traffic before Adam remembered to close his mouth.

eleven

ONCE UPON A TIME, THEY HAD BEEN BROTHERS. TECHNICALLY, he supposed, they still were, having sprung from the same father and mother.

But once upon a time, they had been *brothers*—inseparable in their childish adventures and enthusiasms. Once upon a time, they had stalked through the woods out back of their house, hunting wild Indians with their cap guns. Once upon a time, they had sat mesmerized together before the radio, cradling their cups of steaming Ovaltine as the voice with the chilling laugh caged up inside asked its ominous question: "Who knows what evil lurks in the hearts of men?" And then answered itself with another of those fiendish laughs: "The Shadow knows." And their Ovaltine grew cold because they forgot to drink it.

When George grew up and decided to join the Marines because he knew in his bones there was a war coming and he wanted to be a fighting man and not—as his father would have preferred—some officer pushing paper from one desk to another, Nick, three years younger, had seethed with anticipation of the day he could do the same. "Hope the war isn't over before I get my chance," he had told George when George returned from basic training for a brief leave before shipping out for Pearl Harbor.

And George, conscious of Nick's worship and not above basking in it, had grinned and tousled his hair, knowing Nick hated that, but liked it a little bit, too, and said, "Don't worry about it, kiddo. I'm sure I'll see you on the front lines." Too young and stupid yet to know what he was even talking about, but beaming in the light of Nick's admiration just the same.

Because they were brothers.

And if they hadn't been brothers—real brothers—for twenty years now, since that Christmas Day when Nick had stormed into his bedroom and said, without preamble, "You can't be serious about marrying some nigger!" the truth was that George had always held onto a tattered hope that one day the relationship might be restored. But standing there with the rest home at his back, helpless witness to Nick's casual cruelty toward his son, toward a boy who had never done a single thing to him, George felt stabbed with a cold certainty.

They would never be brothers again.

Alarmed by this certainty, his conscience whispered warnings and contradictions against his ear. God is love, it reminded him. God is redemption. God is forgiveness. How often had he preached those things? How often had he commended them to some man or woman estranged from a parent or sibling?

And what did Jesus say in the Sermon on the Mount?

"Therefore if thou bring thy gift to the altar, and there rememberest that thy brother hath ought against thee; leave there thy gift before the altar, and go thy way; first be reconciled to thy brother, and then come and offer thy gift."

First, be reconciled to thy brother . . .

But it wasn't George who had chosen this path. It was Nick. All George was doing—so he told his troublesome conscience—was acknowledging reality, the fact that Nick had just taken that tattered hope of eventual reconciliation and shattered it like a crystal vase hurled against a concrete floor.

No, they never would be brothers again. Never could be brothers again.

He crossed the parking lot hesitantly, even as Cora's taillights disappeared in the flow of evening traffic. Adam stared after them looking poleaxed, stunned from a blow he never saw coming. Luther's expression bore witness to his own helplessness. George knew Luther had never been comfortable with the lie he had lived all these years for the sake of his sister and her white husband, and now, to have it blow up right in front of his eyes, what must he be thinking?

But maybe, George told himself with that brand of desperate hope that logic cannot abide and common sense cannot penetrate, it had not blown up at all. Maybe it could be salvaged?

"Don't listen to him," he said. The first words that came to mind.

Adam turned as if he had forgotten George was there. "Did you hear that?" he demanded. "What did he mean by that?"

"Don't listen to him," repeated George. "He just wants to hurt you." He put his hands on Adam's shoulders, looked into his eyes. "Don't let him do it," he said. "I've told you how they responded when I proposed to your mother. All of them except my father. They hate Negroes. That's what they learned to do, growing up here, being white. It's what they were taught by their teachers, their friends, even the church. But you have to believe me, Adam: I never learned that. I don't know why, but I didn't. That's why I was able to see your mother for the treasure she was. It's how I got the courage to ask her to marry me."

He was conscious that desperate hope had him babbling. "Don't let him hurt you," he repeated, helplessly.

Adam's eyes were still uncomprehending. "But what did he mean by that?" he insisted.

George caught Luther giving him a meaningful stare. Gently, he shook his head, no, which made Luther grimace. George ignored it. "I have no idea," he replied.

Luther turned away at that, and George knew the gesture for what it was. Condemnation of an overt lie. But what else could he do?

George disregarded his brother-in-law, instead seeking Adam's eyes. "I am your father," he said. This, as far as he was concerned, was an overt truth.

Adam nodded, but his expression remained dubious. George tried to think of what else he might say. He came up empty.

Luther spoke quietly. "We better go," he said.

George was still watching Adam as he spoke. "Yes," he said, "I think you're right." Adam's eyes were vacant as a house the day after moving day.

They piled into the car and Luther backed out, then piloted the old Buick into traffic. "Can you put me up tonight?" George asked him. "I promise, I'll find a hotel room tomorrow. I had intended to stay at our family house since it hasn't been sold yet, but it turns out Nick is there with Cora, so that wouldn't be such a hot idea."

"Sure," said Luther. "No problem. Now, you want to tell us what happened in there?"

George sighed. From the day they first met, Luther had always been straight to the point. There was no subtlety in the man, no artifice. Some days, that gave him a bracing and refreshing honesty. Other days, it just made him insensitive and brusque. George couldn't decide what it made him today. What he did know was that Luther was pushing him—hard—toward a truth he had no wish to confront.

"I'm sure you can guess," he said. "You saw enough."

"I think we rather hear it from you," said Luther.

This brought another sigh. Luther was determined not to take the hint.

"Think we *deserve* to hear it from you," added Luther behind a sidelong glance.

George had had enough. "We argued, okay? Same as we did twenty years ago. Same as we did when my mother died. Nick, he's . . ." A pause. George breathed, trying to settle himself, then began again. "He's like so many other people, down here especially—but in a quieter way, up North as well—who think their skin color makes them special, puts them on a high shelf above everybody else. It's hard not to think that if you're white. The whole country exists to help you think that. Of course, I'm not telling you anything you don't already know."

"So you argued," prompted Luther. The city was flying by their window. They had left behind the canopied streets. The houses and lawns were again growing small.

"Yeah," said George. "We argued. Cora cried. My father yelled at us to stop it. He told Nick he was ashamed of him."

George fell silent, struck now, as he had been in the moment, by the wounded look on his brother's face then. What a thing, he thought, to have your beloved father say to you from his deathbed.

"Can't imagine your brother liked that too much."

George shook his head. "No, he didn't. And the worst thing? Papa was clear. You know, you said he has moments when he's still really sharp and other moments when he's not all there? This was one of those moments when he was sharp. He knew exactly what he was saying and who he was saying it to.

"He told Nick, 'You feel you have the right to say these things because you think you are white. Well, when I came to this country, December 12, 1895, nobody thought I was white.' He told Nick the story of how he stepped off the boat in his shabby clothes, and how people called him a dirty foreigner, a bohunk. It's a story he's told us for years. And when he asked someone what that word meant, they said, 'It means you and me are one step below the micks and one step above the niggers.'"

George glanced over at his brother-in-law. "Sorry," he said.

Luther shrugged and George couldn't tell whether he was indifferent to the word or the apology. "What else he say?" asked Luther.

"He told him how he spent years trying to make himself white, how he did things he's still ashamed of, until he finally decided it was more important just to be a good man, just to try and live in peace with other men. He said, he only had one regret—that he wishes he had done a better job of teaching that to Nick. And that's when he started to weep. You know my father. He never weeps. But lately, as he's gotten older, his emotions are right near the top.

"Cora and I, we told him, 'Don't cry.' She patted his back, but he ignored us both. He looked at Nick square in the face and said, 'So I suppose I take some responsibility for how cruel and selfish and hateful you are. But you are an adult man, thirty-eight years of age, so you must take some responsibility, too, and it makes me sad that I see no sign of that.'"

Luther gave a low whistle. "Damn," he said.

"Yeah," said George. "And that's when he said it. Still looking Nick dead in the eye: 'I am ashamed of you, my son.' Just like that: 'I am ashamed of you, my son.'"

"That's when ol' Nick come flyin' out of there?"

"Like somebody set the place on fire," said George.

"You hear that?" Luther was looking at Adam in the rearview mirror. "His daddy told him off. That's why he was mad."

"But what did he mean by what he said?" asked Adam, and George knew his son would not be deterred. "How could he say he never met my father?"

"I told you," said George. "He was angry. And he's a bigot. He was trying to hurt you, that's all."

Luther implored him yet again with a sidelong look. And yet again,

George ignored it. "Anybody want something to eat?" he asked. "My treat."

Luther shook his head. Adam didn't respond.

They ordered catfish and French fries from a stand on Davis Avenue, the main commercial strip in the Negro section of town. The street was busy and loud, traffic flowing up and back, a boy on a bike weaving in and out around the slower-moving cars. From the speakers over the doorway of a record store, "Stop! In the Name of Love" by the Supremes pulsed against the night. Levi Stubbs of the Four Tops was singing, "*Baby, I need your loving*," when their meals were served up in grease-stained brown paper sacks. Luther drove two blocks down before turning into the alley that ran alongside Youngblood's Barbershop and pulling into the parking lot behind.

"Home, sweet home," he said.

"Good," said George, forcing a grin, "the smell of that fish was driving me crazy."

He looked back to Adam for confirmation that the food smelled delicious. Adam looked right through him.

They climbed the stairs, George lugging his own suitcase, Adam making no move to help, and Luther let them into his small, neat living space. He turned on the television and they ate their meals sitting on the couch. And the night grew old. *Perry Mason* became *Password* became *The Baileys of Balboa* became *The Defenders*. All of it washed over them without leaving a mark. Somewhere during a commercial break—Mrs. Olson pulling her ever-ready can of Folgers coffee from her purse—George recalled Thelma once telling him that Luther didn't even watch television outside of news programs and ball games. He considered the rest of it stupid beyond endurance.

But on this night, all three of them sat there before the flickering blue light. They watched without watching, but they watched because it was there—and because watching filled the time, helped to ward off the silence that otherwise loomed over them like unpaid bills. In a way, George supposed it was exactly that.

Once upon a time, impulsively, romantically, ridiculously, he had stood in a segregated park on Christmas Eve and proposed marriage to a Negro woman he knew mainly from correspondence. Her son, not yet two years old, watched as he did it.

And somehow, they had both agreed—did they ever even speak about it?—that Adam would take George's name, that he would raise the boy as his son. Because to tell the baby the truth—hard enough for her even to admit that truth to herself—was simply unthinkable. If the truth was too crushing for her and she was an adult woman, how could she allow it to fall on a toddler, a baby with pudgy cheeks who pointed at a toy train and called it a "choo choo"?

It had seemed natural, it had seemed easier, it had seemed *right* for the boy to simply call George "Dad." Because George *was* his father and if biology did not agree with that, well, even George himself had forgotten this somewhere along the way. He suspected Thelma had, too. They were a family. She was his wife and Adam was their son and that was all there was to it.

But it turned out—and he knew now that they should have understood this all along—that they were only piling up that unpaid bill, mortgaging tomorrow's peace of mind to pay for today's. Now, somehow, tomorrow had arrived. And with a few hateful words from the embittered man who once had been his brother, the bill had come due, and George had no idea how they would pay it. He had no idea if they could.

"George."

He glanced over. Luther was pointing at the television. Dazed, George looked back at the screen. He blinked in surprise. Somehow, without his realizing it, *The Defenders* had ended. Now there was a man in glasses and a conservative suit reading the news from a sheaf of paper.

". . . has died," he was saying. "Following Sunday's melee on the Edmund Pettus Bridge in Selma, he had come to Alabama from Boston in response to the call from civil rights leader Dr. Martin Luther King, Jr., for a march by clergy in support of his campaign to get voting rights for Negroes. He was transported to Birmingham University Hospital after allegedly being set upon by a gang of white toughs. Three suspects have since been arrested. Reverend James Reeb was thirty-eight."

Luther pointed. "Ain't that the guy—"

George cut him off. "Yeah," he said. He hung his head, closed his eyes. "Yeah, that's the guy."

"I'm sorry," said Luther.

"Me too," said George. He felt exhausted, wrung out by these last two miserable days. "Fellas," he said, "would you mind if we shut it down for the night? I could use some sleep."

Luther agreed that that was a good idea. He retrieved some bedding from a closet, then said good night, went into his room, and closed the door. George brushed his teeth at the kitchen sink, then stripped to his boxers and lay down beneath a quilt on the pull-out. Adam took a pillow and a blanket and sacked out on the floor. He hadn't spoken unprompted for hours.

George turned off the lamp and the room went dark. "Good night, son," he said. Chancing it.

There was a moment. Then Adam said, "Good night."

And that, at least, was something.

George closed his eyes, thinking it might be difficult to fall asleep. When he opened them again, the darkness was beginning to lighten and he was startled to find that it was morning. He had to pee, but he held it, luxuriating in the stillness and the warmth.

As his eyes adjusted to the dim light, he glanced down at Adam's pallet on the floor. It took George a moment to process what he saw: the covers thrown aside, an empty space where Adam should have been. George sat up straight, a sudden foreboding pulling him down, like waters closing above a drowning man. His eyes searched the small space, living room and kitchen, for movement. But all was still. He got up and crossed to the bathroom, pushed the door open, but the small chamber was empty and dark.

And that's when he knew it for sure.

Adam was gone.

twelve

ADAM REALIZED, ONLY AFTER HE HAD QUIETLY DRESSED IN the darkness, only after he had plucked his mother's letters from the metal box hidden on the bookshelf, and only after he had slipped down the stairs and was standing in the predawn quiet of Davis Avenue, that he had no idea where he was going. That is, he couldn't recall the address of his so-called grandfather's house from the times George had taken him there to visit. Adam had only a general sense that it was near a country club roughly north and west of the part of town where colored people lived.

So for two hours, he fumbled his way onto and off of buses crowded with sleepy-eyed rush hour travelers, with colored maids and chauffeurs, mechanics, schoolteachers, janitors, and cooks, going to work on a Friday morning. He asked awkward directions. Once, he transferred onto a bus going the wrong way. But eventually, he found his way to a neighborhood that looked familiar, a community of gated driveways and expansive lawns, of gently winding streets and of houses that sat back and looked down. He stepped off the bus and started walking.

Adam remembered Johan Simek's house as a white mansion sitting at the apex of a horseshoe-shaped driveway, the front door flanked by beveled glass and recessed beneath a columned portico. So he walked the vaguely familiar streets, looking for a house that matched his memory.

He did this for an hour, trudging up and back down the quiet, elegant thruways, but he didn't see what he was looking for. He kept walking. Soon he realized that he was passing some homes for the second time. By this time, it was after nine a.m. He was beginning to tire. He wished he had some water.

When he'd been walking for another half hour, Adam began to feel the sting of his own foolishness. He had run away from home in a fit of pique, run away like a seven-year-old child, and come here because he had some vague notion of confronting his hated uncle—or whatever Nick Simon was—and wringing the truth out of him. But instead, he had become lost in an alien maze of rich white homes, and he was even thirstier now and getting hungry as well.

Adam hated the thought of slinking back to the apartment above Youngblood's Barbershop, of facing George and his uncle having accomplished exactly nothing except to make himself look stupid. He knew they would never say that to his face, but that wouldn't stop them from feeling it. And they might even be right.

But what else could he have done?

Those words—*Nigger, I've never even met your "dad"*—had torn something loose inside him. In the detonation of those seven bomb-shell words, he had lost all foundation, all understanding of his own identity. And Dad's—no, *George's*—idea of a response was to go for cat-fish and watch *Perry Mason*?

Just thinking about it made him angry all over again. Adam took a seat on a sidewalk bench beneath the cool shade of an old oak. A black woman, heavyset and wearing a pink dress and white apron, trun-dled briskly past him, obviously late for work. He nodded a greeting. She gave him a strange look in response and he realized she had prob-ably taken him for white and was now trying to figure out why some unknown white man was acknowledging her. People occasionally did that—even colored people—if they weren't looking closely enough.

The woman went on. Adam leaned back and closed his eyes and let a minute pass, then two. The moment felt like grace.

And that's when he heard the car approaching. Adam opened his eyes and was frustrated but not surprised to find a Mobile police car pulling abreast of him, bubble-top light flashing slowly. He realized belatedly that he should have expected this. He sat up straight and readied himself for the inevitable.

Two officers climbed out. The one on the passenger side approached; he was a tall, rangy man with a long neck and a prominent Adam's apple. His partner, older and thickset, body going over to outright fat, hung back by the car, hand lingering near the weapon holstered on his hip.

The first cop got right to it. "You don't live around here," he said. An announcement, not a question.

Adam kept very still. All his mother's stories about what it meant to be a Negro in the Deep South came rushing back. And the decision to leave the safety of Luther's apartment to go foraging around this unknown city in this utterly foreign state began to seem even more foolish than it had just a moment ago.

"No, sir," he said, confirming the statement that wasn't a question, "I don't."

The driver peered closer. "And you ain't white, neither," he said. Another announcement.

"No, sir," said Adam.

"Look almost white, though."

"Yes, sir."

"Mulatto, I'd say. Half nigra."

"Yes."

"What you doin' here, half nigra?"

Adam considered his responses and decided the truth was the only one that made sense. "I got lost," he said.

"Lost?" For the first time, the almost-fat cop spoke, hand still lingering near his weapon.

"Yes, sir."

"Where you from, half nigra? Sure ain't no place around here."

"I'm from New York City."

"Is that right?" With a low, appreciative whistle, the first cop thumbed his cap back off his forehead and glanced over at his partner. "You hear that, Charlie? We got us a half nigra boy here from New York City."

The one called Charlie said, "Yeah, you weren't kiddin' when you said you was lost, were you? Well, I don't know how it is in New York City, but down here in Mobile, Alabama, when a colored boy goes wandering through a rich white neighborhood, it makes the housewives nervous and they start to callin' the police."

"That they surely do," said the first cop. "Why don't you get on your feet for me, boy, and show me some ID."

Adam had pushed up off the bench and was reaching for his wallet when a woman's voice stopped him. "Officers, there's no need for that."

All three men turned in surprise. The woman who had come upon them unnoticed was slim and white. She was wearing powder blue pants with a white top. A straw hat and cat-eye sunglasses shielded her face. At her feet sat a collie, panting at the end of its leash. It took Adam a moment to realize that this was George's sister, Cora.

"Ma'am?" said Charlie.

"I'm Cora Brockman," she said. "I'll vouch for this boy. I know him. In fact, I suspect he was looking for my house."

"Ma'am?" Charlie repeated it. He seemed confused by this turn of events. The hand lingering near the gun had fallen. "You say you know him?"

Cora smiled sweetly. "I know it's hard to believe, but I do. I'm afraid he's my brother's son."

The two cops shared a look. "Yes, I know," said Cora. "It was all quite the scandal twenty years ago. But as you said yourself, he's obviously half nigra, so you can see I'm not foolin'." Another sweet smile. "Go on, officers, I'll take him with me. I live just around the corner."

Charlie scowled as if he were being tricked and couldn't quite figure out how. But the tall one looked from Adam to Cora and back again, then jerked his head toward the car as if disgusted by the whole business. "Let's go, Charlie," he said in a voice leaden with some unspoken judgment. "Apparently, this lady knows the boy." And he got in the car.

The beefy cop's bushy eyebrows knitted together into one. He regarded Adam and Cora with baleful suspicion. He touched his cap. "Y'all have a nice day," he said, in a tone that wished them anything but.

"They really wanted you," said Cora as she watched the car drive slowly off. "I think I spoiled their fun." Her smile had become faint.

"Thank you," said Adam. "You came along just in time."

She turned to him. "Two blocks up," she said. "Sparrow Lane. Make a left. Two blocks after that, a right on Oriole. You'll see the house on your left."

"Ma'am?" Adam was confused.

She lowered her glasses. "I can't very well be seen walking with you, now can I?"

Adam absorbed this, wishing he had thought of it himself. He should have listened more closely to his mother's stories. "Allow me to get a half block ahead," Cora was saying, "and then you follow. If we're fortunate, no one will think I am being stalked by a Negro brute and call the authorities again."

She didn't wait for an answer, making a kissing sound to the dog instead. "Come on, Punkin," she said. "Let's go home."

The dog came obediently to its feet and led the way. Adam did as he had been told. When Cora reached the end of the block, he started after her. As he passed beneath the gaze of each big house, he tried not to wonder how many eyes were upon him, peering through curtains even now, marking his progress through the quiet neighborhood and maybe even calling the police again. It was hard not to look right or left. Adam made himself focus on just walking straight ahead.

After minutes that felt longer than they likely were, Adam finally saw the house he had spent all morning searching for. It sat as it had in memory, at the bend in a long drive shaped like an inverted U. He started up the drive, only to hear Cora's voice call to him from a copse of trees on the lawn off to his right.

"Where do you think you're going?" she asked.

Adam stopped. "I was going to the house."

"No, you're not," she said. She shook her head. "You really aren't from around here, are you?"

Adam wondered how many times the South and its strange customs would catch him unawares, make him feel stupid and slow. Cora was seated on one end of a long stone bench secluded in the trees. She pointed to a spot at the other end. "Sit there," she said.

She chuckled as Adam complied. "So, what was your plan?" she asked, taking off the sunglasses. "Were you going to go ring the doorbell and punch Nick in the nose for what he said?"

Cora read the answer from his face before he could speak it, and it made her laugh airily. "My God, you were, weren't you? Well, you should be thankful I stopped you. Nick is a marine who's been in combat and you're a child who looks as if he might be bowled over by a strong wind. I'm afraid it would not go well for you."

Adam's cheeks flushed. She didn't notice. Or pretended not to.

"Not that I blame you for being angry," she said, leaning down to scratch behind the ears of the panting dog sitting placidly at her feet. "Nick had no call to say what he said. That was cruel. It was downright mean. And believe you me, I told him so."

"Yes," said Adam, "it was cruel and it was mean, but was it true?"

"That's something you'll have to ask Georgie," she said. A realization came into her eyes. "Does he even know where you are? Does he know you're here?"

Whatever she saw in Adam's face answered the question. "He's going to be very worried about you. I hope you'll at least call him to let him know you're all right."

When Adam still didn't answer, she shook her head. "You really should call him," she repeated.

"He lied to me," said Adam.

"He wanted what's best for you," countered Cora. "That's what my poor brother has always wanted for everybody, ever since we were kids."

She turned a contemplative gaze upon the big white house. "I really do miss him, you know? It's amazing how fast twenty years can go by. Nick misses him, too, though you'll never hear him say it. But they were as close as two brothers can be."

Cora regarded him for a moment. Then she asked, "Do you have any siblings?"

Adam shook his head. "No," he said. Then he thought about it and added, "Not that I know of, at least."

"You should count yourself lucky," she told him. "I'm not saying I don't love my brothers. I do, very much. But nobody can hurt you like a sibling. Nobody else is close enough, nobody else knows all your secrets and your soft spots. If you want to know why Nick did what he did, that's why: it wasn't to hurt you so much as it was to hurt Georgie."

Adam, remembering George's nervous prattling the night before, thought maybe it had hurt them both. He didn't say anything.

"Nick and I," she went on, "grew up idolizing Georgie. He was that big brother every little kid should have. He was capable and sure and knew how to do things. Best of all is that, unlike many big brothers, he didn't mind having a pair of runts like us tagging after him. Other fellows, they didn't want anything to do with their younger siblings, but Georgie was never too busy for us."

Her expression was wistful and distant. "He was a good person, you know. Smart, good-looking, even-tempered. Very serious from a young age, though—especially about the Lord." She rolled her eyes, gave a little laugh. "Nick and I, we went to church because that's what you do in Mobile on a Sunday. But Georgie looked forward to it."

Cora gave him a serious look. "Maybe you're thinking to yourself that I just see him through rose-colored lenses, being his little sister. You might be right on that. I may tend to romanticize, but so be it. As far as I was concerned, my big brother was just about perfect."

She didn't speak for a moment. Adam let her have the silence. He glanced up at the house, looming and silent.

Nigger, I've never even met your "dad."

He wondered who his real father was. He wondered why he had never been told.

After a moment, Cora said, "So what is it that brings you and Georgie down here, anyway? Was it just to see Papa?"

Adam shook his head. "We came down for the voting rights campaign."

She started at the news. "He's involved in that foolishness up in Selma?" Then she chuckled. "Actually, I don't know why I should be surprised. It sounds just like something Georgie would do. He probably thinks that Martin Luther King is the cat's pajamas."

She seemed to realize all at once who she was talking to. A faint guilt stole across her face. "I suppose you do, too," she said.

"I admire him," said Adam.

Her expression turned rueful. "It's a brave new world," she said. "I don't mind telling you, that's difficult for some of us to accept. But Georgie, he saw it coming twenty years ago." A pause. Then she said again, softly, "I really miss my big brother."

"He's not dead," said Adam.

Her head came up sharply, but he didn't care. Adam was tired of her talking about George as if he were no longer among the living, speaking about him in the past tense just because he had married a colored woman and moved away. It was a moment before her features composed themselves into something that wasn't quite a smile. "No," she finally said, "I suppose he isn't. But it's been so many years."

"Twenty," said Adam, who had just turned twenty-one. He had always supposed that he was born out of wedlock, that his folks had fooled around before George shipped out, then got married as soon as George got back. They had always been vague on the timing, though, and now he understood why.

"Yes," she said. "It will be twenty years as of Christmas Day. I'll never forget when he told us about wanting to marry your mother. In a lot of ways, that was the last Christmas I ever had—the last one we ever had as a family, I mean. There was this huge row and things were said that could never be unsaid—especially after Papa took Georgie's side and Mama looked at him as if she no longer recognized her own husband."

Cora gave Adam a direct look. "It broke our family, you know. I suppose it created your family in the same instant, but it broke mine. We were never the same again. We were never even together again, unless you count Mama's funeral. That's what I mean when I say that I miss my brother. I miss my family. I miss the way we all used to be, here in this house."

"And you blame my mother for that." Adam didn't bother making it a question. He felt the heat rising in him. He fanned at a bug that buzzed near his face.

Her expression turned contemplative. "I suppose I do," she said. "I know that isn't quite fair. It takes two to tango and Georgie is the one who asked her. You can hardly blame her for saying yes."

"She said yes because she loved him," said Adam.

Cora pursed her lips as if turning over a thought that had never occurred to her. "I suppose she did," she conceded. "I suppose it's unfair to impute any other motive. But when you're in pain, you don't always think about what's fair."

"You think you're the only ones in pain?" Adam's voice had turned sharp, but he couldn't make himself stop. "My mother, she can't even set foot in this damn state. Can't make herself do it. That's how much pain she carries. She and my uncle, they saw their parents—my grandparents—burned alive at their own front door by some mob of crazy ass white people. Burned alive, you hear me? I just saw my uncle—he's a combat veteran—keel over crying just from talking about it, and it's been forty-two years. And you want to talk about pain?"

He stood, suddenly unable to stay on the same bench with her. The dog's head came up off its forepaws. Cora regarded him in silence. After a moment, she said, "I'll get the car and take you down to the bus stop, so you can get back home. As you've already seen, you don't want to be caught wandering around in this neighborhood."

She stood without another word, made kissing sounds so the dog would follow, and hiked up the driveway. Her gait was stiff and Adam knew he had struck a nerve, knew there was fury caged within that her genteel manners would not allow her to express. She was probably thinking that this strange nigra boy had a hell of a nerve. And maybe he did. But he didn't care. The self-absorption and nerve of her had rubbed his patience raw.

Why did white people think they were the only ones who felt pain? Why did they think their pain was the only pain that mattered?

"I miss my brother," she had said.

Well, hell, give him a call. Write him a letter. That was certainly more than Luther could ever do for missing his parents.

Adam sat there waiting out his own anger.

After a time, the Cadillac came down the driveway. Adam went to the passenger side. He spent a brief moment deliberating whether he should sit in the front or the back—what were the rules, according to the arcane customs of the South? Finally, he said to hell with it and got in the front seat. He was sick and tired of the damned South.

As the car pulled off, he glanced back at the house. Somehow, he was not surprised to see Nick standing under the portico watching him go, hands on his hips. Adam fought down an absurd urge to give the white man the finger.

"I want to call my brother," Cora was saying, "and let him know you're all right and will be home soon." She rummaged blindly in her purse and brought up a small notepad and pen, which she handed to him. "Would you write down the number, please?"

Adam did as she had asked and put the notepad and pen on the seat between them. When she paused at a stop sign, she glanced down and said in surprise, "You've written two numbers."

Adam nodded. "One is for my uncle's house here. The other is back home in New York. You know, in case you ever need it."

She seemed surprised. Her taut features softened almost imperceptibly. "Thank you," she said.

Moments later, they pulled up at a bus bench. "I don't know the buses very well," she said, "as we never rode them, but I'm pretty certain that if you stay on this line, it will take you downtown. From there, you can ask around and someone should be able to direct you back to your uncle's house."

She paused, then took the notepad, flipped to a fresh sheet, and wrote two telephone numbers. Adam questioned her with a look. "My numbers here and in Huntsville," she explained. Something like a smile tugged at her lips. "In case you ever need it."

She looked as if she wanted to say more, then seemed to realize there was nothing more to say. Adam nodded his thank you and stepped out of the car. As the Cadillac pulled away, he sat on the bus bench. Frustration chewed at him. He had wasted a morning and accomplished almost nothing. Yes, the idea of confronting Nick Simon had been a childish one that had made sense only in his outrage. But it would have been good to at least get an answer to the basic question: if George Simon was not his father, then who was?

Which is when Adam remembered the bundle of letters he carried in the breast pocket of his windbreaker. He fished them out, but didn't immediately open them. Instead, he tapped them absently against the palm of his left hand as he argued with himself. The idea of violating his mother's privacy—more, even, than Luther's privacy, his *mother's* privacy—still did not sit well with him. It made him feel sneaky and low.

But she had lied to him. They had all lied to him. For twenty-one years, they had denied him the simple dignity of knowing the truth about his own self, of knowing who he was. So, what did he owe any of them, really? What did he owe even her? They had not respected him. Why should he treat them any differently?

Thus decided, Adam stopped tapping the letters. He thumbed through until he found those that were postmarked from the time of his birth, and he began reading.

He was quickly confused. He did not exist on these pages. There was not a peep or a hint of him. Instead, Mom chattered in her graceful script about doings in the neighborhood, about her grandfather's ongoing feud with the widow woman across the street, about rationing meat and saving used cooking oil, about working at the shipyard on Pinto Island, about sermons heard in church. But there was nothing, absolutely nothing, that suggested she had given birth to a son.

Adam lowered the letters and scratched his head. He couldn't figure it out.

Maybe, as George wasn't actually his father, Mom wasn't really his mother? Maybe he was adopted? It would certainly explain those rare and perfunctory hugs and the brisk, businesslike way she spoke to him. But why would she adopt him if she didn't want him?

Adam felt like a vessel drifting slowly nowhere on a restless sea, anchored to nothing. Who was he? Where did he come from? It seemed the more he asked the questions, the less he understood. Over the course of a day, he had lost everything he had ever known about himself. Why had the truth, whatever that was, been kept from him all these years?

He almost didn't read the last letter. It was dated March 30, 1945—thirteen months after his birth—and it occurred to him that if he hadn't appeared in any letter before this one, there was no reason to believe he would appear now. He was quite sure that if he read this letter, he was only letting himself in for another tedious compendium of things happening to people he didn't care about in a neighborhood where he had never been.

But on the other hand, it *was* the last letter. And he had come this far. So he unfolded it and began to read. His breath snagged almost at once. The letter said:

My dear brother:

I have started this letter five times now and each time I have wound up tearing it up and throwing it away. I think the problem is, I keep looking for some way to tell you the things I need to tell you that won't hurt you. There are so many things I need to say to you, some of them things I should have told you a long time ago, but I was too afraid. But I have come to realize that there is no way I can do this without causing you pain. Even though I don't want to, I have to. You have a right to know.

I guess the first bad thing I should tell you is that our grandfather has passed away. Gramp died just a little over a week ago. I just got back from his funeral, in fact. It was a beautiful service. Everyone from our street was there. Mrs. Foster cried and cried, the poor thing. The minister gave a lovely eulogy, talking about how Gramp was born when our people were in chains and lived to see us find freedom and how the old ones never gave up, either.

I know the thought of Gramp's death will grieve you, but keep in mind that he was blessed to live a very long life and that none of us gets to stay here forever. You should be happy to know that he was healthy right up until the end and that he did not suffer. His body just finally gave out on him, is all. I can report to you that he died sitting in his favorite chair, with a smile in his face, holding his great-grandson in his arms.

That's right, Luther, you are an uncle now. I have a son. His name is Adam Mason Hayes and he is 13 months old. He is just beginning to walk and jabber. I will send you a picture in my next letter.

I can imagine what a shock this news will be to you. Or maybe I can't.

I'm sure you will have noticed from the baby's last name that I didn't go and get married behind your back (smile!). So maybe you think your little sister has turned into a woman of loose morals. Well, it's nothing like that, Luther dear. I would give anything in the world not to have to tell you this, but the truth is, your sister was raped.

I have hardly ever said that word or written that word or even thought that word since it happened. I think I felt that if I never used the word, I could fool myself into believing it didn't happen. But it did. And here is the part I truly fear to tell you, the part that has kept me up nights trying to think of a way to break it to you: the man who did it was a white man.

His name was Earl Ray Hodges and his wife was a friend of mine. She was a very good friend, actually, in spite of her being white. Feeling the way you do about white people, I know you will find that difficult to believe, but it is true. In fact, she was such a good friend that when she found out what her husband had done to me, she killed him—shot him dead. So there is no reason for you to be thinking of ways to retaliate for what this man did.

That's already been taken care of and he will never trouble anyone but Satan again.

As you might probably guess, there is much more to tell, and I can imagine you have many questions. I will try to answer them as best I can, but I have to beg you to be patient with me and let me tell you these things at my own pace. I hope you understand that none of this is easy for me to talk about.

And yes, I know you will be angry with me for keeping this from you for two years. I feel bad for writing you all those letters filled with gossip about the neighborhood, but never telling you anything about any of this. I hope you can forgive me.

But you have to understand, dear, that I couldn't think of a way to tell you these things. It would be hard enough under any circumstances for a sister to say things like this to a brother, but it was even harder for me, Luther, because like I said, I know how you feel about white people. And I also know you have your reasons. No child should ever have to see what we saw. I'm blessed that I can't really remember it, and I guess you've been cursed that you can't really forget. I almost didn't have the baby because of that. I went to a woman who was going to help me get rid of it, but at the last second, I changed my mind.

What I realized, Luther, is that, yes, I know what it is to be angry at white people. Lord knows I do, especially after what that man did to me. But I'm not like you. I don't want to have to hate them all just for being white. I know they hate us, most of them. But I don't want to have to hate them back. I don't see how that makes things better. It seems to me there's enough hate going around. It seems to me that's why the whole world is fighting right now.

That's why I started to get rid of the baby, Luther, because I thought I was going to hate it. I didn't think I could find a way to love it, but I did. It wasn't easy; I admit I had to work at it, but I did. I'm hoping you will, too. That's what frightens me most,

Luther, the idea that you won't be able to love him. I hope you'll be able to. I hope you'll at least try.

I know I've given you a lot to think about, so I'll let you get to it. I trust this letter finds you safe and in good health. Take care of yourself and Godspeed the day you make it back home safe and all of this is over. I love you, big brother. Please don't ever forget that.

Your sister,
Thelma

When Adam lowered the letter, he could barely breathe.

He had wanted to know. Well, now he knew.

He had wanted to know, but he had never once thought about what knowing might cost him. What it might do to him.

And now, knowing, he felt . . . soiled. He felt grubby and small.

"I didn't think I could find a way to love it," she had said, "but I did. It wasn't easy."

And how could he blame her? God bless her for trying. But how could he really blame her even if she had not?

He was not her child, born of love or even lust. No, he was something that had been done to her. He was the product of an emission, the evidence of a crime. And if she had borne the woe stoically and heroically, did that make the woe itself any less?

Now he understood why George had been the hands-on parent, the one down on the floor with him playing trains or race cars, the one to help with homework or college applications. Mom, on the other hand, had been the one to watch, smiling encouragement or offering ideas as needed, her head wreathed in cigarette smoke, caring, yet also remote, as visible yet unknowable as a mountain peak.

Small wonder. It made Adam want to know who this Earl Ray person was and why he had chosen her. And what must she have felt?

Adam thought it a miracle that he was even here to ask the questions. He could not have blamed her if she had abandoned him altogether, left him on a doorstep, left him in a trash can. What was he to her, after all, but a living reminder of her cruelest day? He was the rapist's son.

The bus came grumbling to a stop in front of him then. People climbed off. Then people climbed on. Dazedly stuffing the letters back into his jacket pocket, Adam followed them. When he got on, he patted his pants pockets, belatedly realizing he had no coins. He opened his wallet and gave the driver a single. The man made change from the nickel-plated dispenser hooked to his belt.

"Transfer?" he asked.

"What?" Adam had been thinking of his mother.

"I said, 'Do you need a transfer?'"

Adam nodded dumbly. "Yeah," he said. "Yeah."

The rapist's son. That's who he was. The realization had its teeth in him.

Adam accepted the transfer. The bus rolled into traffic. He took a seat. The streets blurred past him. He had no idea where he was going. He only knew that there was no going home.

He had no home to go to.

thirteen

THELMA WAS BALANCING A STACK OF LEGAL BRIEFS IN THE crook of her left arm as she pushed the door open. The telephone chose that moment to begin jangling. "I'm coming," she told the annoying device. "I'm coming."

She closed the door, dropped the briefs on the couch, flipped on the overhead light, hustled across the room, and plucked the receiver from its cradle. "Hello?" she said. The operator asked if she would accept charges on a collect call from George Simon. She said yes, thinking to herself that with all these collect calls, the next phone bill was sure to make her cringe. She wouldn't be surprised if it was forty dollars or more.

"Go ahead, caller," the operator said.

"Hey, honey," said George's voice.

Just the two words, benign and routine. But they didn't fool her for a moment. Something inside her went on high alert. "What's wrong?" she asked.

It seemed to take him unawares. "How do you do that?" he asked after a moment.

"What's wrong, George?" she asked again.

"Nothing," he said. "Honest. I mean, we're all fine, nobody's hurt."

"But?" she prompted.

She heard frustration push out of him in a long breath. "But Adam left," he said.

"Left? What do you mean, he left?"

"I mean, he . . . *left*. He . . . ran away, I guess."

"Ran away? George, what are you talking about?"

"Thelma, he found out. He knows."

"He knows? He knows what?"

"Thelma," he said slowly, letting her hear the gravity in his voice, "he *knows*."

A chair caught Thelma as she fell, her legs suddenly useless. "Oh, God," she said. With her free hand, she cradled herself against the sudden cold. She couldn't get her breath. "Oh, God," she said again. "How?"

Whereupon George told her a story about an angry confrontation with his brother at the rest home and how Nick Simon had stormed out and taken his rage out on Adam, the awful seven words he had said. George told her how he had awakened that morning to find Adam already gone and how Luther had noticed a box of his wartime memorabilia sitting open on the kitchen table and when he looked into it, the only thing missing was Thelma's letters to her brother.

"Luther said it's like he wanted us to know he had them."

"Oh, my God," she said.

"Cora called this morning to say he had gone to my father's house, looking to punch Nick in the nose. She stopped him from that, at least. But she said she put him on a bus at ten thirty this morning. Thelma, it's after seven."

"Maybe he's just blowing off steam," she said, trying to believe it even as she said it. "Maybe he'll walk through that door any minute now."

"Maybe," said George. "But somehow, I don't think so."

"Lord, what must he be thinking?"

"Thelma . . ."

She glanced to the bookshelf in the living room. Adam grinned down at her from beneath his royal blue high school mortarboard, a replica diploma held diagonally across his chest. "This has been coming for a long time," she said. "It was foolish of me to think I could go the rest of my life and never have to confront what happened, the choices I made."

"It's not your fault," said George. "And it wasn't a choice you made. It was something that was done to you."

She barely heard him. She was thinking.

After a moment, she said, "I'm flying down."

"Flying?" said George.

He sounded surprised. Not that she could blame him. Thelma had never been on an airplane in her life. "I've got some time coming at work," she said. "I can get Claudette to cover for me in court Monday."

"Thelma, are you sure?"

"I'm not sure of anything right now," she said, "except that I've got to get there. I know the ticket is going to be expensive. Probably thirty-five, forty dollars, but we have our savings, and as far as I'm concerned, this is an emergency, so—"

He cut her off. "It's not about the money," he said. "Thelma, you hate Alabama."

And this, of course, was the truth. She hated the backwards state where she was born. Hated the whole damn South because it had first hated her. And more than that, she feared it, feared it to the center of her solar plexus.

"But I love my son," she said.

She paused, giving George a moment to retort. Her husband kept silent and for that, she loved him, too.

"I'll be down tomorrow," she said. "I'll call when I know the time."

fourteen

On that January day in 1946 after they had gotten Thelma and George married and moved into their new home, Luther and Johan had climbed into the rented van for the long drive back to Alabama. His sister had stood there on the sidewalk in front of her new home in this new city with her new husband and her baby, Adam, waving as the truck pulled away. And Luther, her protector since childhood, had been stabbed by an ice pick of guilt and reproach, by the fact that he was leaving his little sister to this uncertain life in this unknown place. Only by force of will had he resisted jumping out in the middle of the street, grabbing her, and throwing her in the truck.

Then Johan had rounded a corner and Luther couldn't see her anymore and it was almost a relief. If he had known how to pray, he would have done so in that moment. Instead, he had simply said, in a soft voice, "I hope she be okay without me."

Johan had nodded and said, "She'll be fine. They'll both be fine." And Luther knew it for what it was—less an expression of confidence than a pantomime thereof.

He had seen her only once since then. That had been eleven years later, the day he stepped off a Greyhound bus into the cacophony of the New York Port Authority and, after being buffeted about by crosscurrents of people, finally found his way to a crowded, rattling subway car that wove its way through tunnels and between buildings until he arrived at 125th Street in Harlem, where he proceeded to walk for a few blocks, suitcase in hand, fending off a man who walked alongside, trying to sell him a Rolex luxury wristwatch from his coat pocket.

Luther had seen his sister before she saw him. She was pacing outside the office of the Legal Aid Society, smoking and scanning the crowded sidewalk. She had thrown down the cigarette when she spotted him crossing the street toward her and they folded each other in a long embrace before he held her at arm's length and took an appreciative look. The years, he thought, had been good to her. His sister looked every bit the modern female lawyer in her navy-blue hat and matching waist-length coat, cinched fashionably tight around the middle. They could have put her on the cover of *Ebony*. She looked like promise and hope, like the very embodiment of Negroes rising. And he knew then that Johan had been right that day the truck pulled away from the brownstone. His sister had turned out just fine.

"Mom and Papa would be proud," he had told her, as a way of conveying to her that if he himself were any prouder, the buttons of his sports coat would go pinging like shrapnel off signs and windows up and down the street. She had beamed in the light of his praise.

Now, eight years later, on a bright Sunday afternoon, Luther stood with George in a lobby of the Mobile airport, waiting to see his sister again. Her plane taxied to a stop and the ground crew rolled stairs up to the aircraft door. The hatch opened and a smiling stewardess stood aside as a procession of travelers began filing out of the plane. Luther might not have recognized her in her oversized sunglasses and hat, but for a quickening of George's breath. It amused him that Thelma still had that effect on this man after almost twenty years of marriage.

"There she is," said George.

And indeed, there she was. To Luther's critical eye, she seemed smaller. Her face—what he could see of it—was taut, her mouth a thin, humorless line. She seemed almost to stand on tiptoe, like a bird ready to leap into flight at the slightest hint of threat. He knew why, of course. Alabama.

Thelma came down the stairs and into the waiting room. George tried to kiss her cheek, but she averted her face. In his happiness at seeing her—in his whiteness—he had forgotten, but this was not New York City. Hell, it was just three years since a trio of colored soldiers had sued after being denied service at a restaurant in this very airport.

Alabama was still Alabama. Still a kingdom of Jim Crow. Or as Governor George Wallace had vowed just a few years before, "Segregation now, segregation tomorra, segregation forever."

"Honey," said Thelma, as she removed her sunglasses. That was the only thing she said, but it was enough. There was an admonition in it that made George take a step back.

"I'm sorry," he said, flustered. "I forgot. I'm just happy to see you."

Luther was thankful he had to abide by no such constraints. He took his sister into a long hug. "Hey, baby girl," he said. "Long time, no see."

"Too long, big brother," she murmured against his cheek. "Too long."

As they went to retrieve her checked baggage, George said, "By the way, we heard from Adam. He called last night."

This stopped Thelma in the middle of the concourse. "He called?"

"I told you he would," said Luther. "He a smart boy. Got to figure he come to his senses sooner or later and stop acting like a child."

"He said he was headed back to Selma," said George. "Took the bus. Said he wants to rejoin the march."

"How did he sound, George? What did he say?"

"He sounded . . ." There was a beat as George searched for the right word. Finally, he shrugged and said, "Well, to tell you the truth, honey, he sounded like a stranger. Maybe it's just that he knows now I'm not, you know, his real father. It felt like when you're talking to somebody, and you haven't been properly introduced."

"You *are* his real father," said Thelma in a tone that foreclosed any debate on the subject.

"He'll be all right," said Luther. "Just need some time. It's a lot to take in." He hoped his confidence did not sound as false as it felt. But George and Thelma seemed not to have heard him anyway.

"I'm scared we might have lost that boy," she told her husband.

"He's upset," said George. "He'll come around. I just wish my stupid brother had kept his mouth shut."

"Your brother's not stupid. He's mean. He's wanted to hurt me since 1945 and he finally got his chance."

"I know," said George. "You're right."

"Come on," said Luther, "let's get your bags and get out of here."

Half an hour later, they left the airport in Luther's Buick, passing a sign that said, above George Wallace's name, "Welcome to Historic Alabama—Heart of Dixie." The words were flanked by an American flag on the left, a Confederate battle flag on the right.

He glanced at his sister, who was sitting across from him. She shook her head as the sign went by. "Them and that damn Dixie flag," she whispered.

"You a long way from New York," he told her.

"And believe me, I can't get back fast enough," she replied. "Do you have a cigarette?"

"Honey, I thought you quit," said George, who was sitting in the back seat. It made Luther wince.

"It's just one cigarette," Thelma told him, her voice brittle. She accepted the smoke and punched in the lighter on the dashboard. Thelma lit the cigarette, took a deep, appreciative drag, blew a long stream of smoke, then rolled down the window and watched the outskirts of the city fly past.

Luther allowed a silence to intervene. Then he said, "So what you going to do?"

The glance she gave him called the question foolish. "I'm going to Selma," she said. "I'll stay here for a day or two. There's a friend I want to look up. And I want to spend time with you, of course. But obviously, I'm going to Selma." Another drag on the cigarette. "That's where my son is."

She said little more on the drive into town. Half an hour later, Luther pulled into the parking lot behind Youngblood's. Because George's ribs were still taped, Luther wrestled both of Thelma's heavy bags up the stairs to the apartment. It had been decided that the couple would stay with Luther for as long as they were in town. With Thelma here, there could be no thought of moving into a hotel. The Avenue was a lot safer for a salt-and-pepper couple than some downtown hotel, even assuming they could find one that would rent to them—or that his sister would take it.

No, the Avenue was the only place that made sense. It was not safe, but it was safer.

Over Thelma's objections, Luther stashed her bags in his bedroom, where the linens had been changed, the bed freshly made, and towels washed in anticipation of her arrival. "It ain't the Ritz," he told her, standing in the doorway, "but . . ."

"It's fine," she assured him.

"I'm glad to have you here," he said. "Hate the circumstances, but . . ."

"I know," she said.

"You going to be okay?"

She nodded. "I'll be fine."

"All right, then," said Luther, clapping his hands together once. "Well, I'm going to give you two some privacy for a while." It was obvious to him that his sister and her husband needed to talk.

Thelma protested. "Oh, Luther, don't let us kick you out of your own place. We haven't even had a chance to catch up."

"We'll talk," he told her. "It's just that Sundays and Wednesdays is when I usually go to visit Johan. He's kind of used to that and I don't want him thinkin' I forgot."

"Why don't I come with you? It would be nice to see George's father again."

Luther, who had been counting on doing this alone, froze. He had no good answer for that. Luckily, George spoke up. "Honey," he said, "you've been traveling all day. Why don't you get some rest first? I'm going to go see my dad tomorrow and you can come with me then. Besides, he's more likely to remember who you are if he sees you with me."

"That's a good point," said Luther.

Thelma's expression was dubious. "Well, all right," she said. "If you think that's best."

George assured her he did, and Luther agreed. He kissed her cheek on his way out the door, promising to return in time to take her to dinner. Luther trotted down the stairs but didn't go immediately to his car. Instead, he unlocked the back door of the barbershop. It was dark and quiet inside, the floors freshly swept and mopped, the room smelling faintly of Glo-Coat, lemon Pledge, and hair. Ordinarily, he liked being in here by himself. The stillness carried the memory—and the fore-knowledge—of Negro men laughing, playing checkers, and shooting the shit as they awaited their turn in the chair, free, if only for that hour or so, to be just men among men, no more and no less. It always brought him a measure of peace to pause in the doorway of the empty shop—*his* empty shop—simultaneously anticipating and remembering.

Today, he did neither. Instead, he went straight to the room that served as his office—a grand name for a space not much bigger than a janitor's closet—pulled open his bottom desk drawer and retrieved the bottle of whiskey he had lately taken to squirreling away there. He plucked a shot glass from the same drawer, blew in it to dislodge any dust or small creature that might be sleeping there, and poured himself one finger. Luther drank it in a gulp. He felt centered by the jolt that followed. It felt so good, in fact, that he decided to take the bottle with him.

Retracing his steps through the pregnant stillness of the empty shop, Luther slid behind the wheel of the Buick. It was, he knew, illegal to drive with an open container of alcohol. But, thanks to Alabama's blue laws, it was also impossible to find a liquor store or bar open on a Sunday, so as far as he was concerned, he had no choice. Because he needed whiskey for this.

It wasn't that he was worried about running into George's mouthy brother. He thought he might actually enjoy popping Nick Simon in the chops after what he had said to Adam and the pain it had caused Thelma. It might even be worth spending the night in jail for.

But the fact that Floyd Bitters slept in a room just down the hall from Johan, that shook him. He hated to admit it, but it did. And he needed something to steady himself.

Luther started the engine and backed out, guided it down the alley along the side of the building. He inserted the car into a break in traffic, then flipped the radio on. Dizzy Gillespie's trumpet filled the car, tracing the frenetic melody of "Salt Peanuts."

In a sense, Luther had lied to Thelma when he told her he didn't want the old man missing the regular Sunday visit. Most of the time, after all, Johan Simek barely knew what day it was. So that wasn't the real reason for this trip. No, the real reason was that Luther didn't want it to be said—if only by himself, in the private corners of his own mind—that Floyd Bitters had made him chicken out, kept him from doing something he otherwise would have done. That man had already taken so much away. Hell, he had taken everything. Luther could not abide the idea that he would take everything, plus this: a regular visit with an old friend on a Sunday afternoon. Yet at the same time, Luther could not face that visit—face that proximity—sober.

So he drank his way across town. He knew it was a reckless thing to do, knew how abruptly the flashing lights of a prowl car could appear behind him, a risk that grew exponentially greater as he transgressed the invisible line separating poor and black from wealthy and white. He dreaded the thought of the field sobriety test, the pinch of handcuffs, the hard, reverberating clang of metal bars closing him in.

Yet, he still sneaked sips from the bottle, glancing surreptitiously about for any hint of a black-and-white Ford parked at a curb or lurking in some inconspicuous alleyway. He drove with exaggerated caution, keeping well below the speed limit, not allowing the grille of the car to intrude even an inch into the crosswalk. When, at last, West Haven Rest Home appeared in his windshield, Luther wanted to congratulate himself on his cleverness. But he was embarrassed by it, too.

He remembered all too well how it was back when he drank every day in search of oblivion and, in the process, made himself an embarrassment to his sister and their grandfather. He had come so far from the man he once had been, yet somehow, it seemed he had ended up right back where he started.

Suddenly disgusted by himself, Luther pulled into a parking space in a far corner of the lot. He left the engine running, took one last sip from the bottle, patted his breast pocket, and brought out a package of spearmint gum. He folded two sticks into his mouth, then screwed the top back on the bottle and reached across to pop open the glove box, intending to stash the liquor away. He was surprised to see that his pistol was still sitting there, waiting to be returned to his bedside. He stared at it for a long time, stared at it as if he had never seen a pistol before.

He stared until the bleating of car horns made him jump. Out on the street, he saw, someone had been slow in taking advantage of the green light. It broke the spell. Luther threw the bottle into the glove box, pushed it closed. But he still didn't turn off the engine. Cannonball Adderley and Miles Davis were performing "Autumn Leaves," the bass and piano cool and portentous before Adderley's saxophone resolved their tension into sweet lyricism.

One of his favorite songs. Luther lit a cigarette and sat there smoking and listening. After a moment, he reached back into the glove box, took out the bottle, took another last sip. Warmth rushed over him in a wave. He eyed the doors of West Haven as he recapped the bottle.

Some white man came walking out, lending his arm to an old lady who tottered as if just learning to walk. He watched their slow progress across the parking lot, watched the man—he had a Clark Gable mustache and wavy black hair—open the door of a late-model Ford and seat the old woman inside, then go around and get in on the driver's side.

There was the sound of an engine coming to life, the car's taillights glowed red and white, and the vehicle backed out. Luther tapped a fingernail on the whiskey bottle. It made a hollow plinking sound. Clark Gable finished backing out and the car turned toward the street. Luther flicked away his cigarette. He put the bottle back in the glove box and turned the ignition off. Miles Davis fell silent. It felt as if the whole world had fallen silent.

He got out of the car. The parking lot seemed to sway beneath him. He waited for it to settle, then walked toward the door. He felt like Wyatt Earp striding toward the O.K. Corral. A foolish image, he knew, but this was a showdown of sorts, wasn't it? Him, facing off against the great terror of his life, him proving that he was no longer afraid.

Luther pulled open the door and stepped into the muted light. The teenage girl behind the reception desk glanced up from a paperback novel—*Return to Peyton Place*—ignored him with a glance, went back to her reading. Had she kept her gaze on him, she would have seen Luther walking with slow caution across the swaying floor.

On the television in the day room, William Holden had lit the tip of Lucy Ricardo's putty nose on fire with a cigarette lighter. Ricky Ricardo's eyes looked like they were about to pop right out of his head. Garish shrieks of laughter exploded from the speakers.

Luther ignored them, concentrating instead on the careful placement of his steps. One or two of the residents gazed up from the television, preferring to watch him instead. Apparently, he was the better show. After what felt like an hour, he stood finally at Johan's door. He lifted his hand to knock, then let it hang there as he glanced down the hallway to where the source of all his loss and fear lay ensconced behind a door just like this one. It didn't seem fair.

But, he reminded himself, he was drunk, so he didn't care. That was the whole point of getting drunk.

Luther knocked on Johan's door and when the voice inside invited him in, he pushed it open gratefully. He found the old man alone, sitting on the edge of his bed, spooning up grapefruit. Johan, magnificently dressed, as usual, in a gray pinstriped suit with matching homburg, glanced up at his visitor, eyes wide.

"Luther? What are you doing in Budapest?"

It took a moment to register and when it did, Luther couldn't help himself. He laughed. Regret overtook him immediately as he saw his friend's face collapse in confusion. But Lord, the laughter felt like relief, felt like a favor from the great beyond. In a word, it felt good. He hated that.

"I'm sorry," he told the befuddled old man as he took one of the visitor chairs and tried to bring the laughter under control. He touched Johan's shoulder. "I'm sorry," he said again. "I'm drunk. I ain't meant no harm."

"You are not in Budapest?"

"Afraid not," said Luther. "I'm just here in Mobile. We both here in Mobile."

Johan looked around as if seeing the room for the first time. "Ach," he said, "so we are." Then his eyes narrowed. "But you say you are drunk?"

"I'm drunk," repeated Luther. "Snockered."

"But it's"—Johan lifted his eyes to an institutional clock on the wall above the door—"not yet four in the afternoon. And this is Sunday. Isn't this Sunday?"

"Yeah," said Luther, "it's Sunday."

"Then, why are you drunk?"

The question carried no accusation that Luther could hear, only honest confusion. Somehow, that made it worse. An accusation would have given him an excuse to be angry and defensive. But the guileless bewilderment in Johan's voice seemed to require guileless truth in response. So Luther gave it to him.

"If I'm drunk," he heard himself say, "I don't have to think."

"I don't understand."

"You remember what you told me last week?" said Luther, and immediately regretted the question because Johan likely didn't remember last week, much less anything he had said then.

But the old man responded without hesitation. "I told you I saw him. I saw Floyd Bitters."

"Yeah," said Luther, surprised, "that's what you told me."

"He lynched your parents," said Johan.

"Yeah," he did, said Luther, suddenly realizing that, while he was very drunk, he wasn't nearly drunk enough.

"When you were only nine years old," said Johan.

"Yeah," said Luther. "Only nine."

"He beat me up once, you know." Johan spoke this in a confiding tone. "He hurt me badly."

"I know," said Luther. "You told me last week."

"We were never able to get justice," said Johan. "We were never able to hold him accountable."

"No," said Luther, "we never did."

"All the evil he did," said Johan, a whisper of wonder rising in his voice, "and he never paid for any of it."

"Not a bit," said Luther.

"Why is that?" asked Johan. His eyes radiated a soft perplexity. An innocent bafflement.

Again, Luther found he could not lie or evade. "He white," he said. "When you white, you can do whatever you want to Negroes. You don't have to pay for it."

"He's white?"

"Yeah."

"So he gets away with it?"

"Afraid so."

"That's not fair."

"No, it ain't," said Luther.

"It's not fair," repeated Johan. "Not after what he did." His voice shivered slightly, like tree leaves under the caress of a passing breeze, and his eyes glittered.

"It's a fucked-up world," said Luther. "Fucked-up country."

He expected Johan, who bore himself with such starchy propriety, to say something like, "I could do without the crude language." Instead, Johan just faced him with his watery eyes. "Yes," he said, simply. "It certainly is."

And what could he say to that? Luther didn't even try. Instead, he turned on the television and they watched the news together. The announcer told them that South Vietnam had bombed a naval base off Tiger Island in North Vietnam. Former Soviet premier Nikita

Khrushchev had appeared in public for the first time since losing power. And there were protests across the country in support of the Negroes who had been brutalized one week ago while fighting in Selma for the right to vote.

"That settles it," said Johan, pointing at the screen. "Wallace cannot hold out against the whole country. Negroes will win their rights."

"I'll believe when I see it," said Luther.

"You are such a cynic, my friend."

"Maybe," said Luther. "Cynics don't get they hearts broken, though."

"Leave room for hope, always," said Johan.

Luther shrugged. "Near as I can tell, world don't care if Negroes hope or not. World gon' do what the world gon' do. Don't matter too much what we think about it."

"You're bitter," said Johan.

Luther shot him a look. "I got a right to be, don't I?"

After a moment, Johan gave a resigned nod. "I suppose you do," he admitted.

When an attendant came in wheeling a cart full of trays to present Johan with his evening meal options, Luther took his leave. In the hallway, he paused as he had when he arrived, gazing down toward the room where Floyd Bitters lived, remembering Johan's honest indignation at learning that white men are not held accountable for the things they do to Negroes.

"That's not fair."

It was a reflection of how decimated Johan's mind had become that he said it like that, like a child in kindergarten denied use of the sandbox, but in a way, it also made perfect sense. It did not take a genius to understand that it was wrong for a man to kill two innocent people in the most brutal way imaginable, then get to live out his life unmolested as if it never happened. No, it was a wrong so obvious and so simple even a child in kindergarten could grasp it. Yet the sovereign state of Alabama could not. More to the point, he thought, Alabama simply didn't give a damn.

Luther returned through the dayroom, through the lobby, and opened the door to the parking lot. There, he paused. Nick and Cora were climbing out of her Cadillac, coming toward him. Luther's body tensed, his fists clenching in anticipation of the standoff.

It did not happen. Lost in conversation, George's sister and brother glanced at him, then brushed past on the way to see their father.

Luther stood there with his mouth agape, feeling the tension recede like a tide going out.

He hadn't even registered on them. That's how little he mattered. That's what being a Negro meant. Suddenly, Luther simply felt tired. He felt drained.

He got in the Buick and turned the ignition key. Charlie Parker came up, his saxophone weaving poetry out of thin air. But Luther was in no mood for poetry. He turned the radio off and wheeled the big car to the lip of the parking lot. He had no idea where he was going. He didn't really care. The going itself was the point. He waited for a break in traffic, gave the car some gas, and, with a sickening crunch, ran smack into the rear bumper of a Ford sitting at the light. The collision drove Luther's head into the steering wheel and he rocked back into his seat, pain galloping through his skull.

God, he thought, could this day possibly get any worse?

Which is when a bubble on the roof of the car he had hit began to flash red and blue, and the doors came open on both sides.

fifteen

THELMA GORDY AND FLORA LEE HODGES HAD MET EARLY IN the war. Flora Lee, a rail-thin white woman with a hill country accent, passed out from sheer hunger one day in the standing-room-only crowd riding the Davis Avenue bus. One sympathetic colored woman had given her a seat, in violation of local segregation statutes, while Thelma, who was returning from the grocery store, had given her a box of Cheez-Its from her bag, in violation of simple common sense.

But what else could she have done? What other Christian, moral option was available? She had asked herself this question many times over the years. She had never found an answer.

Not that Thelma had intended friendship. She had simply fed Flora Lee as she would have fed anybody, and, when the white woman mentioned that she had come to the city looking for work, pointed her toward the shipyards over on Pinto Island, where the demands of war had created an insatiable need for workers, even if they were female.

Then the bus had reached Flora Lee's stop, where her husband—a bantam man with a crippled gait and a ridiculous pompadour—was waiting for her. Through the open window of the sweltering bus, Thelma had borne witness to what happened next.

First, he berated her for riding in "the nigger section" of the bus. Then he saw the box of Cheez-Its and his eyes pinwheeled in their sockets.

"Where'd that come from?"

Flora Lee had lowered her eyes like a naughty child. "One of them women give it to me," she said, "on account I was hungry."

"Uh huh. So I guess you sayin' I don't provide well enough for you.

You got to go beggin' niggers now. Is that what you sayin' Flora Lee?"

She didn't get a chance to answer. He hit her in the mouth before she could. When the bus pulled off, Thelma had been grateful to leave the pitiful woman and her hateful husband behind.

Except, she hadn't really left them behind at all.

She met Flora Lee again when she herself sought work out at Pinto Island. Thelma had tried to discourage the woman from talking to her, but Flora Lee, garrulous and guileless in equal measure, had not taken the hint and began following her around like a stray puppy. And her husband, working as a janitor at the shipyard, continued to abuse her, once knocking her to the ground in full view of the entire day shift.

That was the day Flora Lee accepted a foolish offer from Thelma to come stay with her and Gramp in their little shotgun house on Mosby Street until she could find a place of her own. This, too, was in violation of segregation statutes and simple common sense. But here again, even all these years later, Thelma didn't know what else she could have done.

So maybe everything that followed was preordained, a destiny she could have no more escaped than gravity itself: Earl Ray Hodges catching her alone in the belly of an unfinished ship, slamming her face into a bulkhead, knocking her senseless, and raping her in retaliation for the loss of his wife. "Shouldn't have mixed in white folks' business, nigger," he had taunted.

When she found out about it, Flora Lee had returned that very night to the trailer she shared with Earl Ray. She shot her husband in the neck, then waited calmly for police to come arrest her. Two months later, Thelma, pregnant with the rapist's son, had visited her in jail to say they could no longer see each other. It was simply too dangerous. Amazingly, instead of being angry at Thelma's abandonment, Flora Lee had been empathetic. "It's okay," she said.

"Why you got to be so goddamn understanding?" Thelma had snapped, angry for reasons she couldn't even define.

But her friend had only smiled. "It's all right," she repeated. "You gon' be all right. Both of us, we gon' be all right." Like she knew something Thelma did not.

That was the summer of 1943. It was the last time they ever spoke.

Now, Thelma stepped down from a bus, checked the address she had written on the scrap of paper in her hand, and began walking. She had almost changed her mind about coming here. Following Luther's sheepish call from jail, she had endured a sleepless night, taunted by fears of all that could happen to her brother at the hands of white justice, which was no justice at all where Negroes were concerned. How many times had she preached to Adam that he must never give the police any excuse to even notice him? She would never have thought she'd have to give the same lecture to Luther.

Drinking again? After all these years? And then, of all the cars to hit, he had chosen a police cruiser? Luther, she thought, would be lucky to escape with his life.

But in the end, the arraignment had turned out to be a pro forma affair. The court seemed more amused than outraged over Luther's extravagantly bad judgment—"You hit a police car, son?" asked the judge incredulously, looking up from the charging documents while the bailiff stifled a laugh—and he had walked out of court on bail with the trial to be set within the next two to three weeks.

Thelma had been relieved but also infuriated, and she started in on Luther the moment they stepped out onto the street. What was he thinking? What was wrong with him? Had he lost his damn mind?

Luther had borne her anger stoically. "You right," he kept saying. "You right, sister."

After a few minutes, George had gently reminded her that it was still early, and she had not seen Flora Lee in twenty-two years. Given the way she felt about Alabama, she would probably never have another chance. Wouldn't a visit with her old friend be a better way to spend the afternoon?

Thelma had not been fooled. She knew her husband was more concerned with getting his brother-in-law off the hook than with whether she spent time with an old friend. Still, she could not deny his logic. She could chew out Luther any time. She might never have another opportunity to make things right with Flora Lee.

"Fine," she said, eyes hard on Luther. "I'll go. But"—and here, she leveled a finger at her brother—"we're not done with this."

So now Thelma walked, occasionally consulting the scrap of paper, comparing what was written there to the addresses that passed her by. Half a block from the bus stop, she came to one that matched. But she knew it couldn't be right because she found herself standing not in front of a house or apartment building, but beneath the hand-painted sign of a bookstore. It showed two identical women—both waiflike and blondé—reaching toward one another in a rough homage to Michelangelo's *Creation of Adam* from the ceiling of the Sistine Chapel. "Twin Sisters Books," it said.

The books in the display window included *The Second Sex* by Simone de Beauvoir, *The Feminine Mystique* by Betty Friedan, and *The Bell Jar* by Sylvia Plath. They also included *The Source* by James Michener, *The Man* by Irving Wallace, *Why We Can't Wait* by Martin Luther King, and *Herzog* by Saul Bellow.

"Something for everybody," muttered Thelma.

She was confused. She had searched the white pages for Flora Lee Gadsen—Flora Lee's maiden name—and had found this address. But that made no sense. Surely, Flora Lee didn't live in a bookstore.

Hesitantly, Thelma pushed open the door. A little bell mounted above tinkled to announce her arrival. The lighting inside was soft and the shelves created narrow aisles just wide enough for a single customer. They were labeled according to subject: history, travel, literature, biography. There was one large section called "Women's Liberation."

The store was pleasantly cluttered. What little space was not crowded by books was crowded by tchotchkes—buttons, figurines, pins, and whole families of crocheted dolls watching the room from atop the shelves. This was a space designed to be browsed and lingered in, a room of discoveries waiting to be made. An orange tabby lay on a countertop, watching with imperious uninterest as Thelma looked around. There were no other customers.

"Help you?"

The voice startled her and she realized she was being watched, not just by a cat, but by a large white woman of probably sixty years who sat on a stool behind the counter, her thumb holding her place in a copy of *Armageddon* by Leon Uris. She wore overalls over a blue flannel shirt, her steel-colored hair was chopped short, and a pair of spectacles sat on the tip of her nose.

"I must have the wrong place," said Thelma. "I'm looking for someone, an old friend I used to know. According to the phone book, this is where she lives."

The other woman's face opened in a sudden smile and she laid the novel aside. "I'll just bet you're Thelma," she said, pointing. "I'll just bet."

Thelma was surprised to hear her name from this stranger's mouth, but the other woman gave her no time to respond, plucking the receiver from a telephone on the counter and dialing seven digits. After a moment, she spoke into it. "You have a visitor down here," she said, a note of mischief in her voice.

The woman listened for a moment and then said, "No, I didn't get the name." A conspiratorial wink at Thelma. "Why don't you hurry on down?"

She lowered the receiver and came around the counter, still smiling, her hand extended. "I'm Joan Berglund," she said. "Joanie to my friends."

Thelma was still confused. "So, this is the right address?" she said, as her hand was swallowed in the bigger woman's beefy grasp. "Flora Lee Gadsen lives here?"

Joanie nodded. "We have our apartment upstairs."

She seemed unable to stop grinning. "So, you're Thelma," she said. "I swear, I feel like I know you already. I told Flora you'd show up here. She didn't believe me, but I told her you would."

This was even more confusing. "How did you know I would—"

She was cut off by the sound of her own name, spoken from behind her in a tone of disbelief. "Thelma?"

Thelma turned and saw her standing at the bottom of a spiral stair case that descended from the ceiling into the center of the room, her mouth agape as if she could not believe what she was being told by her own eyes.

It had been twenty-two years, but Thelma would have known Flora Lee anywhere. Still the same thin, small woman with no lips and a little too much nose. All that had changed was that the haunted look had gone from her eyes and she stood straighter than had been her habit, no longer carrying herself as if in perpetual apology for taking up space and consuming air.

These were the only observations Thelma had time to make. Then, the two women were in one another's arms, crying and laughing. Flora Lee held her so tightly that Thelma thought she might never let go. Her own embrace was just as fierce.

Joanie Berglund stepped quietly past them and went to the door. She turned the latch, and then flipped over the sign hanging in the window. The invitation to "Come in, we're OPEN" became an apology instead: "Sorry, we're CLOSED."

In the center of the room, Thelma and Flora Lee were still clinging to one another. "Why don't we go upstairs and have some tea?" Joanie suggested. "Seems like the two of you have a lot to talk about."

Moments later, as a kettle steeped on a hot plate in the kitchenette, Thelma sat in an armchair facing the couch where Flora Lee and Joanie had settled themselves. Up here in this efficiency apartment, as downstairs in the store itself, books were stacked everywhere. And what surfaces weren't covered by books were covered by more of those crocheted dolls in all skin tones and national outfits from around the world. "You did these?" asked Thelma, examining a dark-skinned doll with button eyes and a kente cloth dress.

Flora Lee nodded happily. "We sell 'em in the store. Folk can't get enough of 'em."

"This is where you live?" Thelma's eyes fell upon the single, rumpled bed in the corner.

Another happy nod. "Joanie is my very special friend," she said.

Thelma was not shocked. Living in New York all these years, she had encountered many women—and men, too, for that matter—who preferred the company of their own sex. And surely, being married to Earl Ray Hodges would be more than enough to make any woman swear off men for good.

"You look happy," she told Flora Lee. "I'm glad."

"Thank you, Thelma. I am happy. First time in my life, really."

The kettle began to whistle and as Joanie got up to attend to it, Thelma said, "That takes a load off my mind. I've always felt bad about the last time I saw you. I mean, when I said we couldn't be friends anymore."

Flora Lee's face softened. "Thelma," she said, "I don't know why you worry about that. I told you then and I'll tell you again: I don't blame you for that. I don't think I'd want to be friends either with somebody who brought Mr. Earl Ray Hodges into my life. May he rest in damnation."

"Amen," said Thelma. "I mean, I'm a preacher's wife, so I probably shouldn't feel that way. But amen."

"Preacher's wife?" Flora Lee drew her legs up beneath her as if in anticipation of a good story.

"Uh uh," said Thelma. "You first. What have you been doing? How did you two meet?"

At that question, Flora Lee shot a sidelong glance at Joanie, who was returning with a tray on which rested a porcelain tea kettle, matching cups, and a selection of tea cakes. Joanie laughed as Flora Lee began clearing books from the coffee table. "We met in prison," she said as she lowered the tray.

"Prison?" Thelma didn't think to hide her surprise.

Joanie nodded as she began filling the teacups. "I killed my husband, too," she said as she handed one to Thelma.

Thelma stammered, "I . . . um . . . okay," and then fell silent, because she had no idea what else to say.

Joanie laughed. "It's all right," she said, pouring her own cup and snatching up one of the tea cakes. "I promise you, I'm not a crazed serial murderess. But neither am I ashamed of what I did. I killed Woodrow Chapelle because I couldn't abide that man hitting me one more day."

"He beat you?"

"Beat me?" Joanie laughed again. "Honey, Woody used me as his personal speed bag for seventeen years. Split lip, black eyes, lost teeth, bruised spleen, broken orbital bone, you name it, I've had it. Folks at the emergency room must have thought I was the clumsiest woman in the world, all the times I told them I fell down the steps or walked into the door. Of course, they had to know what was really going on. They'd have been crazy not to. They just didn't say anything. Neither did I.

"And then, one day, sitting there with my nose bleeding all down my dress, I decided I'd had enough. Just like that: I've had enough. I wasn't as bold as our friend here, though," she added with a fond glance toward Flora Lee. "I didn't shoot the bastard in the neck. A little rat poison in his sloppy joe did the trick. Kind of wish I had shot him, though," she mused. "It would have been a kindness. I didn't particularly like seeing him suffer the way he did, much as he deserved it."

Flora Lee said, "When we got to comparin' notes, it was like we had lived the same life. Neither one of us was the prettiest gal in town, neither one of us sufferin' from an overabundance of confidence, both of us easy prey for the first smooth talker who come around with flattery and flowers."

"And then we marry 'em and they treat us more like sparring partners than wives," added Joanie.

"Same life," repeated Flora Lee. "That's why in prison we started calling ourselves twin sisters."

Thelma remembered the sign. "The bookstore . . . "

Flora Lee nodded. "We tell people we're fraternal twins—you know, twins that don't look alike. And that way, they don't mind that we're livin' up here together, 'cause they don't realize we're actually just two horny old broads sharing the same bed. At least, most of 'em don't. I'm sure some of 'em—the women especially—are too smart to be fooled. They just don't say nothin'."

"I can't imagine that would go over too well," said Thelma.

Flora Lee's eyebrows went up. "In Alabama? Hell, no."

"I saw you looking in the display window," said Joanie, "so you know that we sell all kinds of books. But the truth is, that's just to pay the bills and give us cover. Our true purpose is to sell books that help women like the ones we used to be, help them discover themselves and figure out how to be a whole human being without necessarily needing—or wanting—to be defined by a man."

"You mean that section of books I saw downstairs," said Thelma. "'Women's Liberation.'"

"Exactly," said Joanie. "You should see the way some of these poor little housewives sneak in here and whisper that they want a copy of Betty Friedan's book. All the while looking over their shoulder to see who might be listening. You'd think we were selling pornography. But I'll tell you what we're really selling. We're selling change."

Flora Lee nodded. "First time in my life," she said, "I feel like I'm doing something important. Something that matters. I ain't never felt that before."

"I'm so happy for you," said Thelma. "You've certainly come a long way."

"Thank you," said Flora Lee, with a little mock bow. "But that's enough about me. It's your turn. Tell me what you've been up to."

Thelma obliged, sketching out the broad contours of her life since leaving Alabama. She told the two women about George's impulsive Christmas Eve proposal and her equally impulsive acceptance, about moving up to New York City, about the lean years when he was studying for the ministry while she was working her way through college. About Adam, who should be graduating from City University this spring, except that he had taken the semester off to work on the voting rights campaign over in Selma.

"He was on that bridge," she said, "and the state troopers knocked him senseless. My brother had to go get him out of the hospital."

"He's a handsome boy," said Joanie. "You should be proud."

It stopped Thelma cold. "You've met Adam?"

Joanie looked surprised. "You didn't know? We thought you knew."

"Knew what?" asked Thelma.

Joanie's expression turned uncertain. "He came by here"—she turned to Flora Lee—"when was that, honey?"

"Friday," said Flora Lee. "Three days ago. He looked me up, same as you did. Came by, introduced himself, asked me if I would tell him about his father. You know, his real father, Earl. I ain't thought too much about it. I figured he was just naturally curious and, you know, who else can he ask? So I answered all his questions. I was real honest with him. Told how he could be the most charmin' fellow you ever met one minute, turn into a demon the next. Told how he hated colored people."

"What else?" asked Thelma. Her skin felt tight.

"We thought you knew," said Flora Lee. A helpless look toward Joanie.

"That's why I told Flora Lee you'd be comin' to visit her soon," said Joanie. "I figured, if your son was in town, you wouldn't be far behind."

Thelma repeated the question. "Did he ask you anything else?"

"Well, he wanted to know 'bout how Earl . . . you know . . . raped you, and I told him about that, least as much as I knew."

"Is that all?"

"Pretty much. He asked where Earl was from and I told him how we both grew up in Payton County in the north part of the state, where they do the coal mining. You know, Earl's whole family is still up there, last I heard. One reason I'm down here, as far south as I can go without swimmin'."

Flora Lee stopped all at once, a troubled expression seeping into her eyes. "Thelma, did I do wrong?"

The question surprised Thelma. It seemed to come from the old

Flora Lee, the shy and hesitant one who always seemed to be asking permission just to be. Thelma reached across the table and covered her friend's hand with her own. "No, honey," she said, "of course not. Get that out your mind right now. He wanted some information about his biological father and who else could he ask?"

Flora Lee's expression had turned dubious. "I just feel like there's somethin' you ain't tellin' me," she said.

Thelma wished she had a cigarette. She sighed. "He didn't know about the rape," she said. "I never told him. I never knew how. He's grown up thinking George is his natural father."

"But he knew about it when he came here. He's the one brought it up."

"George's brother, Nick," said Thelma. "He never liked George marrying a colored woman. In fact, they haven't spoken in twenty years. He saw Adam at the rest home where they were visiting Johan. You remember him. He was your lawyer?"

Flora Lee nodded. "I remember."

"Well, Nick and George got into it and Adam jumped in, told Nick to leave his father alone. And Nick, that bastard, he told my son"—Thelma paused, eyes stinging, lips pursed angrily—"'Little nigger, I never even met your father.'"

Flora Lee's hand went to her mouth. "Oh, my Lord. That poor boy."

Thelma nodded. "Yeah," she said. "I probably should have told him myself at some point, but I didn't know how. Like you say, it's not easy for me to talk about. But now, he's learned it in the worst way possible. He sneaked out of my brother's house Friday. He went to Nick's house, but thankfully, he couldn't get in and then, I guess, he came here. Nobody's seen him in three days. That's why I flew down here in the first place. I need to talk to him. I need to explain."

"Thelma, I'm so sorry. If I'd known, I would never have opened my big mouth."

Thelma shook her head. "It's not your fault. If it's anybody's it's mine."

"Or this guy Nick," said Joanie. "He sounds like a real piece of work."

"I've never met him," said Thelma. "For his sake, I hope I never do."

"So, what are you going to do now?" asked Flora Lee.

"Well, Adam called Saturday. He told my brother that he's going back to Selma. You know, they're planning another voting rights march."

"Good for them," said Joanie. "It's terrible how they treated those people on that bridge."

"I'm going up there," said Thelma. "I just need to see my son, you know? I just need to talk to him."

"He'll be all right," said Flora.

"I hope," said Thelma.

"No, really," said Flora Lee, and now she was the one who took Thelma's hand. Her eyes locked Thelma's. "You remember what I told you last time I saw you?"

Thelma nodded. "I was just thinking about it this morning," she said. "You told me I was going to be all right. You said we were both going to be all right."

"I believe that," said Flora. "Especially for you. You're a good person, Thelma Mae. I don't think you even realize how rare that is. I might not even be here if it wasn't for you. You gave me a place to go when I needed to get away from Earl and you did it even when you knew it was dangerous, even when your friends told you not to. I never forgot that. I never will. I can never thank you enough."

"Flora Lee, that's very kind," began Thelma, beginning to draw back her hand.

But Flora Lee wouldn't let it go. "No," she said. "I need you to listen to me. I've thought about this for years, I've practiced what I'd say if I ever saw you again and now you're here, I'm going to say it. I know what you been through, Thelma. I hate that you went through it for me. I didn't deserve it; I've always known that. But you, doin' what you did for me, it made me want to be better, it made me want to *do* better. If that's the effect you've had on my life, I can only imagine the effect you've had on that boy of yours."

Thelma felt speared by her gaze. Flora Lee said, "I believe God's got his special people, Thelma, his people that make everything around them better. And I believe you're one of them. That's why I told you twenty years ago you were going to be all right. And I was going to be all right, too, just from knowing you. And I was right, wasn't I? Look at you: got your law degree, livin' with your husband up there in New

York. Me and Joanie, runnin' our bookstore down here in Mobile, sellin' Betty Friedan books to these poor housewives. We all came out all right, didn't we?"

"Yes," said Thelma. She felt a trickle from her eye, wiped at it with her free hand. "Yes, we did."

"Okay then," said Flora Lee, "if I knew what I was talkin' about way back in 1943, then I know it now. So you hear me when I tell you, Thelma. Your son? He's going to be just fine. Everything with you and him is going to be just fine. Okay?"

"Okay," said Thelma.

"Okay," said Flora Lee. She finally released Thelma's hand and sat back. "Okay," she said again.

"Well, all right," said Joanie.

They sat another forty-five minutes, talking, remembering, laughing. For Thelma, it felt as if a boil had been lanced, as if something poisonous had leeched out of her. When Joanie turned the closed sign back around, and she gave Flora Lee a last hug and walked back out onto the street, Thelma felt a sense of lightness—even hope—that she had not known since she got the call from George telling her about the run-in with his brother. Indeed, she had not known this feeling since before Adam first snuck off to this cradle of her nightmares. She breathed and it felt like the first time in forever.

And then she stopped in the middle of the sidewalk and stood stock-still.

Thelma would never know how she made the leap she did in that moment. She would never be able to explain how the knowledge came to her. There was no thread of logic that led her to it, no sudden revelation that made her say, "Aha!" No, the truth was, one moment, it wasn't there and the next, it was, obvious as neon. And suddenly, she knew.

It was a lie. Adam had not gone to Selma.

That boy, that foolish boy, had gone up to Payton County in search of Earl Ray. Or at least, of Earl Ray's family. And that left her no choice. She would have to go there, too.

sixteen

"You can't do that!" There was heat in Luther's voice and it made Thelma stiffen.

Worse, it was the second time he had said it, and she had had enough. Standing there over the stove, she pointed toward him with the tines of the serving fork. "Luther Hayes, I'm gon' need you to stop tellin' me what I can and cannot do. We ain't kids anymore. I am forty-four years old and that is damn sure old enough to decide a few things for myself."

"Really? Well, if I can't tell you, maybe your husband can."

And here, he glared in expectation at George, who was sitting on the couch, watching television, where President Johnson was supposed to give a speech about voting rights at any minute. George looked up with the miserable expression of a man who had been hoping to be ignored.

"Honey," he said, "maybe your brother has a point." His voice reminded Thelma of someone venturing out onto lake ice in the first freeze of winter. She almost felt sorry for him, then didn't feel sorry at all.

"My brother needs to mind his own damn business," she said, turning back to prod the pork chops as they sizzled and browned in the skillet. "My brother has no children, so he cannot possibly understand."

"Yeah, but I got a sister," snapped Luther. "A hard-head, stubborn-ass sister want to go traipsing in some hillbilly county way up in the sticks just 'cause she got a hunch—a *hunch*—her son there."

"I ain't asked you to go, Luther," said Thelma. "I'll go by myself."

"Hell you will," said Luther.

"He's right," said George. "Even if you do go, you can't do it by yourself, Thelma. Be reasonable."

And there it was again, that word "can't."

"You too?" Thelma threw down the serving fork. "You tellin' me what I can't do, George Simon?"

Distantly, she knew they were only concerned for her—and with good cause. But reason had flown from her since that moment on the sidewalk when the realization of where Adam had gone hit her like a fist out of nowhere. Indeed, it had taken every bit of willpower she could muster not to leave right then and there, not to go straight from the bookstore to the Greyhound station and buy a ticket for Payton County.

But she knew that would be foolish. So, she had forced herself to return instead to Luther's apartment to tell her husband and brother what she planned to do. They had been arguing ever since. As the afternoon shaded into evening, she had called Greyhound and learned that the last bus of the day stopping in Payton County had already left. The next one would not leave until seven the following morning. Thelma was determined to be on it. She *had* to be on it.

Yet now, here were her brother and even her husband, her beloved George, treating her like a child, using that word, "can't." Unbelievable.

George regarded her with gentle eyes. When he spoke, he made it a point to keep his voice even. She felt again like some bomb he was trying to defuse. "That's not what I said," he told her. "I said you can't go *alone*. It's too dangerous. If you go, I have to go with you."

At this, Luther made a sputtering sound that was half derision, half disgust. He lifted his hands and walked away.

"Honey, you can't go with me," said Thelma, faking patience she did not feel. "You're white. How do you think it would look, you and me, traveling together, telling those people we're looking for our son? This is Alabama we're talking about, George. *Alabama*. And what's worse than that, it's not even a big city. It's some little coal town nobody ever heard of."

George took this in and shook his head. "That always comes up, doesn't it? The color thing."

"Yes," she said, and she couldn't help feeling sorry for him. "It always will."

"If anybody go with her," said Luther, returning from the far side of the room, "it have to be me. And I ain't doin' it."

"Ain't nobody's askin' you to," snapped Thelma.

George held up a hand to stop her. "Why?" he asked Luther. "He's your nephew. That's your sister. Why wouldn't you go with her?"

Luther gave a bark of laughter. "'Cause she *wrong*, that's why. He ain't up there with them hillbillies. He got better sense than that. He in Selma. You heard it yourself. I heard it, too. 'I'm going back to Selma.' That's what he said. Thelma ain't got nothin' but a hunch. You bet a pony on a hunch. You don't drive three hundred miles."

"I'm his mother," said Thelma. She was forking the pork chops onto a serving dish. "It's more than a hunch."

"Just 'cause you his mother don't give you no magic powers," said Luther.

"There's a simple way to find out," said George, once again holding up a hand to keep her from snapping back at her brother. "Instead of driving, why don't you just call up there in the morning?"

"Who do I call?" asked Thelma. "And what do I say?"

When George didn't reply, she said, "Exactly. Think about it: if you were him and just learned what he learned, what would you want?"

George reflected for a second. Then his head came up. "Revenge," he said. "But on who? The man who attacked you is dead."

"Don't matter," said Thelma. "Long as he has some kin, somebody who can take the blame. Adam is hurt and confused. Maybe he wants to go piss on the grave. Or maybe he wants to find some brother or cousin of . . . that man and punch him in the mouth."

"That's a lot to speculate from a hunch, Thelma."

"Maybe it is," she admitted. "But I'm not wrong. I know it as sure as I'm standing here."

George snapped his finger in sudden recollection. "Luther, you still have the name of the lady where he was staying in Selma, don't you? Why don't you call up there and ask if anybody has seen him?"

"It's going to be a toll call," Thelma told her brother. "Just let me know how much it is when you get your bill and I'll send you a check." It was a petty thing to say, but she was in a mean mood.

"I'll do that," said Luther. Apparently, his mood was no better than hers.

As Thelma filled the serving dishes with canned peas and Rice-A-Roni, Luther retrieved the telephone from his bedroom, brought it into the living room on its extra-long cord, then got the operator to place the call. Steam hissed angrily as Thelma put the skillet into a sink full of foaming dishwater, then she motioned to George to fix himself a plate.

"Aren't you going to eat?" he asked, rising from the couch.

She shook her head. "Too keyed up," she said. "I don't have any appetite." He looked hesitant. "Go ahead, George," she said, motioning again toward the plates.

"Hello, Mrs. Baker?" Luther's call had been answered. "Evenin'," he said. "Sorry to bother you. This is Luther Hayes, Adam Simon's uncle. We met last week?"

The person on the other end said something Thelma couldn't hear and Luther gave a strained laugh in response, shooting her a sheepish glance as he did. "Yes, ma'am," he said, "the one that won the war all by hisself. Reason I'm callin', we tryin' to connect with Adam. He said he was headed back that way."

Luther stopped to listen. "Uh huh," he said. "Uh huh. Really? Okay, well, you call us after that, then. What's that? Yes, ma'am, you can call collect."

He hung up the phone. "She hasn't seen him," said Thelma.

Luther pursed his lips. "No," he admitted. "But she said a bunch of 'em are in the church, gettin' ready to watch Johnson give this speech. She was just headin' over there. Says she'll ask around and call back right after."

"I told you," said Thelma.

"Don't mean he ain't there," said Luther. "It's a big housing project they got 'em in. Plus, some of 'em been doin' protests in Montgomery these last few days as well. He could be there."

"He's in Payton," said Thelma. "And tomorrow, I'm going up there. You see if I don't."

"Let's watch the speech," said George. "Then, when she calls, we can figure out what we're going to do next."

Thelma regarded her brother. "Fine," she said.

"Fine by me," said Luther.

The two men fixed their plates and took seats on the couch. Thelma stood. She couldn't make herself sit.

On the screen, the homely, sad-eyed man who had succeeded the dashing John F. Kennedy stood at the dais waiting out an ovation from Congress. His great, large head filled the little screen. When finally he spoke, his cadence was deliberate, his voice the slow-cooked drawl of his native Texas.

"I speak tonight," he said, "for the dignity of man and the destiny of democracy. I urge every member of both parties, Americans of all religions and of all colors, from every section of this country to join me in that cause. At times, history and fate meet at a single time in a single place to shape a turning point in man's unending search for freedom. So it was at Lexington and Concord. So it was a century ago at Appomattox. So it was last week in Selma, Alabama. There, long-suffering men and women peacefully protested the denial of their rights as Americans. Many were brutally assaulted. One good man, a man of God, was killed."

George had been chewing. At the reference to James Reeb, Thelma saw his face go still. In her single-minded fear for her son, she realized, she had forgotten that poor George had seen a man killed. Could easily have been killed himself. She put a consoling hand on his shoulder. It was like laying hands on a rock.

"In our time," said Johnson, "we have come to live with the moments of great crisis. Our lives have been marked with debate about great issues, issues of war and peace, issues of prosperity and depression. But rarely in any time does an issue lay bare the secret heart of America itself. Rarely are we met with a challenge, not to our growth or abundance, or our welfare or security, but rather, to the values and the purposes and the meaning of our beloved nation. The issue of equal rights for American Negroes is such an issue. And should we defeat every enemy, and should we double our wealth and conquer the stars and still be unequal to this issue, then we will have failed as a people and as a nation. For with a country as with a person, what is a man profited if he shall gain the whole world—and lose his own soul?"

Applause crackled from the screen, some in the audience of graying and balding white men meeting Johnson's challenge with an enthusiastic ovation, many others with stony faces and silence. George whispered a single word: "Preach." Luther watched with unreadable eyes.

"There is no 'Negro problem,'" said Johnson. "There is no 'Southern problem.' There is no 'Northern problem.' There is only an *American* problem"—he had to pause again for applause—"and we are met here tonight as Americans, not as Democrats or Republicans. We are met here as Americans to solve that problem."

He invoked the ideals of the nation's founding and the great and defiant words in which those ideals were encased—ideals and words on which the country had defaulted so many times, thought Thelma, as to render them effectively meaningless. Yet Negroes kept hoping, didn't they? This was the great, resilient miracle of America—or the great, resilient foolishness of colored people. Or both. "I have a dream," Martin Luther King had roared only two years ago, standing at the temple of Lincoln. "I have a dream, deeply rooted in the American dream."

I have a dream.

Spoken to people living in a nightmare.

All the Negroes had cheered, all the world had cheered, she had cheered. But now she wondered: Did King's words encapsulate the miracle or the foolishness? Or was there, in the end, no difference between the two?

She regarded these two men on the couch who had nothing in common but her, these men with whom she had spent her entire life, these men she loved—and knew what each would say about miracles and foolishness. She could see it in their very posture.

George, his concentration complete, leaned forward toward the television, elbows on his knees, hands clasped, his dinner forgotten.

Luther sat back into the couch, arms crossed over his chest, barricading his heart.

On the screen, Johnson was explaining to his audience—and to the watching world beyond—what it was like to be a Negro trying to vote in the South. "Every device of which human ingenuity is capable has been used to deny this right," he said. "The Negro citizen may go to register only to be told that the day is wrong, or the hour is late, or the official in charge is absent. And if he persists and if he manages to present himself to the registrar, he may be disqualified because he did not spell out his middle name or because he abbreviated a word on the application. And if he manages to fill out an application, he is given a test. The registrar is the sole judge of whether he passes this test. He may be asked to recite the entire Constitution. Or explain the most complex provisions of state law. And even a college degree cannot be used to prove that he can read and write. For the fact is, that the only way to pass these barriers is to show a white skin."

She was surprised at the elation she felt in hearing those words. The president had said nothing she didn't already know, of course. Nothing she had not lived. The fact was, the only way to pass a lot of barriers was to show a white skin. But to hear those words from the lips of the highest official in the country reminded twenty million Negroes, and vouched to the rest of the nation, that they were not crazy, that they had, indeed, endured what they had endured, been cheated of their citizenship, just as they had always said.

She had occasionally heard King lauded for what people called "speaking truth to power" and she agreed that it was a bracing thing. Tonight, however, the world was hearing truth *from* power, hearing power testify on the side of the vulnerable and the exploited, and that was simply exhilarating. When you have lived your life down in the shadows on the margins, she thought, it was a hell of a thing to be flooded by light, to be seen.

"Well, damn," said Luther. He was impressed, too. George looked at him, not quite understanding. Then he turned back to the screen.

"Wednesday," said the president, "I will send to Congress a law designed to eliminate illegal barriers to the right to vote."

"There it is," said George. He smiled over his shoulder at Thelma. "He's doing it."

"Yes, he is," she said.

Like other political observers around the country, they had been debating for weeks whether Johnson would take the plunge, introducing ambitious legislation to guarantee voting rights—especially since it had not even been a year since he signed the Civil Rights Act. George had thought he would. Thelma had disagreed. The smart money, after all, said Johnson would feel it was too much, too fast. Yet here he was, making fools out of the smart money, outlining the provisions of a bill that would strip states of the ability to deny colored people their right to vote.

"There is no Constitutional issue here," Johnson was saying. "The command of the Constitution is plain. There is no moral issue. It is wrong, deadly wrong, to deny any of your fellow Americans the right to vote in this country. There is no issue of states' rights or national rights. There is only the struggle for human rights."

The applause was coming at almost every pause now. Thelma felt oddly weightless. She looked down at her brother, he looked up at her, and she could tell he felt it, too, this sense of gravity losing its hold. He was fighting it—he wouldn't be Luther if he didn't—but he felt it, just the same.

Something was happening here.

On the screen, Johnson was recounting the long journey of the 1964 bill into law, how it took "eight long months of debate" to reach his desk and how, when it did, the provisions of the bill that protected Negro voting rights had been stripped away. "This time," he said, "on this issue there must be no delay or no hesitation or no compromise with our purpose."

It was nearly a minute before he could speak again. The chamber erupted in applause and shouts of approbation. The cheers seemed to crest and break like a wave, only to renew themselves, gather strength, and grow louder than before. The camera panned the room and found most of that audience of old white men on their feet lavishing Johnson's defiant ultimatum with praise. It caught others sitting in their seats as if glued there.

Luther's laugh was bitter. "Look at them old honkies," he said. "They can't stand it."

"Yeah, but look at the rest," said George. "They're on their feet cheering like crazy. You always see the glass as half-empty, brother-in-law. To me, that looks half-full."

"That's 'cause you ain't never been thirsty," shot Luther.

He patted George's back in a comradely way to take some of the sting out of it, but Thelma knew he wasn't joking. And he also wasn't wrong. It was easy to believe in possibility when possibility was all you'd ever known. But to grow up colored in Alabama, to live in a shotgun house on a dirt street, to be raised by your grandfather because your parents were burned alive at your front door, was to regard possibility like you regarded the man behind the three-card monte table: with profound and immovable skepticism, worn like armor for self-defense.

And yet, watching Johnson's grave face as he waited through the ovation, she was almost sure she was right in what she felt. The feeling was elusive and ephemeral, to be sure. She couldn't even put a name to it. But it was there, just the same.

Something *was* happening here.

When he was able to speak again, Johnson urged Congress to join him in "working long hours, nights, and weekends if necessary" to pass the bill. "The outraged conscience of a nation," he said, demanded no less.

"But even if we pass this bill," said Johnson, "the battle will not be over. What happened in Selma is part of a far larger movement which reaches into every section and state of America. It is the effort of American Negroes to secure for themselves the full blessings of American life. Their cause must be our cause, too. Because it's not just Negroes, but really, it's all of us who must overcome the crippling legacy of bigotry and injustice.

"And we *shall* overcome."

He narrowed his eyes, physically leaned into those words, speaking each of them separately and distinctly so that no one could mistake his meaning.

George was snatched to his feet, pumping his fist. "Yes!" he shouted, as if he were in the room and the president could hear him. "Yes!"

Luther's arms came down. His jaw came open.

Thelma swept a tear from her cheek.

And she knew that what she had felt was real, if only for this instant, if only for this sliver of time. The president of the United States, standing before both houses of Congress and the world, had spoken the rallying cry of the civil rights struggle. Power was, indeed, aligning itself with the powerless. If that was truly happening, then nothing at all was impossible.

Gravity had given up the fight. It was a heady, disorienting realization. Hope filled her like oxygen.

Johnson spoke for almost fifteen minutes more. He reminded Americans that they were one nation, and that poverty and ignorance are afflictions that beset white Americans as well as colored. He singled out the America Negro as "the real hero" of the struggle to vindicate American ideals, stir reform, and "make good the promise of America."

When the speech was done, as Johnson was making his way out of the chamber and the newspeople were explaining to viewers what they had just seen, George turned to Luther. "What do you think?"

"It was a good speech," said Luther. "Better than I expected, I'll give him that."

"Good speech?" George was incredulous. "Did you hear him speak up for Negro rights? Did you hear him say, 'We shall overcome'? When has a president ever spoken like that? Even Kennedy didn't speak like that."

"It was a good speech," repeated Luther. "Proof be in the puddin', though."

"What does that mean?"

"Mean I'll believe it when I see it," said Luther.

George flopped back on the couch, rolling his eyes to the ceiling. "You're a hard man to impress, Luther."

Luther shrugged. "I just know better than to get my hopes up," he said. "Get your hopes up, this country knock 'em down, every single time."

"This time is going to be different," said George. "Just wait. You'll see."

"I hope you right," said Luther. "But one thing I done learned: if you don't get yourself up too high, you don't have as far to fall."

"What says you're going to fall?" demanded George.

"Experience," said Luther.

George turned to Thelma. "Help me here, honey. Am I wrong to think that was a great speech? It was everything we could have hoped, wasn't it?"

"Yes," said Thelma. "Of course it was."

"But . . . ?"

Luther answered for her. "But every time white folks make colored folks a promise, they renege. Ask the Indians, you don't believe me."

"I think you're too cynical," said George.

"I might be," conceded Luther, "but I'd rather be cynical than be fooled."

"But—" began George. The sound of the ringing phone cut him off. Luther crossed the room to pick it up.

"Yes," he said into the receiver. "Yeah, I will." He listened. He said, "Really? You're sure? Okay, thank you."

Luther hung up the phone and turned to Thelma. She knew what he was going to say before he said it.

"Okay," he told her, "you win. Be ready to leave at seven. Look like I'm drivin' you up to Payton County."

seventeen

A SAXOPHONE SOLO BY STAN GETZ DISSOLVED INTO A COT-tony fuzz of static about a half hour north of Mobile. Reluctantly, Luther snapped the radio off. He knew from experience that he wouldn't pick up another station worth listening to until he skirted the edge of Birmingham three hours from now. Nothing but hillbilly music and farm reports till then. Payton County was almost two hours past that, straddling the Tennessee River up near the border. Angus, the county seat, was pretty much the only thing there that might be counted as a town—and that was if you were being generous. He doubted anyone there had ever heard of Stan Getz.

So Luther knew this would be a long, mostly silent drive unless he cleared the air with his sister. They had spoken barely an extraneous word all morning.

"Look . . ." he began.

She was ready for him. "Don't worry about it," she said crisply.

"I just wanted to apologize," protested Luther.

"No need," she told him.

"Yeah, there is. I was pretty rough on you last night."

"No need," she repeated. "I know you just wanted what was best for me." The windows were halfway down and she was wearing a bright scarf to keep the rushing wind from dismantling her hairstyle. Her eyes were invisible behind oversized sunglasses. Now she shifted in her seat to face him. "But if you want to talk about something . . ."

Oh, shit, groaned Luther, inwardly.

". . . we should talk about what happened to you Sunday."

Luther kept his eyes steady on the road. "Ain't much to tell," he said. "Got drunk and hit a police car. That's the long and short of it."

He was hoping he could just brazen his way through the interrogation he knew was coming. Maybe if he kept his answers short and curt, he could get it over with more quickly.

"'Got drunk and hit a police car,'" she repeated. And Luther threw away all hope that this might be painless.

"Yeah," he said, miserably.

"'Got drunk,'" she said, "'and hit a police car.'"

"You ain't got to keep repeatin' what I—"

"Got drunk. And then hit a police car."

"Go ahead and make your point, sis."

"You could have been killed," she said hotly. "*That's* my damn point, Luther Hayes! You're just lucky they all thought it was funny, your drunk ass rear-ending a police car. That God you don't believe in must have really been looking out for you. It's a wonder they didn't take you into that police station and beat you half to death, then say you tripped comin' out the squad car. It's a wonder they didn't throw you *under* the jailhouse."

"I know," said Luther, miserably.

"You do?" she said, regarding him closely. "Then how you let somethin' like this happen, Luther? As far as I knew from your letters over the years, you hadn't had a drink since—what?—1942? Isn't that what you told me?"

"Yeah," he said. For years, he'd drunk himself to oblivion every night just to get through, just to be able to collapse in his bed without being tormented by the memory of what happened when he was nine. He had gone on the wagon while in army training.

"So, is this a recent change?"

A sigh of surrender. "Yeah," he said.

"Then what I can't understand is, why'd you start up again after so many years?"

"No reason," said Luther. "Just thirsty. Just wanted a drink, is all."

"Uh huh," she said. "'Just wanted a drink is all.'"

He shot her a look. "You gon' keep repeatin' every damn thing I say?"

She volleyed the look right back at him. "Depends. You gon' keep lyin' to me?"

Luther made a disgusted sound and returned his attention to the road. Theirs was the only car on the highway as it wended its way through a thick strand of loblolly pines. The trees were tall, and at this hour, the sun lay close to the horizon, which lent the shadows an illusion of twilight. All was silent, except for the rustle of tires against asphalt and the faint cry of a red-tailed hawk circling above. Luther put a cigarette to his lips, punched in the lighter on the dashboard.

"Apparently, you went by the old farm last week?"

There was a tentative note in Thelma's voice. Luther gave a long sigh. The lighter popped up and he touched fire to his cigarette, exhaled a long gray plume that was shredded in the breeze from the window.

"Yeah. I guess Adam told you?"

"Last week," she said. "Day after you went, in fact. He called me collect, worried. Apparently, you wouldn't speak to him for a day or two. He thought you were angry with him."

Luther glanced over. "Wasn't mad at him."

"I know," said Thelma. "That's what I told him."

"Just mad, period," said Luther. "Hurt, if you want to know the truth."

"I know," said Thelma again.

"He was askin' questions. He wanted to know about it. And I figure, he got that right. They was his grandparents, after all. Would have been, at least. He got a right to know why they ain't around."

"He does," she said. "I agree."

There was a silence.

Then Thelma said, "But it's not easy for you—for you, especially—to talk about it. Or to go to that land. Because you saw it. You remember it."

"He had a right to know," repeated Luther.

"I know he does," said Thelma. "I'm not arguing that. In fact, I'm not arguing at all. I'm just saying, I know it's hard for you. And maybe that's why you felt like you needed a drink?"

He looked over at her. Her eyes were hopeful. She needed to believe she had doped out why he was drinking again. Never mind that Luther had been hungover the very morning she called, asking him to rescue Adam from Selma. Never mind that when she asked about his woozy demeanor, he had told her it was just a headache.

He had lied to her then. Now he had a choice of whether to com-
pound the lie or at last be honest, to tell her he had come face-to-face
with the monster who had haunted his dreams for four decades. It
wasn't a difficult decision. He lied.

"Yeah," he said, "that was it."

Not that it hadn't been painful, being on the old farm. Not that
he hadn't needed a drink afterward. But that wasn't what had returned
him to the bottle after all these years. Luther didn't know how to say
that to his sister, didn't know how to express—or even understand for
himself—the shame he had felt after walking into that room and finding Floyd Bitters alive and staring up at him.

Bad enough he had been helpless as a nine-year-old boy. Now he
was helpless again as a man pushing fifty-one years.

"Well, I understand," she said. "But you have to get back on the
wagon now. You know that, don't you?"

He nodded. "Yeah, I know."

"Don't want to go back to the way things were."

The way things were. Such a gentle way to describe the awful years
when he drank as a matter of necessity. Luther smiled despite himself.
"No," he said, "don't want to do that." He shook his head and added,
"You know, I'm the one supposed to be givin' you a hard time. I'm the
big brother."

"You're the *only* brother," she corrected. "Outside of George and
Adam, you're the only family I have in the world. If you think I'm not
going to be concerned about you, you've got another think coming."

Luther was touched. "Well, you know I feel the same," he said.

He allowed a silence to intervene. The car rumbled over a bridge,
past a field where a tractor was pulling a plow ahead of a fantail of dust.

Luther said, "So, let's talk about today. Assuming you right about
Adam being up here, what you going to do? How you going to find
him?"

Thelma was looking out the window. She shrugged. "Not sure," she
admitted. "Figure I'll just ask if anybody has seen him. If that doesn't
work, I'll try to find the Hodges family. That's what he would have
done."

"They not likely to take too kindly to you," said Luther.

"I know."

"Probably didn't take kindly to him, neither."

"I know."

There was another silence. Then Thelma said. "That's what scares me, Luther."

"What's that?"

"As you say, they probably didn't take kindly to him asking questions. He went up there three days ago. Three days. And we haven't heard from him since. What could have happened to keep him from calling us for three days?"

Luther touched her shoulder. He knew what she was thinking.

She was thinking Andrew Goodman, James Chaney, and Michael Schwerner.

She was thinking Medgar Evers, James Reeb, and Jimmie Lee Jackson.

She was thinking Carole Robertson, Denise McNair, Cynthia Wesley, and Addie Mae Collins.

She was thinking that the South was ever the South.

And her boy was missing.

"He be all right," said Luther. "I'm sure he fine." He spoke with confidence he did not feel. "You and your mother's intuition. Like I told you, he probably in Montgomery, chasin' after some gal."

He forced himself to laugh. And he pressed a little harder on the accelerator.

They stopped a few hours later at a country crossroads on the outskirts of Birmingham. The new civil rights law said that they could go right downtown, if they so desired, to the lunch counter in Tutwiler Drugstore and order anything off the menu that looked appealing, but neither Luther nor Thelma was willing to test that. So instead, they ate the bologna sandwiches she had packed that morning and washed them down with lukewarm Coca-Colas. They took turns peeing in the woods, they got some gas, and they were back on the road in under an hour.

It was just after two in the afternoon when they crossed the Tennessee River, passing a sign welcoming them to Payton County. Minutes later, they entered the town square in Angus, a cluster of dusty little buildings centered around a bronze statue of some reb soldier standing guard, his rifle at the ready, his eyes lifted to the North.

Mountains loomed over the town. Luther found the effect vaguely claustrophobic, like someone constantly looking over your shoulder.

He parked in an angled space behind the reb statue, then checked his watch. "We got about five hours," he said. "Call it four to be safe."

Payton was a sundown county. Negroes were not allowed within its borders after dark. This, too, would be illegal under the new civil rights law, but he doubted Payton County gave a damn about that. He remembered his grandfather telling him about a sign he had once encountered at the approach to some hick town back when he was wandering the roads after the Civil War. It said, "Nigger, if you can read this, you'd better run. If you can't read, run anyway."

The South was ever the South.

"Four hours," said Thelma. "Doesn't give us much time."

"No, it don't," said Luther. "On the other hand, there ain't that many places to look. Come on."

He climbed out of the car and they stood a moment, getting their bearings. There wasn't much foot traffic in the square and what little there was was all white. Passersby allowed their eyes to linger on the two Negroes standing there.

"You'd think they never saw colored before," said Thelma.

"Ain't just that," said Luther. "This one of them towns where everybody know everybody. They wonderin' who we are."

The Angus town square was ringed by storefronts. There was a chicken restaurant, a hamburger stand where you ate at picnic tables outside, a café, a thrift store, a church, a market, a couple of saloons, and a two-story building marked as county offices. A sign indicated that the post office was to be found in the grocery store. Another indicated that the café doubled as the Greyhound station.

"So, what do we do now?" asked Luther.

Thelma indicated the café. "Let's try there first," she said. "That's where he would've come in."

Luther shrugged and they crossed the square and pushed open the restaurant door. The tables were unoccupied, the entire room empty but for an old white woman in a ridiculous paper soda jerk's cap who stood behind the single counter where meals were ordered and bus tickets purchased. "Help you?" she said, looking up from a Bible at the sound of the door.

Then she squinted, light catching on the lenses of her glasses as she got a good look at her visitors. "We don't serve you all in here," she snapped. "I don't give a good goddamn what the goddamn federal government says. We *don't* serve niggers."

Luther's body went rigid at the insult. Except for going to visit Johan twice a week, he had long made it a point to have as little interaction with white people as he possibly could. This was why. He was ready to turn right around and walk out, but to his surprise, Thelma removed her sunglasses, lowered her head, and smiled, somehow seeming to make herself smaller. "We wasn't lookin' to eat, ma'am," she said.

His sister hadn't had to deal with white people's hatefulness for twenty years. Not Southern white people, at least. She had gone away from here, gone back to school, built a new life, accomplished something. Yet, how readily she slipped back into the old pattern of making yourself harmless, putting white folks at their ease. It made him sad.

"Well, if you lookin' for a bus ticket, you go outside and go around to the window," said the woman, hooking her thumb to an opening in the wall at the end of the counter where she sat. "You should know that."

"Beg pardon, ma'am," said Thelma, "but we ain't from here. And we wasn't lookin' for no ticket. We lookin' for a boy might'a come through here couple days ago. Tall boy, young, thin. Mulatto. He look 'mos white. His family ain't heard from him and his mama got worried, so we come lookin' for him. You seen anybody look like that, miss?"

The old woman glared. "I don't pay no attention. They come off the bus out there in the square and they go on their way. That's all I know. Now, you two, git!"

Her tone was exactly as if she was shooing a bad dog. Luther's teeth clenched and he looked somewhere else. But he heard the smile in Thelma's voice. "Thank you, ma'am," she said. "You have a good day, now."

"Uh huh," grunted the woman, licking her thumb to turn a page in her Bible.

Luther pushed open the door. Thelma stepped through and he followed her. They stood there for a moment. "Lord, but I hate Alabama," whispered Thelma. "I hate the whole goddamn South."

She didn't wait for an answer, moving instead to the service window around the side of the chicken restaurant next door. A fat white man, sweat glistening on his pink cheeks, met them there.

"What y'all gon' have?" he asked.

Thelma was smiling again. "Beg pardon, sir, but we didn't want nothin' to eat."

"Oh?" One eyebrow pushed itself up against the paper cap covering his bald pate. "Well, then what you stop here for? This here's a place for people want somethin' to eat." He laughed, amused by his own wit.

Thelma obliged him with a chuckle. "Yes, sir," she said, "and it sure do smell nice. But right now, we lookin' for a colored boy got off a bus here three days ago. We was wonderin' if you seen him. He ain't from these parts and his mother scared he might of got lost, got off at the wrong stop, maybe. Tall, thin, look 'mos white."

The man shook his head. "Ain't seen nobody like that," he said, "but I'll tell you one thing."

"What's that, sir?"

"If he did get off here, I hope he had sense enough to get out of town before the sun went down. Hope that for his sake. Same go for you all, too, by the way."

Thelma grinned into his warning stare. "Yes, sir," she said. "We know. Thank you, sir." And she backed away from the window.

"Can't imagine he'd have gone into that thrift store," said Luther, once they were back out on the sidewalk. "You want to try one of these bars?"

Thelma shook her head. "I've been thinking," she said. "He hasn't been seen in three days. If he did come here—and I believe he did—then there's only three logical reasons for him to be out of touch." She ticked them off on her fingers. "One, he's in the hospital. Two, he's . . ."

She stopped, exhaled a deep, shuddering breath. Her eyes blinked at a sudden tear.

"You ain't got to say it," said Luther. "I know what you mean."

She nodded gratefully. "Or three," she said. "He's in jail." And she inclined her head toward the building on the far side of the square marked with a raised, art deco sign that said "County Offices."

"Or maybe he in Montgomery sniffin' after some young gal like I been sayin'," said Luther. But Thelma was already crossing the square and Luther had to trot to keep up.

They pulled open the glass door and entered a small vestibule feeding into a hallway that extended the length of the building. A stairwell with tattered red carpet rose off to the right. Thelma studied a building directory on the wall, then turned to Luther. "It says the sheriff's department is upstairs."

Moments later, they found themselves standing before the counter of an open bullpen beneath the loud hum of fluorescent lights. Wanted posters were thumbtacked on a bulletin board above a single file cabinet. An oscillating fan atop the cabinet swept the stale air, the breeze from the blade in the wire cage fluttering papers on the four desks that occupied the room. Only one of the desks was in use. He was a tall, thin man with a sallow face and hound-dog eyes, and he sat reading some paperwork. A brass nameplate pinned to his khaki shirt opposite a five-pointed star identified him as Deputy Stewart.

He made them wait for perhaps a minute. Finally, he glanced up with little interest. "Yeah?" he said.

Thelma smiled. "Yes, sir," she said, "I'm Thelma, this here is Luther. We lookin' for a boy we think come through here on Saturday? Family ain't heard hide nor hair from him since then, and we startin' to get mighty worried."

Stewart's sudden grin showed tobacco-stained teeth and no amusement. "Mulatto boy, frizzy hair, thin build, got a mouth on him?"

Luther and his sister shared a look. Then, Thelma said, "Yes, sir, that sound like it might be him."

"He's back there," said the man, indicating the door to a hallway. Above the frame was a brass sign that said simply, "Cells."

Luther said, "Why you holdin' him?"

His sister touched his arm and he knew he had spoken too sharply. "What he do, sir?" she asked the deputy from beneath humble, lowered eyes.

Stewart gave Luther an appraising glance that said plainly, *I'm going to keep an eye on you*, then lifted a paper off his desk and gave a quick glance before turning to Thelma with another of his humorless smiles.

"We got him for assault and battery," he said. "Seems he busted up a bar."

"I see," said Thelma. Luther marveled at the steadiness of her voice. "And you mind tellin' me, sir, who did he assault?"

"Man named Gil Hodges. Real popular fella. Well known in these parts."

"So what happens now?" asked Thelma.

"Now? Oh, he'll be our guest till he go to trial. That'll likely be next week sometime. I expect he'll end up in the state prison after that. Look like a pretty open-and-shut case. Lot of witnesses. And I can tell you for a fact, the judge we got, he don't much cotton to public brawling. I'd say this boy is lookin' at a good five years, minimum. And that's if the judge is in a good mood. Five more if he ain't."

"Yes, sir," said Thelma. "Sir, is there a reason he didn't call his family? Don't he get a free phone call?"

"Didn't want it," said Stewart.

Thelma's eyes narrowed. "You told him he had a phone call comin', but he didn't take it?"

"Yep. That's about the size of it."

"I see," said Thelma. "Well, can we see him?"

"I suppose there ain't no harm in it," said the deputy with a shrug, removing a ring of keys from a peg on the wall. "Need to see some ID, though. And I'm gon' have to search this buck you brung with you."

Wordlessly, Luther lifted his arms as the deputy came around the counter. He endured the rough, fast pat down, then reached into his wallet and pulled out his driver's license as the deputy was mashing at Thelma's hair—"You'd be surprised what some gals stick in there," he explained. Finally, he examined the driver's license she proffered from her wallet.

"You're from New York," he said.

"Yes," said Thelma. "Born here, though."

He was paging through the photos and cards in her wallet. He stopped when he saw a studio-posed portrait of George and Thelma beaming with a young Adam between them. "Look at the happy family," he said, grinning. "I suppose this here is the boy's daddy?"

"Yes," said Thelma. Her voice was still light and sociable.

"Guess they allow all kinds of stuff up there in New York City." Stewart paged to the next card. Luther saw that it was an ID card from the New York State Bar Association. The grin fell from Stewart's face. "You a lawyer?"

"Yes, I am," said Thelma.

Whereupon Stewart snapped the wallet closed, returned it to her purse, and handed it back. "Suppose I should tell you, then," he said, "your boy put up a real struggle when they come to take him in. It's a wonder they didn't add resistin' to his charges. He got banged up pretty good, though. Nothin' that won't heal," he added, "but he sure is a sight." He gave a queasy chuckle.

Thelma was not amused. Something flared in her eyes as the white man laughed his uneasy laugh. But whatever it was didn't make it to her voice. She said, "Thank you for letting me know," and her tone was so deferential and polite she might have been talking to a mechanic who had just told her she was almost due for an oil change.

"Can we see him now?" asked Luther.

The deputy nodded and waved them to follow him into a dimly lit hallway. There were two cells with floor-to-ceiling bars, a stone wall between them. In the first, marked above the door with a paper sign reading "White," five men were caged, two lucky enough to be reclined on cots, three more sitting on thin mattresses on the concrete floor. In the second cage, marked with another paper sign, this one reading "Niggers," a lone man lay sprawled haphazardly on a cot, one leg drawn up, the other trailing the floor, a forearm thrown over his eyes. His shirt had been white. Now half of it was the coppery red-brown of dried blood. He stirred at the sound of people moving outside his cell. The arm came down and what they saw made Thelma's hand fly to her mouth to catch a sob.

"Mom?" he said.

Adam's voice carried surprise, but also dismay. Luther could tell from her eyes that his sister had missed this. She was fixated on the ruined face. Not that he could blame her.

Her son's right eye was a plum, as round and black as the juiciest summer fruit on the tree. His cheeks and temple were nested with abrasions. A *V* of old blood began at his nose and ran to a point on his chin.

She stared an accusation at the deputy. "He resisted," said Stewart. His voice had risen an octave.

Thelma said, "Yes, I heard you say that." Her own voice had gone cold.

There was a moment. Then the deputy made an awkward retreat. "Y'all take your time," he called as he exited the hallway. "No rush."

Adam winced as he stood and moved in an old man's shuffle toward the bars. "What are you doing here?"

"Where else would I be when I hear my son has gone missing?" asked Thelma.

"You came all the way down here? You didn't have to do that."

"You're my son," she said simply.

"But I know how much you hate it here."

"You're my son," she said again.

Adam sighed. "Well, how did you find me?" he asked. "How did you know I was here?"

"That's your mother's doing," said Luther. "Women's intuition, I guess."

"Why didn't you call?" asked Thelma.

"I didn't want anybody to see me like this. I didn't want you to worry."

It made Luther angry. "You didn't think we'd worry when George went back to Selma and didn't see you there?"

Adam's expression turned sheepish. "I guess I didn't think about that," he admitted.

"That's about the dumbest goddamn thing I ever heard in my life," snapped Luther.

He'd have said more, but Thelma gave him a look and he just shook his head and turned away.

Adam said, "Mom, when I found out what happened to you, when I learned . . ."

Thelma raised her hand like a traffic cop. "We'll talk about that later," she said, briskly.

"You gon' tell us what happened?" asked Luther.

"Yes," said Thelma. "This deputy claims you assaulted some man named Gil Hodges, then resisted arrest."

"He's lying," said Adam. He regarded his mother. "I'm so sorry," he said. His voice was soft, and Luther knew the apology encompassed more than this predicament.

"What happened?" pressed Thelma.

Adam sighed. "I got off the bus," he said. "I was looking for anybody from that guy's family, that Earl Hodges. I don't know what I wanted. Maybe just to scream at one of them for what he did. I know that makes no sense. I think maybe I also wanted to see who it is I come from, who my family is. I guess I wasn't thinking straight."

"Go on," said Thelma.

"Not much to tell," said Adam. "I wandered around for an hour. Started at the bus station, went to the thrift store, the grocery, the church up there on that hill. Told them I was tryin' to find my father's family. They all asked me who my father was, and I told 'em it was Earl Ray Hodges. They acted like they never heard the name, but I could tell they were lying.

"I went into one of those bars on the square and was talkin' to the bartender when these three fellas came up behind me and one of them tapped me on the shoulder. When I turned, he said, 'I understand you're asking about my brother.'"

"Small towns," said Luther. "Everybody know everything."

"Yeah," said Adam, "I guess I didn't really understand that. He told me his brother was dead. I told him I knew that. He asked me what I wanted. I told him Earl Ray Hodges was my father—my biological father, at least—and I guess I just wanted to see what kind of people I came from."

Adam paused, looking down. "I'm sorry, Mom," he whispered.

"What happened next?" prodded Thelma.

"He got mad. I mean, *real* mad. Called me a goddamn liar. Said people have been lying on his brother ever since 'that bitch he married' killed him, and he was sick of it and he wouldn't stand for nobody dirtying his brother's name. He said Earl Ray never needed to rape nobody to get sex. He called you a whore, said you probably wanted everything you got."

His eyes were steady on her. Thelma didn't flinch. "And what did you say?" she asked.

"I'm your son. I couldn't let him get away with that."

"What did you say?" repeated Thelma.

"I told him to take it back or I'd kick his ass."

Thelma pinched the bridge of her nose.

"I wasn't going to just let him say that!"

"That's when the fight started," said Luther, not bothering to make it a question.

Adam nodded. "Wasn't much of a fight. He shoved me, told me I better get to kickin', 'cause he wasn't takin' back a goddamn thing."

"I swung at him, I admit that, but I hit nothin' but air. Next thing I knew, it seemed like the whole bar landed on top of me, people coming out of corners with fists and pool cues and me at the bottom of it, just trying to cover up, protect myself."

Adam fixed his wounded gaze on Thelma. "I thought I was going to die. I probably would've, but somebody ran across the square and got a couple of those sheriff's deputies and they pulled me out of there, threw me in here. They say Hodges is pressing charges against me for assault. I didn't hit him. I didn't hit anybody. I'm the one who got his ass kicked."

"Alabama," replied Thelma.

"Alabama," echoed Luther.

"Do you see why I didn't want you coming down here?" said Thelma, her voice an angry hiss of steam. "Now, do you see?"

"I see," said Adam. Pause. "But I wish you hadn't come, either."

Thelma looked at him, her head going slowly from side to side. "I guess neither of us is getting what we want," she said.

Luther said, "What are we going to do?" He checked his watch and saw that it was 2:55. "Whatever it is, we got to be quick about it. Remember where we are."

Thelma's hand cupped her mouth. A vertical concentration line appeared between her eyebrows. She was silent for a long moment. Finally, she said, "Let's go."

"Go? Where we goin'?"

Thelma had already started down the hall. Now she stopped and turned. "We've got to see this Gil Hodges," she said, as if it were the most obvious thing in the world. "We've got to make him change his mind."

eighteen

SHE FELT IT AS SURELY AS A TOUCH, HER BROTHER'S WORRIED gaze on her as he navigated a crushed-gravel path so narrow that tree limbs scraped the car doors. "Thelma," he finally asked, "are you all right?"

"Yes," she said. But his eyes were unconvinced. "I'm okay," she insisted.

She was lying, but how could she not? How could she explain that she was actually in two places—two years—at the same time? That she was sitting here and now, in March of 1965, in Luther's Buick, on the way to plead with Earl Ray Hodges's brother, but that she was also crouching, in May of 1943, behind a bulkhead in a compartment of an unfinished warship. That her heart was lunging against her breastbone, that her breathing was shallow, and that Hodges, with his gimp walk and his stupid pompadour, was out there, calling after her like a stray dog.

"Here, nigger, nigger, nigger. Here, nigger, nigger, nigger."

Sometimes, she still heard it in her sleep, echoing.

Here, nigger, nigger, nigger.

"I see now why that deputy ain't wanted to give us no address," Luther was saying. "Address be pretty much useless up here in these hills. Hard enough just to follow that map he drew."

A tree limb slapped hard against her window and Thelma jumped. It was as if the road was closing in on her. As if Alabama itself was.

"You sure you all right?"

"Yes," she said.

Here, nigger, nigger, nigger . . .

And then he had entered the compartment, his eyes delighted at finding her at last, helpless and alone, and she had moved away from him, pressed herself back against the bulkhead, the hard cold of the metal against her back telling her she had nowhere left to run.

And he grinned.

Sitting there next to her brother, twenty-two years later, Thelma wanted to scream, needed to scream, almost screamed. But some stern thing within her refused to allow it, commanded her to impose order on her scrambled thoughts.

No, it said. *Scream later. Right now, you have work to do.*

She drew in a deep breath.

"This must be it," her brother was saying. He brought the car to a stop. They found themselves with no more road, sitting opposite a rickety cabin in a crushed-gravel clearing. Smoke piped from a brick chimney. A rust-eaten old Ford truck—circa the late '40s, if she had to guess—sat next to the building. Two coon hounds tethered to a tree stump by long chains bayed hoarsely at them. A balding white man in stained overalls, gray beard stretching to his chest, stood there puffing at a stubby cigar, watching them closely. He held a shotgun loosely in his left hand, the barrel touching the gravel.

Thelma nodded. "And that must be him," she said. With a silent prayer, she pushed open the door and stepped onto the gravel. She could feel the rocks poking her feet through the thin soles of her shoes. Thelma forced herself to smile as she moved forward, taking care to stay clear of the dogs.

"Mr. Gil?" she said. "Mr. Gil Hodges?"

"Who's askin'?" His voice was like a metal rod drawn across concrete.

"I'm Thelma. This here my brother, Luther." She nodded to where Luther stood behind her, having not moved from near the car door. She had asked him to let her handle this on her own and he had reluctantly agreed.

Hodges took a long draw on the cigar. He blew out smoke, removed the stub from his mouth, contemplated it for a moment, flicked away ash, then stuck it back. "Ain't in the habit of receivin' niggers at my home," he finally said.

"Yes, sir," said Thelma, "I imagine you ain't. I wouldn't have imposed on you like this, I would've called, but sheriff say you don't have a telephone, and this kind of important."

"Speak your piece, then." Before she could get a word out, he wheeled on the dogs, who had never ceased barking and bellowing. "Elvis! Brutus! Shut up!"

Chastened, the dogs whimpered into a silence, then lowered their heads to their forepaws, watching him with sorrowful, accusing eyes. Satisfied, Hodges turned back to Thelma and repeated himself. "Go on and speak your piece so you can be on your way."

Thelma chanced a step closer. "It's about the boy," she said, "Adam Simon."

He spoke around the stump of the cigar. "Uh huh," he said. "I figured as much."

"I come here, sir, to ask you, to beg you, to drop the charges."

"You're his mama, I suppose?"

"Yes, sir."

"Well, can't nobody blame a mama for trying to help her son, but I'm afraid you come up here for nothin'."

"Please, sir. He a good boy. Ain't never been in no trouble a day in his life. He active in our church. His father—stepfather—is a preacher. And he be graduatin' college soon. With honors. Gon' have a BA in education. I'm hopin' he go on to law school, like I did."

Hodges took the bait, as she had hoped. "You're a lawyer?" he said. He didn't bother trying to hide his surprise. "Nigra woman lawyer?"

"Yes, sir. Passed the bar ten years ago."

It was a calculated risk to tell him this. There was the chance he might realize that if she was educated, if she had a law degree, then her demeanor here, all the smiling, the bowing, and the fractured grammar, was a put on designed to set him at ease. But she thought the risk a small one—white people rarely bothered to actually see or hear Negroes; it was what made it possible to put them on in the first place. And she wanted it in the back of his mind that she had other ways of defending her son if it came down to it.

But that was for later. For now, she gave him another bright smile, another bowing of her head. "You seem like a good man," she said. "I know you don't want to see this boy throw away his whole future just on account of some foolishness."

"Yeah, well, the problem is, your boy assaulted me."

"Beg pardon, sir, but we both know that didn't happen." It was another risk, though this one was bigger. If he reacted poorly, he might shut down entirely. But Thelma was gambling the man would be more intrigued than offended by her boldness. And she wanted him off balance, a little less certain of himself.

Hodges drew the cigar from his mouth and his eyes widened. "Are you callin' me a liar?"

She felt, rather than heard, Luther shift behind her and she prayed he would not intervene. She smiled. "No, sir. No, no, no. Ain't in the habit of callin' no white man a liar, especially when he got two mean dogs and a shotgun, and I ain't got neither. It's just, well, I seen my son, sir—he might not never have use of that eye again, by the way—and I seen you and I made the obvious conclusion. I expect he tried to assault you, would've done it if he could, but near as I can tell, he never had the chance."

Thelma stopped talking to give Hodges room to respond. Instead, she saw him watching her closely. He stuck the cigar back in his teeth. She proceeded cautiously.

"Seem to me, sir, it probably wasn't so much what the boy did that upset you as what he said. About your brother, I mean."

She paused again. Still, Hodges regarded her silently, squinting through the smoke from his cigar. She had to get him talking.

"You and him, y'all grew up in these parts, didn't you, sir?"

Hodges nodded, slowly. "Him and me, my ma and pa. Had a younger sister name of Janey, but the fever took her, 'long about '28. She weren't but five."

"Sorry to hear, sir. So it was just you and your folks and . . . your brother?" All these years later, and still, she couldn't call his name out loud.

Another nod. "I practically raised him myself. Papa was in the mines, Mama was in the bottle."

"Must have been hard."

"Look around. Ain't nothin' up here easy. Especially not for Ray, what with that bad leg, kids givin' him shit about it. Callin' him Gimp Hodges and all like that."

"I'm sure it hurt you to have him die like he did. And then, somebody tell you this boy askin' around town about him, sayin' he did some terrible thing."

Hodges' eyes turned sharp. "You think that boy is the first? Ever since that bitch in Mobile shot him, we've had to live with people whisperin' 'bout what Ray supposed to have done. Near 'bout broke Mama's heart 'fore she died, folks talkin' 'bout how he s'posed to raped some nigger." Hodges stopped. His eyes bored in on Thelma and she realized that he was only now making the connection.

"Raped *you*," he said. "You're that boy's mother. Hell, that means you the one who said it, ain't you? That Ray raped you?"

"Yes, sir, I'm the one. I said it."

He roared. "Well, I say you're a goddamn liar!"

Thelma heard Luther moving behind her. She held up a hand to stop him, but her gaze never left Hodges, who had turned red in his indignation. "Ray ain't never raped nobody. You hear me? *Nobody!* He ain't never had to do that. He could get all the tail he wanted. Never had to force nobody! You lied on him! Lousy bitch! You lied!"

His grip on the shotgun tightened. The dog's heads came up from their forepaws and they looked around, as if sensing the charged emotions like electricity riding a storm.

Thelma's mind whirled in desperation. It was all going wrong. It had not occurred to her—it should've, but it hadn't—that he might not have even accepted what his brother did, that he might hold her responsible for his brother's death. Now, her calculated gambles, her sly manipulations, were crumbling down right in front of her, and as a result, she would lose her son, her only child, to a state prison. All because the brother of that hated man could not face the truth. But maybe if she relieved him of the need . . . ?

"You're right!" she heard herself cry all at once. "Lord help me, you're right. I lied on that poor man!"

She heard Luther behind her. "Thelma, no." She ignored him.

"For twenty-two years, I done lied on him," she said. Thelma hoped the confession did not sound as false as it felt. She was no actress, after all, no Bette Davis or Katharine Hepburn, and to her ears, her performance sounded melodramatic and overwrought. But she plunged ahead anyway. "I lied," she repeated, this time in a soft whisper meant to convey deep remorse. "Couldn't let nobody know the truth."

She paused to gauge the effect of her words. Hodges seemed to stare down at her from a great distance. "And what was the truth?" he demanded.

Thelma felt a great stillness within her as she took a breath and then began to pluck lies from the air, hoping to weave them together on the fly into a cohesive narrative to satisfy what this man needed to believe. "Me and him," she said—even at this extreme moment, she still could not call the bastard's name—"we was sweet on each other, see? I knowed he was married, plus he was white on top of that, but I didn't care. I just wanted to be with him."

The words felt like maggots writhing on her tongue. But she pushed on. "I, you know . . . seduced him, I guess. We only done it the one time, then I come up pregnant. His wife, she found out somehow. And that's when she shot him. I ain't wanted nobody to know I was carryin' a bastard child, so I just said he raped me. See?"

It was a flimsy skein of lies, each more bizarre and outlandish than the last, and she was terrified he would see right through. What had possessed her to think she could get away with it? For a long, silent moment, Gil Hodges regarded her. His expression was cool and contemptuous, and Thelma waited for him to call her a liar again. At least this time, he'd be right. But instead, he said, with bitter satisfaction, "Finally, the truth come out."

Thelma sagged from sheer relief. "Yes," she said. "I been carryin' that all these years."

"Wasn't never no rape. You wanted him to do what he done. You wanted my brother."

"Yes," agreed Thelma. More maggots writhing. She thought she might vomit right there at his feet. But her son's life was at stake, so she said it again. "Yes, I did. I wanted it."

Hodges shook his head. His voice was heavy with contempt. "You lousy bitch," he said. "You lousy bitch."

"Okay, that's enough!" Luther was at her side. "You need to watch your mouth, motherfucker, or I'm gon' watch it for you."

Hodges flung the cigar butt away. "Both of you," he said, motioning with the rifle barrel, "get the fuck off my land."

Glaring at Hodges, Luther took Thelma's shoulders. "That's enough," he whispered in her ear. "You tried your best." He was steering her toward the car. That was it, then, thought Thelma, dazedly. She had failed. She had lost her son. She had lost everything.

That realization propelled her. Thelma spun away from her brother's grasp and threw herself to her knees at the feet of this man who had called her a nigger and a bitch, this man whose brother had brutally raped her. She ignored Luther calling her name. She ignored the gravel cutting her flesh. She ignored the snarling and barking of the dogs.

She grabbed Gil Hodges's big hand in hers, surprising both of them. "Please, sir," she wailed. Tears streamed down her cheeks. "Please, sir!"

Luther touched her back. "Come on, Thelma. You ain't got to do this."

She twisted away. "Please, sir," she cried again, louder. "Don't punish the boy for my mistake! He only come up here because he believed the lie I told him. It ain't his fault, it's mine."

Hodges stared down at her. She kissed the back of his hand, felt the wiry hairs against her lips. "Get up," he said. She kissed his hand again.

"Stop doin' that!"

"He's your own nephew!"

"Ain't no kin to me!"

"Hell he ain't! I just told you how it was. He your brother's son. Don't matter how he got here. *He your brother's only son.* That make him your nephew!"

"That don't—"

She cut him off. "You say it ruined your family name when folks heard your brother was accused of rape? How they gon' act when they find out he loved a nigger woman? And they had a son? And you threw that son in jail? Your own nephew. What they gon' say then?"

Finally, she saw his eyes flicker in thought. Finally.

Fervently, Thelma pressed her lips once more to the back of his hand. "Please, sir," she said. "Please."

"Look," he began. And then he whirled toward the dogs, who were still barking furiously. "Elvis! Brutus! I told you to shut the fuck up!"

When the dogs were silent again, he turned back toward Thelma. "Get up," he said, as he extricated his hand from her grip.

Thelma climbed slowly to her feet, Luther bracing her. She felt blood trickling down her calves. Gil Hodges regarded her for a long moment. Finally, he said, "Go. Y'all need to get out of here."

"But, sir . . ."

"Go," he repeated. There was a moment. Then Hodges sighed. He shook his head. "I ain't got no phone, as you said. But Dewey Coolidge, he lives up the hill a ways, he's got one. I'll call down and tell Stewart he can let that boy go. They should be cuttin' him loose by the time you get back down."

Thelma's hand came to her mouth and fresh tears gushed from her eyes. "Oh, thank you, sir! Thank you so much! God bless you, sir. God bless you."

He held up a hand to stop her. "Just go," he told her, "before I change my mind. And don't y'all never come back up here, you hear me? Tell that boy the same."

"Yes, sir," said Thelma. "Yes, sir."

She felt Luther's hand on her elbow and allowed him to guide her back to the car. She never took her eyes off Hodges. It was silly, she knew, but she had a superstitious sense that if she didn't watch him closely, some connection between them would be shattered and he would change his mind. Hodges watched her, too, his eyes on her all the way to the car, still on her as Luther turned around in the clearing and began the journey back down the treacherous road to the little town below. And then they were out of sight of one another, and all Thelma could do was hope Hodges would keep his word. Her knees ached. She looked down and was faintly surprised to see the cuts and the dirt and the coagulating blood. Softly, she wept.

Luther said, "Thelma . . ."

She said, "I can't, Luther. Not now. I just can't."

"What you did . . . what you told him . . ."

"Luther, please." She looked at him. She sighed. "Let's just be glad he's letting Adam go. Let's just leave it at that."

Her brother nodded. His face was a portrait of uncertainty, but he didn't push her and for that, Thelma was more grateful than she would ever be able to say. She felt as if she was made of glass, as if talking would shatter her into a million pieces.

She had said things that made her hate herself all over again, things that made her feel unclean. But what else could she have done? If she hadn't done what she did, she would have surely lost Adam, and that, she could not bear. To lose her son would be to lose herself.

So she had done what horrified her, what made her disgusted, what was necessary. And Thelma knew she would carry it in her from now until the day she died. It would be a part of her, every bit as much as the rape itself.

Half an hour later, they parked again in the square and Thelma found herself standing in the shadow of the reb soldier's statue. The inscription on the bronze plaque read: "In memory of all the men and boys who answered duty's call when their nation was in peril." A brown-and-white crust of pigeon shit streaked the bronze soldier's face.

Luther said, "I'll go over there to the county building to see how long it'll be."

"Be careful," she told him. She nodded toward a phone booth. "I'm going to call George," she said. And they moved off in opposite directions.

Moments later, Thelma heard the operator say, "Go ahead, caller." When George came on the line, she said, simply, "We found him."

"Oh, thank God," said George. "Oh, thank God. I've been praying so hard."

"I guess God heard you," she said, her voice breaking. And then she started to cry. Again. Her tears seemed inexhaustible.

"Thelma, are you all right?"

"I'm fine."

"Thelma, I have ears. You're crying."

"Yes," she admitted.

"Is it because you're happy?"

"Yes," she said, because lying was the easiest thing. But she wasn't happy. She thought she might never be happy again.

"Is Adam all right?"

"I'm not sure. I hope so. George, they had him in jail. And they beat him up something fierce."

"What? Why?"

"Because he asked questions they didn't like. Because they knew they could."

"But he's out now? He'll be all right?"

"I think so. Luther's gone to get him."

"He's strong," said George, and it sounded as if he spoke as much for his own reassurance as for hers. "He's young. I'm sure he'll be fine."

"Yes. I'm sure he will." Lying again.

"So, what happened?"

"I'll tell you about it when we get back. I don't want to run up Luther's phone bill any more than I already have. Just wanted to hear your voice. We should be home before midnight."

"I'll be waiting," said George. "By the way, Cora called me."

"Your sister?" Thelma was surprised. "What does she want?"

"Invited me to dinner this evening. Said she wants to clear the air between us."

"Just the two of you?"

"She wants to bring Nick along."

"I see," said Thelma.

"I told her no," said George. "If it wasn't for him, none of this with Adam would have ever happened. She said she's coming over anyway."

"You should go," said Thelma.

"Really?" He sounded surprised. "Why?"

"Your brother almost got this boy killed. I want to know what he has to say for himself."

"Thelma . . ."

"I want to know, George." She felt a spike of heat in her chest. She heard her voice turn brittle. "I really want to know. Why do white folks have to be so mean and evil all the time, huh? I wish your brother would tell me that. Why do they do colored so bad? Why can't they just leave us alone? We're human beings just like they are! Why can't they just leave us be?"

"Thelma, I don't—"

"You ask him that for me, George! I want you to ask him that for me!" She was surprised to find herself yelling into the receiver.

"Thelma, I don't know . . ."

"You go on to that dinner, George." Thelma lowered her voice to a rasping hiss. "You tell your brother he like to got this boy killed. You ask him if he's happy with himself. You ask him if that makes him feel like a big man. Do that for me."

There was a long, strained silence. Thelma closed her eyes, tried not to feel the weight of that man's big hand in hers, her lips pressed against it.

George said, "I'm so sorry, Thelma."

"What you sorry for?" She was chagrined to hear herself snapping at George.

"For Nick. For everything. For whatever it is you had to go through up there that you haven't told me yet."

This made her sigh. "I apologize, George. I shouldn't take it out on you."

"I'm your husband," he said, simply.

"Look," she said, "it's your decision whether or not you go to dinner with them. I support you, either way. But I just really want to know how he can live with himself. If you do go, I hope you get a chance to ask him that for me."

George said, "If I do, I will." He paused a beat. Then he said, "It's not that I wouldn't like to be reconciled with them, Thelma. They're my sister and brother for goodness' sake. But I'll never apologize for being with you, for loving you and Adam. You two are the best part of my life. And I don't want to be reconciled with them if they can't respect that. To hell with them both if they can't respect that."

"Well, pray on it," said Thelma. "God will tell you what to do." All at once, she simply felt drained. "I love you, Mr. Simon."

"I love you, too, Mrs. Simon," he said. "See you soon."

Thelma hung up the phone. She stood for a moment, simply breathing. She surveyed the square. Some voice of practicality within nudged her toward the chicken restaurant. They had a long drive ahead of them. They would need something to eat.

The fat man poked his head through the walk-up window at her approach. "Where's the window for colored?" she asked him.

The man shrugged. "Ain't got one," he said. "Used to have one, but they passed that law last year, said we can't no more. Got to follow the law, right?"

She couldn't tell if he was mocking her. She decided she didn't care. "Yes," she said, "I guess you do."

She ordered three large fried-chicken dinners and three large Coca-Colas, then took the bags of food back to Luther's car. She set them on the dashboard and waited. Thelma could not remember the last time she had felt so hollow.

After a moment, the glass door stenciled "County Offices" swung open. Luther came through. Adam came hobbling behind.

Thelma watched them walk toward the car, her brother and her son.

She began to weep again and could not stop.

nineteen

THEY CAREENED THROUGH DARKNESS, THE LIGHTS OF
Birmingham an indistinct glow above the shadowy tree line behind
them, Mobile still hours ahead. Adam stared ahead sightlessly, worn
down by all that he felt—by all that he now knew and wished he didn't.

He was the rapist's son.

He was the *rapist's* son.

It was four days since he had come into this knowledge and still it
lodged sideways in his throat, a lump he could neither swallow through
nor breathe past.

He was the rapist's son.

Mom, the rapist's victim, lay curled in the back seat. The soft exha-
lations of her snoring and the hum of tires on macadam were the only
sounds in a lonely world. His uncle concentrated on his driving. Few
words had passed between them since Luther wheeled the big car
around the small-town square and aimed it south, and for this, Adam
was grateful. He thought of the silence as a sort of kindness.

Mom had bought chicken dinners for them, but only Luther had
eaten, tearing into a drumstick with one hand, holding the vehicle
steady with the other.

Adam had declined the proffered meal. He knew he should have
been hungry—ravenous—after four days of bologna sandwiches and
runny eggs, but he had no appetite. His mother had gone to sleep
instead of eating. It looked like she might sleep through the entire journey. This, too, Adam considered a kindness.

And miles passed beneath the tires of the big car.

Then, without preamble, there came a sudden rustling of rain, big drops pattering hard against the roof of the car. Luther turned a silver knob on the dashboard, and with a rhythmic squeak, the wipers began sweeping water from the glass. Adam closed his eyes. More miles passed.

"You all right over there?" His uncle finally spoke out of the darkness.

"Yeah," said Adam.

"You want to talk about it?"

And this was unexpected enough that Adam opened his eyes and glanced over. Since when did his stony uncle offer to talk about anything? Luther must have read his surprise. He shrugged. "Yeah, I know," he said. "But still . . ."

"Nothing to say," said Adam. "I wanted to find out, and I did."

"Yeah, you did. You mad?"

Adam shook his head. "Not really," he said. "It just . . . hurts is all. Hurts to know what happened, hurts to find out your mother has lied to you your whole life."

"Don't be too hard on her," said Luther. "She did the best she could. It ain't like tellin' you the truth would have been easy. How you explain rape to a five-year-old?"

"I get it," said Adam. "But I still wish she had told me." He gave his uncle a pointed look and added, "Or *you* could have."

"Wasn't my place," said Luther.

"Well, I guess now, at least, I understand," said Adam.

His uncle glanced over. "Understand what?"

"Last week, when I asked you why you didn't like George—I misread that, didn't I? It wasn't that you didn't like him, it was that you didn't like to hear me calling him 'Dad.'"

It took a moment. Finally, Luther said, "Yeah." Another moment. "I never liked havin' to lie."

Adam took this in. Then he said, "Luther?"

"Mmm?"

"You never liked me, either. Did you?"

He felt the car slow as Luther's foot came involuntarily off the accelerator. Then his uncle caught himself and the car leapt forward again. "Don't know what you talkin' about," he said. "I always liked you just fine."

Adam shook his head. "You don't have to lie," he said. "You just said you don't like lies, didn't you? Besides, I've always known it. I mean, I could tell from the time I was a child, when George would bring me down here. I'm not saying you were mean to me. But you never treated me like a nephew, either. I couldn't figure out what I had done. But now I get it."

There was a moment. The water drummed against the roof of the car. The wipers squeaked.

Finally, Luther said, "It never had nothin' to do with you, Adam. Not really." He inclined his head back toward Mom, still sleeping in the back seat. "It had to do with her," he said. "It had to do with my sister."

"Not sure I understand," said Adam, as Luther shook a cigarette loose from the pack in his breast pocket and punched in the lighter.

His uncle didn't respond right away. The lighter popped up. Luther touched the electric fire to the cigarette. He lowered the window a fraction and blew out gray smoke, watched the wind shred the cloud. At length, Luther spoke again.

"Day she was born, I was six years old," he said. "I remember everything about it. Remember these old women shooing me out the house. Remember how scared I was, hearing my mother screamin' like somethin' tearin' her up inside. And I remember when they brought me in there to meet my sister for the first time. Even let me hold her, though she so tiny I was scared I might drop her and break her. Everybody talkin' 'bout what a beautiful baby. She this little wrinkled-up thing sleepin' with a frown on her face like she mad about somethin'. Tell you the truth, I couldn't see what the fuss was about."

The memory was good for a chuckle. "Thing I remember most, though," Luther continued, "is my father takin' me aside that day, said we needed to have a talk, man to man. He tol' me: 'You got a big responsibility now, Luther. That's your sister in there. That make you a big brother. Big brother has a very important job. He got to look out for the ones under him. He got to take care of them, protect them from gettin' hurt.'"

Luther stared ahead into the rain. "My father the best man I ever knew, Adam. I admired him, looked up to him, wanted to be like him. And here he is givin' me this important job. I mean, Thelma was my sister, so I already loved her, already would have took care of her. But gettin' this trust, this *responsibility*, from my father, that sealed the deal. I've spent near forty-five years now watchin' out for this girl, tryin' to protect her. And mostly, I did. But then I end up going to Europe to fight for a country don't give enough of a damn about me and mine to even prosecute the people that killed my parents."

Luther fell silent. After a moment, Adam finished the thought for him in a quiet voice. "And while you were gone, she got raped," he said.

"Yeah," said Luther.

"You weren't there to stop it."

"No," said Luther.

"So when you see me, it's like a reminder."

"Yeah," said Luther. "Remind me I wasn't there when she needed me. I was off in Belgium or France or some such, fightin' for so-called freedom."

"You feel like you failed her."

Luther's laugh was bitter. "You got a hell of a way with words, boy," he said. "But yeah, you right. I feel like I failed her. Wasn't never about you, Adam. I'm sorry I made you feel bad."

"Probably didn't help that the guy was white. I know you didn't have much use for white people."

It took almost a full minute for Luther to respond. Took so long that Adam thought maybe he wouldn't. His uncle smoked quietly as he navigated through the rain, one hand resting easily on the steering wheel. Finally, he said, "You right. Never had no use for white people after what they did to my parents. I hated them all, if you want to know the truth. They stood for all the evil in the world, far as I was concerned. Them and they fuckin' Jim Crow and Ku Klux Klan and the way they force you—even though you s'posed to be a grown-ass *man*—to tuck your head and grin like a little boy, step off the sidewalk if you see them comin', humiliate yourself every goddamn day if you want to go on livin'.

"Hell yes," he said, "I couldn't stand nary a one of them motherfuckers. Still don't trust all that many. But I try to give them the benefit of the doubt till they show me they don't deserve it. Try to do that much, at least. I learned that some of 'em all right. A few. Your dad, for instance. Your granddad, for another. I seen a lot of 'em out there gettin' ready to march when I went to Selma, so I guess they all right, too." He took a last drag off the cigarette, tossed the butt into the rain and rolled up his window.

"'Some of 'em are all right'? Are you trying to spare my feelings because I'm half white? It's okay, Luther. Say what you mean."

Luther cut him with a glance. "When you ever known me to bite my tongue, boy?"

Adam shrugged. "Almost never," he conceded.

"Exactly. See, there's a part of this you don't understand yet. You know that letter you read, the one you took out of my box?"

"Yeah?" said Adam. He refused to feel guilty for what he had done.

"That letter where she told me about you," said Luther, "it reached me in Germany, right before the end of the war. Never forget it. I was in this bakery givin' these two old krauts a hard time. Her with her SS earrings, him with his Hitler mustache, picture of Hitler on the wall. Kraut bastards. And somebody run up and give me this letter. I tell you, it like to knocked me on my ass when I read it. Any other time, it might have made me hate white people even more than before."

"'Any other time?'" Adam was confused.

"I got that letter five days after we liberated a concentration camp," said Luther. He glanced over. "They teach you any history in school?"

"Sure," said Adam. "Well, I mean, Christopher Columbus, George Washington, the Smoot-Hawley tariff, and like that."

"You don't know nothin' about the camps?" asked Luther.

Adam shook his head. "Camps?"

"Nuremberg trials? Genocide?" Luther's glance was probing. "You know anything about that?"

"No," said Adam, "not really."

Disgust darkened Luther's eyes.

"I don't understand what you're trying to tell me," said Adam.

Luther put another cigarette in his mouth, pushed in the lighter. After he lit his cigarette, he cranked the window down again to vent another gray cloud. Luther smoked quietly for a moment.

Finally, he spoke. "White people killed your grandparents, as you know. And for years that made me hate white people. All of 'em, without exception. But then, as I say, we liberated one of these camps."

"What kind of camps?"

Luther's gaze turned inward. "Death camps," he said. "If there's a worse place on Earth, you don't want to know about it. Barbed wire fencing. Smelled like shit and piss and puke, all mixed together. Couldn't breathe with your mouth open for all the flies buzzing around. Corpses stacked everywhere, like cordwood for a fire. They dead, but they seem to be twitchin' and movin'. Then you look closer and you see it's actually maggots crawlin' all over 'em. A million maggots. That's what make 'em seem like they movin'.

"But the worst part ain't the dead, it's the living—if you want to call 'em that. We seen all these skeleton people, nothin' but bones, walkin' around like they already dead, but just ain't figured it out yet. And one of 'em, she—I think it was a woman, but I ain't never been able to say for sure—she come up and took my hand and start makin' these awful noises and at first, I couldn't even figure out what she was doin'. That's when I realized, she cryin'. Only she ain't got enough water in her to make tears."

Adam looked over at his uncle and was surprised to see his own tears overflowing. Luther made no effort to wipe them away.

"Who were these people?" he asked.

"Jews," said Luther, breathing out cigarette smoke. "The Nazis set up these camps, see, and they killed six million Jews before anyone could stop them. They hated 'em so much, they tried to kill 'em all and they damn near did. And I remember thinking it didn't surprise me that white people treated colored people bad. I seen it all my life. But I never realized till that moment, white people could treat white people bad, too. 'Cause even though they be white, they ain't the right kind of white, you see?

"So, to get back to your question: no, it ain't helped matters none that the bastard who done this to my sister was white. But by the time I find this out, I'm also dealing with what I seen in this camp. So sometimes, it's a little more to it than just, this one bad because he white."

"You're saying there's exceptions to the rule," said Adam.

"I'm sayin' color is simple. People are complicated. Hell, the woman that killed the bastard, she was white, too."

"His wife," said Adam. "Flora Lee."

"Yeah."

Adam said, "He would've gotten away with what he did if she hadn't shot him."

Luther shrugged. "This America," he said. "That's the whole point of being white. Gettin' away with shit."

"It shouldn't be that way," said Adam.

"No, it shouldn't," said Luther. "But it is, just the same."

They were silent for a few minutes. Then Adam said, "You know, in that letter she wrote, Mom mentioned how she almost got an abortion. I wonder if she ever wishes she had gone through with it. Might have made things easier all the way around."

"You know better than that," said Luther. "And if you don't, you should. Your mama love you. Even when you was just a little somethin' curled up in her womb, she loved you. And I tell you for a fact, she ain't never wished she went through with no abortion. Not once."

"Would have been easier," repeated Adam.

"Would have meant life without you," said Luther.

Adam shrugged. "Would that have been such a big loss?"

Luther stared at him. "What are you tryin' to say, boy?"

Adam didn't respond. "You think your mama don't love you? Is that it?"

"You love somebody, you don't act like you can't stand to touch 'em. You love somebody, you give 'em a hug once in a while, don't you?"

Luther looked over at him, "Your mama don't hug you?"

Adam shook his head.

"Not even when you was a little boy?"

Adam shook his head.

Luther was silent for a long moment. Finally, he said, "Okay, I get it. She ain't never showed you affection and that hurt you."

"It *ate* at me," corrected Adam. "It made me think there was something wrong with me."

"Wasn't nothin' wrong with you," said Luther.

"Yes, there was," said Adam. And when Luther looked over in surprise, he said, "I was her rapist's son. I still am her rapist's son. That's what I'll always be."

Another silence intervened. Then Luther spoke quietly. "You know," he said, "you ain't asked how she did it."

"How she did what?"

"How she got that man to drop the charges against you. Don't you want to know how?"

"She talked to him, right? She convinced him."

His uncle shook his head. "Was a lot more to it than that," he said. "This woman went up that hill and begged that man to let you go. I'm talkin' about *begged*, do you hear me? Down on her knees in front of the bastard who beat you up, the man whose brother raped her. *That* man. She even kissed his motherfuckin' hand. And when that didn't work, she lied. Told him wasn't no rape. Told him she wanted it, said she and the bastard who raped her was in love and that she lied about the rape. She even apologized to him. To *that* man."

Adam felt his mouth fall open. "What? Why would she say—"

"Because she knew that's what he needed to hear. So she told him that bullshit. You hear what I'm sayin'? Damndest thing I ever saw. But if she hadn't done that, you wouldn't be sittin' here now."

There was a moment. Then Adam said, "I wish she hadn't done it."

"I wish I hadn't seen it," retorted Luther. "But you her son. You was lookin' at five years, maybe ten. So she did what she had to do. Don't tell me she don't love you."

Luther's eyes held Adam's for a moment. Then he turned back to the road and lit another cigarette. Adam watched the shadowy trees fly past. He was struggling with the idea of his mother kissing the hand that had beaten him, begging for his freedom, downplaying her own ordeal in order to save him. Somehow, that knowledge just made everything worse. Made it harder. Perhaps his uncle knew that, because once again, he gave him the kindness of silence.

And they rushed down a highway swept with rain.

twenty

THREE HOURS AFTER HE GOT OFF THE PHONE WITH THELMA, George heard a heavy tread mounting the stairs and then a fist knocked hard against Luther's door. When George opened it, there stood Nick, saluting at rigid attention in his dress blues, a peaked cap on his head, a cigar tucked into a corner of his mouth.

George had almost worn his clerical collar, but looking at his brother, he was distantly glad he had opted instead for a simple blue blazer and tie. One of them hiding behind the uniform of his calling was more than enough. "At ease, sergeant," he said.

With an easy grin, Nick allowed his body to relax and extended his hand. George considered not taking it, then did. As they shook, Nick made a show of looking past George into Luther's modest apartment and his lips pulled themselves down into something meant to approximate an appraisal. "Nice place you got here," he said.

George chose to ignore the jibe buried none too deeply in his brother's words. "Where's Cora?" he asked.

"Downstairs, waiting in the car. Guess she wanted to see if we could say a friendly hello without adult supervision. But we'd better get down there before your neighbors notice there's a white woman sitting there all by herself."

Another dig. It did not portend an enjoyable evening. "You know," said George, "maybe this is a bad idea."

Nick clapped him heavily on the shoulder, still grinning around the cigar. "Nah, c'mon, it'll be fun. I'll behave myself, promise. Besides, you don't want to disappoint our kid sister, do you? She is very eager for all of us to make nice."

The idea of subjecting himself to an evening of this stranger's smug grins made George want to close the door in his face. He remembered the conviction, solid as a fist, that had struck him just a few days ago, after Nick's act of indifferent cruelty toward Adam.

They would never be brothers again. They never could.

But the words of Jesus, spoken from that mountainside in Galilee, had struck him, too, albeit a softer blow thumping against his conscience like a small boat bobbing against the pilings of the dock. "First be reconciled to thy brother..."

First, be reconciled. The commands of faith were hard, thought George, not for the first time.

He stepped through Luther's door into a cool twilight, pulled the door closed, tested the lock, then gestured toward the stairs with an open palm. "Let's go," he said.

They trotted down. The back door of the barbershop was open and the boisterous banter of men filtered into the parking lot. The disc jockey on the radio finished announcing a call-in contest as drums kickstarted "Nowhere to Run" by Martha and the Vandellas, the horns raising a thunderhead of portent, the piano tickling the edges of the groove.

George shook his head. To hear that particular song at this particular moment felt like God was winking at him. Certainly, the songwriters had neatly captured his predicament. He felt trapped.

Nick was bobbing his head and popping his fingers as he moved toward the driver's side of Cora's car. "What can I say?" he said, when he saw George looking. "This is all the kids listen to in 'Nam. Kind of grows on you after a while."

Cora was in the passenger seat. George opened the back door of the vehicle—a black 1965 DeVille, if he was not mistaken—and slid in behind her. She spun around, her eyes bright, her mouth widened in a red-rimmed smile. "Georgie!" she cried. And George, who had always hated that nickname but never complained because he knew his sister worshipped him, did his best to return her smile.

"Cora," he said. "Good to see you, sis."

She leaned over the seat and took him in an awkward embrace, kissing him on the cheek. "I'm so glad you agreed to come to dinner," she whispered in his ear. "It's been far too long."

Nick plopped into the driver's seat and started the car. He gunned the engine, snapped on the radio, and turned the dial up and down the AM band till the music from the car's speakers matched what was blasting out of the back door of the barbershop. Then he backed the car out of the parking space and aimed it for the narrow alley that led to the street. He tore off into traffic with barely a pause for oncoming cars and they hurtled down Davis Avenue, chased by the dire, chanted warning of Martha's Vandellas. *"Nowhere to run, nowhere to hide..."*

Nick drove aggressively, even recklessly, darting in and out of the Tuesday rush hour traffic, pressing the accelerator to the floor, running through stoplights. Cora kept up a stream of airy chatter, but George could see in the tautness of her shoulders, could hear in the false shrill of her laughter, that she was terrified Nick might wrap her beautiful new Cadillac around a lamppost and the three of them with it. But George knew what his sister did not—that Nick's driving was for George's benefit, a way of testing how much George could take, how far Nick could push things before his big brother would cry uncle. It was, in other words, a contest of their respective manhood.

George, who was not without ego, his calling to the ministry notwithstanding, decided he would not give his brother the satisfaction of complaining. Then Nick braked sharply to avoid plowing into a station wagon that drifted at a sedate pace over in front of them; Cora's hand flew to the dashboard to brace against the sudden arrest of momentum. Her knuckles were white.

George finally gave in. "Nick, slow down," he said.

Nick glanced over his shoulder, smiling. "Going a little too fast for you, Reverend?"

"Yes," said George. "Slow down. Please."

"As you wish," said Nick.

Cora turned to look back over the seat at George. "He does drive a trifle fast, doesn't he?" she said, with a strained, giddy laugh. George could tell she was grateful he had spoken.

"Live fast, die young," said Nick.

"Nicky!" Cora slapped at her brother's shoulder as he changed lanes to move ahead of the station wagon. "What a perfectly horrid thing to say."

"It's from a movie," said George.

"I don't care," said Cora. "It's still a horrible thing to say."

"Doesn't matter much," said George. "Nick is pushing forty. That's a little late for dying young."

Nick glanced back. "Ouch," he said. "You never did believe in soft-soaping things, did you?

"I always believed in the truth," said George.

"Well, none of us are getting any younger," said Cora. "That's why I thought we should get together, since we all happen to be in town at the same time. Life is too short, boys."

"Here, here," shouted Nick.

George didn't respond, instead watching silently as Mobile flew past the window. On the radio, some woman was gushing at having won tickets to an upcoming concert. George wondered where Thelma was. He wondered what she had gone through to get Adam freed. Whatever it was, it had left her sounding more beaten than he had ever heard—at least until he mentioned the call from Cora. Then her sudden anger at Nick had seemed positively hysterical.

Ask him if he's happy with himself! Ask him if he feels like a big man!

In the front seat, Nick was warbling along with Marvin Gaye. *"How sweet it is, to be loved by you,"* he sang, happily off-key. Cora was laughing. George sank into his seat, miserable.

Twenty minutes later, Nick pulled into the restaurant parking lot. To George's surprise, they had come to Pirate's Cove, a seafood restaurant on the causeway east of downtown. When they were children, it had been the place their father brought them for family occasions. George had celebrated his high school graduation here.

Against his will, the memory tickled a smile from him as he stepped out of the car. "Oh, my Lord," he said. "It hasn't changed a bit."

Nick gave him a sour glance. "The sphinx smiles," he said.

"I thought it might bring back pleasant memories," said Cora, coming to stand next to him.

"It does," said George, taking the restaurant in. The façade was of boards painted to look as if they had been ravaged by years of storms and sun, nailed at haphazard angles to suggest a freebooter's shack in some misbegotten bayou. From the front door, a sturdy pier, designed to look like a rickety one, extended into Mobile Bay. Low lights flickering in yellow globes completed the impression that this was a forlorn and forgotten place.

About a half mile to the west, George could make out the conning tower and guns of the USS *Alabama*, a World War II ship that had just opened to the public for tours. A weapon had become a tourist attraction. It made him feel older than his years.

Beyond the *Alabama* lay the shipyards of Pinto Island. This, George remembered, was where Thelma had worked during the war. It was also where she had been raped.

The smile went away and his lips puckered at the thought. Then he heard Nick laugh. "This guy's been here since we were kids," he said, pointing up at the sign over the door, where a pirate with an eyepatch and a maniacal grin beckoned customers inside. "Boy, some things never change."

"Yeah," said George, absently, his gaze still on the shipyard. He ignored Nick's quizzical glance.

Inside, the three of them were led to a table overlooking the water. George sat facing his siblings. The restaurant was weeknight quiet as they studied their menus. It had been almost twenty-five years since he last came here, but George realized he still knew the bill of fare by heart. As far as he could tell, not a single new item had been added. Only the prices had changed.

They ordered their meals, returned the menus to their waiter. Cora leaned back in the chair, lacing her fingers together on the table, appraising her brothers. "Well," she said, with a pleased smile.

"Well," said Nick.

"Well," said George.

There was a silence. George caught Cora shooting an imploring glance toward Nick. Nick caught it, gave a little shake of his head, then cleared his throat. "Look," he said, "about the other day. I just wanted to say that I was out of line. And I apologize."

George looked at him. "I appreciate it," he said. "But I'm not the one you should be apologizing to."

Nick's eyes narrowed. "Really? And who is it you think I should be apologizing to, brother?"

"Adam," said George. "He's the one you hurt."

Nick scowled. "You won't live long enough to see that happen," he said.

"No, I don't suppose I will," said George.

"Boys, come on, now," said Cora, behind a forced laugh.

"You remember what you said to him?" said George.

Nick plucked a roll from the breadbasket in the center of the table. "Yeah, I remember."

"Well, he went looking."

"Looking for what?"

"His real father. Or at least, his real father's kin. Until you said that, he had no idea I wasn't his real father. What you said, what you told him, it changed everything."

"I already told you I was sorry," said Nick, buttering his roll.

George brought his fist down on the table hard enough to make the silverware rattle. "Everything," he repeated.

"You can't blame me for—"

"He took a Greyhound and went up there asking around," said George.

"Up where?"

"Up north. Where his so-called real father was born."

"Okay. So?"

"So the people up there, they beat the hell out of him," said George. "They beat him, and they threw him in jail. All because you tried to use him to hurt me."

"You should have told him the truth a long time ago," said Nick, taking a bite from the roll.

"That's not your call," said George. "For that matter, it's not mine, either. It's Thelma's."

"Look, I already said I'm sorry for shooting my mouth off. I don't know what else you want from me."

"How about you stop treating my family like some sort of joke?" said George. "That would be a nice start."

"Your family?" Nick's eyebrow arched.

"Yes."

"*We're* your family," said Nick, waving his hand in a gesture that took in himself and Cora. "Or had you forgotten?"

"I never forgot," said George.

"Obviously, you did," said Nick. "Else you'd never have done to us what you did."

"Really? And what did I do to you, Nick?"

"Embarrassed us, that's what. Shamed the family name. Poor Mother was never able to hold her head up in polite society again. I don't know why this is so hard for you to understand," said Nick, as if explaining basic math to a not-very-bright child. "White people do not marry niggers."

George's chair clattered as he lunged to his feet, fists clenched. "Call her that again and see if I don't knock your goddamn teeth down your throat!"

Nick grinned up at him. "Oh ho," he said, his voice merry. "Such language from a minister of the gospel. Isn't there something in that book of yours about not taking the Lord's name in vain, padre?"

"Call her that again," said George.

Nick waved an exasperated hand. "Sit down, George," he said.

"No," said George. "I want to hear you call her that again."

His brother made a sour face. He popped the last of the bread into his mouth and turned away as if George were a pest too inconsequential to be bothered with. George heard himself breathing. He could not remember the last time he had been so furious. Cora touched his arm. "Please sit down, George," she said. "People are staring."

It was true. For the first time, George became aware that the restaurant had grown still, the servers pausing in their rounds, the few diners watching them with rapt fascination. Still, he did not move.

Then Cora said, "Please, Georgie. For me."

And he pursed his lips, blew a disgusted breath out through his nose, then pulled his chair back into place with a loud scrape, and sat down. He pointed a rigid finger at Nick. "Don't you ever use that word in my presence again," he said. "You hear me?"

Nick flipped him a dismissive gesture in response. Then Cora said, "Nick, he's right. No matter what you or I think about his decision to marry that woman, there's no need for such coarse language. And at the dinner table, no less. You know neither of our parents would have approved. They both frowned on that kind of talk."

"Oh, come on, Cora," said Nick. "You know you don't agree with him any more than I do. White people do not marry"—he cut his eyes at George and pronounced the word with pained deference—"Negroes."

"That's not what Father thinks," said George.

"Yeah, well, Father"—Nick rolled his eyes—"I'll admit, I don't know how you managed to bamboozle him. Because the man who raised me would never have sat still for you marrying a Negress—much less helped you to do so. And poor Mother . . ."

His voice trailed off and Cora picked up the thought. "Mother was devastated," she said. "It was as if you had died in the war, George." She gave him a meaningful stare. "I'm not exaggerating," she said. "It was just that bad."

"Turned your room into a shrine," said Nick.

"Forbade any use of your name," said Cora.

"I wasn't dead," said George. "I wrote her. I even called. She never responded."

"She was hurt very badly," said Cora.

"Yeah, well, she wasn't the only one."

They were silent for a few moments. Nick craned his head, looking for the waiter. "How long before we eat?" he said. "I'm starving."

"I'm not the reason Father changed," said George, his voice soft.

"What do you mean?" asked Cora.

"Nick said a moment ago that he doesn't know how I managed to, as he put it, 'bamboozle' him. But it wasn't me that changed his thinking. I didn't have anything to do with it."

Nick swung his gaze back to the table. "What are you talking about? Of course, you did."

George shook his head. "No, that was a man named Floyd Bitters, a commissioner up in Stubbs County. Father told me the story that Christmas Eve. He said it like it was something secret, just between the two of us, but after all these years, and with him being sick now, I don't suppose he'd mind if I told you."

"Told us what?" demanded Nick.

"You remember when he changed his name?"

Cora nodded. "Of course. He went back to using Johan Simek, the name he had in the old country. Mother was mortified."

"I always wondered why he did that," said Nick.

"I'll tell you why," said George. "From the moment he got off the boat in 1895, Father was always so proud of being an American. And so proud of being white—at least once he understood what white was. He hated having the stink of being an immigrant on him. That's why he changed his name to John Simon as soon as he could. That's why he worked so hard to make money, to raise himself from being that twelve-year-old boy standing on the docks looking up at the towers of the city for the first time. It's why he hated it so much whenever any of his old accent slipped through. It's why he was so set on my marrying Sylvia Osborn from next door."

"I remember her," said Nick with a low whistle. "Blonde bomb-shell. Dead ringer for Marilyn Monroe. And she was willing to marry your sorry ass."

George ignored it. "Her people supposedly came over on the *Mayflower*," he said. "I don't know how true that is, but that was the scuttlebutt. Father thought that was perfect. He thought by me marry-ing her, having children by her, it would make our family, well . . . more white. That meant a lot to him."

"So?" Nick arched an eyebrow. "Why shouldn't it?"

George shook his head. "You're such an idiot. I wonder that I never saw it before."

Nick's mouth shrank and his eyes hardened. Cora spoke in a warn-ing tone. "Boys . . ."

George sighed. "One day, back during the war, Father went up to Stubbs County. I won't get into the reason, but it's not important here. The thing is, he got crosswise with this Floyd Bitters character. And you know how Father's accent would come out sometimes when he was excited or fatigued? That's what happened up there. So they knew he was not born in this country. This Bitters beat him up something fierce. Stomped his chest and broke his ribs. But I think what hurt Father most is what Bitters said to him as he was lying there in the dirt.

"He said, 'You come up here in your fancy suit pretending you're a white man. You are not a white man. You just look like one.'"

There was a silence. George took in his siblings' stricken expres-sions, then went on. "Father told me he had a revelation that day. He had worked so hard to make himself white, make his whole family white, only to have this loudmouth commissioner from some hick county tell him he still didn't make the grade. He said he asked himself then, 'What is white and why do I need it so much? Why wasn't it enough to just be a man and be good?' He said he decided he would spend the rest of his life just trying to do those things. Just to be a man and be good."

"That's why he changed his name?" Cora looked stunned.

George nodded. "Yes. He decided he could be just as much an American using his real name."

"And this is Christmas Eve when he told you that story?"

Again, George nodded. "It was that last Christmas Eve, the one when I had just gotten home. I went over that same night and picked up Thelma and proposed to her. You see, I realized Father was right. I think I'd known it for a long time, but that was the first time I really *realized* that I knew it. Thelma and I, we had written each other all through the war. She never gave up on me, even when the Marines declared me KIA and everybody thought I was dead. And I loved her. It was as simple as that."

There was a beat. Then Nick sputtered. "What a crock of shit!" Cora gave him a horrified look. He shook his head. "I'm sorry, sis, but it is. 'What is white?' That was Father's big question?"

Nick's left hand shot up next to his head, fingers splayed wide. He pointed to it with his right hand. "This is white," he said, pointing to his pale skin. Then he pointed to a young Negro man who was clearing away glasses and plates two tables away. "And that's not," said Nick. "That's a Negro. It's really not that hard to understand. Don't know why you and the old man have so much trouble with it."

"It's really that simple for you?" said George.

Nick leaned forward. "It's that simple," he said.

George's response was cut off by the arrival of dinner. The waiter, an older Negro man whose blazing smile made George think of Louis Armstrong, placed their plates with a deft hand and practiced ease.

"Here we go," he said. "We have the scallops for the lady, a surf and turf cooked medium rare for our marine, and fried catfish for the other gentleman. Will there be anything else?"

Cora said, "No, thank you. Everything looks lovely."

"Very well," said the waiter. "I'll be back directly to check on you all. Bon appétit." And with a deferential bow and another smile, he retreated from the table.

Steepling his hands, George said a silent grace. Nick, who had already begun eating, looked up from his steak with an apologetic grin. "Sorry about that, padre," he said, swallowing a chunk of meat. "I was starving."

George shrugged. "Don't let me stop you," he said.

For long moments, no one spoke and the table was silent but for the sound of silverware being used. Then Cora said, "You know, excepting Mother's funeral, this is the first time we've all been together since that Christmas. That Christmas really did change everything."

"I know it did," said George. "But that wasn't what I intended."

"Maybe not, dear," said Cora, "but surely you had to have known. When you announced that you had just proposed to this colored woman, you had to know there would be an uproar."

George shook his head. "You want the truth? I didn't even think about it at the time."

"You were so in love," said Nick, his tone mocking.

"I was," said George. "Still am."

"Well, the point I was making," said Cora, "is that that was twenty years ago, and we have missed so much of each other's lives since then. With Mother gone and Father ailing, we are all that we have left. It's a shame we know so little about one another's lives. For instance, George, you have three nephews you've never met. My sons Calvin, Bobby, and Reed—they're all teenagers now, practically grown. Cal is a senior in high school. My husband, Calvin, Sr., is a lawyer, like Daddy. Wait, I'll show you a picture."

She went into her purse and produced a wallet, from which she extracted a snapshot of a handsome family on the porch of a handsome red brick house. She pointed to each of the boy's faces in turn. "This one here is Bobby and here's Cal and here's my youngest, Reed."

"That's a great-looking family, sis," said George. "I'm happy for you."

"I wish you knew them," said Cora. She returned the pictures to the wallet a little sadly and forked up some green beans.

"Well," said Nick, "I haven't been as lucky as our sister. Marie divorced me a few years ago. She just wasn't cut out to be a military wife, something we both realized too late. But I got two great kids out of the deal." From his hip pocket he pulled a wallet, which he fanned open and placed on the table where George could see. From the plastic enclosures two pretty blonde girls smiled up at the uncle they had never known. "This one," said Nick, placing his thumb on the photo to the right, "is Jeannie, my oldest. And the other one there, that's Lisa."

"Good-looking kids," said George.

"Yeah," said Nick.

"They must take after their mother."

This elicited a wry smile. "Yeah," said Nick, replacing the wallet in his pocket. "Guess they got lucky in that regard."

"Well," said George, lowering his fork, "since we're sharing family photos, I'll show you mine." And he pulled out his own wallet and opened it to show two facing studio portraits. The one on the left was of Adam, dressed in a royal-blue graduation robe with a matching mortarboard pressed down on his frizzy hair, grinning at the camera and clutching a diploma like a trophy. On the right was Thelma, in a wine-red graduation robe and mortarboard of her own. She held her diploma to her chest. Her gaze was off center, as if fixed upon some unknown horizon.

Cora leaned forward, studying the photos. "She's quite pretty, George," she said. She turned her attention to Adam, touching the photo with her index finger. "Your boy, he looks almost white. I remember thinking that when I saw him."

"He's a very good kid," said George. "I love him. I love them both."

"I hear he came up the hill the other day looking to kick my ass," said Nick. He was sawing at his steak.

"Yes," said George. "I heard the same thing."

Nick popped a piece of meat in his mouth and chewed it with gusto. "Well," he said, "give the kid points for ambition, if not for common sense. I'm glad Cora got to him first."

Cora cut a glance at George, and he knew she was worried how he would respond to the threat. But George didn't. Not right away. Instead, he forked a piece of fried catfish into his mouth and simply regarded his brother, this kid who had once trailed after him through the woods out back of the house, Gene Autry cap guns at the ready as they stalked renegade Indians and no-good cattle rustlers. How had they gone in such drastically different directions from those halcyon days? How had they begun at the same place and yet become such radically different men? He suspected he would never know.

"Thelma wanted me to ask you a question," he said, quietly.

Nick looked up. "And what was that?" he said.

"She was quite distraught over what happened to Adam. As I said, apparently, they beat him pretty badly. She and Luther had to go up there north of Birmingham to get him. In fact, she's on the way back now. I don't know what she had to go through, but it sounds like it was a lot. And she told me to ask you this: how can you live with yourself?"

A wintry frost came into Nick Simon's blue eyes. "You tell her I live with myself just fine," he said.

"She wanted you to know that you nearly got her son killed. *Our* son killed. She wanted me to ask why white folks always have to be so mean—so petty—to colored people. And it's true, you know. I see it all the time. We white people go out of our way to spit on colored people's lives. We make it a point to humiliate them, even if doing so hurts us in the process."

"Georgie," said Cora gently, "I hardly think that's fair."

Nick dabbed at his mouth with his linen napkin, then tossed it casually on the table. "No, it's not fair," he said. "We're not petty or mean to Negroes, not to the ones who know how to stay in their places, anyway. Fact is, the Southern white man understands the Negro better than anybody. The Southern white man is the best friend the Negro has got."

"'The Southern white man,'" repeated George. He shook his head, chuckling. "Nick, your father was a Hungarian peasant who came to this country as a child in the bottom of a steamship just seventy years ago, lice crawling in his hair, nothing in his belly, unable to speak a word of English. 'The Southern white man.' Do you hear yourself? What the hell does that even mean?"

Nick drew himself up. "If you have to ask," he said, "you'll never understand."

"I guess I won't," said George. He tossed his own napkin on the table. "And I thank God for that."

"You're so superior," said Nick. "You think you're better than me. You always have."

George shook his head, sadly. "No," he said. "You were my brother. I helped Mother to take care of you when you were born. You were my first playmate, both of us toddling around the house getting into mischief. You were my brother and I loved you. But I don't think I ever really knew you."

"Were?" asked Nick.

George hunched his shoulders. "I don't think we're going to see each other again, Nick. Maybe at Father's funeral, if it comes to that. But anything beyond that?" He shook his head. "You're asking too high a price. You're asking me to choose between my wife and son—and you. Between what I know is right—and you. And that's really no choice at all."

Cora said, "Georgie, don't you think that's a little harsh?"

George looked at her. "No," he said, "I don't. It's my job to protect my family, just like it would be your husband's job to protect his."

"Well," said Nick, and his voice was stiff as cardboard, "I guess that says it all, then."

"I guess it does," said George. "I hear the fighting over there in Vietnam is getting pretty rough. I won't ask you to be careful, 'cause we both know that's impossible in combat. But I will say, keep your head on a swivel. Take care of yourself." He turned to Cora. "I think it's time to go," he told her. And without waiting for a response, he lifted an arm to flag down the waiter.

Twenty minutes later, Cora's Cadillac emerged from the Bankhead Tunnel downtown. Nick drove at a moderate speed and the radio played softly. No one spoke. George was struck by a visceral sense that something important had just ended. Its loss left him sobered, yet not quite saddened. Wandering in his own thoughts, he almost missed the bulletin on the radio. Then, realizing what he'd heard, he sat up straight. "Turn that up," he said.

Mystified, Nick did as he was asked. George heard the deejay say, "The final word will come tomorrow, but it looks like it's going to happen, kids. They're finally going to get across that bridge. Federal judge Frank Johnson is expected to issue a ruling tomorrow on a plan submitted by civil rights leaders for a five-day march from Selma to Montgomery, fifty-four miles down Route 80, for a rally at the state capitol. So, get your walking shoes ready and keep it locked right here on your information station to make sure you know the who, what, when, where, and why. Meantime, let's always remember to follow this good advice from the Impressions."

The singers' voices came up in urgent falsetto harmony. "*Keep on pushin'*," they sang. "*Keep on pushin'*."

Nick snapped the radio off. There was silence for a moment. George sank back in his seat. He thought about Jim Reeb.

"That march," said Cora in a quiet voice, "that's the whole reason you came down here, wasn't it?"

"Yeah," said George.

"Didn't somebody get killed? Didn't I hear that?"

"A Negro man got killed a couple weeks before, actually. Then yeah, the night after the second march, a bunch of thugs beat up a white minister from Boston. I was with him when it happened, in fact."

She whipped around to look at him. "George! I didn't know that! You could've been killed."

"Yeah," said George softly. "I could've been. I got off with some bruising. Guess I was just lucky."

"And if they march again, I suppose you're going to be with them?"

"It's what I came here for."

"But *why*, George?" Her eyes pleaded for an answer.

He shrugged. "Because it's what's needed. And it's what's right."

"You were always so concerned about what's right," she said, turning back around and crossing her arms over her chest.

George smiled to himself. "Why shouldn't I be concerned about what's right?" he asked. "Shouldn't we all be?"

Nick sucked his teeth. "Don't know why you can't leave well enough alone."

"Would you want to leave well enough alone if you were a Negro in Alabama?"

"But I'm not," said Nick. "That's the whole point. You claim to be such a holy man, George, such a man of God. Well, God has decreed that on this Earth, there are superior races and inferior races. And by trying to change that, you are messing with God's design, you and Martin Luther Koon and all the rest of these agitators. Can't you see that?"

George met Nick's eyes in the rearview mirror. He surprised himself by laughing. Nick's eyes tightened. "I don't see what's so damn funny," he said.

George said, "I guess you wouldn't. You see, Thelma and I, we went shopping for one of those automatic washers a few months ago. Thought it might be cheaper and easier than constantly going to the laundromat. And you know what they call that thing in the middle of the machine? The part that spins the clothes around? They call it an agitator. The agitator gets the dirt out."

George laughed again. Nick's mouth puckered. Cora turned toward the window, arms still defending her heart.

And that was the last they spoke until the car turned into the alley alongside Youngblood's Barbershop and pulled into a parking slot by the back door. They all got out.

Cora wrapped George in a long embrace. "I love you, Georgie," she said. "I don't care about all the rest."

"Love you too, sis."

Nick came forward, his right hand extended. George did not lift his own hand to meet it. Instead, he shook his head, no. "Take care of yourself, Nicky," he said. Surprise and anger flashed like lightning in Nick Simon's eyes. His mouth opened. But whatever he was going to say was lost as all three siblings turned toward the sudden sound of tires crunching pavement as a cone of light pressed itself against the side of the alley. A moment later, Luther's old Buick heaved into view and pulled into a parking place.

There was a pregnant moment when nothing moved and the only sound was the hissing and popping of an engine that had just completed a journey of over three hundred miles. Then the doors came open.

Thelma was the first one out of the car.

twenty-one

By the time Luther got out of the car, his sister had already closed the space between herself and Nick Simon and now stood glaring at him. It made for a stark, almost ridiculous contrast, the big white gunnery sergeant in his dress uniform, a cigar cocked in one corner of his mouth, towering over the smaller Negro woman, whose print dress ended just above her dirty, blood-scabbed knees.

Luther moved toward his sister, calling her name. George moved toward his brother, doing the same. And then, both men stopped short. It struck Luther that whatever came from this confrontation had been coming for a long time. Maybe it needed to finally happen.

"You're Nick Simon," Thelma said. "You're George's brother."

He sneered at her, gave a tight nod. "And you're Thelma," he said.

"Yes, I'm Thelma," she confirmed.

Then she punched him in the face.

The blow was hard enough that Nick's head snapped back and his cigar flew. Luther thought, inevitably, of his mother doing the same thing when Floyd Bitters came to her door and he wondered if Annie Hayes's feisty courage had somehow leapt across time and death to possess her daughter. Or maybe this was just how any mother would behave toward someone who threatened her family. Maybe they all turned into Cassius Clay.

Luther wanted to get between his sister and the marine before something worse happened, but he was rooted like a tree by his own fascination. Likewise, the other three people in the parking lot—Adam, George, and George's sister, Cora—stood still as statues in the park.

When Nick's head came back around, he had a hand to his jaw.

Thelma had tagged him good, but the marine refused to give her the satisfaction of wincing in pain. Instead, he smiled at her. "Pleased to meet you, too," he said.

Thelma was not amused. She leveled her index finger. "I know you don't like me," she said, and her voice was steel. "I really don't care. But in the future, you keep it between you and me, Nicholas Simon. Whatever you have to say, be man enough to say it to my face. Don't hide behind a child."

Nick's eyes darkened. "You're callin' me a coward, lady?"

Thelma did not flinch. She pointed the index finger behind her toward Adam, but her eyes never left Nick's face. "You see that boy back there? That is my son. You see his eye? That happened because of you. So what I am telling you, Nicholas Simon, is that if you ever hurt my child again, I will see you dead. That's my promise to you."

Nick laughed. Or at least, he tried to. But while his mouth opened in a scornful bark, his eyes refused to cooperate. Instead, they watched Thelma warily as if here was some new and threatening creature they had never seen before. He turned his astounded face first one way and then the other, making a show of looking about to see if anyone else was finding this as funny as he was trying to. Finally, his eyes returned to Thelma. "You're going to kill me? Really? How you going to do that, lady?"

George spoke quietly. "It's time for you to go, Nick."

Nick ignored it, slapping at his chest. "I'm a United States Marine, honey! That means I've been threatened by experts."

George hardened his voice. "Nick, you need to go."

Nick turned, as if he had forgotten George was there. "Some sweet little missus you got there, big brother," he said, pointing. "Said she's going to kill me. Did you catch that? This is what you choose over us?"

Luther took a step. "You heard what he said, man. Time to go."

This brought another forced laugh. "Oh, you too now, huh? You want to get in on it, too, is that it?"

"Nick." He spun toward this next voice. His sister was standing at the driver's side door of her car. "Let's go," she told him.

"Oh, come on, Cora. You're not going to let . . ."

"Georgie's right. It's time for us to leave. We don't belong here." She got behind the wheel of the car without waiting for an answer. Luther thought she looked terribly sad.

Nick turned in a circle, as if searching for a friendly face. Whatever he saw made his shoulders go down. Then his eyes flickered. "Fine," he muttered in the petulant voice of a child, "but I want my cigar back. She knocked it out of my mouth with that sucker punch. I paid two bits for that smoke."

Again, he turned, eyes scanning the pavement. Luther watched him. Thelma and George watched him. He squinted into dark corners of the parking lot. He did not find the cigar. Luther was on the verge of telling him again that he had to go, cigar or no cigar.

Then he heard a slow footfall. Luther turned and was surprised to see Adam moving around the Buick coming toward them, his gait halting. Slowly, he crossed the few feet separating him from his mother and Nick Simon.

He passed behind Thelma without stopping, then grimaced in apparent pain as he knelt to reach into a patch of brown grass clustered about one of the support beams holding up the exterior balcony at Luther's front door. He came up with the cigar stub, which he silently presented to Nick. Nick looked at it, then took it, knocked off a few stray blades of grass, and stuck it back in his teeth.

He regarded Adam's ruined face and for a moment, Luther thought he might say something. Then he grunted, shook his head, and went around to the passenger side of his sister's Cadillac. He slumped low in the seat, puffing on the cigar.

Cora lowered her window. Her eyes were filled with luminous sorrow. They lingered on George—"Georgie," she had called him—and her brother gave her a nod, mouthing some farewell Luther could not hear, though he was only a few feet away. Then the white woman looked at Thelma and the grief in her eyes took on a certain wonder.

She put the car in reverse and backed it out slowly. Luther moved to one side to give her room and she wheeled the Caddy down the narrow driveway toward the street. Luther heard her as she accelerated into traffic.

For a moment, no one spoke.

Then Adam broke the silence, "Good night, everyone," he said. "I'm going to bed." He climbed the stairs without waiting for a reply.

As they heard him let himself into Luther's apartment, George looked a question toward his wife. "It's a lot to deal with," she explained. "Plus, I'm sure he's tired. We're all tired."

"Ain't that the truth," said Luther. "Only thing I want right now is some shut-eye."

But finding shut-eye would prove impossible. Six hours later, he was wide awake in a tangle of sheets on his foldout couch, having long since given up trying. Exhausted though he was, Luther could not still his mind, could not impose silence upon it. Instead, he just lay there, as the night pushed toward the dawn. He heard the occasional car go whooshing past on Davis Avenue, heard the light snoring of his nephew, who lay on the floor beneath a thin blanket with a couch cushion as a pillow.

He tried not to think of Adam's bright, raw pain—

"I am her rapist's son."

—or of Thelma, down on her knees, kissing that white man's hand and telling lies that betrayed her very self. He tried not to think of the fracture that now divided them, that consigned mother and son to opposite shores of guilt and shame. He tried not to think of how many of his own demons these last few days had awakened.

Luther tried not to think of many things, but he thought of them all anyway, his worries circling like relay runners on some endless track, one leading to another, that one leading to another, that one leading back to the first. Adam muttered something unintelligible, and Luther marveled that the rest of his family was able to get any sleep.

Which is when he saw his bedroom door open and Thelma come creeping through, wearing a thin nightdress. She paused in the darkness to get her bearings, turned toward the shadowy lump that was her only child and stood there a full minute, looking at him, listening to him breathe. Then she moved through the room, silent as a wraith but for the creak of the door as she pulled it open and stepped out onto the balcony.

Luther gave her a moment. Then he swept the useless sheets aside and padded after her, clad in red pajamas she had given him for Christmas two years back. When he opened the front door, he found her sitting on the top step, smoking from a pack of cigarettes he kept on his nightstand.

She turned at the sound of him. "Luther," she said. "Hope I didn't wake you."

"No such luck," he said. "Ain't been able to sleep."

"Same," she said.

He sat beside her, shook a cigarette from the pack between them and lit it. "Surgeon general ain't gon' be too happy about you pickin' up the evil weed again," he told her.

Thelma regarded the cigarette burning between her index and middle fingers. "You're right," she said. "I was doing so well, too." She took a deep drag.

Luther leaned around so that he could see her face. It was troubled. "Thelma, are you okay?"

After a moment, his sister shook her head. "No," she said, "I am not."

"Anything I can do?"

Another shake of the head. "I'm just tired, Luther. I just feel so tired."

"Tell me about it," said Luther. "A twelve-hour drive will take it out of you."

A sad smile. "I wasn't talking about the drive," she said.

"I know," admitted Luther.

Thelma said, "He's right, you know."

"Who's right?"

"Adam. He told you I never hugged him. He was right. I didn't realize it until he said it."

Luther sighed. "I'm sorry you heard that, Thelma."

"I wasn't trying to eavesdrop. He raised his voice and it woke me up and I heard him say that."

"Did you hear him ask me why I ain't never liked him?"

She shook her head. "No. I must have dozed back off. He asked you that?"

"Yeah."

"What did you say?"

"What could I say? I told him it wasn't never about him. It was about the white bastard who, you know . . ."

"Raped me," she said.

"Yeah," said Luther, "who raped you." He breathed out a stream of gray smoke.

"For the longest time, I could never say that word," said Thelma. She stubbed out her cigarette, flung the butt away. "It was like, if I didn't say it, it didn't happen. Foolish, huh?"

"Not foolish," said Luther. "You get by the best you can."

A moment passed. Then she turned toward him. "Luther, what am I going to do? I think I may have lost my son."

He shook his head with more determination than conviction. "He be all right. Just got a lot to sort through."

"I can't imagine. I don't even know what to say to him."

"Maybe say nothin'," suggested Luther. "Maybe let him come to you when he's ready."

"Does he hate me?"

"If he hate anyone, I think he hate hisself. He called himself 'the rapist's son.'"

"Oh, my Lord," said Thelma.

"I don't think he understand how you can love him, comin' out of that. I told him if he could have seen what I seen, up there on that mountain, he wouldn't have no question."

"You told him about that?"

"Yeah. I still don't know how you did it."

Something inexpressibly sad drifted into her eyes then. "I don't know, either," she said. "I just knew it had to be done."

"That fool actually thought you were tellin' him the truth," said Luther, marveling. "About havin' feelings for his brother, I mean."

Thelma's smile was rueful. "It's what he needed to believe," she said.

"If you hadn't loved that boy—I mean, loved him *hard*—ain't no way you could've done that. I know it wasn't easy."

"Hardest thing I've ever done," said Thelma. "It made me feel . . . dirty all over. It still does. I wish I could just unzip my skin, climb out, and leave it behind. That's how dirty I feel. I swear, I was in the tub for an hour, trying to get rid of that feeling, water hot enough to cook a lobster. I like to scrubbed my skin off, but it didn't help." She chuckled. "You know, with all these people using your bathroom, I bet when you get your water bill, it's going to be . . . going to be . . ."

And then her voice crumbled, and she wept. Luther put an arm around Thelma's shoulder and drew her to him. "Shush," he said, softly. "Ain't nobody studdin' no damn water bill." He felt her shudder against him as she cried, felt the warm dampness of her tears on his chest.

After a moment, Thelma said, "You know, when he was looking for me in that ship, to . . . to rape me, that man called after me like a dog. Did I ever tell you that?"

"No," said Luther. Beyond what she wrote in her letter, Thelma had never told him anything about that day. He had never been sure he wanted to hear. Now he kept very still.

"Yeah," said Thelma with a little nod. "'Here, nigger, nigger, nigger.' That's what he said. 'Here, nigger, nigger, nigger.' Just like you call a dog."

"I'm so sorry, Thelma," said Luther.

"I'm sorry, too," she murmured against his chest.

"Hateful bastard," said Luther.

"Yeah," she said. "That's something I've never understood, Luther. Why are they like that? Why do they hate us so bad? What did we do to them for them to treat us that way?"

"I don't know."

She drew back from him now. Her eyes were glistening and earnest. "I mean, we didn't buy and sell them like cattle. We didn't rape them and use them and cheat them. We sure as hell didn't burn them. They're the ones who did all that to us. If anybody has a reason to hate, we do."

Luther thought about it for a beat. Then he said, "Maybe that's the reason."

She frowned. "How do you mean?"

Luther shrugged. "Maybe when they see us, it reminds them of all the dirt they done to us, knowin' we ain't never done nothin' to them even though we had plenty reason. Maybe they can't stand it."

Thelma considered this, pursed her lips. "So that makes them do more dirt?"

Luther shrugged in reply.

"That makes no sense," she said.

"Don't none of it make no sense," said Luther. "It never has."

They fell silent then. Luther lit another cigarette. The two siblings sat there, each lost in their own thoughts, as the rising sun began carving shadows from the darkness.

twenty-two

WHEN THE SUN WAS FULLY UP, LUTHER STUBBED OUT HIS cigarette and rose to go back inside. "Got to get ready for work," he said.

"I'll be in in a minute," said Thelma.

The door closed behind her brother, and Thelma was grateful to be alone in the stillness. It felt . . . cathartic. She sat for long minutes, breathing in the morning, listening as the city roused itself. When she reached absently for another cigarette, she realized Luther had taken the pack with him. This, she knew, was his subtle way of helping her to stop backsliding on her determination to quit; her big brother was still looking out for her. The thought was good for a tiny smile as she stood to head inside.

She found the pull-out bed folded back into the couch and Adam sitting there with the telephone receiver pressed to his ear. He glanced up at the sound of her and nodded. "Good morning, Mom," he said, his voice soft.

"Good morning, Adam," she said.

For an awkward moment, she stood there, waiting for more. Adam, she could tell, was waiting for the same. But no more words presented themselves, so she went into the bedroom and woke George. He stumbled groggily into the bathroom to shave as she pulled on a summery dress from her suitcase.

By the time she came out of the room, Adam was attacking a mound of eggs and bacon. Luther fixed her a plate, placed it pointedly on the dinette table at Adam's elbow. Thelma took it and went just as pointedly into the sitting area instead. This earned her an imploring look from her brother, but she ignored it, took a seat on the couch instead, and began picking at her eggs.

238 | Leonard Pitts, Jr.

What Luther didn't understand was that this was not some stubborn, angry silence waiting to see which party would be first to give in. No, this was the kind of silence that is found at the limits of language, a silence of not knowing what to say. She reached over and turned on the television, hoping the morning news might drive the painful stillness from the room, but it didn't. It only filled it with ambient sound no one heard, like the hum of a refrigerator.

Or at least, no one heard it until the white man on the screen announced that negotiations between federal judge Frank Johnson and the SCLC were soon expected to result in an agreement that would allow the Selma to Montgomery march to go on. Her brother perked up at this. "Look like Martin Luther gon' get his march after all," he said. He turned to Adam. "Too bad you ain't in no shape to join 'em."

"I'll be there," Adam said. "I was just on the phone with some of my friends from SNCC. They're sending a car down to get me. Should be here in a couple of hours."

"That's great." George was just coming through the bedroom door, shrugging into his sports coat. "You think maybe I could hitch a ride?"

Adam said, "I think the car's going to be full, Dad. And besides"—a guilty glance at Thelma—"I think I'd like to be on my own for a while, if it's all the same to the two of you?"

"I see," said George. "Well, I guess that makes sense."

Nothing showed on his face, but even so, Thelma could tell he was hurt. Nineteen years of marriage, she supposed, made you a kind of mind reader. "George," she said, "are you sure?"

"I'm sure," he told her. "I'll catch the Greyhound."

Thelma looked toward Adam, who was suddenly very interested in his plate. She almost asked him to reconsider, then didn't. In that moment, she felt something essential go out of her. Her eyes met Luther's and he gave her an almost imperceptible shrug. Moments later, when her brother went down to open his shop, he seemed grateful to escape. Thelma could not blame him. She wished she could escape, too.

Instead, she sat there as long minutes turned to long hours, heavy with the weight of things not being said. George called Greyhound to get their schedule, Adam went into Luther's room to bathe and dress. A game show came on television. Thelma sat with her hands clasped between her knees, facing the screen, but not really seeing it. The silence grew heavier.

Her only child had become a stranger. Thelma sneaked a glance, saw that Adam had escaped into one of Luther's books. He might as well have been in another state. George, sitting at the dinette, saw her looking and gave a sad half smile that was meant, she supposed, as encouragement.

She tried to return the smile, wasn't sure that she did. It struck her that, after all these years as a family, as mother, father, and son, suddenly, they were just three people sharing a space, people who nodded politely to one another but really had nothing to say. They might as well have been strangers in a bus station waiting room.

Thelma wanted to cry.

At eleven, there came a vigorous honking from the parking lot below. Adam glanced up. Wordlessly, he returned Luther's book to the shelf, hoisted his bag, and headed to the door. He paused with his hand on the knob, head lowered.

"I'll see you in Selma," he told George.

George nodded. "See you there."

He turned to Thelma, took a deep breath. "Bye, Mom," he said.

First words they'd spoken in three hours, and it was just a mundane farewell of the type they'd surely spoken a thousand times before. *Bye, mom.* Words that seemed so small, useless against the needs of the moment. But, she realized to her chagrin, she didn't have any that were better.

"Bye, Adam," she said.

He looked for an instant like he might say more, but instead, he stepped out of the house. Moments later, there came the sound of young people exchanging greetings in the parking lot below. George said, "It'll be okay, Thelma."

Thelma didn't answer. No response seemed the kindest response. But she knew in her bones that things would never be okay again.

And Lord, she was tired . . .

George went down to the barbershop to get a trim. An hour later, Thelma went down and borrowed the keys to Luther's Buick. She drove her husband to the Greyhound station, neither of them speaking. Trailed by a porter carrying the bag George had trouble managing because of his broken ribs, they walked out onto the platform where the driver was collecting tickets. The porter placed his bags in the compartment under the bus. George tipped him, then turned to Thelma. He told her not to worry. He told her again everything would be all right.

She tried to hear him, but it was as if his voice emanated from one of those little transistor radios someone had thrown into a well. His words seemed to come from somewhere far away, seemed not quite real. Apparently, George realized this. He took her hand, used his other hand to lift her chin, bring her eyes to his, and said . . . *something*. It was something earnest, something to comfort her and give her strength, but still she couldn't quite hear it. His words were so far away.

Then Thelma's gaze happened to drift beyond her husband, to where some white-haired white woman stood staring at them, staring with force and, indeed, impunity, at the white man and his Negro wife. She saw Thelma seeing her and her gaze only sharpened.

Of course. Alabama.

And Thelma snapped back into herself like a rubber band that has been pulled taut and then released. Without warning, she pushed roughly past George and poked a stiff index finger into the other woman's pink brocade blouse. "Who the *hell* do you think you're staring at?" she demanded. She flung the index finger back toward George. "Yes, that white man is my husband. Is that what you were wondering? You got some problem with that? You got something you want to say?"

The other woman's thin lips twisted. "My dear," she began in a voice like January in Chicago, "I can assure you I don't—"

"Shut up!" shrieked Thelma. "I don't want to hear a word from you, understand? Not one goddamn word." She was dimly aware that the entire platform had gone still, that people were staring. She didn't care. George had a restraining hand on her arm, but it was a weight she barely felt. Her entire being was focused on this wrinkled old lady with the powder-dusted face and the smell of some perfume that brought to mind caskets and roses, who regarded her now with imperious, impervious eyes.

"You white people," said Thelma, a choking fury rising in her as she poked again at the brocaded chest, "you think you have the right to treat colored people any way you want, and we're supposed to just keep putting up with it. Like we enjoy taking shit from you. Well, this is one Negro who's had enough, you hear me? Enough! And if you don't stop eyeballing my husband and me, I am going to beat your old ass up one side of this bus station and down the other. Don't try me! I am the wrong woman, and this is the wrong goddamn day!"

The old woman glared. There was a moment. The thin lips came open as if to speak again, but whatever she saw in Thelma's eyes clamped them shut again. Finally, she lifted her nose with as much righteousness as she could muster, and abruptly turned her back on Thelma, who stood there, small in the large silence, her chest heaving, her husband softly patting her back.

"Maybe I shouldn't go," he told her after a moment. His voice was anxious and soft.

"Go on," she said, finally turning back toward him. "Luther and I will meet you in Montgomery at the end of the march like we said." They had made this plan only the night before.

"But Thelma..." protested George.

"Go on." She touched his chest. "I've got Luther here to keep an eye on me. I'll be fine."

"Everything's going to be all right, Thelma," said George. "You'll see."

"I know," she said. "Now go on, before the bus leaves without you."

He was reluctant and for a moment, she thought he might insist on staying. Then he leaned down and kissed her. In public. In Alabama. "I'll call you when I get there," he said. And he boarded the bus.

It pulled out moments later, George's palm pressed against the glass. She waved to him. When the bus was out of sight, her hand fell like a weight.

Thelma went back to the car and drove out of the parking lot, but she didn't immediately return to Luther's apartment. Instead, on a lark, she drove south to Mosby Street, searching for the little one-bedroom house on a dirt road with an open sewer where she had grown up with Luther and Gramp so many years ago. But the house wasn't there. In fact, to her surprise, the whole neighborhood was gone, replaced by a housing project. She drove slowly through the warren of red brick buildings, some with old Negro men sitting out front on kitchen chairs, drinking beers and talking loudly. They marked her passage with mild curiosity and Thelma decided there was no point in stopping to seek out old neighbors in a neighborhood that no longer existed.

This was a different place now. It bore no memory of her, held no memories for her. It was just a street, as if the life she had lived here had never happened, as if it were all just a product of her imagination. Thelma worked her way back to the main avenue and drove toward Luther's apartment. On the way, she stopped at a drugstore. There, she bought a box of Kotex, a bottle of sleeping pills, and, after hesitating and considering it for a full minute, a pack of cigarettes.

Back at Luther's apartment, she turned on the afternoon news and found that it was official. The judge had lifted his injunction. The great march to Montgomery would begin Sunday.

George called two hours later.

"Just wanted to let you know that I got in all right," he told her.

"Bet that old lady was giving you funny looks the whole way," said Thelma.

"I'm not worried about her," said George.

By which he meant that he was worried about Thelma. She decided not to notice the implication. "Are there a lot of people?" she asked.

"Yes," he said, "and everyone is so excited."

"Have you seen Adam?"

"No. Like I said, there are a lot of people here. More coming in by the hour. When he wants to be found, he will be."

"I'm worried about him," she said.

"I'm worried about *you*," he told her, the implication now made plain.

"You don't have to," she said. "I'm just fine."

She was lying, but she figured there was nothing wrong with lying to put someone else's mind at ease. Especially if telling the truth would only hurt them worse.

They talked another few minutes before she told him to be careful and they hung up the phone. By the time Luther came upstairs, she had dinner—fried chicken, mashed potatoes with gravy, green beans— waiting for him. They watched television for a few hours and then she went to bed.

The next two days passed quietly. Both mornings, she had to talk herself into getting out of bed. Both afternoons, she napped on the couch. When she was awake, she watched television—more accurately, she used the sound from the television to fill the silence of the apartment. She thought of going back to visit Flora Lee again, but she didn't.

She thought of going to Gramps's grave, but she didn't do that, either. She had no energy. She had no real desire.

Instead, for two days, she slept, made dinner, and sat before the television. When Sunday came, Thelma awoke thinking she might like to borrow Luther's car and go to church. She had a vague sense that going to church might do her some good.

Then Luther mentioned at breakfast that he would be visiting with Johan today, and she gave up on the idea. He asked if she'd like to come along, and Thelma was tempted to say yes. But she did not relish the idea of seeing her father-in-law in his present condition. Besides, he likely wouldn't know who she was—they hadn't seen each other since 1946—and that would only agitate him.

So she said no instead. As she heard Luther's car roar to life in the parking lot below, Thelma rinsed the breakfast dishes. She washed them, stacked them neatly, then went into the bedroom, sat on the edge of the bed, and tried to think of what she would do with the day. She considered taking a nap. It was not yet noon.

The march was scheduled to end Thursday. Then she would drive back to New York with George, Lester, and Reverend Porter. Adam, she assumed, would find his own way back with his SNCC friends. He would return to school and she would return to work, to deposing witnesses and filing motions and listening to arrested people, evicted people, exploited people, dispossessed, despised, and wretched people tell her their sad stories. She would go back to trying to squeeze a few drops of fairness for them from the great rock of American justice, to celebrating small victories because they were the only kind available. Soon enough, she supposed, she and her son would find words again and things would go back to more or less the way they had been before. Except different.

Forever, different.

Here, nigger, nigger, nigger.

Like she was a dog.

Lordy, she was exhausted.

She went into the bathroom, poured water into one of the disposable cups Luther kept on the counter. She came back out, rummaged in her purse for the sleeping pills she had bought a few days before.

Wasn't never no rape. You wanted him to do what he done. You wanted my brother.

Yes, I did. I wanted it.

Maggots writhing in her mouth full of lies. Rocks cutting her knees. And that wounded expression on Adam's face.

Exhausted.

She broke the seal on the bottle, unscrewed the cap. Thelma poured out a handful of pills and then quickly, before she could stop herself, before she could talk herself out of it, she threw them into her mouth, chased them with the cup of water, swallowed them down.

And then

And then

And then.

Thelma sat on the bed. After a moment, she lay back on the pillow, clasping her hands on her stomach. After a few moments more, she felt her thoughts growing watery, felt them disconnecting from one another like toy train cars. She felt the world growing distant. And she felt the jumble of her fears—so many fears—grinding to a welcome halt. It was so much easier this way, so much simpler when you just stopped fighting it. Stopped fighting . . . everything.

She marveled that she had never realized this before.

Thelma Mae Simon smiled. Then she closed her eyes and allowed the darkness to pull her in.

twenty-three

THE DAYROOM WAS QUIET THAT SUNDAY MORNING AS Luther passed through, one old man nodding off in front of a dark television screen, a janitor mopping. At Johan's door, he lifted his fist to knock, then paused. Standing there, just a few feet removed from the enfeebled monster down the hall, always seemed to demand as much. He looked toward Floyd Bitters's door and immediately felt his stomach tighten. He remembered what he had told Adam a few nights ago.

"That's the whole point of being white. Gettin' away with shit."

His nephew had seemed surprised. But for Luther, the reality of white folks getting away with shit had been one of the earliest lessons of his life.

He wrenched his gaze back from the hallway to the door in front of him. He gave it a perfunctory knock, then pushed it open. The room he entered was wreathed in shadow. The old man was still sleeping, his breath escaping in soft whistles. Luther was surprised. He had always known Johan as an early riser. The senility, he supposed.

Then one of the shadows moved and Luther started, a hand going to his chest.

"It's just me," said George's sister, even as the door closed itself behind Luther. She was standing on the far side of the bed. "Sorry to give you a fright. I'm driving back home today and I wanted to say goodbye to Papa. I've been waiting for him to wake up."

Luther's eyes adjusted and he was able to make her out. Pink blouse, matching hat, navy-blue jacket. "Beg pardon," he said, lifting his hat. "I ain't meant to interrupt."

"You're not interrupting," she said. A glance toward Luther's case. "What's that?"

He held it up for her to see. "Just my clippers and some other things."

"Oh, that's right," she said. "You're a barber. You cut Papa's hair for him."

"Yes, ma'am. Every two weeks."

"And you visit him in between, don't you? The staff told me."

"Yes, ma'am."

"You like my father."

"I suppose I do, ma'am."

"You're probably more attentive to him than his own children have been."

There was no answer for this, so Luther didn't try.

"Poor Papa," she said. She stroked his hair fondly.

"Well," said Luther, backing toward the door, "I don't want to wake him."

She laughed. "Stay. You couldn't wake my father with a nuclear war. You never saw such a sound sleeper."

"Well, in any case, I don't want to intrude." The idea of being alone in a room with this white woman made his skin itch.

"I told you you're not intruding," she said. "Indeed, I ought to be thanking you for taking such good care of him."

"No need for that, ma'am."

"And I suppose I owe you an apology, as well."

"Ma'am?"

"Nick's behavior these last few days has been absolutely beastly. You all have every right to be furious with him. I told him so in no uncertain terms."

"Yes, ma'am," said Luther—he hated all the "ma'ams" he heard suddenly coming out of his mouth—"and speaking of your brother, I really think I should be gettin' on. Don't want no more confusion."

"Oh, you don't have to worry about that," she said. "I poured Nick onto a train yesterday morning. By now, I expect he's halfway back to Vietnam. Probably nursing a terrible hangover, too, if I'm any judge. But try not to think too harshly of him. All of this is hard for him, you know? Hard for all of us. Except for Georgie, I suppose."

Something else for which there was no good answer. Luther kept silent. He wished a nurse would come in.

"So," said the white woman with sudden, forced brightness. "I suppose we're family, eh? Been family for a good many years, even though we've never rightly met. You'd be my—what?—brother-in-law? I'm not even sure I know your name. It's Lucius, right?"

"It's Luther," he said. "Luther Hayes."

"Well, Luther, pleased to meet you, albeit twenty years late. I'm Cora Simon. Well, I used to be Cora Simon. It's Cora Brockman now." Luther was grateful she did not extend one of her gloved hands across the bed for him to shake. He was walking on new ice here. He had no idea what the rules were yet. In a way, he supposed, that was an apt description of the entire country just now.

"Pleased to meet you, Miz Brockman," he said. There was no question of calling this white woman by her first name.

"So, tell me, how do you and my father know each other? I know that Georgie and your sister met—"

"Thelma."

She blinked. "Beg pardon?"

"My sister name Thelma."

"Yes, of course. I know that Georgie and 'Thelma'"—she spoke it as if she had trouble with the pronunciation—"met when the military asked him to pay a courtesy call on her after Pearl Harbor, when her husband died saving his life. But how did you and Papa meet?"

"It's a long story," said Luther. He wasn't about to talk about Johan showing up to rescue him from the drunk tank. "He done me a favor once."

She smiled fondly. "That sounds like Papa," she said. "Always helping others. He and George have such big hearts. They see things the rest of us don't."

"What kind of things?" Luther was curious, despite himself.

"The future," she said. "I suppose that would be the best way to put it. Like all of this that's going on now with that Martin Luther King and all these marches all over the country? Civil rights? Georgie saw the need for that twenty years ago. The rest of us never saw anything that needed changing."

"'The rest of us,'" said Luther. "You mean, white people?"

She conceded the point with a small, indifferent shrug. "Yes," she said, "I suppose I do."

There was a silence. Then she said, "Tell me, Luther, what did you think when you first heard my brother wanted to marry your sister?"

Luther did not hesitate. "I thought they was both crazy."

"Exactly," she said, laughing as if vindicated—as if here was someone who finally understood.

"Not 'cause they was wrong to love each other," said Luther quickly, annoyed by her laugh, annoyed that she might think his disapproval back then gave them common ground now. "No, I thought they was crazy because gettin' married meant they was gon' have to fight every day of they lives. It meant they was gon' have to take a lot of "—he almost said "shit," but decided at the last second to choose a more decorous word for this white lady—"grief from people who, like you say, never saw nothin' that needed changing. Especially when the rest of us knew that *everything* needed changing."

He heard the new ice creaking ominously beneath his tread, knew he had probably said too much. But he could not just stand here and trade idle bullshit with this woman. If he was going to be forced to stay in this room and talk to her, he would tell her the truth.

Her smile shrank as she processed his meaning and that gratified him. It frightened him, too. Finally, she said, "I never thought of it that way."

"I ain't never thought of it no other way," said Luther.

"*Everything* needs changing?" She said it as if to confirm that she had heard correctly.

"That's the way colored people see it, yeah. Schools, jobs, police. Ain't none of it made for the colored man. You grow up like us, you feel the same way."

"I understand," she said. "But if you grew up like us, you'd realize what a frightening proposition that is."

"Don't need to grow up like you to know white people scared," said Luther. "I'm a Negro, ma'am. I been understandin' white people my entire life. Had to in order to survive."

He heard the ice grumble. Tried to ignore it. Reminded himself that he would not stand here and bullshit.

"Oh, come now," she said, with a little chuckle. "Aren't you being a little dramatic?"

Luther shook his head. "No ma'am, I'm not."

"But you really think we're that easily understood?"

Luther said, "You got a husband, right? Brockman you said was his name?"

"Calvin, yes. But I don't see what that has to do with anything."

"Can you read him, ma'am?"

"Of course," she said. "Like a book."

"Can Calvin read you the same way?"

She blinked. Her mouth opened, then closed. "Well," she said, finally, "I suppose that's one way to look at it."

"Yes, ma'am. That's one way."

"Well, anyway," she said, "you can see why what you're saying would scare some people."

"Don't seem to scare George none," said Luther.

"Well, George is . . . George," she said. "He's different."

"Yes, ma'am, that he is."

Luther was lifting his hat to his head, thinking this might be an opportune time to make his escape. Then she said, "I suppose he's returned to New York? He and Thelma and your nephew?"

Your nephew, too.

Luther thought this, but did not say it. He lowered his hat. "No, ma'am. Well, Thelma still here, but George and Adam in Selma."

"Oh," she said. "For that march, I suppose."

"Yes, ma'am. Voting rights."

"Georgie and Nick were arguing over that very thing the other night on the way back from the restaurant. Nick was saying how the way things are is ordained by God and outside agitators shouldn't mess with that. As I'm sure you can imagine, Georgie disagreed."

"Yes, ma'am. So do I."

"I'm sure you do," she said. "And I'm sure you have good reason."

"Yes, ma'am. I believe so."

"You know, George was hurt on one of those marches. He was with that Yankee preacher who got himself killed."

"Yes, I know."

Exasperation crimped her lips. "Of course, you do," she said. "I don't know why I even said that. You knew it before I did. And you're not even blood kin."

"No, ma'am. Just a brother-in-law."

"I'm his sister," she said. Her eyes glittered. "I should have known. God, I hate what all of this has done to my family. I hate that we're so far apart. I hate that we barely know each other. I hate it all so much."

"Yes, ma'am," said Luther. "I imagine you do."

She tossed her head bitterly. "I used to hope one day we'd all reconcile. But now I doubt that's ever going to happen. The other night, Georgie spoke to Nick as if . . . he didn't ever expect to see him again. He told him, 'We were brothers.' Not 'we *are*' but 'we were.' Nick was hurt. I was, too."

"I'm sure that's hard on you," said Luther.

"It's a dagger in my heart," she said.

"Why George say somethin' like that, you don't mind me asking?"

She closed her eyes for a long moment. George wondered if the new ice had finally cracked open and he was about to fall into the icy depths below. Finally, Cora Brockman opened her eyes. "He said that Nick was asking him to choose between his brother and his wife and son, between his brother and what he knew to be right. And he wouldn't do it."

"I see," said Luther.

"You know George," she said.

"Yes, ma'am, I do."

"So you know how he is about doing the right and moral thing."

"Yes, I do."

Her smile was bitter. "I don't know how it is being his brother-in-law, Luther, but I can tell you it's hard being his sister, hard living with someone who aspires to be a saint. You never quite feel as though you measure up."

Luther shook his head. "George ain't no saint," he said, "and as far as I know, he ain't never tried to be one. He just a man who think it's important to do right by people. All kinds of people."

"I suppose he is," she conceded. "But it's difficult to know just what that is, don't you see? The things I thought were right twenty years ago all seem to be wrong now. The world is changing so fast and it's hard for some of us to keep up."

"'Some of us,'" said Luther.

"Very well," she conceded, "white people. It's hard for *white people* to keep up, to understand what colored people are trying to say. But I hope you know," she added, "that we're not all like Nick. Some of us are at least trying."

It seemed a plea for some absolution Luther had no power to give—and no desire to, either. He was struggling with how to respond to this when he heard Johan say, "Who's that? Who's in my room?" His voice was taut with distress.

His daughter patted his chest. "Shush. It's just me, Papa. It's Cora."

Luther was grateful for the opportunity to escape. "I'm gon' give you two some privacy, ma'am," he said, placing his hat back on his head. "I'll be out here." He was through the door before she had a chance to protest.

Luther went to the parking lot, where he leaned on the hood of the Buick and smoked a cigarette. Then he smoked another. The whole encounter unsettled him.

Some of us are at least trying.

What did this white woman want from him? Was she expecting sympathy? Did she think she deserved a medal?

Some of us are at least trying?

Well, damn, he thought, try harder.

So cocooned was he in the bitterness of his thoughts that Luther didn't register Cora Brockman approaching him in tears, dark rivers of mascara running down her cheeks, until she was almost upon him. Startled, he threw down his third cigarette and stood straight.

"Miz Brockman? What is it? What's wrong?"

"It's Papa," she said.

An icepick of dread stabbed through him. "Johan? What's wrong with Johan?"

She shook her head. "It's not that. It's . . . he didn't know me. I kept telling him who I was, told him I was his daughter, his little girl, but he would have none of it. He became agitated, accused me of trying to poison him. He screamed for me to get out, then started yelling in some Hungarian gibberish."

The memory unleashed fresh tears. It occurred to Luther that this was the moment, if she had been a colored woman, when he might have put a hand on her shoulder and tried to comfort her. But there was no possibility of that with this white lady. He had already walked on new ice and managed to escape safely. He wasn't about to push his luck by hitting it with a sledgehammer. So Luther could only stand there awkwardly, sympathizing from the safety of four feet away.

"I'm sorry," he said. "But you know he ain't meant it. He not in his right mind. You know that man in there love you, miss. He wouldn't hurt you for all the world."

She lifted her eyes and they were garish—bright-red orbs framed by runny black makeup. "Has he ever screamed at you and told you to get out?"

"Well, no, ma'am," admitted Luther. "But that don't mean he won't do it next time I go in there. It's the condition, ma'am. It ain't him."

She closed her eyes, shook her head ruefully. "You always think there'll be more time," she said.

"Yes, ma'am," said Luther. "But beg pardon, ma'am, he be eighty-two years old in November, right? How much more time did you think there would be?"

She regarded him closely, then smiled a smile that reminded him of a broken vase poorly glued back together. "My God," she said, "but you do have a... unique way of putting things, Luther. No sugarcoating for you."

"Yes, ma'am," he said. "Sorry, ma'am. I been told that before."

She held his gaze a moment longer as if he were some species of fish or fowl she was struggling to identify. Then, without another word, she walked over to her car. Luther watched as she backed it out and pulled onto the street. After she was gone, he turned back to the rest home and spent a moment contemplating it. Finally, he lifted his barber's case and headed for the door, wondering what he might find.

When Luther entered the room, Johan was sitting up in bed watching television as he spooned up a chunk from the grapefruit on his breakfast tray. "Luther!" he called, his voice jovial. Then, noticing the barber's case, he added, "Is it haircut day again so soon?"

"Afraid it is," said Luther.

"But you're early, aren't you? I'm not even out of bed yet."

"Yeah," said Luther. "Sorry about that. But the march startin' today and I didn't want to miss none of it. I thought we might watch together."

Johan's brow crinkled like paper. "March? What march?"

"Voting rights march. Remember? Martin Luther King. Selma to Montgomery."

The old man's brow released. "Oh, yes," he said. "The march. Of course. Is that today?"

"Yes," said Luther, setting his barber's case aside. "George is going to be in it. Him and Adam."

"George? My son?"

"Yes."

"And who else, did you say?"

"Adam. George's son."

"George? My George? He has a son?"

"Yes," said Luther. "Wife and a son."

"Isn't that wonderful," said Johan. He waved Luther toward one of the two chairs in front of the television. Some Sunday morning church service was playing. "Sit, sit," he said.

Luther put his hat on a wall hook and lowered himself to one of the chairs. He turned it and pushed back a bit so that he could see Johan behind him while also keeping an eye on the screen.

"George has a wife and son," Johan was saying, as he spooned up more grapefruit. "Imagine that. You know, I have a wife. And another son. And even a daughter. I haven't seen any of them in a long time, though. Do you know what happened to them? Do you know why they don't come by?"

Luther glanced to the television, afraid his eyes might give him away. "I'm sure they come by as often as they can," he said.

"You're Luther," said the old man.

"Yes, sir, I am."

"I saw him, you know."

Luther's eyes came back around. He was surprised to find Johan's cheeks suddenly wet with tears.

"You saw who?"

Johan's eyes flicked from one corner of the room to the other, as if the shadows might be listening. "I saw that Floyd Bitters," he whispered. "He's here. Did you know that? He's here."

Luther lowered his head. "I know he is," he said.

"Don't let that man get me, Luther. Please, don't let him hurt me again. He hurt me so badly that day. I could hardly breathe. I thought I was going to die."

"He ain't gon' hurt you," said Luther. "I promise. He can't hurt nobody no more."

"He killed your parents," said Johan. It was as if the realization had suddenly struck him.

"Yeah," said Luther, "he did."

"You must hate him, too."

"Yeah," said Luther, "I hate him, too."

"Does he still scare you, as he scares me?"

It took a moment and when finally Luther answered, his voice was as soft and harsh as sand falling on paper. "Yeah," he said, "I guess he still do."

Then Luther noticed that the Sunday morning preacher was gone, replaced by a sign that said "Special Report." He swung his attention to the television. "Look," he said, "the march about to start."

twenty-four

A COLD SUN BEAMED DOWN. MARSHALS WEARING ARMBANDS encouraged people to get into formation. A military helicopter thrummed heavily in the sky above. And the great march finally stepped off from Brown Chapel on Sunday afternoon, March 21, at 12:46, almost three hours after it had been scheduled to begin.

It was the climax of an extraordinary two days in which sleepy little Selma had abruptly become an absolute ant colony of activity. For two days, the air had crackled with static-filled transmissions from two-way radios as army Jeeps hurried to and from. Green trucks with the letters "U.S." stenciled on the doors lumbered through town, ferrying soldiers of the Alabama National Guard, which had been federalized by President Johnson. Other trucks hauled giant tents across the Pettus Bridge to prepare the campgrounds. Still others had borne portable latrines to be placed along the highway. Thirteen ambulances, a mobile hospital, and a "healthmobile" had arrived to handle medical emergencies. Food had been shipped in by the ton and a church basement had been converted into a storehouse, stuffed with sacks of oranges, tubs of apple sauce, big cans of peas.

And the people . . .

Delegations of them had poured in from all over the country, swelling by thousands the population of a tiny city that was home, in normal times, to just twenty-eight thousand citizens. As a result, there was not a motel or hotel room to be had; these had been commandeered by reporters and dignitaries. The clergymen, students, housewives, mechanics, janitors, librarians, and other ordinary Americans who had felt compelled to join the great parade found it necessary to sack out wherever they could find space: on church pews, in storage rooms, on the living room floors of Negro families.

Among the newcomers was a group from Hawaii who marched beneath a banner declaring, "Hawaii Knows Integration Works." As was the tradition in their state, just before the march began, the Hawaiians had draped garlands of flowers—leis—about the necks of the march leaders, including Martin Luther King, Jr. And then, one arm linked with his top aide, Reverend Ralph Abernathy, and the other with Maurice Eisendrath, head of the Union of American Hebrew Congregations, he stepped off onto Sylvan Street, leading the human flow behind him down the ribbon of red dirt that ran like an artery through Negro Selma.

They followed a flatbed truck bearing a group of news photographers and television cameramen. The latter were capturing the event on film that would be flown back to New York City to air on the evening news. One of the cameramen joked grimly that the man who failed to capture the rifle shot that felled King mid-step would never work again. Unbeknownst to that cameraman—and, for that matter, to King—a group of volunteers had been assigned to flank the great man on either side to obscure the sightlines of any would-be snipers.

Not that hateful people were without means of expressing themselves. The procession passed a white boy in a red roadster with his car radio cranked up high. It was playing "Dixie." Another car drove past the marchers, a message crudely whitewashed on its windows: "Coonsville, USA," it said.

Adam, clad in denim overalls and carrying a backpack, walked somewhere in the middle of the throng, joined by friends from SNCC who had temporarily put aside their antipathy toward "de Lawd" and his showboating methods in a spirit of solidarity with SCLC and respect for those who had been brutalized on the bridge. Even his friend Jackson Motley had been inspired to join. But the spirit of goodwill had its limits. Silas Norman, the director of SNCC's Selma project, was studiously ignoring the march and concentrating his energies that day on doing chores around the office.

The purple bruise that had closed Adam's eye for a week had shrunk and faded to a sickly yellow streaked with patches of violet. It was still obvious he had been slugged, though, and people assumed it was the remnant of an injury he had sustained on the bridge. Adam didn't tell them differently. The truth was too complicated—and too painful—to get into.

He was elated that morning, energized not just by the fact of standing shoulder to shoulder with like-minded people in a nonviolent army three thousand strong, but also by the fact that a volunteer doctor had, just an hour before, pronounced him fit to march. Under terms of the agreement negotiated with the federal judge, only three hundred marchers would be allowed to participate in that part of the demonstration that passed through rural Lowndes County, where Route 80 narrowed from four lanes to two. It had been said that in deciding who would be allowed to join that leg of the journey, priority would be given to those who had been beaten and gassed in the first attempt to cross the bridge.

Adam had been told he might be one of that three hundred, provided he got a doctor's approval. He was exhilarated to know there was a chance he would be marching tomorrow. He was also a little frightened. Local people had warned him repeatedly that Lowndes was nothing to fool with, that it was the most virulently racist county in a virulently racist state. Its bogs and swamps were said to provide many excellent places for the easy disposal of a body—a function they had served countless times over the years.

Adam had heard all this, but tried to ignore it. What good was it to think about a thing over which you had no control? All he had—all anyone had—was this moment, here and now. And in this moment, he felt like the crest of some mighty wave as he walked down Sylvan, arms linked with people on either side of him. Someone started a chorus of "We Shall Overcome," and he sang along joyfully. On this hopeful afternoon, at least, the song's soaring promise felt as if it just might be within reach.

And so, they proceeded down Sylvan Street, then turned right on Alabama Avenue, a motley parade of ponchos, letterman jackets, cassocks, fedoras, nun's habits, blue jeans, suits, church hats, sweatshirts, and fur-lined coats. One young couple pushed a baby in a stroller. Military police stood guard between the procession and small knots of white people who congregated on the sidewalks taunting and jeering.

"Look at all the white niggers!" one woman said to another in loud, mock amazement.

"You ever seen so many white niggers in all your life?" another replied.

Other women singled out a clutch of nuns walking together. "Hey, sister, how many of those niggers can you take on at one time?"

"Hey, sister, which one of those bucks will you be spreadin' your legs for?"

Adam saw a white nun walking near him go pale at the insults. But she pursed her thin lips, lifted her patrician jaw, and affected not to hear the abuse.

Then they turned left onto Broad Street and there it was again, the Edmund Pettus Bridge. Adam swallowed. He had to fight an urge to just stop there on the sidewalk and take it in. After everything that had happened beneath its tower, the bridge seemed to demand that reverence. But the line kept moving and he stayed with it.

"Third time's the charm, right?" said Jackson Motley.

"I sure hope so," said Adam.

At the sound of his voice, a girl in the row ahead of him turned to look back. "It's you," Emma said. She had to raise her voice to be heard over the freedom song—*"Ain't gonna let Sheriff Clark turn me around, turn me around, turn me around . . ."*—"Been lookin' all over town for you. You saved my life on this damn bridge. That's what people told me, anyway, 'cause I was knocked out cold. I never got a chance to thank you."

Adam shook his head. "They give me too much credit," he said. "I just tried to move you out of harm's way. Then I got clobbered myself."

She shook her head. "Hell of a thing," she said.

He nodded. "Hell of a thing," he agreed.

They approached the bridge. Some white man had set up speakers and Peggy Lee serenaded the marchers, her voice meditative and mournful against a feathery cushion of guitar and piano, the drummer keeping time with soft brushstrokes.

Motley arched an eyebrow. "They playin' 'Bye Bye Blackbird' for us? That's our send-off? Hell, that song's a hundred years old, ain't it? Least they could do is play us somethin' hip."

"Ray Charles," suggested Emma.

Motley pointed a finger. "There you go," he said.

And as if on cue, the three of them started singing "Hit the Road Jack."

They broke up laughing, but laughter wilted under the gimlet glare of one of the marshals who materialized without warning at the end of their row. He spoke only one word, raising his voice to make it heard above the tumult.

"Dignity," he said.

The three young people fell into an embarrassed silence at that and a line of humanity half a mile long climbed the span. At the apex, where two weeks before he had found himself facing a line of possemen on horseback and blue-helmeted state troopers, Adam saw that the road was clear. The moment struck him with an emotional force for which he was not prepared.

"My God," he said.

Motley glanced at him but knew enough to say nothing. And so the great march crested the bridge. As they passed under the span of metal with the Confederate hero's name on it, the Alabama River rushing beneath them, Adam felt something exuberant running through his chest like electric current. He wanted to pump his fist the way you do when your football team scores a winning touchdown, but refrained—*"Dignity"*—from doing so. He could not help smiling, though.

Emma looked back at him. "Maybe the third time really is the charm," she said. She was smiling, too.

"Maybe it is," replied Adam.

As the procession came down off the bridge, they were met by scattered jeers from white onlookers. Some waved Confederate battle flags. One drove past in a car with another message whitewashed onto its windows: "Martin Luther Koon!" Someone held up a sign that said, "I hate niggers." Someone else lofted a sign that said, "Too Bad Reeb." A tow-headed white boy no older than six paced back and forth along the line screaming, "Good-bye, niggers! Good-bye, niggers!" His voice was raw, his cheeks bright pink.

Adam was stunned that a child could have packed so much hatred into so few years. But it seemed to have possessed the boy, the words spewing out of him like some benediction of evil.

"Good-bye, niggers! Good-bye, niggers! *Good-bye*, niggers!" White men and women behind him laughed in tolerant amusement.

Adam caught Emma's eye. He shook his head, disbelieving. She returned a palms-up gesture. And on they walked.

He had made it across the patch of pavement where he was clubbed senseless just two weeks before, the same spot where Martin Luther King had led his forces into a humiliating turnaround just a few days later. Now the highway stretched open before him, before all of them, and the possibilities—and the threats—seemed endless.

Adam plunged doggedly ahead, telling himself that he was prepared to meet either. The little white boy never stopped his awful screeching, but with each step it grew fainter. After a few minutes, it could no longer be heard at all.

twenty-five

THE TELEVISION WAS ON, BUT SOMEHOW, THE APARTMENT felt quiet. Luther closed the door behind him.

"Thel?" he called. "You here?"

It was late in the afternoon. He was surprised not to see her in the kitchen, getting something ready for dinner. In just the few days his sister had been here, Luther had grown quite used to the idea of having someone else do the cooking, if only because it spared him from having to eat his own. Even after all these years of bachelor life, Luther had never managed to become much of a cook. It was one reason he took so many meals at diners and carryout joints.

Hungry after missing lunch, Luther went into the kitchen and got some bologna from the refrigerator. He thought of frying it, but that was more work than he felt like doing. Instead, he slapped the lunch meat and a slice of processed cheese down on a piece of bread, smeared another piece of bread with mayonnaise, and put it on top. He reached into the refrigerator for a can of Coke, poking two holes in the top with a can opener on his key ring. He noted absently that his sister hadn't answered him yet. "You not watchin' the march?" he called, after taking a long pull from the red-and-white can.

Luther took his sandwich back into the living room, sat on the couch, and watched the news for a moment. Still no response from Thelma. Maybe she was out? But why would she leave the television on? Where could she have gone? Wouldn't she have left him a note?

So she was taking a nap, then. That made sense. Certainly, she was sleeping a lot, lately.

But still . . .

There was something about the quality of the silence, the oppressive weight of it, that made him uneasy. For a long moment, Luther sat there just listening and chewing, trying to put a name to his anxiety. It was like trying to grab Jell-O in your fist. Whatever it was, his mind could not hold it. It kept squirming free.

"Thel?"

Luther got up and moved toward the bedroom.

"Hey, Thelma, you in there?"

The door to the bedroom was about six inches from the jamb, light from his table lamp leaking through. Why would Thelma be sleeping with the lamp on?

And right then, for no solid reason he could define, Luther felt anxiety twist his gut hard, like wringing out a dishrag. He knocked on the door. No answer. He knocked again. Then he pushed it open.

In that first instant, he thought she was only napping after all. She lay on her side. Her eyes were closed, her face was at peace.

But there was a stillness about her that unnerved him. And . . . something, some whitish substance, was dribbling from her mouth, pooling on the coverlet. Vomit. The bottle of pills, open on the nightstand, completed the picture.

The shock of it vibrated Luther's body like a tuning fork. A taste of copper flooded his mouth. His mind refused to process

could not process

reality had become

too real, too much *there*

like being plunged face-first into ice water from a dead sleep

Then his mind jolted into gear and he screamed her name, two long syllables of pure anguish. "*Thelma!*"

Luther grabbed his sister, pulled her to her feet. She was heavy and limp, a sack of wet sand with arms that hung straight down. Luther shrieked without realizing it, bawled like a terrified boy.

He patted her cheeks. Nothing. He slapped her hard. Slapped her again. "*Thelma!*"

There. Did her eyelids flutter?

Yet another slap, harder still.

Yes, her eyelids definitely fluttered.

"Oh, thank God, thank God, thank God," whispered the atheist,

Luther Hayes. "Come on, Thelma, come on. Don't do this, you hear me? Don't you do this!"

Not even in tank battles during the war had Luther felt such raw fear. He didn't know what to do. Had no idea what to do. What should he do?

The telephone. Of course. The telephone.

No, not the telephone. How much time would he lose trying to find an ambulance service that accepted Negroes? Theoretically, that was no longer an issue since they passed the civil rights law last year, but he wasn't about to risk Thelma's life on a theory.

Instead, Luther hoisted the dead weight of his baby sister in his arms. "Hold on, Thelma," he whispered. "You hold on."

He carried her through the living room and down the stairs. In the parking lot, he lowered her to her rubbery legs, leaned her against the car and fished for his keys. When he had managed to fumble the passenger side door open, he deposited Thelma awkwardly in the front seat. Above him, his front door gaped wide, and Luther wondered distantly if he would still have a television when he got back home.

But he didn't have time to care.

The car started with a roar. Luther backed out with a screech of tires, floored it down the short alley, swung a left that made four lanes of Sunday drivers skid to avoid collision. He barely noticed, pushing the accelerator down as far as it would go, weaving in and out of traffic, jumping through red lights. With his free hand, he alternately hammered his horn and slapped Thelma's cheek. Limp as a rag doll, her body jerked this way and that as Luther yanked the wheel right and left, darting across lanes. Suddenly, some old white man in a pickup truck drifted over in front of him, forcing Luther to brake hard. Thelma's forehead made a thunk like somebody plucking a watermelon as it slammed the dashboard.

"Oh, shit!" cried Luther, pushing her back, watching the traffic, blowing his horn. "I'm sorry I'm sorry I'm sorry." But he did not slow down.

Behind him, horns blared. Tires shrieked. People cursed. Luther drove through it all with a single-minded mania. He had to save Thelma.

Unless it was already too late.

This thought kept trying to intrude. Luther kept pushing it back. He gritted his teeth. He snarled. He drove.

It only took six minutes. It felt like an hour, but no, just six minutes, and Luther brought the car to a hard stop in front of St. Martin de Porres, a Catholic hospital for colored. He scrambled out of the car, snatched open the driver's side door, pulled Thelma into his arms, and began to drag the weight of her toward the building.

He pulled the glass door open, startling a group of white women in white nun's habits who were talking together at a reception desk. "Help me here!" he cried. "I need help!"

There was a shocked moment when nothing happened. Then one of the nurses, an older woman, started barking orders. "Sister Ruth, page Dr. Sullivan! Sister Miriam, get a gurney!" She turned to Luther. "What happened to her?"

"I don't know," he said, helplessly. "She took some sleeping pills."

"What's this on her forehead?"

Luther was surprised to see that blood was dripping from a hairline cut. "I guess she smacked it on the dashboard when I hit the brakes. I was driving fast," he added, his voice apologetic.

"What is her name?"

As Luther was supplying this information, the gurney came, a young Negro doctor in a lab coat trotting behind it. He surrendered his sister to these strangers, and they lifted her up on the stretcher and wheeled her through swinging doors into the exam area, already cutting away her clothing.

Luther tried to follow, but the older nurse held up a restraining hand. "No," she said, "you'll only be in the way. Wait over there." She pointed to a room of straight-back wooden chairs, magazines, and Bibles on the coffee table, a television mounted in a corner. "We'll come get you when there's any word."

Luther tried to protest. "But . . ." he began.

"You did your job," she told him. "Now, let us do ours."

"She's my sister," he protested feebly. But the nurse was already gone.

So Luther took a seat on one of the pitiless chairs and there he waited, his arms folded, his head pressed back against the wall, trying not to weep as his mind fed him a litany of horrors.

The doctor and the nurses coming out with grim faces to give him the bad news.

"We tried our best, but..."

"We're sorry, Luther, but..."

"Maybe if you'd gotten her here sooner, but..."

He had stopped to eat a bologna sandwich while his sister lay dying just a few feet away! A fucking bologna sandwich! The thought made him nauseous. It bloated him with reproach.

And from the television overhead, a chipper announcer promised "shipwreck hijinks" on the next episode of *Gilligan's Island*.

What would he tell George? How would he explain?

And how would they break it to Adam?

The strained silence between him and his mother before he left for Selma. . . . If it turned out that was the last time he saw her, the boy would be devastated. He would be ruined.

No, Luther reminded himself sternly, wiping at his tears. He was way ahead of himself. Thelma had *not* died. She was alive. She would recover from this and go on to live a long life. This, he told himself, was what he would believe, until somebody came through those doors and told him different. Until then, all these grim thoughts amounted to nothing, just his mind torturing him, like some bad little boy pulling wings off flies. But the pep talk he gave himself didn't do Luther much good. Fear still rode him like a jockey. It still knifed him like some back-alley mugger. Luther couldn't help himself. He started weeping again for his dead sister. He wished he still remembered how to pray.

Minutes piled up and became an hour. Luther tried to decide whether it was a good thing that it was taking so long. They wouldn't still be working on her if she was dead, right?

As if in perverse reply to his unvoiced question, the chipper-voiced man on television now promised "spook-tacular laughs" on the next episode of *The Munsters*.

Luther wanted very much to throw something through the screen.

Why had she done it? Why hadn't he realized something was wrong? Yes, he had known she was depressed, but he hadn't known she felt bad enough to do something like this. That had never even occurred to him. He had completely missed it.

"Big brother has a very important job. He got to look out for the ones under him. He got to take care of them, protect them from gettin' hurt."

His father had given him a very important charge. And he had failed. Again.

"Mr. Hayes?"

Luther started at the sound of his name. Somehow, the doctor was right in front of him, but Luther hadn't even seen him there. He leapt to his feet.

"Did you hear what I said?" the doctor asked.

"N-no," stammered Luther. "I'm sorry. I guess I wasn't . . ."

"No problem," said Dr. Sullivan, pushing a pair of glasses up on his nose. "I'll repeat myself. It was a very near thing, but we were able to revive her and get her stabilized. We'd like to keep her overnight for observation, but I expect to be able to discharge her in the morning."

Luther was not certain he had heard right. "She's going to be all right?"

The doctor nodded. "Yes," he said, "physically."

Luther sagged. He felt fresh tears spring to his eyes. "She's going to be all right?"

"Physically," the doctor said again, and there was steel in his voice now. "Mr. Hayes, your sister tried to kill herself. That's nothing to fool around with. My advice would be to encourage her to get some psychological help as quickly as possible. You may not be as lucky next time."

Luther's heart thumped hard at the mention of a next time. "You saying she's crazy?"

The other man shook his head, emphatically. "I'm saying it's pretty obvious she's deeply troubled. She's dealing with emotional issues she can't resolve and she needs help."

"Can I see her?"

Sullivan nodded. "They're putting her into a room. The nurse will come get you as soon as they've got her situated."

"Thank you," said Luther. He extended his hand and the doctor took it. "Thank you for everything."

It was another half hour before the nurse—it was the same older white woman who had taken charge when he burst through the door— came for him. She led him up a stairwell and down a long hall. She didn't say anything until she reached a closed door midway down. There, she stopped and faced him squarely.

"Just so that you know," she said, "your sister might not be happy to see you."

"Beg pardon?"

"It's pretty common in attempted suicides," she said. "There's a certain amount of embarrassment at having been caught, having failed, as it were. It usually manifests itself as hostility. I'm not saying that it will, but I am saying that it could. I just wanted you to be prepared. Follow her lead. Don't get into an argument with her." Her eyes sought his. "Do you understand?"

Luther nodded. She said, "Try not to be too long. We don't want to overtax her." And with that, she pushed the door open and Luther walked through. It was a spartan room. A door in the corner leading to a toilet and shower, a dark, silent television on a wheeled cart, a window looking out on a fleet of clouds sailing the twilight, and, in the center, a bed, where Thelma sat in a white hospital gown, propped against pillows. She looked over at the sound of Luther entering the room. Then she turned away and watched the clouds.

"Thelma," he said.

She didn't answer. He moved to a plastic chair next to the bed. He turned it so that it was facing her, took a seat. "How you doing, sis?"

After a moment, she spoke in a dark voice he had never heard before. "You should have just let me die," she said, still watching the clouds.

Luther was scandalized. "Thelma! Don't talk like that."

She went on as if he hadn't spoken. "It would have been easier on everyone."

"Wouldn't have been easier on me," he said.

"Would have been easier on *me*," she replied.

"That's bullshit," he sputtered, remembering a second too late the nurse's admonition against getting into an argument.

But Thelma just glanced at him. "Don't you see?" she said. "I've made a mess of everything."

He shook his head, emphatically. "You ain't made no mess out of nothin'. All your life, all you ever done is try to make the best of the situation. That's all you ever done, Thel."

If his words made any difference, he couldn't see it on her face. After a moment, she turned back toward the window. "Are you going to tell George what I did?"

"I ain't thought about it," he admitted. "I was focused on gettin' you here. You don't think he should know?"

A little shrug. "I don't know," she said. "I guess he has a right to. Poor George. He's going to be hurt."

"Yeah," said Luther.

"I don't know how to do that," she said. "I don't know how to hurt him."

Luther spoke gently. "Fine," he said. "I'll tell him. Ain't gon' be able to reach him till after the march, though."

"He's going to think I'm crazy," said Thelma.

"He your husband," said Luther. "He love you." Which, he knew, wasn't quite an answer.

"This doctor thinks I'm crazy," she said. "He wants me to see a shrink as soon as I get home."

"He don't think you crazy," said Luther. "He told me that himself. He said you dealin' with some emotional problem got you messed up inside."

"Well, that's true enough," she said. "It's been really hard, these past few days."

"Yeah," said Luther, "but that ain't all of it."

Her gaze sharpened. "What do you mean?"

"I mean, I know these last few days was hard, but that ain't all there is to why you took them pills. You been sad a long time, sister. I just ain't realized it before."

She smirked. "Oh, so you're a psychologist now?"

Luther shook his head. "No, but I ain't no fool, neither. I got eyes and ears. Hell, you tried to tell me yourself, that day we talked on the phone and you started sayin' how you ain't been a good mother to that boy. You tried to say it, but I just didn't want to hear. Thelma, you been sad for years."

Her stare challenged him. Luther wanted to turn away, but that was the whole problem, wasn't it? Turning away. Him, her, all of them, turning away. So instead, he met the force of her gaze. And he watched as it slowly crumpled, as her lips trembled and her eyes moistened.

The confession escaped her in a whisper. "God, I feel like such a failure."

"You ain't no failure, Thel. You the best person I know. And I ain't sayin' that 'cause you my sister. I'm sayin' it 'cause it's true."

She gave him a long look. Then she said, "Luther, I'm sorry."

Now Luther felt his own eyes growing wet. "You scared the shit out of me, Thel. Don't you never do that again. If you feelin' that bad, you talk to me. You talk to *somebody*, you hear me? And if we don't listen, you *make* us listen."

She wiped her eyes. "You sure you don't think I'm crazy?" she asked, smiling a little to make it a joke.

But Luther knew it wasn't a joke. He shook his head emphatically. "No," he said. "It's the world that's crazy, Thel, not you. Feel like it's spinnin' out of control, and you just out here like the rest of us, tryin' to hold on the best you can."

"Well, I guess I'm not doing so good," she said, through a tiny, reflective smile. "I slipped off today."

"But I caught you," said Luther.

A somber look. "You caught me," she agreed. "I don't know whether I should thank you for it or not."

"Thelma," he said, and then he stopped because he didn't know what else to say.

His sister regarded him with something like pity. After a moment, she reached out her hand and Luther took it in his own. Thelma gave him a tight smile and returned her gaze to the window. They sat there together for a long time, watching as the day's last light bled from the sky.

twenty-six

THE SUN WAS HANGING LOW, CARVING LONG SHADOWS ON the ground, when the marchers, stiff and footsore, reached their campground, seven miles out of Selma. The temperature had plunged, and Adam wished he had brought a coat. Instead, someone supplied him with a thin blanket, which he wrapped around his shoulders like a superhero's cape as he stood in line for a supper of spaghetti, pork and beans, and cornbread served from brand-new galvanized garbage cans. As he was waiting, one of the marshals approached and told him he had been selected to make tomorrow's march through Lowndes County. She gave him an orange vest and told him to make sure to wear it in the morning; it was how the three hundred marchers chosen for this leg of the journey would be identified.

Once his plate had been filled, Adam went to look for Motley. He found him with some other young marchers sitting cross-legged by an oil drum fire outside one of the men's field tents. "What was that about?" asked Motley, nodding toward the marshal.

"She told me I got picked to march tomorrow through Lowndes County," said Adam.

"Bloody Lowndes," replied Motley, twining some spaghetti on his fork. "Ain't that what they call it?"

"That's what I hear," said Adam. He could see his own breath.

Motley snorted. "Better you than me, then, baby," he said.

"I'm not afraid," said Adam, around a bite of cornbread. He was lying.

Motley rolled his eyes. "You'd better be. Being afraid might help you stay alive."

This was a point Adam couldn't argue. "How about we change the subject?" he said.

"I'm just sayin'. You know, a girl told me those crackers have gathered up a bunch of snakes from the swamps and they plan to let 'em loose at the campsite tomorrow night."

"How does she know this?" asked Adam.

"I don't know," admitted Motley. "I didn't ask her."

Adam shook his head. "You can't listen to every crazy rumor," he said.

Motley shrugged. "I believe her," he said. "You can't say it doesn't sound like somethin' they would do. And you know what?"

"What?"

"When those snakes start bitin', I bet ol' Martin Luther will tell y'all you can't stomp 'em or chop 'em with a hoe. Got to be nonviolent all the way." He drew himself up self-importantly and spoke in imitation of King's preacherly baritone. "I have a dream that one day, the men and the snakes will sit down to the table of brotherhood! I have a dream today!"

Around them, people looked up. Adam glanced about, worried that one of King's lieutenants might have heard the mockery. "Man, are you crazy?" he hissed. "You can't be talking like that. What if one of King's men heard you? What if King himself heard you?"

Motley made a gesture of indifference. "What I care?" He pointed toward a pink-and-white house trailer that sat in the middle of the camp. "You see where they got de Lawd sleepin'? No hard, cold ground for him, no sir. No snakes, neither. Bet it's nice and toasty in there, too. What do you think?" He hugged himself against the chill.

Adam said, "I think you're going to get yourself kicked out of here. And me, too, just for being with you."

"Maybe that wouldn't be the worst thing in the world," muttered Motley.

"What do you mean?"

Motley didn't answer immediately. He took a sip of punch from a Styrofoam cup. A pair of military police went by, chatting quietly. Adam saw John Lewis getting into a car for the ride back to Selma; his doctor had only allowed him to march on the condition that he not spend nights in camp. A few feet away from them, a young white guy with a guitar was singing a serviceable version of "Blowin' in the Wind" by Bob Dylan as people circled him, swaying to the music.

Finally, Motley said, "What are we doing here, Adam?"

Adam was confused. "You and me?"

Motley shook his head. "SNCC," he said. "What are we doing following all these country preachers around like we're their junior varsity? Got us singing their freedom songs and practicing how to get busted upside the head and don't hit back. De Lawd say he got a dream? My dream is, I hope one of those crackers does try to hit me upside the head. I'll make sure I'm the last nigger he ever hits."

Adam said, "Come on, man."

"I'm serious," said Motley and indeed, the eyes that met Adam's were clear and purposeful and contained not the faintest suggestion of humor.

"But nonviolence is our middle name," said Adam. "Literally. Student *Nonviolent* Coordinating Committee, remember?"

"I know that," said Motley, impatiently. "But maybe the time for that is past. Maybe it's time we did something else because I've got to tell you, I've had it with letting white folks push me around while all I do is pray for them. Watching what they did to you and John and all the others out there on that damn bridge, it made me sick. I'm glad we got across today—I know that was a big deal—but I'm just saying I don't know if I can go along with this nonviolent stuff anymore. And a lot of brothers and sisters feel the same way I do."

"Yeah, I know," said Adam. He had heard the same murmurs of discontent.

"Some of us have some ideas," said Motley. "Some of us think there's a whole 'nother way to approach this."

As a preacher's son, Adam Mason Simon had been raised to trust in the movement of things not seen, to believe faith had a weight and a gravity all its own. But that belief was at war with the fact that he was twenty-one years old and already impatient with the preening hypocrisy of white people who sang paeans to the nobility of freedom whilst sitting in suppression of twenty million Negroes. Anyone with sense would see that something had to give, something had to break. How long could things go on this way? How long were Negroes supposed to put up with daily denial and humiliation? How long did they have to wait to be free?

It had already been too long. And black people needed more than just preachers counseling patience.

At that very moment, as if his thoughts about the shortcomings of preachers had conjured him, Adam spotted his father—*stepfather,* some voice within him corrected—standing in line for his evening meal. He was wearing his clerical collar and his eyes were bright as if he were lit from within by some righteous fire of determination and belief. If George had any doubts about the virtue of the struggle, that fire had long ago burned them to ashes.

It made Adam ashamed for reasons he couldn't quite define.

And the shame, in turn, made him defiant. Was he not a grown-ass man with a mind of his own? He turned to Motley. "Tell me more," he said. And they talked deep into the night.

Morning came. And on they walked.

Martin Luther King, with his wife, Coretta, by his side, took the lead. They wore matching green earmuffs and had their heads down, reading newspapers. Behind them came a station wagon with Mississippi plates bearing doctors from a human rights organization. Adam spotted John Lewis marching doggedly ahead. Like Adam, he was wearing an orange vest.

The Alabama sun increased its hateful glare until it was impossible to believe the air temperature had been below freezing just hours before. Adam rolled up his sleeves, then went into his backpack for a white bucket hat. It made him look like Gilligan, but just now, he didn't care.

He was pulling on the drawstrings to tighten it when he caught sight of a pair of dark-skinned boys who had found another way to fend off the sun. They'd slathered their faces with thick, white sunscreen and with their fingers, inscribed a single word on their foreheads: VOTE. It made Adam smile.

And on they walked.

Past barren fields, through strands of trees, down lonely stretches of empty Alabama road.

"How many miles we supposed to be doing today?" someone asked Adam.

"Seventeen," he replied.

"Lord, my aching feet."

"Forget about your feet," said another marcher. "Worry about the snakes."

"Ain't no snakes," said the first marcher.

"But I heard—"

The first marcher gave an emphatic shake of her head. "That's just a rumor. They had a press conference this morning and somebody asked the government man about it. He said there's nothin' to it. Army has checked out the field and they've got it under guard."

"No snakes?" The second marcher sounded relieved.

"No," said the first marcher. "Whoever spread that around is just trying to scare us." She tapped her forehead. "We've got to stay strong."

Adam nodded, pleased to have at least one of his worries authoritatively resolved. Then, from above, he heard the faint sound of an engine. He shielded his eyes and glanced up to where the angry sun had perched. It took him a moment to spot the source.

A light airplane was diving toward the marchers on the highway. By now, everybody was looking up and pointing. It occurred to Adam belatedly that this made them all perfect targets if, God forbid, the pilot meant to strafe them. Military helicopters buzzed the little plane, but it kept coming straight on, as if the pilot intended to crash into the march like some kamikaze from the war.

Just as Adam was tensing himself to run, the plane banked away, trailing a sudden blizzard of white papers that came fluttering to the ground. Adam snatched one out of the air. He found himself holding a leaflet that said, "An unemployed agitator ceases to agitate." It bore the legend of something called the Confederate Air Force.

Glancing up, Adam saw his own confusion mirrored in the faces of the people around him as they read the flyer. One man stared after the departing plane as the papers continued fluttering down, some landing in a creek that rushed by beneath an overpass.

"There it go," he drawled in a laconic voice, "the Confederate Air Force."

Someone chuckled. Someone else joined them. And in the next moment, laughter broke through like water from a leaky dam.

"The Confederate Air Force," said some stout woman with her hands on her hips. She shook her head, chuckling. "Lord, have mercy. Now I done seen everything."

And on they walked.

Some people waved from passing vehicles. Others shot single-digit salutes. After a while, Adam was too tired to respond to either. He fanned at flies, wiped at sweat that had collected between his collar-bones. A group of crows jeered at the line of people from atop a tree.

They took a break just before the point where the highway narrowed. Adam sat right down on the pavement, hot and exhausted. A few moments later, someone handed him a bologna sandwich, and he demolished half of it in a single bite, washing it down with a long draft of water from his thermos. A couple of army Jeeps went by. A man jabbed an elbow lightly into Adam's side.

"See 'em?" the stranger said. "Them the demolition experts."

"Demolition experts?"

The man nodded sagely. He spoke around a bite of bologna sandwich. "I heard one'a them army fellas say they check for bombs and booby traps along the road."

"Wow," said Adam.

"Yeah," said the man. "They done trained for a war zone. That make 'em fit to handle Lowndes County, I guess."

Moments later, one of King's aides began addressing the marchers. "All right," he called, "this is where we part company with some of you for a little while. The highway narrows to two lanes up ahead and it stays narrow for twenty-two miles. In order to comply with Judge Johnson's order, only three hundred of us can walk on this leg of the journey. Now, those of you who have been chosen, you should already have received your orange vests. When we tell you to, we're going to need you to line up on the highway."

A Negro teenager raised her hand, but started speaking before she could be recognized. "Excuse me, but that ain't fair," she said.

"What isn't fair?" asked the aide.

The girl pointed to where a group of other young Negroes sat cross-legged. "We the ones who can't vote. We the ones who started this here protest. We the ones who get shoved around every day by Sheriff Clark when we try to demand our rights. Not meanin' no disrespect"—she glanced at a white man wearing one of the coveted orange vests—"but if only three hundred of us can go through, then them three hundred should all be Negroes. Don't get me wrong: we thankful for the white people who come down here to help us, but it's our protest, ain't it? It's a Negro protest."

A murmur of approval rippled through the assembly. A white woman said, "Maybe she has a point."

King's aide lifted a hand for silence. Then he said, "I appreciate everybody's input. And young lady"—a nod toward the Negro girl—"you make some good points. Nevertheless, we're going to go ahead as planned. There are two main reasons. The first is that Dr. King feels—and I happen to agree—that it would be morally wrong to abandon allies who have refused to abandon us, who have made their own sacrifices and, in some cases, even had to defy their own communities, in order to stand with us. That's important because, while this is a Negro protest, they know it's also, in the larger sense, a human rights protest.

"And if that doesn't persuade you," he added, "then there's the simple fact that having white folks march with us draws more attention to our cause than if it was just Negroes marching alone. It also gives the white bigots we will be confronting another target for their hate, thereby reducing the level of abuse all of us must face. Because what do white bigots hate even more than they hate Negroes?"

Adam spoke without thinking. "They hate white people who help Negroes."

King's aide pointed toward him. "Exactly," he said. "So y'all rest a minute and then let's get ready to move out."

The Negro teenager who had spoken up took all this in with a skeptical expression, but she didn't press the issue. "Fine," she said. "But we'll be back."

"We'll be lookin' for you," said the aide.

Moments later, after buses had ferried the excess marchers back to Selma, the remaining three hundred formed themselves into columns three abreast. King waved them forward like the leader of some wagon train of Old West homesteaders. "Let's move out," he called. "Pick it up, now!" His dark face beamed.

Adam followed the column past a green highway sign lettered in white: "Enter Lowndes County," it said. The narrow road crossed through a swamp, the waters on either side dark with mystery, lily pads floating on the surface, misshapen trees rising, wraith-like, from the depths. Adam caught his breath. These waters, he knew, held many grim secrets.

As if they were all sharing the same fear, someone piped up at that moment with a freedom song. "*Ain't gonna let nobody turn me around*," the unseen man sang. Adam joined his voice to the chorus that responded, "*Turn me around, turn me around, turn me around.*" It made him feel braver than he knew himself to really be. But feigning courage, he reasoned, was almost the same as having it.

At least, he hoped this was true.

And on they walked.

After a while, they began to encounter bands of colored people standing by the road to encourage them. In Lowndes County, Adam knew, even so small a gesture constituted an act of defiant courage. Children gazed upon them with shy, solemn expressions. Young women in head rags and faded housedresses covered the gaps in their smiles with self-conscious hands. Young men stood with arms folded, watching with flinty eyes as the marchers walked by.

And then there were the old people. Bent and hobbled, leaning heavily on canes, sitting in tattered wheelchairs, they waited at the roadside as if they had been hoping for such a procession longer than a few minutes, longer even than a few hours, as if they had been hoping for it all their lives. In some sense, Adam supposed, they had. And when the marchers came into view, these grandparents and great-grandparents, these shriveled refugees from another century, grew fidgety and agitated as toddlers on Christmas morning.

Yellow eyes glistened moistly. Delighted smiles showed gums as innocent of teeth as a newborn's. Hands left shrunken and fleshless by age and arthritis reached out to offer fleeting, weightless handshakes, or simply to touch, as if just that was enough. Especially when King passed by. They gazed upon him with unnerving reverence. Old men pumped his plump, soft hand. Old women threw arms around his neck.

"Thank you, Lord," they cried. Adam couldn't tell if they were thanking the Lord for King, or if they thought the Lord was King. Not that it seemed to matter. "Thank you, Lord!" they cried.

For one woman, hugging King's neck was not enough. She planted her lips on his cheek, then cried out in triumph. "I done kissed him! I done kissed him!" Tears shone in her eyes.

"Who?" someone challenged. "Who you done kissed, Juanita?"

"I done kissed the Martin Luther King!" she said.

"The" Martin Luther King. As if the name were a title, like "the" queen or "the" president—as if it was so revered, she couldn't even approach it directly, had to use a grammatical advance guard to convey the awe it deserved. It made Adam feel uneasy for all the times he and Motley and others their age had scorned King for puffery and pretense. These old people saw nothing of the sort. To the contrary, they stood there and sat there by the side of that road as if they had lived all their lives hoping, praying, and persevering for just such a man to someday come ambling by, bringing with him the promise that eventually, even they might be free.

And on they walked.

The marchers made camp that night in a field that turned out to be infested with red ants. Adam spent half the night slapping at the ferocious little beasts, awoke scratching at angry welts on his wrists, forearms, and elbows. It occurred to him that he'd have almost preferred the snakes.

Almost.

Then it began to rain.

The first drops fell during breakfast, just as Adam was receiving his dollop of oatmeal in his disposable bowl. By the time he had scurried back under cover of a green field tent, the porridge had become soup. He lifted some of the watery concoction with his spoon, watched it dribble back into the bowl and decided he was not so hungry after all. He dumped the bowl into the trash barrel at the entrance to the tent.

The weather had cleared up by the time Adam and the other marchers were again underway, but it would turn out the morning shower was only the prelude to what the day had in store. Two hours later, the skies cracked opened in earnest, water cascading in fat, heavy drops upon the three hundred souls who trudged up Route 80 through the wilds of Lowndes County.

Those who had thought to bring umbrellas along opened them up. Those who had not made do. Empty cornflakes boxes were converted to rain hats. Plastic sleeping bag covers became ponchos. It made for a ragtag parade.

From the side of the road, watched carefully by a contingent of national guardsmen, a group of white men cackled at the sight of the bedraggled marchers. "Well, this thing is all over now," said one, whose name was Rufus. He and the other men were dry and comfortable, drinking bottles of Coca-Cola beneath the awning of a service station as they watched the procession go by. "A nigger can't stand the rain," he added with pontifical certainty. "That's a known fact. Absolutely cannot stand the rain."

"Hell," said yet another man, whose name was Philpot. "I hear ol' Martin Luther Koon had to pay 'em fifteen dollars a day to march in the first place. 'Voting rights' my ass."

This brought more laughter. Then Philpot stopped abruptly and jabbed an index finger toward the road. "Hey!" he cried. "Look at that." One of the marchers was carrying an American flag on a pole draped over his shoulder. The flag was upside down, a universal signal of dire distress. Not that Philpot understood this or would have cared, even if he did. "Damn niggers don't even know how to carry the flag proper," he grumbled.

Philpot made a megaphone of his hands. "Hey, nigger!" he called. "You got your flag upside down." He gestured helpfully with his index finger that the flag should be turned right side up. If the flag bearer heard the instruction, he gave no indication.

"I think they're doing it on purpose," Rufus said.

Philpot's eyes narrowed. "You think so? Goddamn it, then, that's disrespectful. They're disrespectin' the flag of their own goddamn country."

"Somebody needs to set them straight," said Rufus, pushing his sleeves up on his forearms and taking a menacing step toward the road.

One of the national guardsmen, a young white roofer from Birmingham, moved to bar his path. He carried a rifle with the bayonet fixed. "That's far enough, sir," he said. His voice was calm, but firm.

Rufus was apoplectic. "Let me pass, boy. Don't you see what they're doin'?"

"I have my orders, sir."

Rufus jabbed his finger toward the road. "I shed blood to defend that flag, boy, first in France, and then in Korea. That flag stands for freedom. I won't stand by and see it disrespected by a bunch of niggers!"

The guardsman's voice did not change. "I know how you feel, sir, but I'm afraid I can't let you interfere. Like I said: I have my orders."

Rufus's mouth shrank to a petulant grimace, and he took a reluctant step back. "I swear, I don't know what's going on in this country these days," he complained. "Niggers got more rights than us." He spat in the dirt. The other men nodded and grumbled their agreement.

The guardsman just stood there, a few feet beyond the shelter of the awning, rainwater glistening on his poncho and dripping from his helmet, wishing he was back home in Birmingham playing with his newborn daughter. The baby—his first—had his mother's startling blue eyes and soft hair the color of sunshine and he loved her endlessly. But no, instead of being with her as he should have been, he was here, standing out in this miserable rain with these miserable men on this godforsaken stretch of nowhere, watching over a bunch of jigs to make sure nobody gave them what they had coming. "Fuckin' niggers," he muttered in a voice that reached no ears but his own.

Adam was barely aware of the men by the side of the road yelling at the marchers. Angry white men were hardly a novelty by this point, and he was more concerned about the stabbing pain that had reduced his long stride to an awkward limp. Last night in camp, he'd had a blister on the ball of his right foot lanced by a doctor but had declined the doctor's suggestion that he catch a ride back to Selma to rest for a day. Adam was determined to walk every mile of this journey.

A car, its windshield wipers working furiously to sweep water from the glass, pulled abreast of the procession then. A beefy white man leaned out of the driver's side window. Adam braced himself to be cursed, or even for a gun to appear in the man's hands. Instead, the man howled, "Hey, niggers! Think we'll get any rain today?"

His laugh was as loud and sudden as a shotgun blast. The woman next to him rebuked him. "They're wet and they're weary," she said. "I don't think it's funny."

The white man's grin curdled as he glanced back at her. "Oh, hell, Elizabeth, I'se just funnin'." He leaned back into the car and sped away.

"Can this marriage be saved?" One of the marchers intoned the question with the portentous solemnity of a soap opera announcer, and everyone laughed. Adam had learned to be thankful for laughter, to pass up no chance to enjoy whatever amusement this experience offered. It gave respite, if only momentarily, from the hardship of the journey.

And on they walked.

Adam was drenched to his skin. His hat was sodden and shapeless. It sat heavily on his head, the hair beneath it drooping in a tangled, defeated mass. Even his underwear was soaked. He was so wet that water didn't even matter anymore. When the occasional car went by, spraying the marchers with fantails of rain, Adam didn't bother to flinch. What did a little more water mean to him at this point? He was soaked with it. He was drenched.

And the low, dark clouds promised still more to come. The road stretched ahead of them into an abyss of gray. The marchers seemed to have the whole world to themselves. It was a lonely sensation.

Just as Adam was beginning to feel sorry for himself, he caught sight of a white man with one leg stumping gamely along on his crutches, his face set in a mask of stony resolve as if to say to all who merely looked at him that he refused to be defeated by any of this—not the rain, not the road, not his infirmity. It made Adam resolve to stop whining, even to himself.

The road rose steeply. Great trees rustled in the warm breeze. An eighteen-wheeler barreled past with an emphatic blatting of its airhorn. Rain rushed down from a dismal gray sky containing not the merest patch of blue.

And on they walked.

twenty-seven

THAT AFTERNOON, THE MARCHERS FINALLY TURNED OFF
Route 80 onto a farm field, where they immediately sank to their ankles
in mud, a mire so thick it pulled at their shoes with every step.

A man with a megaphone pleaded for patience and promised the
situation would be rectified. Twenty minutes later, a fleet of flatbed
trucks arrived bearing bales of hay. The trucks parked on the road so
as not to get mired in the muck. Adam, exhausted, joined some of the
other exhausted men in forming a relay to unload them. They spread
hay around the campsite as makeshift sidewalks, arranged it beneath
the field tents as makeshift bedding.

The mud was not impressed. It tried to swallow the hay as it tried to
swallow everything else, but eventually, there was enough of it, spread
thickly enough, to offer the tired marchers—those who were not too
picky, at least—some islands of dryness upon the sea of muck. Adam
was one of those who was not especially picky. He sank, mud-spattered,
drenched, and drained, onto a relatively dry patch of hay beneath one
of the field tents.

After a moment, he unlaced his muddy tennis shoes, pulled off his
wet socks, flexed his toes in the open air, and received in response a stab
of pain. The gauze that had been applied to his blistered foot the night
before was drenched by blood and rain. It hung limply, the adhesive
of the tape all but gone. Adam considered unpacking his bedroll, then
decided that was too much work. Instead, he lay on his side on the straw
with his knapsack still strapped on, pulled the sopping wet Gilligan hat
from his sopping wet head, and made a pillow of his clasped hands.

It was midafternoon, sunset still hours off, and all around him was cacophony. Some teenage girl was shrieking as if having a nervous breakdown, and a group of nuns was trying to calm her. Some young guy with an acoustic guitar was singing Sam Cooke's "A Change Is Gonna Come" in a warbling tenor more earnest than tuneful. Someone else, trying, like Adam, to take a nap, growled, "Kid, if you keep up that noise, I'm gonna shove that goddamn guitar up your ass!" Army Jeeps grunted their way along Route 80. Walkie-talkies squawked. The rain beat down steadily upon the tent. Adam ignored it all.

His stomach groaned in hunger, but he ignored that, too. Feeding himself would require him to stand up and go looking for food and that was more energy than he was willing to expend. So instead, Adam lay there and endured the pangs as he endured the noise. A dark-skinned Negro woman walked by carrying a guitar. Her face was framed by kinky hair that had not seen a pressing comb in recent memory—the new style people had taken to calling a "natural." Adam was almost certain the woman was that folk singer, Odetta. She looked regal.

It was his last coherent thought before his eyes slid shut and sleep swallowed him down. All about him, the cacophony went on. The kid on the guitar asserted his right to keep on playing but knew better than to start up again. The nuns managed to get the hysterical girl into a car, headed back to Selma. Two photographers nearly came to blows jockeying for position to snap shots of a Unitarian minister who had dozed off while sitting on a hay bale and was precariously close to toppling into the muck. And a cheer went up when, miracle of miracles, a shipment of air mattresses arrived, rewarding the patience of those stubborn souls who had refused to lie down on hay-covered Alabama mud.

Adam slept dreamlessly through all of it, aware of none of it, his body surrendering itself to deep exhaustion.

It was the smell of food that lured his eyes open hours later. In that first confused moment of awareness, he had no idea where he was, only that his clothes were heavy and damp, that his foot ached with a dull throb, and that he was starving. Adam gingerly pulled his socks and shoes back on and limped out of the tent. The rain had finally stopped. The sky was finally clear. To his surprise, it was still light out. The sun was deep into its long fall toward night, but had not yet touched the horizon. Adam's stomach, more impatient than ever, made a grinding noise like a heavy vehicle shifting gears and he was reminded of the necessity of sustenance. He had barely eaten in almost twenty-four hours.

Adam meant to remedy that, but first, he sought out a doctor. The physician took one look at the foot and pursed his lips doubtfully. "I don't suppose there's any chance of getting you to stay off it for a few days," he said.

Adam shook his head. "I want to finish what I started," he said.

"Well, as a human being, I admire your fortitude," the man told him, "but as a doctor, I really wish you'd reconsider."

"Can't do that," said Adam.

"Didn't think so," said the doctor.

He snipped dead skin from the edges of the lanced blister, cleaned it thoroughly with water and soap, then applied a topical antibiotic and a loose gauze. When Adam reached to put his damp socks back on, the doctor snatched them from his hand and tossed them into a waste bin. Before Adam could get a startled question out, the doctor handed him a new pair of white athletic socks. "Use these," he said. "So many folks coming in with blistered feet and filthy socks that we sent somebody into Montgomery to buy out a department store. And I know this sounds ridiculous given that we're basically sitting in a field of mud, but do try to keep your foot dry and clean."

"I'll do my best," said Adam, pulling one of the new socks over his wounded foot. As he finished tying his shoes, the doctor produced a hypodermic needle with a syringe and a vial of liquid. "What's that?" asked Adam warily as the man drew the liquid into the syringe.

"Penicillin," said the doctor. "Between the mud and the rain, you've probably got some nasty little beasties swimming around inside that wound. Might as well get a jump on them. Roll up that sleeve for me, would you?"

Minutes later, a Band-Aid on his bicep, Adam finally went off in search of food. He ended up with a plate of tuna sandwiches, two bags of potato chips, and a can of off-brand cola. Adam planted himself on an air mattress and began to dig in. It was, he thought, the best meal he'd ever eaten.

"Adam," said a voice from behind him.

Surprised, he spun around, and through a mouthful of tuna, said the first thing that came to mind. "Dad."

His father was standing above him. He smiled a thin smile as he lowered himself to the mattress. "You mean 'George,' don't you?"

"What are you talking about?"

"I had a chat with Luther. He told me that's what you call me now. He said, all the way back to Mobile, it was 'George' this and 'George' that. I guess we're on a first-name basis now?"

Adam sighed. "Look," he said, "I'm sorry. I was just—"

Dad waved the words off. "Don't bother," he said.

"But I want to explain—"

"There's no need. Adam, we're okay, you and me. I know who I am: I'm your father, even if you try to tell me I'm not. So, I'm not angry with you. I just figured I'd give you a few days to figure it out."

Adam sighed in chagrin. "Okay, Dad, fair enough. But what are you doing here? You weren't one of the Lowndes County marchers."

Dad shook his head. "No, I wasn't. But since I had a day off from marching, I volunteered for support staff. We're the ones who drove these air mattresses out here to keep you all from sleeping in the mud."

"You march tomorrow?"

"Yes. My plan is to march the rest of the way into Montgomery. Your mother is going to meet me there. She and Luther are driving up." Dad watched him closely, as if to see how he would take the news.

"Great," said Adam, his voice neutral.

"Look," said Dad, "I know you're having trouble with all this and I get it. It's a lot to take in. And I know it hurts you that your mother was never really . . . warm toward you."

"Dad, we don't really have to talk about this now."

"Yes, I think we do," his father said. He sighed, ran a hand through his hair, took a moment to gather his thoughts. Finally, he said, "Your uncle also told me what happened up on that mountain, what your mother did to convince that man to drop the charges. I don't mind telling you, it broke my heart."

"Broke mine, too," said Adam. "I wish she hadn't done it."

"Yeah," said George. "But if she hadn't, you'd be on your way to some prison farm right now, wouldn't you?"

He waited for a response. Adam had none.

Dad gave a thoughtful smile. "You and me, we had some good times when you were a kid, didn't we? I mean, I know it wasn't always easy for you, being seen out in public with your white father . . ."

"Dad, no. I didn't—"

His father waved the protest away. "It's okay," he said. "I understood. My point is, we had fun together. We went to baseball games, we built models, we worked on your science projects, all those father-and-son things. Your mom didn't do any of that stuff with you, did she?"

Adam felt his eyes burning. He swallowed. "No," he said.

"Sometimes, it felt like she didn't even want to touch you, didn't it?"

Adam's voice was a grainy whisper. "Yes."

"So now, you find out about all this, and you think maybe she didn't really love you. Maybe that's the reason she stood back from you. But love doesn't always look the same in every person or every relationship, son. What your mother did up on that mountain, what she did by even choosing to bring you into the world . . . that was pure love, Adam. Pure love. None of this has been easy for her."

"I know."

Dad stabbed him with a look. "Do you? Do you really?"

"Yeah, sure, I—"

But his father cut him off. "I imagine it was hard on you," he said, "finding out about this man who raped your mother."

"Of course it was."

"I'll bet it made you question everything you thought you knew."

"It made me feel like I was evidence of a crime," said Adam.

Dad nodded. "I can understand that. But can you imagine how hard it must have been to be the *victim* of that crime? I think about that sometimes. I think about it a lot, to tell you the truth. I mean, he didn't just violate her, Adam, terrible as that would have been. But he also brutalized her something awful."

"Dad . . ." These were things Adam was not comfortable hearing.

But his father ignored him. "Your mother doesn't know it, but I've seen the police report. Left you with your uncle one time and I went and looked it up. She had two black eyes. Lacerations and contusions about the head and face. A broken wrist. Vaginal and anal tearing."

"Dad!" Adam raised his voice in alarm.

Still his father ignored him. "Can you imagine what that must have been like?" he asked. "And then to find out, while you're still dealing with that trauma, that you're pregnant by the man who raped you? That means you can never escape him, never escape what he did. Some part of him, some part of that awful experience, is going to be with you forever."

"You don't think I know that?" cried Adam. "You don't think I feel bad about it?"

And yet once again, his father would not stop. "Can you imagine," he said, "what it takes for a woman to endure all of that? To go through with having that child, to raise him on her own while working full time and taking care of a blind grandfather? And then, to put her trust in a man again? And a *white* man at that? To leave the only home she's ever known, to travel over a thousand miles with that man to some place she's never been and build a new life there? Can you imagine what that must have taken?" His father's eyes glowed with wonder. "And then, to come flying back down here, to this place she hates, to confront her worst nightmares, all because her child is in trouble . . . What kind of person does that, Adam?" He shook his head. "I am in awe of that woman."

"Dad, why are you telling me all this?"

"I'm telling you because you need to know. And because you owe her something, Adam. We both do."

"What do you mean?"

This brought a sigh. His father regarded him with an expression that mingled both fondness and reproach. "I guess I'm telling you that there's something your mother needs to hear, son—something she *deserves* to hear. Like I said, she hasn't heard it often enough from me, and she's *never* heard it from you."

"And what is that?"

Dad smiled. "Think about it," he said. "If you're half the man I think you are, you'll figure it out."

Adam was confused, but before he could ask another question, his father rose from the mattress with a grunt. "Now, if you'll excuse me," he said, "I've got to catch a ride back to town. I'll see you in Montgomery, son. Be careful out here."

"Dad, wait."

But his father ignored him one final time and Adam was left sitting there, stunned. After a moment, he picked up the sandwich he had been eating. Then he put it back down, disgusted, and pushed the plate aside. He had no appetite. He felt as if he might never have one again.

The litany of his mother's suffering sat heavily on Adam's chest. Black eyes? Anal tearing? How could he reconcile such horrors with the mom who had bundled him up on snowy days and grounded him when he acted up in school, the mom who was distant and prickly sometimes, yes, but who was always there? Adam was angry with his father for telling him these things, resented being dragged into this small circle of cruel knowledge.

He was immediately aware of his own hypocrisy. After all, he had just gotten over being angry with them both for what they had *not* told him.

And then there was that challenge his father laid down, the thing his mother "deserved" to hear. For the life of him, Adam could not figure out what Dad meant.

"If you're half the man I think you are, you'll figure it out."

Like his father was challenging him. Or more accurately, thought Adam, *testing* him.

But what was it he was supposed to do? The plate of sandwiches offered no clue. And Adam Simon slept restlessly that night.

The marchers returned to the road the following morning under a blessedly dry and sunny sky. They hadn't been walking long before they passed a sign that read, "Entering Montgomery County."

This was good for a victory shout. They had survived "Bloody Lowndes."

No snakes, no snipers, no bombs. Just rain.

Even better, now that that rural county was behind them, Route 80 widened again to four lanes, which meant no more restriction on the number of marchers. Very soon, reinforcements came pouring in by the hundreds—cars, buses, and vans pulling alongside to disgorge fresh bodies unspattered by mud, unburdened by fatigue, feet not yet blistered, skin not yet burned by exposure to the sun, spirits not yet dimmed by hardship.

It was, for those who had been walking since Sunday, as if someone had given them a shot of adrenaline. They stood straighter. They walked taller. Morale lifted like a balloon on a string. And they sang their freedom songs with new gusto: "Ain't Gonna Let Nobody Turn

Me Around," "Oh, Freedom," "Kumbaya," "Walk With Me, Lord."

At one point, Adam picked out from the chorus of voices one he knew—husky, warm, and just now, raised in passionate defiance. He craned his neck until he spotted the singer, a short white man with dark hair and a roman nose who was marching in the front ranks with King. From where Adam was, behind them and to the left, he couldn't quite see the man's full face, but he didn't really need to.

He turned to a white woman next to him, pointing. "Isn't that the guy who sang"—Adam snapped his fingers, trying to recall the title— "'I Left My Heart in San Francisco'?"

The woman, her eyes half-closed above a blissful smile, nodded as if in a dream state. "Tony Bennett," she said.

"Yeah," said Adam. "Wow."

He looked behind him and got another wow. The number of marchers had swollen until he could no longer see to the end of the line. There were at least a thousand of them out here now, a train that stretched back maybe a mile. And reinforcements kept coming.

On they walked. Past cotton fields and tumbledown shacks. Past ramshackle country stores and a mechanic's garage. Past a knot of sullen white people, one dolefully carrying the Confederate battle flag, which hung flaccid and indifferent. A paunchy white woman in sunglasses held aloft a crudely lettered sign that read, "White People Have Rights Too."

"Hey, everybody, listen at this," a young Negro woman said, holding up one of those little transistor radios that fit in the palm of your hand.

The people around her shushed and Adam heard an announcer report on a resolution just passed by the Alabama legislature branding the march an orgy of wild sex parties from which "young women are returning to their respective states apparently as unwed expectant mothers."

Loud laughter went up at the absurdity. "That's crazy!" cried Adam. "We've only been on the road since Sunday, but somehow these girls are already home and the rabbit's already died? I guess nature works faster in Alabama."

"No, it's just that these Southern segregationists are obsessed with the idea of fornication between Negroes and white people," said John

Lewis, a broad grin splitting his face. "They always have been. Why else do you think you see so many shades of brown on this march?"

Adam, the high yella biological son of a white rapist, had been laughing along with everyone else, but at Lewis's words, his laughter stilled itself guiltily. He thought again of his mother's suffering and his father's challenge.

If you're half the man I think you are . . .

And on they walked.

In the front rank of the procession, one of the ministers teased King. "Moses, can you let your people rest for a minute? Can you just let the homiletic smoke from your cigarette drift out of your mouth and engulf the multitude and let them rest?" King smiled at the jibe. He did not slacken his pace.

A man with a megaphone walked back and forth along the line. "Tomorrow, when we get to Montgomery," he said, "there are some precautions you should take for your own safety. Don't talk to people you don't know. Travel in groups: don't go off anywhere by yourself. If some segregationist says something to you, don't answer back; that just adds fuel to the fire. And when the mass meeting is over, do not linger in town. Get out and go home as quickly as you can."

He had to raise his voice to be heard over the sound of their laughter, their singing, the tromping of their feet against the pavement. They were an army now, a legion of righteous indignation come to petition Alabama's government for a redress of grievances, and there was something majestic in the very motliness of them, different people from different places with different minds and different stories all come together upon a single uncompromised belief: every American, Negro or not, had the right to be heard. Jim, the white amputee, was still stumping along, flanked by a young white man and a young Negro man, both bearing American flags. There was a rough-hewn gravity to it all, a kind of pomp that was all the more imposing and impressive because it was made not of gold and silver and high and mighty, but of denim and sweat and determination and grit.

Farm fields began to give way to homes and stores. They passed the Montgomery airport and moved into the outskirts of the city. Soon enough, the isolated scatter of people that had met them along the road turned into crowds of people who melted into the march.

Thus, it was a large and unwieldy parade that began filing into the fourth and final campground—the campus of City of St. Jude, a Catholic hospital—that afternoon at about three. There, they were met by still more Negroes, locals from Montgomery, who waved and cheered.

Someone produced a fife and played "Yankee Doodle." The man marched in place as the columns of the nonviolent army passed him by.

twenty-eight

THE LAST NIGHT IN CAMP TURNED OUT TO BE A FRIGHTEN-
ing and chaotic affair. To George, it felt at times more like a street riot
waiting to happen than a high-minded crusade for the vindication of
human rights.

March organizers had scheduled a show—a rally called "Stars for
Freedom"—featuring a cavalcade of Hollywood headliners. So people
came, both from Montgomery itself and from the surrounding coun-
tryside, and soon, the encampment grew packed, jammed with people.
Worse, a mobile generator failed, leaving the field completely dark but
for a disinterested half-moon parked in the sky above, flashlight beams
probing the blackness, and the headlamps of passing vehicles carving
the mass of people—some thirty thousand of them by this point—into
long, weird shadows on the ground.

For hours, they milled about, growing increasingly agitated, even
as march marshals pleaded for patience and calm. But things kept getting worse. A brief but fierce storm blew in out of nowhere, breaking
two poles and nearly collapsing the field tent they were supporting.
People began to pass out from heat and exhaustion, forcing stretcher
bearers to push and plead their way through the crowd to carry the
stricken to the camp hospital. There was some shoving and pushing and
a few people found themselves jammed up against the stage, which was
actually a platform built atop stacks of coffin crates loaned by a local
Negro funeral home. Shelley Winters, the actress, administered first aid
to some stricken girls who wound up laid out on the stage because there
was no other place to put them.

Meanwhile, children, neither knowing nor caring one bit about heat exhaustion, voting rights, or Shelley Winters, were having the time of their lives. Freed for a night from the tyranny of bedtime, they climbed into the trees ringing the vast lawn, spun the merry-go-round in the playground and came off reeling with dizziness and shrieking with laughter, played jacks and jumped rope in golden squares of light cast by the hospital's windows.

And like everyone else, they waited as the hours dragged themselves by, and the crowd's mood of surly impatience only deepened. They had been promised a show, a grand closing-night performance by some of the many celebrities who had descended upon the march to bestow Hollywood's benediction. But there could be no show where there was no power, and as the darkness showed no sign of abating, some resolved to remedy that on their own.

They clambered onto the stage and there, danced with abandon to tinny music from the speakers of a transistor radio. Soon, marshals were pleading with the interlopers to clear the stage. None of them—they all seemed to be teenagers—paid any heed.

"Bet'cha old Sheriff Clark and them Alabama state troopers could clear them young'uns off that stage in no time flat," cracked a man who paused near George. They stood at the edge of the playground, where George had fled to escape the pushing and shoving. He could barely see the stranger in the darkness, couldn't even tell if he was Negro or white.

"I'm sure he could," he said. He kept his voice neutral, unsure if the man's comment was a wry joke or a serious suggestion from some local white man who had infiltrated the camp.

Then, to George's relief, to everyone's relief, the lights came on. He checked his watch. It was midnight.

Things progressed quickly from there. The teenagers were dispossessed of the stage, the marshals managed to cut an aisle through the crowd for the entertainers to reach the platform, and the show finally went on. Dozens of singers, actors, and dignitaries trooped forward to offer brief songs or skits or just words of encouragement. Peter, Paul and Mary performed "Blowin' in the Wind." Coretta Scott King read a poem by Langston Hughes. Harry Belafonte sang one of his calypso numbers, "Jamaica Farewell." The conductor Leonard Bernstein had no performance planned. "I just wanted to come down to be with you," he told the crowd. Mike Nichols and Elaine May briefly resurrected their old comedy team with a sketch mocking Governor George Wallace. Sammy Davis, Jr. performed, as did Nipsey Russell. And author James Baldwin beamed. "This great march," he intoned in his precise and manicured baritone, "is the beginning of the end of Negro enslavement."

The crowd went wild at that. Why not? thought George. In that shining moment, it did not seem at all an outlandish thing to believe.

Six hours later, on barely five hours sleep, George stood in line waiting for a serving of trash-can oatmeal as, all around him, the march stirred itself to life one last time, four thousand people stretching and yawning and scratching and going in search of sustenance or to perform their morning ablutions. Some warmed themselves at makeshift firepits. Some read from pocket New Testaments. Some talked quietly in groups of two or three as they sipped coffee from Styrofoam cups.

George felt anticipation fluttering in his chest, like a butterfly in a cage. It was going to be a good day. He didn't know how he knew this, but he did.

The last segment of the march began almost at noon—two hours later than scheduled—following a debate over protocol. The marshals' original plan, to give orange vests and a place of honor up front with Dr. King to those who had walked all fifty-four miles, was challenged by a handful of self-important dignitaries who, having parachuted in for the final leg of the journey, now wanted to claim the honor for themselves.

"No, that simply will not do," one of them complained as the last of the coveted orange vests was handed out to a Negro teenager in denim coveralls. "Dr. Jonas was explicitly promised that he would walk arm in arm with Dr. King."

Another cried, "Our president told us Dr. King wanted us to march with him."

The marshal began pleading. "Gentlemen," he said, "please be reasonable."

It was too much for one of the young men in the orange vests. "All you dignitaries got to get in line behind *me*," he ordered. "I sure didn't see any of you fellows in Selma and I didn't see you on the way to Montgomery. Ain't nobody going to get in front of me but Dr. King himself."

The older man drew himself up as if profoundly offended and turned on the marshals, not deigning to even acknowledge the teenager who had just called him out. "You expect me to march behind kids?" he complained.

But the young man did not back down. "These kids have marched all the way from Selma, sir. What have you done?"

"Look at his shoes," someone else cried. "Ain't a speck of mud on them shoes. I tell you what he's done. He done sat somewhere comfortable and clean while we out here walkin' through the swamps. You better line up in the back, Jack."

"Make way for the originals!" someone called out.

It became the young people's chant.

"Make way for the originals," they cried. "Make way for the originals!"

George, who was down in the middle of the scrum with Lester and Reverend Porter, didn't know what to do. But thankfully, Reverend Porter did and he raised a hand to plead for quiet. It took a moment for the chants to die down. Then he said, "All those of you trying to bully these young people ought to be ashamed of yourselves. These are the veterans of the Selma struggle. We are here to support them, not supplant them."

As the orange vests applauded and nodded, Roy Wilkins, the head of the NAACP, said, "That's exactly right. You young people deserve to go first. I, for one, will be honored to march behind you."

This brought more applause and shouts of approval. The tension seemed to leak out of the confrontation like air from a balloon.

But peace and order were short-lived. When King finally appeared, ready to lead the march, the dignitaries surged toward him like iron filings to a magnet, pushing for position. He was like a planet unto himself, exerting gravitational force. The scrum of people trying to get close was so unruly that George saw an older Negro woman in glasses shoved out of the crowd. She stumbled to the sidewalk, where she stood looking forlorn. It was Rosa Parks.

After still more long minutes of delay, order was restored. It was decided that the orange vests would precede Dr. King as a kind of vanguard. He would march accompanied by assorted aides, by Wilkins and UN under-secretary-general Dr. Ralph Bunche, by his wife, Coretta, and by Cager Lee, the eighty-two-year-old grandfather of Jimmie Lee Jackson, whose murder by an Alabama state trooper had ignited the whole crusade.

And finally, it was time.

Helicopters rumbled across the sky overhead. Support vehicles started their engines. Banners and flags were raised high. Photographers squinted through their viewfinders. Someone up ahead said, "Let's go." George muttered a brief prayer. "God be with us," he said.

And the line began to move.

twenty-nine

LUTHER AND THELMA SAT WAITING ON THE STEPS OF MARTIN Luther King's old church, Dexter Avenue Baptist. They had been there for a few hours now, having arrived in Montgomery just as daylight did. Luther had parked in a colored neighborhood—he could tell because the street was unpaved—and they had walked downtown following a service station map.

"Let's sit here," he had announced when they stood before the red brick building with twin staircases curving up from the sidewalk.

"Yes, massa," Thelma replied.

He had sighed, knowing this meant his sister was still upset with him for the way he had treated her the last few days—like a child, to hear her tell it. But all he had done was remove from the house every razor, knife, scissors, and screwdriver he owned. And move his pistol to his locked desk down in the barbershop. And flush all his sleeping pills, pain pills, and blood pressure medication. And forbid her to be alone, requiring her to sit with him all day in the shop.

"Luther, this is crazy," she had told him Tuesday night. "I already promised you I would take the doctor's advice and talk to someone when I get home. And besides, if a person really wants to hurt themselves, you can't stop them, no matter how many knives or pills you get rid of. Hell, I could just as easily hang myself. Did you ever think of that?"

So he had taken her bedsheets.

They had spoken hardly an extraneous word since. Now the siblings sat in silence on one of the staircases serving the church, which stood almost literally in the shadow of the Alabama capitol. George had called from a phone booth the night before to say he and Adam would meet them here after the march.

The street, which had been dark and quiet in the predawn hours when they arrived, had grown steadily more crowded in the hours since then, and Luther was pleased with himself for getting there early enough to secure a good vantage point from which to watch the speech. Security was tight, intersections blocked by military Jeeps and sawhorses, the sidewalks by panels of plywood, to prevent anyone from leaping into the street. Soldiers patrolled the area, eyeing everything and everyone with suspicion. The serious, clean-shaven men with helmets pulled low and rifles slung across their backs seemed so young, almost like boys playing soldier. Luther knew that simply reflected the fact that he himself was getting old.

Just then, he heard a man on the radio announce that the march, officially scheduled to arrive at the statehouse by noon, was more likely to get there an hour or two later. CP time, he thought, shaking his head and checking his watch. He reached into the backpack he had brought with him, producing a bologna-and-cheese sandwich and a can of Coca-Cola. He offered both to Thelma along with his can opener. She accepted them after a moment's hesitation. "Thank you," she said.

Luther nodded. "Welcome," he said, hoping her civil response signaled a truce of some sort. He got a sandwich and a can of soda pop for himself. He was eager to get this over with, to hear the speech, to say goodbye to his family, and begin the journey home. Luther had never had much use for the civil rights movement. Or for its leader.

There was nothing personal in his disdain for King. Unlike Malcolm X, who had often seemed to take wicked delight in personally demeaning him, Luther thought the preacher was a decent enough man—even a brave one. But King spoke a language to which Luther Hayes had no access and in which he had no interest. It wasn't just that he wove Biblical allusions through his words while Luther had lost God the same night he lost his parents.

It was also because so much of King's approach lay in appealing to white people's conscience and Luther wasn't at all sure most of them even had one. So he had little patience for King's so-called "dream," which, as near as he could tell from excerpts of the 1963 speech that he had seen on television and read in the newspaper, had to do with some promised land beyond race where black children and white children would be brothers and sisters, where the color of their skin would have no bearing on the way his own "four little children" would be received, and where Southern governors would reform themselves and their societies out of the habit of violence—physical, mental, social, economic— against colored people. It was, King seemed to believe, a vision that would come true if only Negroes pleaded hard enough for it, if they marched on muddy roads and carried signs for it, if they pointed out like it was news a fact that had been plainly obvious for almost two hundred years. Namely, that America was a glaring hypocrisy, an ongoing failure to be, or even try to be, what it said it was.

Sweet land of liberty, of thee I sing?
All men are created equal?
With liberty and justice for all?
What nonsensical bullshit.

He cast a covert glance at his sister, beaten, raped, emotionally brutalized to the point of suicide by white men, sitting there now sipping soda pop, and he felt his chest grow tight.

There was no dream. This, Luther Hayes knew with a certainty. There was only the nightmare that, for colored people, had begun on a beach in Virginia in 1619 and showed no signs of ending. That was America.

It had always made Johan cringe when he said things like that. The old man believed in this country with a kind of hopeless devotion Luther supposed was only natural for an immigrant who had been taken in from a storm-tossed sea.

"America is no nightmare," Johan had scolded him once as Luther was snipping his dark, wiry hair. "Why would you say such a thing?" Johan's Negro driver, Benjamin, had been sitting in the next chair, where Smitty was giving him a trim. He and Luther shared a sidelong glance.

Then Luther said, "We ain't all come here by choice, Johan."

"Of course not," said Johan. "I know this."

"All right, then," said Luther. "So you know some of us ain't never seen no liberty and justice for all. This country been hypocritical from jump street."

"You tell him, brother!" piped up a man who sat waiting his turn beneath a shelf where the radio was crooning "Only You (And You Alone)" by the Platters.

"Hypocritical, yes," conceded Johan, his tone turning lawyerly. "But hypocrisy does not preclude hope. And that is good, because without hope, we are dead. Without hope, what is the point?"

"Hope," said Luther. He had chuckled. "That's an easy word to say, old man. At least it is when you can look around you and actually see shit gettin' better. But that ain't never been the case for Negroes."

"It will be," Johan had promised.

"Really? How long will it take?" Luther had demanded, his hands working fast, his eyes meeting those of a man in the corner whom he knew to be just two months removed from the chain gang. The man was following their conversation with unfathomable eyes. "You come here as a boy," Luther continued, "and you worked hard and you made yourself rich. And that's great. But you think it's that same way for everybody. You think we all have that same opportunity, and we don't. Me and mine, we been waitin' a long time."

"I know we don't all have the same opportunity," Johan said. "I'm not foolish, Luther. But what I'm saying is, it will come."

"How long?" demanded Luther again.

"You ask me to put a time limit on it? I can't do that. I can't read the future. But what I can say is that it will happen. America is a land of constant reinvention. It is an ongoing revolution. Here is where a boy can arrive, as you said, penniless and unable to speak the language and through hard work, perseverance, and luck, make something useful of himself. It is also where men like your own Dr. Ralph Bunche can grow up from nothing to win a Nobel Prize or, like Joe Louis, become the heavyweight champion of the world. Only here are such things possible."

The man in the corner had given a dismissive snort at Johan's passionate monologue and lifted a magazine to his eyes. Luther had laughed again. "He don't mean no harm," he explained.

Johan had surprised them all by addressing the skeptical man directly. "You, sir, in the corner. He's right. I mean no disrespect. I understand that you are impatient, that every colored man is impatient for this country to finally treat him like a man, and I don't blame you, not a bit. All I am saying is, don't give up on your country. Prod it to do better, to live up to its high ideal of all men being equal. The ideal is a good one. It is the people who are not so good, who refuse to live up to what they claim to believe. And they must not be allowed to get away with it. America belongs to you as much as it does to me. It is still the greatest country in the world."

The other man's mouth had sprung open for a sharp retort. Luther had cut him off. "Let's talk about somethin' else," he said.

Benjamin had piped up helpfully, "Do you all think Brooklyn is going to finally win the Series this year? Jackie gettin' a little long in the tooth. Not going to have many more chances."

The other man had scowled, but he didn't push it. The talk turned to baseball. And the moment passed.

But Luther had always remembered that particular exchange in late August of 1955 because of what happened the next time he saw Johan, two weeks later. The whole world had changed by then—certainly the whole Negro world—and when he spotted through the window Johan's Packard sitting in traffic, waiting to turn into the alley, Luther heaved a heavy sigh. He supposed he ought to not be surprised to see him appearing at the shop just as if everything was the same as before. Johan was a good man, but he was a good white man, which meant he would always be a little oblivious.

"I see your friend is here," muttered Smitty from the next chair over as the car swung left into the alley.

Wearily, Luther had nodded. "Wish he had gone somewhere else," he said. "Just this one time."

Instead, the bell over the door in back jangled a moment later and Johan walked in as he always did, Benjamin trailing behind looking as if he'd rather be anywhere else. Luther could see in Johan's eyes that he knew instantly something was wrong. He'd have been a fool not to. A leaden pall had fallen on Youngblood's Barbershop these last few days and it remained there today. Count Basie was not playing on the radio. No one was crowing over a checkmate or slamming down a domino.

Instead, they trained their eyes on the white man like machine guns, tracked him as he walked to a seat. With a hesitant smile, Johan nodded to faces he knew. No one nodded back.

Years ago, when Johan had started coming here for his haircuts, there had been some grumbling among the regulars about what this overdressed white man was doing here in their place on their side of town. Wasn't it bad enough they had to deal with honkies everywhere else? Did one have to follow them into the barbershop, too?

But they all knew Luther liked him, was even related to him by marriage, so nobody made too much of a fuss. It was Luther's shop, after all, and besides, the old white man seemed harmless enough in an old white man kind of way. After a time, he had become a regular himself, which is to say, just another piece of the furniture, just something else you expected to see when you went down to Youngblood's for a trim.

But this day in September of 1955 was different. Luther had watched Johan take a wary seat, turning his hat in his hand and stealing sidelong glances at the unfriendly faces studying him, not quite sure what was going on. Luther couldn't help it. He felt sorry for him.

"Give me a minute," he told the man whose hair he was cutting.

Luther was conscious of the whole shop watching as he came out from behind the chair, but he ignored the stares as best he could. Wiping his hands on his barber's smock, he stopped at a table cluttered with an unruly assortment of magazines—*Ebony*, *Time*, *Newsweek*— and plucked a small one off the top. It was called *Jet* and it carried a black-and-white cover photo of a pretty Negro girl in a bathing suit and a headline promising "Strange Facts About the Moore-Marciano Fight." But no one who bought that particular magazine cared about Archie Moore and Rocky Marciano. Luther opened it to a page he knew by heart and approached Johan.

The old man looked up at him. "This is about that boy, isn't it?"

Luther didn't reply. He just placed the open magazine on Johan's lap and let the picture do the talking. It depicted the body of Emmett Louis Till. But what had once been a cheerful, prankish teenager had been hammered and gouged and battered and crushed, then dumped like garbage into a river, so that all that was left was this dead and bloated lump captured by the camera, this blasphemous obscenity in white shirt and dark jacket, this mangled, once-human thing upon which had been visited like the biblical scapegoat all the hatred, fury, and fear of the white race entire.

"*Istenem.*" Johan spoke in a voice soft with horror.

"Yeah," said Luther, his own voice weary, "*istenem.*" It was something his friend said when he was truly stunned, a word in his native Hungarian that meant, "My God."

"So maybe," said Luther carefully after a moment, "this ain't the best place for you to get your trim right now. Maybe you should go somewhere else. Just for today, you know what I'm sayin'?"

It took a long moment for the old man to answer, and Luther knew he was still processing the awful image. Finally, he nodded dumbly. "I'm sorry," he said, coming stiffly to his feet. "You're right, of course. I should have thought of it myself."

He surveyed the room as if there was something he wanted to say to the men watching him so closely. To Luther, he looked suddenly haggard, even older than his then-seventy-one years. His mouth hung open, but no words came out. He turned the homburg twice in his hands. Finally, he put it back on his head and nodded to Benjamin, who followed him toward the rear door. At the last moment, the driver turned, and his eyes found Luther's. There was something inexpressibly sad in his gaze. "Tried to tell him it was a bad idea," he said, as if by way of apology. And then both men were gone.

It was almost Christmas before Luther next saw Johan. That was when Johan showed him the note he had sent the dead boy's grieving mother.

He and Luther had never again debated American dreams.

Ten years later, his friend was sinking slowly into himself, disappearing into his own mind bit by bit, like a sandcastle in the encroaching tide. And here Luther was, sitting on church house steps, waiting for Martin Luther King to talk to him about dreams.

Dreams.

It had been only a few days since he had discovered the man who killed his parents alive if not quite well in a nursing home. Only a few days since he'd found himself weeping like a baby into the same soil that drank their blood. Only a few days since he'd seen his nephew beaten and swollen-eyed in jail for telling white men the truth. Only a few days since his sister had had to fall to her knees and kiss a white man's hand while he, her big brother and protector, had helplessly, impotently watched. Only a few days since Thelma had tried to kill herself.

So Luther Hayes was unimpressed by dreams. Yet for all his skepticism, he was also aware of a deep hunger in him to be proven wrong.

Indeed, he sat there in a kind of quiet desperation, willing Martin Luther King—*needing* Martin Luther King—to speak to his anger and despair, to provide some sort of safety valve to bleed off the steam pressure of a rage that made his chest ache.

The drumming of helicopter blades overhead broke Luther's reverie. He glanced up in time to see the aircraft swoop low over George Wallace's house before banking south. A truck with the logo of one of the three television networks lumbered down Decatur and parked at the barricade. Looking down the sidewalk, he saw clusters of spectators, most of them colored, forming behind the barricades. There were still hours left to go, but the signs were unmistakable.

The dreamer was on his way.

thirty

PEOPLE KEPT MELTING INTO THE GREAT PROCESSION AS IT wended its way in from the outskirts of town, so that before long, the marchers walked more than ten thousand strong.

Jim with his one leg was there on his crutches. John Lewis with a heavy gauze protecting his broken skull was there. Adam Simon was there, marching proudly in the front ranks, the pain in his foot just a footnote to the moment, a small price to pay for the privilege of being present. George Simon was there, too, unable to stop smiling. James Baldwin was there, walking among the masses like he was just another colored man. Pastor Columbus Porter and Reverend Lester Williams were there, thinking that it was all worth it, that the time, effort, and expense of driving down to Alabama, of staying in town in hopes the march would finally take place, was more than justified by the electric exultation of this moment.

And yes, Martin Luther King was there, smiling and waving at people he knew from the days when he had lived and pastored and led a historic bus boycott here. They called to him familiarly from the sidewalks, from the pool hall and the barbershop, from the porches of tumbledown houses, shanties of exposed wood on dirt streets.

As the procession moved into downtown, leaflets tumbled from the window of one of the office buildings. They carried an image of a much younger King seated attentively among an integrated audience in what looked to be a classroom. "Martin Luther King at Communist Training School," blared the headline. People shook their heads. People laughed and crumpled the paper. People marched on.

They reached the fountain at Court Square, turned east onto

Dexter Avenue. The white dome of the Alabama capitol was visible six blocks down.

The marchers spanned the wide avenue. They came singing "Battle Hymn of the Republic" and "God Bless America." They came laughing and joyous. They came in suits and ties and overalls, came toothless and ancient, came toothless and brand new to the world. They came bearing children on their shoulders. "This is history," they whispered eagerly to their young. "Always remember this day."

They came marching under flags from various U.S. states— Kentucky, New Jersey, Oregon, Hawaii. Someone even lofted the red maple leaf flag of Canada. And of course, American flags fluttered everywhere. Except, that is, from the dome of the Alabama capitol. Only the state flag and a Confederate battle flag hung there.

"Looks like Alabama has seceded again," Adam said to no one in particular. People around him laughed.

The marchers kept coming. The minutes stretched to half an hour. The half hour doubled to over an hour. And still, they kept coming.

On a makeshift platform mounted in front of the statehouse, King's aide, Andrew Young, announced the purpose of the convocation over loudspeakers. "This is a revolution," he called, "a revolution that won't fire a shot. We come to love the hell out of the state of Alabama."

And the crowd, still gathering, thundered its approval.

Then Harry Belafonte, tall and handsome, skin the color of walnut shells, joined a group of white folk singers, including Mary Travers and Joan Baez, and sang hope songs to the strumming of a guitar. They sang "Go Tell It on the Mountain." They sang "Blowin' in the Wind." They sang "Michael, Row the Boat Ashore." They sang "Come and Go with Me."

"*Come and go with me to that land where I'm bound*," they sang, harmonies soft and soaring.

Ain't no kneelin' in that land.
Ain't no mournin' in that land.
There'll be singin' in that land.

Impulsively, Mary Travers kissed Harry Belafonte on the cheek. It was a gesture of affection, not sex. But white people swamped network switchboards with complaints over the awful implications of this blonde woman's lips touching that brown man's skin. CBS switched to a soap opera.

And still the crowd kept coming. Luther and Thelma moved to the landing atop the church stairs—the staircase was rapidly filling with spectators—to get a better view. Down in the crowd, Adam was grateful to be tall.

On the platform, Whitney Young of the National Urban League was rallying the crowd, reminding them that this march was not an ending, but a beginning.

"Will you march to the polls?" he demanded.

And the cry came back: "*Yes!*"

A parade of other dignitaries trooped to the microphone: the union leader A. Philip Randolph spoke, Ralph Bunche, Roy Wilkins, James Peck of CORE. Rosa Parks addressed the crowd, her voice slow and deliberate.

"The last few days in Selma," she confided, "actually, I almost lost faith. I almost didn't come here today because so many people told me not to come. I said to myself, I could not come here seeing what happened to people in Selma, who were armed with only love. However, I came here with a hope and a faith and you have given me back that faith today."

"What do you want?" Ralph Abernathy demanded of the crowd.

"Freedom!" they shouted.

"I can't hear ya!" he called, cupping a hand to his ear. "What do you want?"

And the cry was louder this time, more emphatic. "*Freedom!*"

"When do you want it?"

"Now!"

"How much of it do you want?"

"All of it!"

Abernathy grinned a folksy grin. "Aw shucks, now!"

Then he launched into a lavish introduction of the man he called "our leader," and Martin Luther King stepped to the microphone. Luther, watching from the landing of the church steps, found him smaller than he'd have expected, a slight man in a dark suit with taller, more imposing men towering over him from behind. Then King spoke in the commanding baritone so familiar from a hundred newsreels and somehow, he became taller.

"They told us we wouldn't get here," mused King. "There were those who said that we would get here only over their dead bodies. But all the world today knows that we *are* here and we are standing before the forces of power in the state of Alabama saying, 'We ain't gon' let nobody turn us around!'"

"Yes, sir!" cried his amen corner. "Yes, sir!" Approving cheers broke out among the audience.

The Selma campaign, King told his listeners, was exposing the root cause of racial segregation in the South. It had not come about, he explained, as a natural result of enmity between the races. Instead, it had been born as a political strategy, a divide-and-conquer ploy used by conservative Democrats to cleave white working men from colored ones and thereby reduce the ability of all of them to demand better conditions or higher wages.

He went on to explain how the politicians and the industrialists used the doctrine of white supremacy to keep white and Negro workers from coming together and forming what would have been an irresistible coalition for change. White workers labored under the threat that if they became too boisterous in demanding higher pay or better working conditions, the bosses would fire them and hire Negroes to work for even less pay in worse conditions. Thus, instead of working in cooperation, the Negroes and the whites were kept always in competition.

King, noted Luther with some surprise, was not so much preaching as teaching. There was only faint applause from people who had come for inspiration and were now receiving a history lesson instead. Even the encouragements from the amen corner began to seem more perfunctory than heartfelt.

Luther, who had read the same histories from which the great man was drawing his speech, was disappointed. Because King was exactly right. And the country would be radically changed—made radically *better*—if only more Negroes and white people understood the implications. Namely, that segregation was ultimately a con job used by those with money and power to keep those without it, whether black or white, in poverty and servitude. Luther was pleased to finally hear someone—particularly someone of King's stature and visibility—speak this explosive truth. But was any of it getting through?

Judging from the apathetic demeanor of the crowd, Luther had to conclude that it wasn't.

But King pushed doggedly on. "They segregated Southern money from the poor whites," he cried, "they segregated Southern churches from Christianity, they segregated Southern minds from honest thinking, and they segregated the Negro from everything."

"Yes, sir!" exhorted the amen corner, still trying to lift him up. But the applause was meager. King, thought Luther, was on the verge of losing his audience.

Perhaps the great man sensed the same thing. He shifted gears then, to describe the marchers as a people "on the move," defiant in the face of racism, of churches burned and homes bombed.

It was as if a brisk wind had caught the sails of a drifting boat. "Let us march!" he repeated, over and over again, describing a righteous and determined advance that would desegregate housing, improve schooling, end hunger, and drive demagogues from public office. "Let us march!" he cried.

"Let us march!" the people echoed, their voices building to crescendos of urgency as they strained toward the utopia he described.

Then King said, "I know you're asking today, 'How long will it take?'"

And Luther, who had spent that very morning recalling the time he had challenged Johan Simek to answer that very question, stood straighter at those words, listened more intently, even as King answered his own question.

"I come to say to you this afternoon, however difficult the moment, however frustrating the hour, it will not be long, because truth crushed to earth will rise again.

"How long? Not long! Because no lie can live forever." The crowd was with him now, echoing the thunderclaps of his refrain.

"How long? Not long! Because you shall reap what you sow.

"How long? Not long! Truth forever on the scaffold, wrong forever on the throne, yet that scaffold sways the future and behind the dim unknown standeth God within the shadows keeping watch above his own." And now King seemed caught up in the whirlwind of his own words, taken to some high and holy place far beyond the streets of this little Alabama town, lifted to some lofty promontory from which he could see the very curve of history's horizon, the shape of worlds yet to come.

"How long?" he roared. "Not long! Because the arc of the moral universe is long, but it bends toward justice.

"How long? Not long? Because 'Mine eyes have seen the glory of the coming of the Lord. He's trampling out the vintage where the grapes of wrath are stored. He has loosed the fateful lightning of his *terrible* swift sword. His truth is marching on. He has sounded forth the trumpet that shall *never* call retreat.'" King bore down hard on the word "never" as if daring someone to contradict him. And the stanzas of the old poem by Julia Ward Howe—"Battle Hymn of the Republic"—rang vibrant with his defiance.

"'He is sifting out the hearts of men before his judgment seat,'" declared King, swept up now in the rushing passion of the poet's words. "'Oh, be swift my soul to answer him, be jubilant, my feet. Our God is marching on. Glory, hallelujah! Glory, hallelujah! Glory, hallelujah! His truth is marching on.'"

He turned from the podium then. People banged their palms together in ovation. They cried out in words that had no language. They wept. And Luther, who had lost God so long ago, could have sworn he almost felt something, some quickening in his chest, some slight pressure behind the eyes.

"How long?" cried a happy woman near him.

"Not long!" answered a man on the other side.

Luther felt himself being drawn toward an unfamiliar shore. He felt powerless to resist. He wasn't even sure he wanted to.

In that moment, it was almost possible to believe—*almost* possible to believe—that change, that the dream about which both Johan Simek and Martin King had rhapsodized, was inevitable if not actually right at hand, that vindication was upon them all, that justice was just a short walk from here.

But he knew better than that, didn't he? He was still the orphaned son of Mason and Annie Hayes, wasn't he? This was still America, was it not?

True, all of it. Yet, Luther still felt . . . shaken.

He looked down on his sister. She was pounding her hands together, screaming with joy. Her eyes beamed.

"How long?" someone else cried.

"Not long!" another voice replied. Laughter. Slapping palms.

Luther shook his head, lit a cigarette with suddenly unsteady hands. He wiped impatiently at a lone tear that came straggling down his cheek.

thirty-one

"I'll say this for him," said Luther, dragging on his cigarette, "the man can give a speech."

Her brother gazed down expectantly, and Thelma knew he was waiting on her response to gauge if she was still angry with him. She was, at least a little, but she also knew they would be parting company in a few minutes—him driving back to Mobile, her and George catching a ride to Selma, from which they would set off for New York City in the morning—and she didn't wish to leave on bad terms. After all, Lord only knew when they would see one another again. So Thelma nodded and made her voice amiable. "Yes," she said, "he sure can."

The anodyne response seemed to please him. He held out his cigarette pack. "You want one?" he said.

She did, but Thelma shook her head. "No," she said, "I'm going back on the wagon."

He nodded. "Good for you," he said.

They stood in companionable silence there at the top of the church house stairs, watching as workmen began to dismantle the platform from which King had spoken just moments before, while the vast crowd drifted apart. Then Luther said, "Thelma, I know you think I been treatin' you like a child these last few days. I ain't meant to make you feel like that. It's just . . . I'm scared. I don't know what to do."

"Well," said Thelma, and she tried to keep her tone agreeable, "you don't have to worry about it anymore. After today, I'll be George's problem."

She knew from the exasperation in his voice when he said her name—"Thel . . ."—that she had not managed to maintain her affable front. The truth was that Thelma had felt put upon and mistreated ever since she woke up—alive—in that hospital, and apparently that sentiment still managed to leak, loud and clear, into her words, even when she didn't want it to. She raised her hand like a traffic cop to forestall his protest. "I'm sorry," she said. "That was mean."

"Thelma," he told her, "you ain't my problem. You my sister and I love you. I just want what's best for you, that's all."

It was a statement so direct, so shorn of artifice, that it made her uncomfortable and she didn't know to respond. Then she did. "I love you, too, Luther," she said. "Try not to worry. I'll be all right."

And in that moment, at least, standing there in the wake of the triumphant event, still high on the power of Martin Luther King's words, Thelma felt as if she just might be all right, at that.

"There they are," said Luther after a moment. He pointed and Thelma saw Adam and George making their way toward them. The sight of her husband tightened her stomach a little. What would he say when he learned what she had done? Or tried to do? How would he treat her? Could she ever repair her family?

She followed Luther down the stairs and the four of them met on the street corner in an exchange of hugs, handshakes, and kisses. Thelma found herself watching Adam as Luther had watched her, parsing his tone for some clue to his mood.

But he seemed fine. He said, "Hi, Mom," and pressed his lips to her cheek. Thelma was surprised at the relief that flooded her at this, and for the first time, she even felt a little foolish for trying to take her own life. It had seemed to make sense at the time. She remembered the realization that had come upon her when she swallowed those pills: how much easier things were, how much simpler, when you just stopped fighting. But with her son kissing her cheek, what had felt like a revelation now felt like some foolish thing someone else had once thought wise a long time ago.

"So I assume you're catching a ride back to Selma with your friends?" she asked him.

"Yes, ma'am."

"How long before you get back home?"

"I'm not coming back," said Adam. "At least, not for a while."

Luther and George had been talking about the speech. Now they, like Thelma, grew still. "What do you mean, you're not coming back?" she asked.

"Mom, there's still work to do here."

"What work? You completed the march. Johnson already sent a voting rights bill to Congress. The work is done."

He shook his head emphatically. "No, it's just beginning," he said. "There's a lot more to do. Me and some of the other fellas, we've been talking about this, and we're not sure this strategy of nonviolent protest works for us anymore. We think that if the Negro is going to get ahead, it won't come from begging white folks to treat us right. It'll come from seizing political power."

"What are you talking about?" demanded Thelma. "You're making no sense."

In response, he pulled his backpack around to the front and began rummaging inside until he produced a mimeographed piece of paper. It carried a pencil sketch of a stationery design. At the top, in a stairstep, were the words "Lowndes County Freedom Organization." Above that was a drawing of a black panther crouched low, prowling toward the viewer.

"I don't understand," said Thelma, as George and Luther came around to peer over her shoulder. "What is this?"

"We're going to start a political party for Negroes," said Adam. "It makes no sense if our people get the right to vote and they don't have anybody to vote for—I mean, somebody who has their interests at heart. So we're going to run a slate of candidates. A lot of our people down here can't read, so we're using the panther as our symbol. When they see that, they'll know it's us."

"You're staying down here?" Thelma was still trying to make his words make sense.

"You know, that symbol doesn't exactly scream 'nonviolence,'" mused George. "More like confrontation. Or even a threat."

Adam shrugged. "Like I said, some of us, we're not so much into that nonviolence stuff anymore."

"So you're pushing—what?—armed revolution?"

Adam laughed. "No, not at all. As I said, this is about political power. But we do think if someone hits us, we should have the right to hit them back. Why is the Negro the only one who has no right to defend himself?"

"I see," said George stiffly and Thelma noted that her husband seemed more put out by this philosophical disagreement over a logo than by the absurd idea of their son staying in Alabama.

Luther, meantime, poked out a contemplative lip as he appraised the drawing. "I like it," he finally said, drawing a questioning glance from George. "I'm probably biased," her brother admitted. "Black Panthers, that's what our tank regiment was called back during the war."

Thelma felt as if she were sealed inside a soundproof bubble screaming her head off, and nobody was hearing her. "You're staying down *here*?" she repeated, raising her voice.

"Yeah," confirmed Adam. "For a while, at least."

"What about school?" asked George, asking a reasonable question in a reasonable voice as if any of this were even the remotest bit reasonable. "You've only got a semester left till graduation."

"So I guess there'll be one less English teacher in the world," said Adam with a shrug. "Doesn't seem like such a big loss. Especially considering what's at stake."

"Still," said George, "it's a shame to quit when you're so close to graduating. Are you sure this is what you want to do? This is a big move. This is the rest of your life we're talking about."

"I know," said Adam calmly. "I'm sure."

"Are all you out of your minds?" Thelma looked from her brother to her husband to her son as if they were spouting alien gibberish. As, indeed, by her lights, they were. "This boy cannot stay here. Adam, you can't stay here. It's too dangerous. I won't allow it."

She had expected the ultimatum to produce confrontation and braced herself accordingly. But instead, Adam's eyes caressed her face fondly and he spoke to her in a voice gentle as spring rain. His words, however, were firm.

"Mom, I'm staying."

"What do you mean? You can't—"

"Mom," he repeated, "I am staying."

She looked again to her brother and her husband, seeking support, but seeing in their eyes only a vague pity. "You'd better talk to your son," she told George. "He's lost his mind if he thinks I'm going to let him stay down here."

"Mom."

Her eyes returned to her son. His gaze shimmered as it settled upon her. He said, "I'm twenty-one years old. That's old enough to make my own decisions, don't you think? When Dad was my age, he was in a POW camp. When you were my age, you were taking care of Gramp and working at the shipyard. I'm not a child, Mom, no more than you guys were when you were my age."

"But Adam . . ."

"Mom, I'm staying. Try to understand. This is important to me. It's something I need to do."

"Adam, these people down here . . ."

"Mom, I know all about these people down here. I was on that bridge, remember? And I was in that jail."

"Yes, but I still wish you'd reconsider."

"I've been thinking about this for a long time. My mind's made up."

"I see," said Thelma. Arms folded across her chest, she went to turn away. Adam touched her shoulder and she stopped.

"Wait, Mom," he said.

"Wait for what?" she asked. "You've made up your mind, remember? You're a grown-up now. You don't need me." She went to turn away again, but the touch on her shoulder hardened.

"I'll always need you," he said. "I always have."

She felt a prickle of guilt in those last words. He had always needed her, but had she always been there? Or hadn't the fact that he was her rapist's son always stood as a barrier between them, an obstruction she could never get past? He was the fruit of that evil seed, the fruit of a man who had hunted her through the bowels of an unfinished warship

Here, nigger, nigger, nigger . . .

Here, nigger, nigger, nigger . . .

and then violated her unspeakably, the man who had soiled her body, her mind, her spirit, her dreams, her future, her very self. The man who had left her . . . contaminated.

Certainly, Thelma had done the best she could with her life, with her husband and son, despite it all. She had not been everything she wanted to be for either of them, but on balance, she thought, most days, she had been all right. But now, here stood the rapist's son—*her* son— implicitly asking for what she did not have to give, what she had never had to give.

"Adam," she began.

He put a finger to his lips. "Mom, I need you to hush for a minute. Let me say what I need to say, all right?"

An army Jeep rumbled by. A helicopter patrolled the sky above. And all about them, people were still chattering, still asking each other, "How long?"

It all went away. The entire world was just Thelma and her son. "All right," she said.

He took a deep breath. "Three things I need to tell you, Mom. The first is that I'm sorry for how I've been acting. It's just that when I found out, it was such a shock. It hit me like a truck. I felt angry that no one ever told me before. But I also felt guilty for what you had to go through. I felt like I was the cause of it somehow."

"Adam," she said, "you weren't—"

He cut her off. "Let me finish," he said. "The second thing I want to say is that I love you." There was mischief in his sudden grin. "All things considered, I think that I'm a pretty decent guy, you know? I'm smart, I get good grades, people seem to like me, I help old ladies cross the street. But whatever I am," he said, his gaze again turning serious, "is because of what you and this guy over here"—a nod toward George—"put into me over the years. I love you to the end of the sky, Mom. Don't ever doubt it, don't ever forget it.

"Which brings me to the third thing," he said. "The third thing..."

His voice thickened on these words and he had to cough it clear. She saw tears standing in his eyes. "The third thing," he said, "is just ... thank you." He glanced at George, and Thelma wasn't sure, but she thought she saw an almost imperceptible nod of approval pass from father to son.

"Thank me for what?" she managed to ask.

Adam's eyes upon her were almost unbearably tender. "Mom," he said again, "*thank you*. For everything you went through, for everything you sacrificed, for all of it. You're the greatest mother in the world and I want you to know that I appreciate you, more than I can ever say."

Before she could respond, Adam grabbed her in a sudden embrace. "Thank you, Mom," he whispered in her ear.

And Thelma, who knew—who had always known—that she was far from the greatest mother in the world, was shocked. She tried to

318 | Leonard Pitts, Jr.

endure the embrace, to wait it out. But it showed no signs of ending. She tried patting Adam's back a couple of times to let him know that that was enough, that he could let her go now, but her son still held her tightly, held her as if determined to draw from her some needed sustenance.

Adam began to weep. "Thank you, Mom," he said again, this time through tears. "Thank you." Her son's hold on her did not ease. Only then did she begin to understand the embrace for what it was. A demand.

Thelma didn't know what to do. And then, she did.

Slowly, as if the motion were unfamiliar, Thelma's arms rose until they met across Adam's back. He wept. She wept, too.

She felt something leave her then. Something bleak and sad, something forlorn that had been part of her for so long she could not remember herself without it, lifted from her heart. In its place came a sudden lightness that left her almost dizzy.

From somewhere far beyond this sacred space, Thelma heard her brother beckon her husband. "Come take a walk with me," he said. "Somethin' I need to talk to you about."

She knew what it was, of course. But she didn't care. It didn't matter.

Thelma Simon hugged her son.

thirty-two

ALL THE WAY BACK DOWN TO MOBILE, LUTHER WAS TOR-
tured by the question of whether he could have done a better job. By
the time he saw the city lights on the horizon, he had come to a conclusion: there is no good way to tell a man that his wife tried to kill herself.

George's eyes had gone wide at the news and he had staggered as
if from a blow. He asked all the obvious questions, then asked them
again. Then he cried and blamed himself for Thelma's despair. Luther
had talked him patiently through it, tried to reassure him that she had
seemed all right since coming home. He pointed out as a reason for
hope the fact that she had agreed to follow the doctor's advice and con-
sult a psychologist. And he made George promise to stay in close touch
and keep him apprised of his sister's progress.

By the time they returned to where Thelma and Adam stood waiting, George was composed again, if a bit wobbly. Thelma had given her
brother a meaningful look as she took her husband's hand.

They said their goodbyes there on the sidewalk before King's old
church. More hugs, handshakes, and kisses were exchanged. He had
told Thelma to take care of herself. "I love you, big brother," Thelma
had told him as they parted. "You be careful driving home."

He had not bothered to correct her, but he'd had no intention of
going home. At least, not yet. First, he had a stop to make.

Darkness had pulled itself like a blanket over Mobile when Luther
turned into the parking lot of the West Haven Rest Home. The man on
the radio was reporting on the murder of a white woman—Viola Liuzzo
was her name—who had been shot on Route 80 while driving back to
Montgomery to provide transportation for some of the marchers.

First Jimmie Lee Jackson, then James Reeb, and now, thought Luther, they were even killing white women. It just never stopped. He shut off the Buick, took a last drag on a cigarette and sat listening to the ticking of the engine.

After a moment, he stubbed out the butt in the overflowing dashboard ashtray and climbed out of the car. He mounted three steps, walked through the front door. The lobby was dark and quiet, the front desk empty. There was no one in the dayroom, either. For once, the television screen was blank. Visiting hours were technically over for the day, but he wasn't worried about that. They all knew him here and besides that, enforcement of the rules tended to be lax.

Still, he was glad he wasn't seen as he strode across the room and into the hallway, where he knocked lightly on Johan's door. After a moment, he heard the voice from inside say simply, "Come."

He found the old man sitting in a chair before the television, on which some middle-class white family in some middle-class white house was having a middle-class white argument about something that was quite hilarious, to judge from the explosion of canned laughter. Johan, dressed in a brown suit with a matching homburg, turned and smiled at the sight of him.

"Come, come," he said, patting the chair next to him. "Have a seat."

"Don't mind if I do," said Luther, tossing his hat on the bed. He unbuttoned his sports coat as he sat. "How you doin' this evening?" he asked.

"I am doing quite well. Thank you for asking."

"You know, I went up to the march today."

"That's nice."

"That Martin Luther King, he gave a hell of a speech. You'll probably see some of it on the news tonight."

"How wonderful."

"And I saw George and Thelma. They drivin' back to New York in the morning."

"You saw George?"

"Yes."

"George is doing all right?"

"Yeah, George just fine."

"That's good to hear."

Luther inclined his head toward the television. "So, what we watchin' here?" he asked.

"Just watching the scenery go by," said Johan. "Such beautiful country this is, don't you think? Especially in the fall when the leaves begin to change?"

"The . . . scenery?" Dread trickled down into the pit of Luther's stomach.

The old man's nod was enthusiastic. His eyes gleamed with joy. "It's really quite lovely, don't you think?"

"Yeah," said Luther. "Really lovely." He regarded his friend, consumed by a sudden sorrow for which he had no name.

"How far are you going?"

"How far?"

Johan chuckled at Luther's confusion. "Yes, young man, how far? Will you be getting off the train at Baja or Kalocsa, or perhaps Dunaföldvár? I myself am going all the way to Budapest. It's where I was born, you know."

"Yeah," said Luther, "I know."

He struggled to keep his face neutral, but within, he mourned. If there was one thing his five decades had taught him, it was that life is a series of losses. You lost loved things, you lost loved places, you lost loved ones. Yet somehow, each time, loss still managed to come as a surprise.

The old man's smile was impish. "I am so looking forward to seeing my papa again," he confided. "And my dear *anyuci*. It has been so long since I was home."

"I bet your mama and papa lookin' forward to seein' you, too," said Luther.

They sat for a moment in companionable silence broken only by shrieks of mechanical laughter. Then Johan said, "So what are you doing on this train? Are you traveling for business or for pleasure?"

"Pleasure, I guess," said Luther. "I come to see you."

The eyes behind the glasses widened in surprise. "You came to see me? Why?"

Luther made himself smile. "Well, we friends, ain't we?" he said. "And that's what friends do. They come see about one another."

"You are my friend?"

"Yeah," said Luther, "I'm your friend. And you mine."

"What is your name, friend? I'm afraid I don't recall."

Luther swallowed hard. He extended a hand. "I'm Luther Hayes," he said. "Glad to know you."

"Johan Simek," said the old man as Luther's hand swallowed his own. "And I am pleased to know you, as well."

They sat for a long time just watching the television. After a few minutes, the sitcom family resolved its problem. There were commercials selling Chevrolets, Folgers coffee, and Quisp, some new breakfast cereal for kids. Then came the theme song for another sitcom about another middle-class white family. This one was called *My Three Sons*. Luther had never heard of it. The window was open a few inches and the room was cooled by a slight breeze. It carried a hint of moisture that made him think they might get some rain before the night was over.

Johan fell silent for a long time. After a while, Luther thought maybe he was asleep. Or perhaps, he was still wandering about in his own mind, enjoying the train trip across the landscape of his long-ago childhood. From out in the dayroom came the faint sound of the janitor running a buffer across the floor. The father on *My Three Sons*— Luther recognized him as a film actor named Fred MacMurray—was looking befuddled over some confusion between his boys when Luther checked his watch and saw that it was getting toward nine o'clock. He started to push himself up from the chair.

The movement stirred Johan, who turned toward him, eyes bright. He said, "I saw him, you know."

Luther was confused.

"You saw who?"

"That man who hit me. The one who knocked me down and stomped me. I saw him. He's here."

"Yeah," said Luther. "I know he is. Hell of a world, ain't it?"

"Hell of a world," agreed Johan.

Luther pushed up from the chair. His knees registered protest and he was reminded, not that he needed it, that he was getting old. He patted Johan on the shoulder. "This my stop," he said. "Got to leave the train now."

"What train?"

"I just meant that I got to go."

"Very well," said the old man. "Good night, my friend. Sleep well."

After retrieving his hat from the bed, Luther stepped back into the hallway. He paused there a moment in the stillness. He took a deep breath. And then, instead of turning right, which would have carried him back through the dayroom and out to the lobby, he turned left, which carried him deeper into the hallway. At room 106, he entered without knocking.

The room was dark but for a small circle of light from a lamp on the nightstand. It was as if the old man hadn't moved in the almost three weeks since Luther discovered him there. He lay in the same position, on his back, his head turned to face the door. His face was still slumped, and as pallid as that of some creature of the deep sea that has never seen the sun. His right hand still angled up from his body, tracing aimless curlicues in the air. And his eyes were still alert. They watched Luther with friendly curiosity as he came into the room. Floyd Bitters made a sound of apparent greeting.

Luther shook his head. "I can't understand what you tryin' to say," he said, "but I can guess. You wonderin' who I am."

Luther found a chair and pulled it closer to the hospital bed, letting it scrape unpleasantly against the floor. "My name Luther," he said, taking a seat, "but that won't mean nothin' to you. You and me, we already met, though, long time ago. Real long time. Forty-two years, in fact."

The old man made another of his inarticulate sounds. Amiable confusion fogged his eyes, as if a really good joke were being told and he wasn't quite getting it.

Luther shrugged. "I told you I don't understand you," he said. "'Course, I don't need to. Ain't nothin' you could say to me I really need to hear. Not at this point."

Another grunt from the old man.

"Yeah," said Luther, "I know. What I want with you, right? Why I come in here to bother you in the middle of the night? Well, like I said, my name Luther, Luther Hayes. You and me, we met one night when I was nine years old. Me, I was small for my age and you was still a big man back then—more mountain than man, tell you the truth—and you snatched me up from the porch. I was so scared, I pissed myself. You remember that?"

Bitters's brow creased as if all this was ringing some vague alarm bell somewhere deep within.

"You still havin' trouble rememberin'?" Luther smiled. "That's all right. Happen a lot more as we get older. Especially if we get in the kind of shape you in. Well, here somethin' might jog your memory: my daddy's name. It was Mason. Mason Hayes. You remember that name? You should. See, you killed him that night. You and a bunch of other drunk-ass crackers. Burned him alive at his own front door. My mama, too. Her name was Annie. You remember any of that?"

Instantly, the watery gaze sharpened. Luther leaned in. "Yeah," he said softly, "I believe you do remember, don't you?"

He did. It was obvious. The hand moved faster in its aimless course. Bitters made more of his wordless sounds. They had taken on a note of agitation.

"Shhh," said Luther, almost as if calming a colicky baby. He even patted Bitters's left arm, which lay still as a stone. "Ain't nobody here but you and me," he said. "And I been wantin' to talk to you about this for a long time, so you might as well just settle in and let me have my say."

He regarded the old man for a moment. Then he said, "It was all about a hog, you remember that? Big, black som'bitch, way I hear. But my papa, he wouldn't sell it to you. Said he wanted to keep his hog to feed his family. Seem to me a man got a right to decide if he want to sell his own property or not, so I can't see nothin' wrong with that, but you sure did. You got a mob together and you came to the house, and you tortured both my parents and killed 'em. Took your time with it, too. Worst death I ever seen, and I been to war."

The old man had stopped making his sounds. His eyes had turned feral with terror. Luther would have thought seeing fear in those eyes— the eyes that had once glared down at him with such haughty disdain—would be gratifying, somehow. But he didn't feel gratification. He didn't feel anything. It scared him a little.

"Worst death I ever seen," he repeated. "What you did to them, you wouldn't do to an animal. Ain't never been able to figure how you white people could get enough hate inside you to do them kind of things. And then, to top it off"—he chuckled and it was a bleak and bitter sound—"all this supposed to been over that there hog and you all didn't even take the damn thing. You shot it and left it there to rot. So it wasn't never about no damn hog at all, was it? Not really."

He paused to see if Bitters wanted to add another of his meaningless sounds. The old man was silent. His right hand continued to flutter above him.

"No," said Luther, "wasn't about the hog. It was about you hating a Negro for having something you couldn't have. For that, you came to his house and you burned him and his wife."

Luther paused again. He lit a cigarette with trembling hands, blew out a long stream of smoke.

"You know what it do to you when you ain't nothin' but a boy and you see your parents killed like that? It fucks you up, man. It fucks you up, bad. I mean, I'm doin' better now, I suppose. Better than I used to. Used to be I couldn't close my eyes without seeing them. Had to drink myself stupid just so's I could sleep. But you know, you get older, you learn to deal with the bad shit you seen. Then my nephew, he come to town with that civil rights thing up in Selma—you probably heard about it—and he ask me, want to know what happened to his grandparents. So, I took him there and I told him about what you done, and I swear, it like to killed me—took me right back to that night. I guess it was already on my mind, though, 'cause a few days before that I come here to visit my friend and what do I find but you, lyin' in here, all fucked up."

Luther knocked ash from the cigarette onto the linoleum floor. "Life is a bitch, ain't it? One minute, you's the king of the world. Next minute, you's lyin' in the old folks' home, can't even wipe your own ass."

As if in response, there came a sudden percussive boom that rattled the glass windows in their frames. The old man flinched, hunching his narrow shoulders. "Thunder," Luther told him.

He crossed the room to the window in time to see the rain begin pouring from the sky, an angry deluge that thumped against the glass. Jagged bolts of fire lacerated the clouds and there was another hard rumble of thunder.

"Big storm," said Luther. "Look like it's gon' go for a while." He finished the cigarette, mashed it against the window ledge, stuck the crumpled butt into his coat pocket.

For another moment, he stood there watching the rain. Then he crossed the room back to where the old man could see him. "So, what happened to you anyway?" he asked, taking his seat once again. "Stroke, I'm guessin'? That's sad. Hell of a way to go. Like you's a prisoner in your own body, I imagine. That friend I told you about down the hall? He done turned senile. Barely remember his own name. I guess gettin' old ain't no fun, is it? I ain't lookin' forward to it, I tell you that."

Luther glanced around the nightstand. "I don't see no pictures," he said. "You got no wife? No family? Wow. So did they all die on you, or they just don't give a damn about you?"

There came a series of agitated grunts. "You right," conceded Luther, "none of my business. Maybe they didn't die. Maybe you never had no family to begin with."

A pause. Then Luther said, "I had a family, though."

His eyes met the old man's. Bitters's gaze was made of fear and yet also a certain prideful defiance.

"I had a family," repeated Luther. "And you destroyed it, sure as if you took a wrecking ball to a house. When you killed Mason and Annie Hayes, it's like you killed all the hope I had in life, all the joy, all the faith. It's like you hurt me forever. And the thing that always bothered me, almost as bad as the murders themselves: you never paid no price for what you did. To me, that was like sayin' it didn't matter what you did. It was like sayin' *they* didn't matter. Like nobody cared that these two people was here on Earth one minute, raisin' their children, mindin' their business, and then the next, they was just . . . gone.

"But they mattered to us, you see? To me and my sister, to my grandfather. They mattered to *us*. And it ain't right that you could just do that and go on with your life for another forty-two years like nothin' never happened."

Bitters grunted, still groping for words.

"Shut up," snapped Luther. He shook his head in disgust. "What you gon' say to me, even if you could talk? Ain't nothin' you can say, man. Not a goddamn thing. So you might as well just lie there and listen."

Luther fished out another cigarette. He lit it, exhaled a stream of smoke, picked a fleck of tobacco off his tongue, looked at it, flicked it away. He laughed. "Bet you ain't used to nobody look like me talkin' like that to you, huh? World's changin', what can I say? I'm sure you don't like that very much. Guess I can't blame you. Must be nice to be white. Do whatever the fuck you want to colored people and don't never have to answer for it. Dance to the music all night long and tell the piper go fuck his self.

"But I got to say, Floyd, that don't seem right to me. Ask yourself— be honest with me, now—do that seem right to you? It don't, do it? I guess that's why I'm here. You may think Mason and Annie Hayes was just some more niggers you could treat any old kind of way and their lives ain't meant much. But see, they was my mama and my papa. And they meant everything to *me*. So that's the reason I come to visit with you, old man. I come to see that the piper get what he got comin'."

Luther watched without interest as the words registered in the old man's colorless eyes, watched his hand flop about in the air like a fish on a pier. Floyd Bitters croaked out more of his stunted vocabulary of sounds, reaching desperately for language that had deserted him long ago. It surprised Luther how little he felt. Not sorrow, not malice, not triumph. He might as well have been washing the dishes for all he felt. Might as well have been taking out the trash.

He stood up, moved toward the bed. "I used to believe in God, you know. Used to know, sure as I knew my own name, that He was up there, keepin' watch over His world, makin' everything right. I don't believe in God no more, though. Somethin' else you took away from me. Right now, I hope I'm right about that. Hope there really ain't no God. 'Cause if there is, I'm surely goin' to hell for this."

A pause. "But if I do, I'm pretty sure I'll see you there."

He clenched the cigarette in his teeth then, reached out with his right hand and clamped the old man's nose shut. The skin was oily to the touch and he had to reposition his hand to get a tight grip and keep his fingers from slipping. Then he used his left hand to block the old man's mouth. Floyd Bitters's eyes flared in panic and he grunted frantically in his stroke language, the one hand flopping desperately in the air. Once, twice, it struck without effect against Luther's arm.

Luther ignored it, concentrating his attention on the murderer's eyes, watching the terror there seep into a pleading sorrow. Of course, they would both be murderers now, he supposed. And that realization made him wonder what Bitters might see in his own eyes.

He hoped it was the ghosts of his mother and father. He hoped it was the forty-two years of hatred, rage, sorrow, and pain that had come to define his life.

He hoped Bitters saw some tiny fraction of that.

Then he saw that the old man's eyes had changed yet again. Terror had become panic and now, panic had segued into a dull surrender. And in that moment, some part of Luther Hayes viewed the scene as if from above, saw a healthy man, a man with his physical and mental faculties still intact, standing above a sickbed smothering the life out of an old man helpless to defend himself, a man decades removed from the person he had been and the crime for which he was being killed. Some voice within him pointed out to Luther that this was a forever thing he was doing, an irrevocable line he was crossing. It reminded him that there were those who would call this an act of evil and that there was still time to pull back from the edge, still time to not kill Floyd Bitters.

Luther registered all of this. He thought about it. And then he dismissed it. He squeezed tighter on the old man's nose, clamped his palm more firmly on his mouth. It was taking Bitters an awful long time to die, he thought.

And just as he thought this, the hand that had been flapping about in midair fell to the bed like a dead bird tumbling from the sky. Luther marked this. He held the old man's airways closed a few seconds longer. Finally, he pulled away and regarded what he had done.

The eyes that had shone confusion, pride, anger, defiance, panic, and finally, resignation, now shone not at all. They were empty, gazing blankly upon infinity. Luther stepped back. He wiped his left hand, wet with the old man's saliva, absently on his pant leg, dragged a forearm across his sweaty brow, surprised at how much effort this had taken.

He stood there for a long moment, gazing down upon the carcass of the man who had killed his parents. Luther waited to feel regret at what he had done. Part of him even wanted to feel it. But still he felt nothing. Then he thought all at once of Martin Luther King's majestic words of persistence, his eloquent assurance of triumph, inevitable.

And finally, he felt something. He felt cold.

How long?

Forty-two fucking years.

How long?

Too goddamn long.

Luther thought of closing the old man's eyes but didn't. Instead, he left him there as he had died, eyes vacant, mouth slack. He stubbed out his second cigarette, put the butt in his coat pocket, put the chair back in place, then opened the door and stepped through into the hallway. He did not look back.

The janitor, a portly Negro man, was still running the buffer in the dayroom. He wore headphones to muffle the sound and did not look up as Luther walked through. Luther stepped out into the rain, got behind the wheel of the old Buick, and seconds later, steered into the street. The red and white lights of traffic made indistinct smears on the windshield. With a steady thunk, the wipers swept the glass clean. Luther drove without thinking.

When he reached the Negro side of town, he pulled to the curb in front of a package store. He ducked through the rain and emerged a moment later with a brown paper sack containing a fresh carton of cigarettes and a bottle of bourbon.

Moments later, Luther turned in to the alley that ran alongside his building and pulled into a parking slot. He climbed the stairs to the covered porch, but did not open the door into his apartment. Instead, he took a seat in one of the two chairs he kept out there, flanking a little circular table. He pulled the bottle of amber liquid and an opaque plastic cup from the bag, cracked open the bottle, poured the cup half full, then placed them together on the table. For a long moment, Luther just sat there and regarded the drink warily.

Thunder rumbled heavily above. Water hissed against the pavement below. And then, from somewhere far away, came the sound of a siren. Luther tensed, thinking to himself that it sure had happened fast. The wailing rose to a piercing crescendo. And then it faded, the emergency vehicle passing by on the street out front. Luther's body relaxed.

He gazed again at the plastic cup of brown liquid. After a moment, he lifted it and tossed the contents over the porch railing into the rain. He set the empty cup back on the table, recapped the bottle of bourbon, lit a cigarette, and gazed out over the low-slung buildings of the town where he was born—little more than shadows on this dark night of storm and wind.

At length, with a tired exhale of smoke, Luther sat back in his chair. He watched the rain sweep down from the sky and waited, cold sober, to see what would happen next.

acknowledgments

M<small>Y</small> <small>FIRST PUBLISHED NOVEL,</small> *B<small>EFORE</small> I F<small>ORGET</small>,* <small>CENTERED</small>
around a relatively young man who is grappling with a diagnosis of early
onset Alzheimer's disease. In order to research the condition, I read a
few books and articles and sat in on a support group. Four novels later,
the book you hold in your hands also features a character contending
with dementia, but this time, there was little need for research. All I had
to do was recall visits with my Aunt Mildred.

She was a vivacious and spirited woman reduced by disease to
confusion, confinement, consternation, and the endless repetition of
questions because the answers, no matter how many times they were
given, simply would not take root in the quicksand soil of her mind. My
aunt—my late father's last sibling—died in May of 2017. She is greatly
missed. The rhythm of Luther's exchanges with Johan in this book
are very much informed by my last conversations with her, so it seems
only fitting that she receives the first acknowledgment in this book's
acknowledgments section.

Beyond that, my grandson, Timothy William Smith II—you never
saw a kid more proud of his full government name—is a car buff who
helped me get some details right regarding the vintage vehicles mentioned on these pages.

Dr. S. J. Rao patiently answered my medical questions.

Kelly Harris helped me nail down some legal issues.

Stephen Posey and Crystal Drye of the Selma Dallas County
Public Library dug out vintage material for me to look at and helped
me to get a handle on the geography of the 1965 struggle.

The Paley Center for Media in New York City gave me access to rarely seen footage of the voting rights march on its triumphant entry into Montgomery.

Among contemporaneous reporting on the three voting rights marches, Renata Adler's work for *The New Yorker* and Roy Reed's, John Herbers's, and Gay Talese's stories for the *New York Times* stand out. Their colorful, detail-rich accounts were invaluable in setting the scene. I also leaned heavily on several books, including: *Jimmie Lee & James* by Steve Fiffer and Adar Cohen; *Protest at Selma* by David J. Garrow; *From Selma to Sorrow* by Mary Stanton; *Selma, Lord, Selma* by Sheyann Webb and Rachel West Nelson; *Selma 1965* by Charles Fager; and *At Canaan's Edge* by Taylor Branch.

Ava DuVernay's staging of Bloody Sunday in her film *Selma* never fails to send a hard shiver riding through me. It was quite useful in helping to set an emotional tone for my own recreation of that event.

I thank my first readers—Judi Smith, Marlon Pitts, Maria Majors, and Ernestine Wilson—for their encouragement and advice. I also thank Judi for her usual vigilance in snaring inconsistent spelling and comma misuse and abuse.

I thank Amanda Gibson for her eagle-eyed copyediting; she helped me avoid more than one embarrassing continuity error.

I thank my editor, Doug Seibold, for his insightful attention to details of character and motivation. The book is significantly better for having him at the helm.

I thank my wife, Marilyn, for forty-plus years of love and support and for being sunshine on my cloudy days.

And I thank God for grace, which is, as the songwriter testified, amazing.

LEONARD PITTS, JR.
BOWIE, MD, DECEMBER 28, 2023

about the author

LEONARD PITTS, JR. IS THE AUTHOR OF THE NOVELS *THE Last Thing You Surrender*, *Grant Park*, *Freeman*, and *Before I Forget*, as well as two works of nonfiction. He was a journalist for more than forty years, including a long tenure as a nationally syndicated columnist for the *Miami Herald*. He is the winner of the 2004 Pulitzer Prize for commentary, in addition to many other awards. Born and raised in Southern California, Pitts now lives in suburban Washington, DC.